"*Glory Road* brims with faith and family, second chances and new horizons. Three generations of women may well remind you of your own as they face transitions and find paths as winding and sweet as those in a lovely garden on a summer's day."

—LISA WINGATE, NEW YORK TIMES BESTSELLING
AUTHOR OF BEFORE WE WERE YOURS

"Rich colorful characters capturing my heart, combined with a story that kept me up till the wee hours, *Glory Road* is a perfect read. Lauren Denton has done it again!

—LISA PATTON, BESTSELLING AUTHOR OF RUSH
AND WHISTLIN' DIXIE IN A NOR'EASTER

"Once again Lauren Denton brings her lyrical writing and compelling characters to a story that will enthrall readers from page one."

—MARYBETH MAYHEW WHALEN, AUTHOR OF
ONLY EVER HER AND CO-FOUNDER OF SHE READS, FOR GLORY ROAD

"Denton crafts a beautiful story with well-drawn, complex characters about the bonds of family, the trials of parenting, and the power of love to soothe the difficulties of daily life. Suggest for readers of Jane Green."

—LIBRARY JOURNAL FOR HURRICANE SEASON

"Any reader who values the comfort of family, the possibility of second chances, and the simple truths of love and sisterhood will devour Denton's novel. In many ways, *Hurricane Season* feels like the calm before a storm that changes everything—for the better."

—BOOKPAGE

"Refined language and dialogue, along with beautifully descriptive scenes will draw readers right into [*Hurricane Season*]. Well-developed, genuine characters and a well-crafted plot that embodies the tenuous ties between family are the highlights of this story. With a Southern backdrop, this poignant tale about sisters . . . will resonate with readers. A truly remarkable read."

—RT BOOK REVIEWS, 4 STARS

"Denton has created a heartwarming, character-driven story that will appeal to fans of Southern fiction."

—PUBLISHERS WEEKLY FOR HURRICANE SEASON

"Perfect for readers looking for low-drama women's fiction."

—BOOKLIST FOR HURRICANE SEASON

"A poignant and heartfelt tale of sisterhood, motherhood, and marriage, *Hurricane Season* deftly examines the role that coming to terms with the past plays in creating a hopeful future. Readers will devour this story of the hurricanes—both literal and figurative—that shape our lives."

—KRISTY WOODSON HARVEY, NATIONAL
BESTSELLING AUTHOR OF SLIGHTLY SOUTH OF SIMPLE

"Inspiring and heartwarming fiction that will please many a heart. After making us love her characters and feel every ache of their journey, [Denton] brings us full circle through a beautiful story, reminding us all that *this too shall pass.*"

—JULIE CANTRELL, NEW YORK TIMES AND USA TODAY
BESTSELLING AUTHOR OF PERENNIALS, FOR HURRICANE SEASON

"It's true what they say. There's no place like home. And reading a Lauren Denton book feels like coming home. With characters you'll want as friends, a setting you can step into, and a poignant story of sisters and family ties and all the messiness of a wonderful life, Denton has penned another tale that will settle in deep and stay awhile, long after the last page is turned."

—CATHERINE WEST, AUTHOR OF
WHERE HOPE BEGINS, FOR HURRICANE SEASON

"An engaging, lyrical story of sisterly love. *Hurricane Season* is sure to add to Denton's growing fan base."

—RACHEL HAUCK, NEW YORK TIMES BESTSELLING AUTHOR

"Denton's delicious debut [*The Hideaway*] is a treat for the senses and the heart. Her exquisitely lyrical writing and character-driven story is a must-read."

"*The Hideaway* is the heartwarmingly southern story about the families we are given—and the families we choose. Two endearing heroines and their poignant storylines of love lost and found make this the perfect book for an afternoon on the back porch with a glass of sweet tea."

"This debut novel is the kind of book you want to curl up with on a rainy day or stick in your beach bag for your next vacation. It is poetic and compelling, emotional and full of life. Its haunting beauty will linger long with readers."

"In this fine debut, Denton crafts a beautiful, heartbreaking story of true love that never dies. This book will please inspirational, contemporary, and historical fans alike."

"Denton's first novel charms readers with her idyllic settings and wonderful cast of characters . . . *The Hideaway* is a deeply satisfying exploration of family, friendship, and the meaning of home."

"From the opening of *The Hideaway*, the reader is captured by the voice of a woman who has for too long kept a story that must be told, one the reader wants to hear. Denton has crafted a story both powerful and enchanting: a don't-miss novel in the greatest southern traditions of storytelling."

Glory Road

OTHER BOOKS BY
LAUREN K. DENTON

The Hideaway
Hurricane Season

Glory Road

Lauren K. Denton

THOMAS NELSON
Since 1798

Glory Road

© 2019 by Lauren K. Denton

Published in Nashville, Tennessee, by Thomas Nelson. Thomas Nelson is a registered trademark of HarperCollins Christian Publishing, Inc.

Interior design: Susanna Chapman

Thomas Nelson titles may be purchased in bulk for educational, business, fund-raising, or sales promotional use. For information, please email SpecialMarkets@ThomasNelson. com.

Publisher's Note: This novel is a work of fiction. Names, characters, places, and incidents are either products of the author's imagination or used fictitiously. All characters are fictional, and any similarity to people living or dead is purely coincidental.

ISBN: 978-0-7852-2522-5 (HC library edition)

Library of Congress Cataloging-in-Publication Data

Names: Denton, Lauren K., author.
Title: Glory Road / Lauren K. Denton.
Description: Nashville, Tennessee : Thomas Nelson, [2019]
Identifiers: LCCN 2018039780| ISBN 9780785219705 (trade paper) | ISBN 9780785219637 (ePUB)
Classification: LCC PS3604.E5956 G58 2019 | DDC 813/.6--dc23 LC record available at https://lccn.loc.gov/2018039780

Printed in the United States of America

HB 08.07.2023

To my family,
with all my love

CHAPTER 1

Everyone knows the weather in lower Alabama can be fickle.
Christmas with the AC pumping or an early June cool snap aren't
the strangest things that happen down here. If you're not careful,
quick changes like these can wreak havoc on your garden. A little
advice: Research before you plant and plan ahead for potential
problems. However, despite research and planning, a good gardener
knows sometimes you have to rip it all out and try something new.
—CANDACE GOOCH, ALABAMA GARDENING FOR BEGINNERS

JESSIE

I'd been on the porch steps shelling purple hull peas for less than an hour and my thumbnails had already turned purple. A bucket sat on the step between my knees and a plastic grocery sack full of empty hulls was perched next to my feet. Our red dirt road was always quiet in the early mornings, but today it seemed even more hushed than usual. With no sound other than the soft thuds of peas filling the bucket, a lone cricket chirping somewhere in the flower bed next to the house, and an occasional hawk cry in the treetops, the silence of Glory Road lulled me.

I'd gotten into such a rhythm—pinch the hull, pull the string, slide one thumbnail in, and flick the peas into the bucket—that my coffee had grown cold. When the front door opened behind me, I jumped, sending a handful of peas skittering down the steps to the grass below. I'd forgotten Evan was still inside sleeping.

I turned and smiled at my daughter as I leaned down to pick up the scattered peas.

"Morning," Evan mumbled. She rubbed her eyes with the heels of her hands, reminding me of her at two or three wearing her Hello Kitty pajamas, holding her stuffed kitty by the tail and asking for a cup of milk. Today, instead of cartoon pj's and milk, it was a faded Fender guitars T-shirt with a stretched-out neck, a pair of my pajama pants, and a glass of orange juice. Her thick blonde hair—full of natural highlights some women would pay big money for—was gathered into a messy ponytail.

She sat on the swing at the end of the porch, tucked one leg underneath her, and pushed off the floor with the other. The chains squeaked a familiar tune. "Don't you need to open up the shop?"

"It's only eight. Mama's over there now waiting on the seed delivery. You know she likes to putter around when no one's there."

"That's so she can sneak succulents back to her house without you knowing."

"Oh, I know it. She only thinks she's being sneaky. When they disappear from the tables, I know exactly where they've gone."

My mother had obsessions, but at least they were harmless—potted succulents, Johnny Cash, and peach cobbler.

Evan sat up in the swing and fanned her shirt away from her skin. "It's so hot out here." She'd never been a fan of hot weather. She wasn't a fan of cold weather either, really. Evan liked everything to be balanced, under control, with nothing out of the ordinary. I worried about her starting high school in just a few short months. High school was a petri dish of weirdness, the exact opposite of ordinary.

"Why aren't you shelling those things inside? Only you would be sitting outside in the heat before you go off to work all day in the heat."

I crooked my head. "It's not that hot yet. But it's summer—it's like this every year. And anyway, I like the heat."

She stood and walked over to the top step, then plopped down next to me and sighed. I breathed in—not quite the same as the baby scent she once had, but still full of sleep and her own essence. I reached an arm around her, pulled her close, and kissed the top of her head. Thankfully, she didn't push me away.

"What do you have planned for today? Mama can take you up the road for a burger if you want. She told me last night she was at Jack & Mack's the other day and her onion burger wasn't up to snuff. I think she wants to talk to them about it." I elbowed Evan. She didn't like going anywhere with Mama alone. I knew how to rein in my mother when she got scrappy, but Evan, for all her unconventional ways, never wanted to be disrespectful. Not too much, anyway.

"Ruth's coming over later and we're going down to the Icebox to swim. If that's okay."

I nodded. I wanted to ask if anyone else was going with them—any boys, any older kids—but at fourteen, Evan was wiser than her years. An old soul. Her track record told me she wouldn't get into trouble, and I trusted her. It was the path I'd chosen—trust her until she did something to break the trust. We both knew that was the deal. Glory Road—all of Perry, really—was about as safe as a room full of cotton balls, but I still felt nervous anytime Evan left my sight. She and Mama were all I had.

"That's fine. Just don't forget your phone. I want you to be able to call me if you need me." Evan must have been the only teenager in the country—in the world, maybe—who was averse to smartphones. She said they made kids stupid. It was hard to argue with that.

"You mean you want to be able to check up on me."

"I won't do that. I know you hate it. But you'll understand one day."

3

"I know, I know." She stood and reached her arms over her head in a big stretch and a yawn. "I'll understand when I'm a parent. A million years from now."

"It only feels that way." Evan was just ten years younger than I'd been when I had her. Ten years—a blink. Sometimes it felt like only yesterday that I sat on Mama and Daddy's porch, rocking on the swing, killing time before going to the Icebox with friends.

I raised my head when the sound of a car roaring down the road made it to the porch. In my peripheral vision I saw Evan look up too. We heard rocks spitting out from under the tires and the soft *whoosh* of red dust before we could actually see anything.

I knew every car that drove past our home and my garden shop, Twig, right next door. Anyone who drove on by, deeper into the tunnel of pines and oaks down Glory Road, belonged there and had likely lived there most of my life. This wasn't one of those cars, yet I still knew it. It was just an image, an intangible picture that occasionally floated back to me in soft threads of memory. Funny how a car can be familiar after nearly twenty years.

It was an old Jeep Grand Wagoneer, blue with brown paneling. The sensations came back in a rush—the softness of the leather seats, the Armor-All shine of the dash, and the scent: a mix of gasoline, fresh pine, and lemons. I closed my eyes and the years peeled back. I could smell, see, and feel it all. Ben used to work on the Jeep every weekend. It was old even back then. I used to joke with him that he was fighting a losing battle, but he was determined to keep it running smooth until it took its last breath.

The Jeep drove a little too fast and music spilled from the open windows. I couldn't name the band or the song, but the rhythm thumped in my chest, making it ache, but not from pain, exactly. A boy sat in the passenger seat, his arm out the window, his dark hair whipping in the breeze.

"That's him," Evan said behind me.

Her words registered, but I was still focused on the music and the memories. Eyes still closed, I didn't answer.

"Did you see the guy in the passenger seat? That was the guy from school."

"Hmm?"

"Mom? What are you doing?"

I opened my eyes and shook my head to clear the fog. "Nothing, nothing." I leaned out to catch a last glimpse of the Jeep, but it was gone. All that remained was a haze of dust in the road. "What guy from school?"

"I stood next to him in line yesterday when I went to pick up my registration packet." She shrugged. "His name's Nick. He's new—or at least he wasn't at the middle school. He's a little older, I think. And different."

I turned to Evan. Her big blue eyes held a faraway gaze. "What does that mean?"

"I don't know, he just stuck out a little. He wore a black T-shirt, for one, and he was listening to music on his phone the whole time we were in line."

I studied my daughter. "How do you know it was music?"

"His head was moving a little, like . . . I don't know." She shrugged again. "It's just a guess. Anyway, he didn't look like he'd been mucking out a chicken house or drinking steroid shakes for breakfast."

"Farming or football," I murmured. Outside of school hours, most young men in Perry—our small, south Alabama blip on the map—were either in the fields or on the field. Either that or getting into trouble. It had always been that way. "I know someone else who likes to wear black T-shirts and listen to music."

"Very funny. But he was different. He didn't seem to care that he stuck out. That he didn't look like all the other guys around here."

Evan may not have recognized it, but I knew she was doing her thing—Eric Clapton and Bob Dylan, the Converse high-tops and

Fender shirts—to make herself stick out. To separate herself from the crowd. She wasn't a girl from a country song—tight cutoffs, bouncy hair, pink lipstick—and she wanted everyone to know. I also knew that despite her difference from the other girls, actually *being* different—not blending in—was hard. I loved her so much for trying though.

"I'm going to make some breakfast. You want anything?" she asked.

"I'm fine. I'll be going over to the shop in a little bit. Let me know when you head out, okay?"

"Sure." She opened the screen door, then paused, halfway into the cool stillness of the house. I bit my tongue and waited. It was a new thing I was trying these days—instead of asking too many questions, I was trying to stay quiet and let Evan speak when she was ready. We were both still learning how to navigate her new teenage emotions and sensitivities.

"You're not really going to dinner with that cop, are you?"

I sighed and rested my elbows on the step behind me. Jimmy Kellan was the new police chief in Perry. He was also single and handsome, which naturally sent the ladies in town into a frenzy. The DIVAS—Divinely Inspired, Victorious And Serving—from Perry Baptist were all over him in an attempt to "welcome him to the community," which everyone knew was code for "If I can't date him, I'll be the one to set him up with someone who can."

Mama had used no such false front. Last Saturday night, enjoying a milkshake from Jack & Mack's with Evan and me, she'd marched up to Officer Kellan's patrol car on Center Street, tapped on his window, and asked him if he would mind accompanying her daughter to dinner.

I shook my head. "No, baby. I'm not."

"How'd you get out of it? Gus was pretty determined."

"I just told her I wasn't going. I said if she didn't call him and let him down easy, I'd make sure I was wearing my oldest pajamas when he came to pick me up."

Evan laughed. "I bet she hated that."

"She didn't talk to me for twelve whole hours."

"I'm glad you're not going."

I looked over my shoulder at her. Framed by the doorway with one hand on the jamb and one on her hip, she was one part sassy, one part vulnerable, and I would do anything to protect that vulnerable side, to keep it innocent and sweet. "Why are you glad?"

She shrugged, and for a moment I thought she might actually let me in on something deep in her heart, some truth she needed to unload. Instead, she let the door close a couple more inches before tossing out, "You're too old to date anyway."

I grabbed a small handful of peas and threw them at the door, but she'd already let it slam closed. She disappeared down the hall to the kitchen, her soft laughter winding its way back to the porch.

I reached down and tied the handles of the grocery sack together. A few of the empty hulls edged out of the top and fell to the step by my feet. I grabbed the escaped hulls and poked them back in.

Too old. Of course, in the eyes of a fourteen-year-old, thirty-eight seemed ancient, but I didn't feel ancient. Sometimes I didn't feel a day over eighteen. An age when everything felt ripe with promise and possibility. When it felt like everything would work out perfectly, because why not?

Behind me in the house, the phone rang. Evan answered it, paused, then groaned. "Gus, it's too early for your singing."

I smiled. It wasn't perfect, but it was good.

CHAPTER 2

*Tomatoes need consistency over all. Establish a regular watering pattern
and stick to it. If you water them too little, then you overcorrect and
water too much, your tomatoes can explode—or at least crack. Not a
preferable situation for anyone, not least for the tomatoes. They can do
quite well with little interference if given the proper growing conditions.*
—EDWIN NICKERBOCKER, 1916 TREATISE ON TOMATOES

EVAN

I t had felt so strange yesterday to walk down the wide center hallway of the high school during the summer when it was quiet and
mostly empty. I imagined how it would be in a couple months when
I sailed through the doors as a ninth grader. Probably weird and awkward, but that was nothing new—middle school had felt like that most
of the time.

I hadn't realized until I opened the front doors of the school that
I had no idea how to get through the maze of hallways. Mom, having
been a student here eons ago, would have been able to tell me exactly
where to go, but I'd made her stay out in the car while I ran in to pick
up the packet of information the incoming students were supposed to
collect. I wanted to do it all on my own, but I ended up feeling kind of
lonely. Every time a door opened, I hoped to see Ruth's face.

Ruth Simms was just about the happiest, perkiest girl I'd ever met.

Even her hair was perky—her dark curls were often out of control, bouncing and springing everywhere. Looking at us, no one would think we'd be friends, but somehow we meshed. Probably because we were both outsiders. Ruth came from strict fundamentalist Christian parents who didn't approve of rock music, shorts, or tank tops. They probably didn't approve of me either, but my obsessions—*Eat a Peach*, *The Sky Is Crying*, my vintage concert tees—weren't the worst they'd seen from kids in Perry, so I guess that made me okay.

Ruth and I hung out a lot during school and after, although we rarely talked about anything deeper than homework, music (she had a secret love of Joni Mitchell), and our dreams for after college. But I was thankful for her friendship, especially since we were both about to enter this strange new world of high school.

I finally made it to the gym. Still no Ruth. Two lines of students zagged across the basketball court and led to two long tables set up in front of the bleachers. A handful of bored teachers sat behind the tables in folding chairs, handing out thick white envelopes and directing the students where to sign their names. I took my place in the shortest line and kept my head down but lifted my eyes to scan the kids in front of me. Who would be annoying me come September? Who would maybe, just maybe, be a new friend?

As the lines crept forward toward the desks, I heard his voice before I saw who the voice belonged to.

"Nick," the voice said. "Nick Bradley."

His voice was deep—deeper than the guys in eighth grade for sure. I lifted my head. The voice had come from a guy standing a few feet away at the head of the other line. He must have been at least a junior. His phone was tucked into his back pocket and red earbuds snaked up to his ears. He moved his head to a beat only he could hear. I so wanted to ask him what he was listening to, where he came from, something.

My line shifted then, passing me to the front. When the teacher behind the table asked for my name, I said it quietly. She squinted up from her clipboard. "Name?" she repeated. Loudly.

A few feet to my right, Nick glanced at me. The look plainly said, *"Poor kid."*

The woman said it yet again, and I muttered my name, my cheeks roasting.

"Say it one more time, dear. It sounded like you said Evan."

"I did. My name is Evan Ashby." I enunciated so she wouldn't ask again. Out of the corner of my eye, I saw Nick grab his packet and head for the glass doors at the back of the gym. I turned and watched him go. Just before he pushed the metal bar on the door, he looked back over his shoulder.

Later on, when I met Ruth at the Gas-N-Go for slushies, I wanted to ask her if she'd seen the guy at school or around town, but talking about boys was something we rarely did. Ruth wasn't allowed to—I wouldn't have been surprised if her parents had a secret tape recorder in her backpack to make sure she didn't talk about anything sinful— and I didn't often see anyone worth getting worked up over.

But there was something about this guy.

As I'd sat on the front porch with Mom this morning, watching her shell those slippery peas, part of me wanted to tell her how Nick had made me feel—all loosey-goosey inside, as Gus would say. Like my stomach and intestines and whatever else was sliding around, bumping into each other. But my mom wasn't the right person to ask about love.

Not that the thing with Nick was love—that'd be ridiculous. He was just some guy I'd probably never see again in the sea of seven hundred kids at Perry High School. But the jittery feeling—what was I supposed to do with that? I'd spent the last twenty-four hours trying to keep my mind from bouncing back to this dark-haired boy with the earbuds and those low-slung black jeans. No way would Mom understand feelings like that.

There hadn't been a man around our house in—well, ever. Other than Mr. Rainwater who occasionally came up the road smelling like the wrong end of a horse. But it was fine. Better than fine, actually. It had been just me, Mom, and my grandmother Gus for as long as I could remember. My dad was around at one time, of course, but I only had a few memories of our life back in Birmingham before me and Mom moved 250 miles south to Perry, Mom's hometown. I was only five when we moved. I rarely saw my dad now, and that was fine too. I did worry a little about Mom though.

Once in a while I'd catch her with a faraway look in her eyes when she thought no one else was around. Sometimes it seemed like she was thinking of something nice, when the corners of her mouth would pull up a little, like she was remembering a good dream. Then other times I knew she was thinking of bad things. Or at least sad ones. A line between her eyebrows sank in when she was concerned about something. When that line showed up, I tried to say something, anything, to make her smile.

This morning there was no half smile, but no wrinkled brow either, and the tightness in my chest unclenched a little. She usually seemed fine on her own with me and our house, her garden, and Gus down the road. She never acted like she needed or wanted anything else. But that look on her face when she saw the Jeep fly down the road? That meant something. I just didn't know what.

The only thing Mom ever said about my dad was that he was a part of her life that was gone for good. And that she liked this part of her life better. I did too. Our little three-person family had made it this far on our own, and I saw no need to add any unnecessary surprises.

CHAPTER 3

Certain plants can alert us to insect intruders, warn us of coming
rain or snow, or foretell an especially warm spring. While there's no
plant or flower that can warn us of major life changes, the very act
of gardening can be a solace to us in the midst of those changes.
—SELA RUTH MCGOVERN, THE WISDOM OF GARDENING

JESSIE

Long before my parents moved to Perry, maybe even before they were born, this area was nothing but woods. Fifteen miles northwest of Mobile, Perry was incorporated as a town in 1924, but it never grew much past the small, two-intersection town that sprouted up among the oaks, pines, and hickories that dominated the landscape. The smallness of it must have suited everyone just fine.

These days, most folks lived closer to the town instead of out on the roads and lanes that swirled through the countryside. It was lovely out here though—long sweeps of wildflowers in the summer, fields dotted with cows and horses, straight rows of corn and cotton and soybeans lining the roads.

My home and the cottage next door that now housed my shop were two of the first houses to pop up alongside this seam of red dirt that was plowed but never paved. Glory Road itself hadn't changed much between the time the first houses were built and today, as I squatted in the dirt behind my shop with a big bag of potting soil.

From the road, the driveway split—curve to the right and you'd meander to the front steps of Twig. Curve to the left and you'd arrive at the front door of the yellow house, where Evan and I lived. Sometimes when customers were scarce, I'd head home and make myself lunch or a cup of coffee, returning when chores beckoned or customers appeared.

After a hot minute of searching for a pull tab, I finally poked my fingernail through the plastic and ripped a hole in my new bag of Potter's Mix soil. Scissors would have been nice, but I'd forgotten my best pair up in the shop when I headed out to the field beyond my back fence, and I had no reason to preserve the cleanliness of my fingernails. Not with a job like this.

I ripped the hole open wider and inhaled. I loved the smell of earth—what was once something else mixing with the essence of what already is. The scent of life permeating life. And if it was a day when Harvis Rainwater's truck was working right, the sharp aroma of manure would soon be mixed in too.

Mama hated the days when Mr. Rainwater's truck rumbled up the road from his spread down at the end of the street. As soon as she heard the boatlike *chug-chug-chug* of the truck's engine, she'd pinch her nose with her red lacquered fingernails and beat a trail inside. If we were already inside, she'd just pout.

"I'm sorry, Jessie Mae," she'd say. "I know it's natural and it makes things grow, but can't you just use a normal bag of fertilizer? Why must you insist on the stink? It offends my nose."

When I heard the truck today, Mama was repotting a small rosebush in the shade near the back porch of the shop, her hands and forearms sheathed in elbow-length rubber gloves to protect her manicure. I shook the soil from my hands and stood. My knees protested a little too much for my taste, reminding me that squatting for so long wasn't good for my legs. That plus the early summer heat wave made me wish I had an extra employee to share some of the heavy lifting.

As it was, Gus and Evan were my only employees, and I used the term lightly—they were part-time at best. During the school year, Evan helped out as much as she could after school and on weekends, and Mama occasionally rang up customers or helped me with simple tasks around the shop. She preferred not to get her hands dirty, and gardening was nothing if not dirty.

The chugging grew louder, and Mr. Rainwater's truck appeared around the bend in the road. A flash of Mama's denim shirt and the slam of the back door told me she'd seen him too. The rosebush lay abandoned on its side next to the new pot, with dirt scattered all around it on the flagstone patio.

By the time I made it around the side of the shop to the driveway, he was already at the back of his truck, lifting a plastic storage box full of Loretta and Patsy's offerings. "His girls," as he called his elderly but still robust mares, unknowingly contributed to the success of my business. Their "contribution" didn't help so much on the herbs, but for flowers it was unbeatable, if a little stinky.

"How do?" he said when I reached the truck. "Loretta found her way into a big bag of grapes I left out in the barn, so she's been running a little rich. Maybe this will help that hydrangea bush you're having trouble with." He rested the container on top of the wheelbarrow he always kept tied down in the back of his truck.

"Maybe so. Not much else has helped. Not even the slivers of peach pie Mama set out at the base of it a few days ago."

He laughed. "Augusta up to her antics again?"

"Not again." I wiped my damp forehead with the back of my hand. "She never stops. She thinks her pies and cakes can save the world's problems. Beginning with my stubborn hydrangea."

"I tend to agree with her. Her cobblers have solved many a

problem here on Glory Road." He took off his cap and used it to fan his face. "I remember once Mrs. Teebo's son got into a fistfight with Al Sparkman's nephew. His nephew was a bit of a pill, but he was here for the summer, so we put up with him. Everyone except Nelson Teebo. He punched that poor boy square in the jaw and would have kept at it if your mama hadn't slammed out her front door. She carried two slices of cobbler on one plate and a pair of forks. All that squabbling stopped faster than you can say jump-in-the-truck."

It was a good story—one I'd heard at least ten times. "Augusta McBride always did know how to stop men in their tracks."

"I heard that," she called from the front porch of the shop.

"Come on out, Mama, and help us with this wheelbarrow, will you?" I winked at Mr. Rainwater. He shook his head.

"I'm not coming within twenty yards of that stinking mess and you know it," she yelled.

Mr. Rainwater shook his cap, then placed it back on his head, gray hair sticking out over his large ears. "I'm not hanging around to see this." He steered the wheelbarrow toward my garden in the back where I grew hydrangeas and azaleas, gardenias and zinnias. I loved their colors, their scents, and the stems they provided for small arrangements I tried to keep on hand for customers to take home. I followed him behind the greenhouse to the plastic swimming pool I used to store the manure. A tarp weighted down with bricks kept critters and curious deer out of my stash—not to mention keeping the aroma in check.

When he'd dumped the load and tied his wheelbarrow into the bed of his truck, Mr. Rainwater pulled a red bandanna out of the pocket of his overalls and wiped his face, then climbed into his seat. "I've been meaning to tell you, Gus's sign out on the highway looks good."

A month ago, at Mama's request, Mr. Rainwater had tacked up a wooden board directly below the sign on the main highway that pointed down Glory Road to the shop. Her hand-painted words read: Slice of Gus's World-Famous Pie or Cobbler Free with Purchase.

"Has it brought in any new customers?" he asked.

"I don't know about new, but just about everyone who's walked in here has left with a slice of something. She's charging them for ice cream though."

He laughed. "Tell her I said hello and good-bye, would you? I'd tell her myself, but I don't want to bother her any more than necessary."

"I'll do that." I patted his hand on the window ledge.

He slid into reverse but then paused. "Has she been . . . ?" He tapped his fingers against the steering wheel. "She been feeling okay lately?"

I shrugged. "She seems fine to me."

"That's good." He nodded. "She just seemed a little off last time I saw her."

I smiled. "You mean sassier than usual?"

He shook his head. I thought I saw a faint blush on his cheeks, but it could have just been the heat. "Something like that."

He tipped his hat and chug-chugged back down the way he came. I watched him until the truck disappeared around the bend in the road. As I turned back to the front steps, I pondered his words. Mama had been a little different in recent months. Nothing bad, just . . . well, just "off," as Mr. Rainwater said. I'd dismissed it, but his mention of it made me wonder if I'd been too quick in my dismissal.

"You can come out of hiding," I called to her when I reached the top step. As I approached the door, I almost bumped into tiny Elma Dean on her way out. She held a small potted tulip in her hands.

"Thanks for stopping in, Elma," Mama chirped after her.

Elma teetered down the steps and carefully placed the pot in the cup holder of her Honda Civic. From the porch, I could see the three pillows she had to sit on to see over the dash.

She tooted her horn as she drove away, gravel crunching and

spitting under the tires. Inside, Mama poked around the shop, casually dusting here and there as if everything were right in her world. She even hummed under her breath.

"How much did you charge Ms. Dean for the tulip?"

"First rule of business, my dear: don't charge your friends. And she's been my friend since we were in Mrs. Collins's first-grade class in the two-room schoolhouse on Mauvila Avenue. You know, the one that's a Gas-N-Go now?"

"Yes, you've mentioned that." My mother could go on a tear about how things used to be. Every time one of the old buildings in Perry was bulldozed to make way for a shiny new CVS or Shell station, she said we were one step closer to the Rapture. "But you do know that you're friends with every single person in Perry, and if you follow your first rule of business—which is not a real rule, by the way—we won't have any business?"

Mama waved the thought away as if it were a pesky fly. "Friends will stick by you when the going gets tough. What did those tulips ever do for you?"

"Pay for that fancy manicure, for one." I muttered it under my breath, but I knew she heard me because she held out her hand and flicked a speck of dirt off her pinky.

Mama had been giving away occasional free tidbits to her friends since the day I opened Twig's doors almost eight years ago. Usually I was able to turn a blind eye, but lately things were changing. With the recent arrival of Earl's Green Thumb Garden Center less than a mile away, even some of my most loyal customers had been lured in by the promise of $4.98 trays of begonias, no matter that they were poor quality and didn't come with a slice of Mama's cobbler on the side.

After washing my hands in the deep sink along the far wall, I ducked out the back door, catching the screen with my foot before it slammed behind me. The back of the shop was covered by an arbor draped with lavender wisteria and sweet Confederate jasmine. The thick vines and dainty tendrils created a deep, welcome shade.

Years ago, I stuck an old rocking chair back into the corner behind the door, and sometimes I sat there even while customers streamed in and out. They'd pass on by, not noticing the slight movement of my chair. Today the shade beckoned with cool, soft fingers and I sank into the chair, rested my head on the back, and closed my eyes.

It was hard to believe this small two-room cottage that now held birdhouses, decorative flowerpots, wind chimes, and other assorted gardening gifts once held the neighborhood's junk. When I was young, the cottage was home to Perry's House of Salvaged Goods, an emporium of sorts run by Mr. Berkeley, an old man who'd lived in the cottage "since time began," as Mama liked to say.

The cottage, and the yellow house next door that Mr. Berkeley also owned, had been vacant for years by the time I moved back home with five-year-old Evan and our Mercedes SUV stuffed with everything we owned, which pretty much amounted to our clothes, books, and Evan's toys. I hadn't wanted to bring anything else—I no longer felt a connection to any of it. Not even to Chris's last name. In our divorce proceedings I requested permission to change my name back to McBride. The change felt right. Natural.

I moved back into my childhood home with Mama, just down the road from Mr. Berkeley's spread, while I figured out how to navigate my new life and dodge the deep crack Chris had gouged into my heart. That crack remained for months, as raw and jagged as the day I found out about *Tiffani*, despite Mama's best intentions to bury my grief in fruit cobblers and buttermilk biscuits.

The sugar helped in the short term, but what really served as a balm to my spirit was the road itself. The split rail fences, the fields, the quiet. For the first time, I appreciated this place that had been the backdrop to my childhood, the place I wanted to escape after high school. Now I saw its particular beauty and the sacrifices my parents made to give me a happy, stable childhood in this place of freedom and fresh air.

I'd been here six months when I saw a man tapping a For Sale sign into the red dirt in front of Mr. Berkeley's cottage. That sign triggered something in me. Glory Road was the same stretch of land it had always been, but somehow it felt like a new version of itself. If it could feel new, maybe I could be a new version of myself too. All at once, I knew this would be where I could stand boldly on my own two feet and grow—and Evan and Mama could grow right along with me. Love had let me down, but now I could bloom for myself.

Three days later, I sat at a long cherrywood table and signed a half-inch-thick stack of papers that transferred ownership of the cottage, its grounds, and the yellow house next door to me.

As soon as Evan and I were settled in the yellow house—a sweet 1947 three-bedroom home with original hardwood floors, six-inch crown moldings, and large airy windows—I got to work. I'd always been interested in plants and gardens—I used to dream of backpacking across Europe to visit the gardens of Versailles, Giverny, and Villa d'Este—but never entertained the idea of opening my own garden business until the opportunity blossomed right in front of me.

The closest place to buy plants and flowers was five miles away, and my idea was to create a welcoming space where folks in Perry and the surrounding areas could not only buy plants to beautify their homes and yards, but also relax, learn, and get their hands dirty. I wanted to show them life could be coaxed from even the driest, most unforgiving ground. I decided on the name Twig because I liked what it represented: something alive and growing. Wanting to be so much more, but not quite there yet.

I sold the Mercedes and used that profit, plus a small business loan from the bank, to build a greenhouse behind the cottage. The one-acre property already boasted an impressive display of flowering shrubs and fruit trees thanks to Mr. Berkeley's near-obsessive gardening habit. I pruned those and added to them, then built up an inventory of trays, pallets, and pots of annuals and perennials, bought mostly from Alabama growers. I took master gardening classes at the public library and the Botanical Gardens in Mobile to hone what I already knew and add to my knowledge.

It took nearly a year before I felt ready to open the shop to customers. By then, I was so steeped in the gardening world, I felt I'd been born to do it. As if all the time before—my young years at home, my years with Chris, all my hopes and regrets and half-blurry dreams—had been seeds dropped down into deep holes that were just now peeking their heads aboveground and stretching up toward the sky.

I lifted my feet off the ground and let the rocking chair coast to a slow stop, the old boards sighing in relief. Above me, the fan Mr. Rainwater had wired onto the arbor sent down a surprisingly forceful breeze, stirring the scents around me into an intoxicating mixture of honey, vanilla, and rich, dark earth.

When I'd first moved back home, I'd craved something, anything, that couldn't be taken away from me. All I had was Evan and Mama. Not even my sweet father was there anymore—he'd died while I was pregnant with Evan, four months shy of meeting his only grandchild. I felt like a weary traveler desperate to claim something as my own.

Eight years later, I still couldn't believe my luck in walking up Glory Road the day the agent stuck the sign in Mr. Berkeley's yard. That I was given a chance to claim my spot on the map before anyone else took it. My home with Evan in the yellow house, Mama down the road, my life's purpose in the greenhouse and tucked into pots scattered around Twig—this was my life now. Keeping things small—close to home—meant no one could take it away.

CHAPTER 4

*Creativity is a crucial characteristic of a good gardener. Just about
anything can creep in and ruin your hard work. When this happens,
it's the gardener's chance to make do. To be creative. However, a
good gardener also knows when it's time to call for help. Sometimes
it takes more than just one set of hands to make things right.*
—SALLY JO MCINTYRE, CONTEMPLATIVE GARDENING

JESSIE

It was almost the end of the workday and I could practically feel
my Nikes wrapped around my feet, my legs pumping down Glory
Road, my mind blissfully free for forty-five minutes. The run didn't
happen every night—sometimes several days would pass without me
lacing up my shoes—but I always returned to it. It would be waiting
for me, like an old friend ready to listen.

It wasn't that Twig was an especially difficult place to work. I
got to keep my hands in the dirt, run my business fifty yards from
my home, and keep an eye on Mama during the day. But some days
the combination of heat and grime, money worries, and certain fussy
customers almost did me in.

Today Birdie Davis had spent my entire lunch break bemoaning
the black spot of death on her climbing roses and how I'd sold her a
defective product (which I hadn't). Major Gregg, an eighteen-wheeler

21

of a man who regularly drove all the way from Sweet Bay just to buy flowers at Twig, had badgered me for twenty minutes about slugs on his petunias. Then I'd discovered a wasp nest the size of a football under the eaves of my potting shed. Unfortunately, I discovered it with the end of my rake, sending hundreds of wasps into a frenzy and scaring away my customers. Days like today, I was ready to hang a Closed sign in the window and hop a plane to an island somewhere.

But then there was that dreamy purple-and-blue hour—the slip of time after the sun went down but before it got dark—when I'd sit on the front porch after a long run and look out on what I had. My little house with the wavy glass in the windows. The tin-roofed, plank-walled shop with overflowing window boxes and flowering vines creeping up and over the porch rails.

Mama and Evan would be in the house chatting about this or that—maybe Mama was telling her about the exact point at which Johnny Cash's music turned from dark to holy, or maybe Evan would be explaining how Joni Mitchell's "Come In from the Cold" has some of the most achingly perfect lyrics of any song ever written.

Whatever had happened during the day, however much we sold or didn't sell, whatever prickly or lovely customers strolled in, it all faded when I saw our spread of land in the falling light.

For now, Mama was still in the shop, dusting and rearranging. Though she wasn't Twig's owner, she often acted like she was, insisting that everything had to be lined up just so and that no speck of dust sat on a shelf unnoticed. I appreciated her fastidiousness because it meant I didn't have to spend precious hours during the day on housekeeping.

The clock on the wall told me I only had fifteen minutes until closing, so with an empty gravel lot out front, I began processing the day's transactions. This part of the day was usually the most tense—seeing how big a bite Earl's Green Thumb had taken from Twig and mulling over the lingering financial effects our rare cold spring had had on the business. Plus, my computer had been acting funny lately.

22

Granted, it was ancient, but other than a few long phone calls to customer service centers in India, it had been mostly reliable, and I hadn't wanted to find the money to upgrade. It had been taking longer to boot up in the mornings though, and just recently it started going dark for short periods during the day. Mama joked that it was taking its afternoon siesta.

I was chewing a fingernail and squinting at the screen—did that column show I sold a whole four thousand dollars less this month than the same month last year?—when it released a high-pitched beep and the screen went completely black.

"What in the world?"

"What is it, dear?" Mama was on the other side of the room dusting the rack of wind chimes, making such a racket she almost had to shout.

"I think my computer just died."

I ran through my usual arsenal of cures—press the power button a few times, jiggle the mouse, check to make sure the cord was plugged in securely—but the screen stayed stubbornly blank. I leaned over and planted my forehead on the surface of my desk.

"Why don't you try unplugging it? That usually does the trick."

I fought the urge to roll my eyes. "I don't think that'll help."

Finished with the wind chimes, she crossed the room and peered at the screen. "I don't want to say I told you so, but . . ."

"But you told me so?" My forehead was still pressed against the smooth wood of the desk.

"If you'd just use a simple credit-card swiper with the carbon paper and a plain old bank ledger, you wouldn't be in this mess. Never trust a computer. Or a politician." She patted my hand. "I'm headed to the house. I'll check on your peas and add a little water, make sure they're not burned to the bottom of the saucepan. Oh, and I'd call Cliff if I were you."

With a swish of her short gray bob, she was gone.

I picked up the phone and called the only computer repair place in Perry, Cliff's Computer World. I knew Cliff well because he asked me to plant the flower beds in front of his shop each season.

"Did you try plugging in the laptop?" he asked when I explained my problem. "Maybe the battery just died."

"Well, the battery won't stay charged. I keep it plugged in all the time."

"You keep it . . . ?" He sighed. "Okay. Why don't you try unplugging it? Count to ten, then plug it back in."

I reached around and yanked the cord out of the wall, then did a quick "one-Mississippi, two-Mississippi" and plugged it back in. "I got nothing."

He went over a few more options to try, then exhaled. I heard his chair squeak as if he was leaning back and propping his feet on the desk. "And how long have you had your laptop?"

"Let's see. I got it just after Evan was born, so fourteen years. Thereabouts." As I talked, I pushed away from the desk and opened the front door. The porch of the shop was in the shade now, and I sat in the glider by the door.

Cliff laughed, one sharp snort followed by a little giggle. "Fourteen years? And it's a PC? It's likely your motherboard's gone out. You're lucky it's lasted this long. I can check it out, but it'll take me a little while to get to it. The fire department just dropped off one of their computers that's on the fritz."

"How long is 'a little while'? This is the only computer I have." I watched as Mama ambled through the grass to my house. Halfway there, she stopped and patted her front and back pockets, then stood completely still. She stayed that way for so long, I stood, thinking something was wrong. But as soon as I did, she patted her pockets again, shook her head, and continued on to my house.

"Doesn't the fire department have some computers in reserve they can use?" I asked, my mind partly on Mama, partly on my laptop.

"Ms. McBride, it's the fire department. I do whatever they ask."

"Yes, yes. I know." By this time, Mama had made it to the house and opened the front door. I rubbed my left eye, the one that always twitched when I felt stressed. I sat back in the glider and blew my bangs out of my eyes. "The fire department comes first, obviously."

"I'll call you as soon as I have an opening, but just know if the motherboard is fried, won't be anything I can do to fix it." An image of Mama's fried eggs flashed in my mind, the yellow yolks slip-sliding across the plate. "You may want to start thinking about a replacement. And if you'll hang on just a sec . . ." He rummaged around a moment. "Here it is. A buddy of mine sells computers. Let me give you his information. Now, his name is Hank . . ."

I took a deep breath and let it out in a thin stream. Money for a new computer wasn't in the budget. Even a trip to Cliff's Computer World wasn't in the budget.

"Are you writing this down, Ms. McBride?"

"Oh yes, I'm writing it down." I rested my head on the back of the glider and closed my eyes.

※

By the time I locked everything up and got back to the house, it was too late to run without food in my stomach. I'd have to squeeze it in after dinner. I kicked off my rubber boots on the front porch and opened the screen door. When it slammed behind me, both Evan and Mama looked up from where they were hard at work in the kitchen.

"Close that front door, hon," Mama called. "No need to invite all that muggy heat inside." Like it was her house and we just lived in it.

In truth, Mama lived next door, although three acres of trees and brush stood between our houses. Since she helped out in the shop during the day, she tended to use our house as a landing base until the three of us had eaten dinner. After cleaning up the kitchen, something

25

she insisted on doing and I wasn't about to argue, she'd gather her things from the day—the large-print crossword puzzle book, a stack of magazines, her denim jacket—and start the quarter-mile walk back to her house. Rain or shine, freezing cold or blazing hot, she always walked home. One evening, during tropical storm Dawn a few years ago, I had to force her into my car to drive her home. She was mad for two days.

"What are y'all working on?" I leaned over the pot of peas on the stove and gave them a stir. They were perfect—brown, almost creamy.

"Gus is teaching me how to make The June," Evan said.

"The June, huh? She reserves that one for only the most special people."

"That's what she told me. I've been sworn to secrecy, although who am I going to blab it to? None of my friends care about cobbler recipes."

"All the same," Mama said. "Best just keep it to yourself. Especially when I add the secret ingredient."

I loved watching the two of them, their heads bent over the bowl of milk, butter, eggs, and vanilla. Mama would give a baking tutorial to a pecan shell if no one else was around. Evan liked to pretend she didn't care about Mama's recipes, but her expression before they heard me come in told me she did care. She was rapt, watching as Mama cracked the eggs—one-handed, Julia Child–style—and whisked in the milk with swift strokes.

When Evan slid the peach-and-blueberry cobbler—including a generous pinch of cinnamon and nutmeg—into the oven, we sat down at the scratched and dinged oak table. A friend had once offered to sand off the top layer to take out all the scratches. "It's a shame to see an antique piece like this all marked up."

I thanked her but kept the scratches and marks. The woman didn't know it, but most of the scratches were actually indentations from pens and pencils. I'd done my homework at this table, as had

Evan. Those "scratches" were two generations of algebra headaches, English essays, and foreign language verb conjugations. Mama had passed the table on to me when we moved into the house and didn't have a place to eat our dinners. I hadn't realized how much I'd missed its presence until I was back to sitting at it three times a day. The table was a part of us, like most everything else on Glory Road.

"How's the computer?" Mama dolloped a serving spoonful of peas onto her plate, then turned to Evan. "It refused to wake up from its afternoon siesta today."

I propped my elbow on the table and sank my chin into my hand. "Cliff thinks it's fried."

"Maybe you can do without," Mama said. "Customers can use cash instead of cards. All you'd need is a notebook to jot everything down and a zippered pouch for the money."

"No one carries cash anymore. Everyone uses cards. No one will take me seriously if I tell them I only accept cash, then shove it into a pencil pouch. Not with Big Earl offering everything from free gardening classes to buy-one-get-one-free terra-cotta planters. I've got to keep up with them somehow. Starting with a working computer."

"So go buy a new one."

I stretched my neck, taut from the day's frustrations. "Do you have an extra thousand dollars lying around? Or even seven hundred? I don't. Twig doesn't."

Mama cut a slice of cornbread and slid it onto my plate. "You'll think of something, hon. You always do."

I sighed and turned to Evan. "How was your day? Did you and Ruth make it to the Icebox?"

"Yeah. It was so cold. I don't understand how the water can be that cold when it's two hundred degrees outside."

"It comes straight from Alaska," Mama said around a bite of rice, as if that town legend made a bit of sense. She gestured with her fork. "It bubbles up from the ground to make Perry's finest swimming hole."

27

Evan looked at me with raised eyebrows.

I shrugged. "It's what they say."

"Who's 'they'?"

"Who knows, but whoever they are, they were saying it when I was a kid too."

"Well, it was freezing. After a while, we just sat up on the rocks and stuck our feet in."

We ate in comfortable silence for a few moments until Mama broke it.

"Oh, did I tell you Elma came in today? She wanted something special for her Sunday school teacher. Poor Georgia's in the hospital with another kidney stone."

I searched her eyes to see if she was making a joke.

"What?" Mama asked. "Kidney stones are serious. They're like childbirth all over again. Elma just wanted to cheer her up."

"I saw Elma. I was there when you sent her out the door with a tulip."

"What? No you weren't. You were up at the . . ." She pointed her finger and gestured over to her left.

"No, Mama. I was there. We talked about you giving away things for free."

"You were not there, Jessie." Mama's voice was harsh, and my stomach swirled. "You were gone, I treated my friend to something nice, and then I stood on the top step and watched her drive away." She took a deep breath, defusing her anger. "You were not there. That's all there is to it."

Silence wrapped around the table and she picked up her fork again. I glanced at Evan. Her eyes were wide. I gave a little shrug like it was no big deal, but the truth was, I wasn't sure. I thought about Mr. Rainwater's words this morning. His concern. And then there was that nagging little voice that had sneaked its way into my brain over the last several months. I told myself it was nothing. Forgetfulness was normal. Quick zaps of anger or anxiety were normal. Mama was fine.

"Anyway," Mama said, then swallowed her bite. "Elma Dean is the sweetest little thing, isn't she?"

"She is. And I hope next time she comes in, I'm there to say hi. And to make sure she doesn't leave with something she didn't pay for."

"Elma's not like that."

"You're right. *Elma* is not a thief." I narrowed one eye, but Mama's face stayed as calm as a spring day.

"Oh, that reminds me." She tapped her red fingernail against her water glass. "I've been meaning to tell you about this idea I had. I know you've been a touch nervous about the shop lately. I still think it'll all come out in the wash, but have you thought about getting into the wedding business?"

"The wedding business? As in . . . ?"

"As in wedding flowers. It's a big business, you know. I saw a flyer on the window of Coleman's Bakery advertising some big wedding-palooza at the civic center in Mobile for brides-to-be. It said over a hundred vendors would be there, including florists. You could get some business cards made up, get you a card table, and tell those brides to call you."

Evan smirked and I shook my head. "No. I'm not in the wedding business, nor do I want to be." I crammed a bite into my mouth. "I know enough about weddings to know brides—not to mention their mothers—are not the kind of customers I want."

"Shoo." Mama waved her hand in the air. "You're a genius with flowers. You could do it if you wanted. And it could be a boost for the shop. A big one. You know how fathers who dearly love their daughters will pay hand over foot for whatever the daughters want." She cocked an eyebrow in my direction.

"Yes, I know that." My dad had paid extra at the last minute because I'd caved and asked for out-of-season lilies for the bridesmaids and grandmothers-of-the-groom bouquets. I'd never had the heart to tell Mama I'd only done it in the hopes of making Chris's mother happy. I didn't even like lilies—the smell always gave me a headache. Fifteen years later, I still wanted to kick myself for having the gall to ask my sweet father to pay even more money just to make an unhappy woman like me.

"Not gonna happen. I don't need that kind of drama in my life, thank you." I pushed back from the table and wiped my mouth. "I'm going to change into my running clothes." I kissed Evan on the top of her head and walked back toward my bedroom.

Just before I closed the door behind me, Mama called out, "What you need in your life, Jessie Mae, is some magic."

I sighed and leaned back against the doorjamb. She was always telling me that. She never specified what brand of magic she was referring to, but knowing Mama, she was talking about a man. As if they grew on trees way out here in Perry. As if I wanted one, anyway.

CHAPTER 5

Sweet peas are an old-fashioned favorite in any garden. A bouquet of
sweet peas can fill a room and your senses with its exquisite, haunting
aroma, almost a memory of a beloved scent rather than an actual smell.
—LUCY LANGWORTHY, GUIDE TO FRAGRANT FLOWERS, 1945

JESSIE

Ten minutes later, I stood at the end of our driveway clad in running shorts, a tank top, and my worn-but-still-sturdy running
shoes. It was seven thirty, later than my usual after-work run, but
the almost deafening roar of the early evening cicadas and the fully
shaded road made me rethink my routine.

Glory Road was three miles long, full of houses that looked almost
exactly the same as they had when I was a child playing kickball in
the middle of the red dirt. Roads in the rest of Perry were paved,
but for some reason, the city had never made it to our road. Folks
on other roads, in other neighborhoods, might have complained, but
those around here seemed to like it. Something about the lack of
asphalt kept everything a little bit quieter, a little calmer. Like the red
dirt dimmed noises and soothed tempers.

I rarely saw anything out of the ordinary on my evening runs. The
same neighbors sitting on the same front porches. The same bright-
blue bug zappers dangling from porch eaves. The same sounds in the

31

trees, almost like whispers welcoming me back. The fact that nothing changed on the road was part of the reason it had been such a relief to settle here after Birmingham. It was a comfort to come back and find it mostly untouched, steady as always. I didn't appreciate or even recognize that steadiness when I was a teenager—the quiet solitude came across to me as *too* rural, *too* country—but I relished it now.

My habit was to turn off Glory about a half mile past my house. I'd take one of the handful of smaller lanes that forked off the main road and run until my legs felt like jelly, then turn around. I never let myself think too hard about why I tended to avoid a certain portion of the road. It was an almost-subconscious veering of my feet and I let them take me where they wanted. Tonight, however, they kept me heading straight down Glory Road.

I was lost in thought—Mama's outburst, the dead laptop, Evan's face, so pure and startling, and the boys who would soon begin to notice it—when I paused to retie a shoelace that had flapped loose. At another time, when my mind wasn't so free and endorphin-soaked, I might have taken more detailed notice of where I'd paused, but it didn't register until I saw the dog.

He trotted down the adjacent driveway toward me, sniffing and smiling as only a dog can. I had no problem with dogs, but I did have a problem with unpredictability, so my first inclination was to keep my eyes locked safely on him. But then details of the scene before me unveiled themselves one by one: the chocolate Lab's red-and-black plaid collar, telling me he was someone's well-loved pet. The familiar ranch house, long and low, with the bright-blue door. And the Jeep Grand Wagoneer in the driveway. In the exact same spot where it used to sit. The porch light was on, and a lamp in the front bay window gave off a welcoming glow. Blood roared in my ears and sweat prickled at my hairline.

Meanwhile, the dog sniffed at my shoes, then my legs, then my ear. I leaned back to keep him a comfortable distance from my face, then straightened up again. He regarded me with hopeful eyes and a wagging tail. With one eye on the front window, I reached down and scratched his ear. "You're pretty cute."

Before I realized what was happening, he was on his hind legs, his front paws propped all the way up on my shoulders. His tongue slurped the side of my face.

"Sorry, sorry," I heard behind me. "I'm coming."

The dog slid his paws from my shoulders as a boy—a young man, really—jogged down the driveway. When he reached us, he grabbed the dog's plaid collar, knelt next to him, and spoke firmly. "Sit, Stanley. No jump." Then he stood and faced me. "Sorry about that. I thought I latched the gate in the back, but he must have nosed it open."

"It's all right." I wiped the side of my face with the back of my wrist. My mind raced, trying to place this kid and the house and the Jeep behind him. "Are you . . . ? Do you . . . ?"

"I'm Nick. We just moved in." He gestured to the stack of flattened cardboard boxes by the garage. "A few days ago. Stanley's still checking everything out, as you can see."

Nick. The dark hair. The kid in the passenger seat of the Jeep. The one Evan had seen at registration.

Stanley pushed his nose into my thigh and I reached down again. Smoothed my hand across the top of his head. "So are you . . . ?" I cleared my throat. "I'm sorry. I'm a neighbor. I live just up the road. I've known the Bradleys for . . . for a while. Did they move?" Ben's parents had lived in this house my whole life, and I hadn't heard a thing about them moving out. I also couldn't figure how this kid fit into the picture. Not to mention the Jeep. It was so remarkably like Ben's, but that was crazy—no way could it still be running this many years later.

Then another thought skittered through my consciousness, so quick I almost couldn't grab it. But it was there. *Could it be?* I could have figured it out if my brain wasn't such a scramble, but as it was, my math skills were lacking.

"Yep, they moved down to Florida. Some retirement place. They like to call it a resort." He shrugged. "They always said they wanted to live at the beach one day."

Stanley nosed around a pile of leaves at the edge of the driveway. "So the Bradleys are your . . . grandparents?"

"Right, yes. Sorry, I should have mentioned that."

Without realizing what I was doing, I began to back away. Stanley trotted over to me and sniffed around my knees. My shoelace had come untied again, but I didn't stop to fix it. "I need to get going." I jerked my thumb in the direction of my house up the road.

Nick smiled and reached down to grab Stanley's collar again.

I took a few more steps, then paused and called out to him. "That Jeep—is it yours?" I knew, but I needed to hear it.

He shook his head. "It's my dad's. He's been driving that thing since he was my age."

I turned and began walking toward home. After fifty feet or so, I picked it up to a jog, then ran faster until a curtain of trees separated me from the house and the sound of cicadas drowned out Stanley's excited barks.

❧

When I arrived back home, breathing harder than usual after a run, Mama was on the front porch. The sky had darkened quickly after the sun set, the edges fading to the color of a bruised peach.

"See anything out of the ordinary?"

I sat on the top porch step and stretched my legs in front of me. I shook my head. "Status quo."

"Old Harvis wasn't out there feeding his horses grapes again?"

"Nope. All's quiet on his end."

"Humph," she snorted. "He's always up to something." Mama creaked back and forth on the porch swing. In the trees around us insects thrummed loud and off pitch. "I may run up the road tomorrow with a pound cake for him. No telling what baked goods he gets these days, being a widower and all."

"He's in church every Sunday and most Wednesday nights. You know the DIVAS must bring him pies by the dozen. They've been doing it for years."

"Those women wouldn't know a good pound cake if it sailed through their window and took out their TV. I'll bring him one tomorrow. Maybe add a small pitcher of whipped cream. Little cinnamon on top."

I smiled but hid it quickly when she raised an eyebrow at me. I held my hands up. "I didn't say a thing."

"Don't you dare. I just have to hold my own with those women, that's all it is. Everyone knows desserts are my territory. I have a reputation to uphold, whether they're part of the faithful or not."

I lifted up loose tendrils that had fallen from my ponytail and fanned the back of my neck. "Mama, I wouldn't want to encroach on your territory if it was the last space on planet Earth."

"That's my girl."

She swung and I sat, silent except for the symphony happening in the trees around us. The pound cake had been a nice distraction, but I returned to thoughts of Ben. Both of us back on Glory Road. Both with nearly grown kids. Surely neither of us would have imagined, all those years ago, that we'd be back here again. At least not like this. I rolled my head side to side, trying to work out the tension in my neck and shoulders.

The Bradleys had lived in the same house all this time, but Mrs. Bradley had always been a low-maintenance gardener. She kept a row of neatly trimmed azaleas along the front of their house and hostas in the shady spots. She stopped at Twig only a couple times a year to purchase her spring and fall annuals. When she did, we always chatted politely, but neither of us tried to extend the conversation any longer than necessary. It wasn't that anything devastating or horrible had happened between Ben and me. It's more what hadn't happened. And what hadn't happened was probably what a lot of people—including Ben, and maybe even me—expected would happen. And he and I went seventeen years without laying eyes on each other. Until now. I closed my eyes and propped my elbows on the step behind me.

With him right down the road, his son and Evan going to the same school, we were bound to run into each other. Even if he avoided Twig, we'd surely still see each other at the school. Or bump into each other in the grocery store. Or I'd see him or his wet-nosed dog on my evening runs. Perry, Alabama, was small. Glory Road was even smaller.

"Jessie." Mama's voice was loud.

"Hmm?" I jerked my head toward her. She pointed to the door.

"Geez, Mom. I've called you three times." Evan poked her head around the screen door, her hair a waterfall of blonde waves. "Where's the popcorn?"

"Oh, uh . . ." I tried to visualize where I'd put the box after my last grocery run. "Maybe near the cereal? Or the peanut butter. It's in there somewhere."

Evan ducked back inside. I reached my arms up over my head and stretched my sides. Everything felt loose, like bendy rubber.

"What's going on with you?" Mama asked.

"Why didn't you tell me the Bradleys had moved out of their house?"

"Oh, did they?"

"Don't give me that. You know everything that happens around here."

"I ran into Elaine a few weeks ago and she mentioned she and Charles were thinking about moving, but you know how they are, always flitting around, traveling here and there. I didn't put much stock in it. They never put up a For Sale sign so I forgot about it. Why? What'd you hear?"

"I didn't *hear* anything. I just met Ben's son. Nick. They've moved in."

The expression on Mama's face didn't change, but her leg moved almost imperceptibly, rocking the swing back and forth just a touch harder. "Is that so?"

"It is. Apparently the Bradleys moved to Florida. Some retirement resort."

"Ben Bradley back on Glory Road." She chuckled under her breath. "Well, if that ain't something to add a little kick."

"Yep. It's something."

In the house behind us, the familiar strains of *The Princess Bride*, Evan's favorite movie, echoed from the TV, but Mama and I stayed on the porch. Her mind was likely drifting into the past just as mine was. Around us, the air was rich with scents—sun-warmed dirt, thick St. Augustine grass in need of a good soak, and that sweet just-before-the-rain smell. Then, far off to the south, a deep rumble of summertime thunder.

CHAPTER 6

Difficile piperis—better known by its common name, "the difficult pepper"—tests even the strongest-willed gardeners. In rare and lucky circumstances, the gardener will learn to give the plant some leeway and the ensuing relationship will be beneficial to both parties. The plant will have an "owner" who understands its particular needs, and the gardener will be blessed with a plant of great temerity and strength of spirit.
—KAYE BUCKLEY, *PEPPER PLANTS FOR LIFE AND LOVE*

GUS

Ninety-five percent of the time, when two people get married, it's easy to tell which one married up. For Tom and me, we both married up. It's rare, I know, but that's just how it happened.

My sweet Tom was not the handsomest or most refined man to walk the streets of Perry. His ears were a little too big, his eyes too narrow, his hair a little thin on top. He was lanky as a coat hanger and had a bad habit of stuffing used Kleenexes in the pockets of his Carhartts, which left me picking bits of white fluff out of the dryer vent for weeks. He took a job working at his daddy's lumber mill after high school and eventually made a solid career there, though he started off shoving wood chips into piles with a push broom.

But oh, he was kind and he loved me so well. I was a spitfire. Thought I knew all there was to know about men and women, the ways of the world, and how to get exactly what I wanted. But the day eighteen-year-old Tom McBride threw a foul ball that bounced up and broke my cheekbone, I realized I didn't actually know much of anything. All my flirting and sassing and batting my eyelashes amounted to nothing in the face of this man who gently held my hand the entire five hours I spent in the emergency room. He hardly let go of that hand for the next thirty-seven years, until he fell off our ladder while cleaning hickory leaves out of the clogged gutter.

So we both married up. I added some color to his world—showed him there was more to life than just blue-collared work shirts and chores around the house. I signed us up for dance lessons and we learned the cha-cha, the Charleston, and the Carolina shag. We dressed up and went out to nice dinners once a month and occasionally saw a movie at the theater in Mobile. I liked to think he appreciated me opening his eyes to a wider world.

And one of the things I appreciated most about Tom was that he slowed me down. He'd take my hand and lead me to the front porch swing to listen to a thunderstorm as it rolled by. Turn off the lamps and light a candle so we could talk, long and slow, into the night. Tell a ridiculous joke about two preachers walking into a bar, but tell it in such a way that tears rolled down my cheeks and my heart just about caved in my chest at my luck in marrying that good, sweet, honest man.

Jessie grew up seeing the love between Tom and me. It wasn't always perfect—we had our fair share of fights, mainly because my selfishness would butt up against his calm benevolence and it annoyed the stew out of me—but it was real. And I knew Jessie wanted that for herself. You can't blame a girl for wanting love and passion in her life when she grew up with a father who adored his wife, day in and day out. Who wouldn't want that kind of love? She just went about it the wrong way.

But I learned early on that a mother can't change her daughter's

39

ways by forcing her. Or by telling her she's wrong, though Lord have mercy, I wanted to so often. By nature, my Jessie was not the cheerleader type, but that's who the boys in Perry wanted, so that was the identity she took on. She lightened her hair, could have bought stock in that sticky pink lip gloss all the girls wore, and hiked her cheerleading shirt up as high as she could and still get out the door under Tom's watchful eye. She became the "popular girl," though deep down, I think even she knew it didn't fit.

Truth be told, I always thought Ben Bradley was more her speed. He was quiet, smart, not your average football player. He was also humble, which I appreciated. He and Jessie spent many after-school hours together, and I saw how he looked at her. Dare I say, it verged on adoration. She said they were just friends, but I had my doubts. I kept waiting for her to come home one day and let it slip that she and Ben were an item, but it never happened. Next thing I knew, Jessie left for college, then she met Chris. Then rumor spread that Ben had gotten a girl pregnant, and that was that.

It wasn't until she moved back home that I took in my first full breath of air since Tom died. In the six years I'd been on my own, I'd forged ahead, working at Kim's Café downtown to help supplement Tom's life insurance and pension, but the years were empty. Jessie didn't completely fill the void he left behind—no one could—but I no longer felt as lonely, and the three of us started a new life together.

Seeing Jessie sitting alone on the top step tonight made me wonder if we were on the verge of something new yet again. Something swift and unexpected.

Then again, my mind had been doing strange things as of late, so who was I to talk of things we never saw coming?

CHAPTER 7

*Novice gardeners—especially those intent on impressing the neighbors—
tend to buy fancy, overpriced fertilizer to give their plants a boost. But just
as you shouldn't oversalt your food, beware of introducing a fertilizer that's
too rich for your plants. All you need is a good dose of kitchen scraps and
lawn clippings. If you have a healthy horse or cow around, all the better.*
—ANNA-LEE COLE, GROWING THE GARDEN YOU WANT

JESSIE

I was out past the back gate when I heard a car coming down our
road. The low roar filtered through the trees and around houses,
finally winding its way to me. I paused and closed my eyes, listening
for the telltale deceleration, which would mean I had a customer.
When I heard it, I pulled my hands out of the potted azalea and
stood. With one last glance behind me at the forlorn azalea, now
sitting crooked in its pot, I turned toward the shop.

Inside, I expected to see Mama at the front desk, but instead,
through the front window, I spotted her dozing on the glider. On my
way to the door, a slight movement caught my attention. I stopped
and retraced my steps backward. Elma Dean lurked in the corner
behind a spinner rack of seeds, one hand behind her back.

"Afternoon, Elma."

"Gus said I could take a pack of morning glory seeds," she blurted.

"I'm sure she did." I stuck my head out the front door and peeked around to the glider. "Mama, it's not even lunchtime. Wake up."

Her head jerked up at the sound of my voice. "What? I'm awake."

"Right." I waited a moment to be sure she wouldn't nod off again, then ducked back inside to wash the soil from my hands. I heard the car pull to a stop out front as I dried my hands and grabbed a bottle of water from the small cooler we kept at the back of the shop. After taking a long sip, I capped the bottle and made my way back to the porch.

I'd expected the customer to be someone I knew—likely someone from the road—but the man who climbed out of the sleek black Land Rover was unfamiliar. He was older than me, in his fifties, maybe. Close-cropped salt-and-pepper hair and tanned skin, as if he spent a decent amount of time out in the sun and open air.

Mama whistled low. "Think he's lost?"

"I know it's supposed to be there," the man said into his cell, which he'd clamped between his ear and shoulder, his deep voice tight and controlled, "but it's not, is it? It's not my . . . I can't do anything about it right now, I'm . . . in a meeting. I'll deal with this when I get back." He punched a button on his phone and dropped it in his pocket before slamming the car door closed and turning to face us on the porch.

"I'm looking for Gus," he called out, then climbed the steps. "The one with the cobbler?" He swung his gaze back and forth between Mama and me as if trying to decide who was who.

"That'd be me." Mama stood from the glider. "I'm Gus McBride. I have fresh peach and a bit of yesterday's blueberry left over. Care for a slice?"

"That'd be wonderful. I'll take blueberry."

"Mm-hmm." She studied him a moment, then turned. From inside she called out, "You'll take peach. Trust me."

He opened his mouth, then closed it.

"Can I help you find anything?" He didn't come across as some-one who'd know his way around a flower nursery.

"I . . . I don't know. I just left a meeting and was thinking about how hungry I was, then I saw your sign out there." He held up his hands as if to say, "Here I am."

Mama appeared behind me with a slice of peach cobbler, a dol-lop of vanilla ice cream right on top. "Can I get you some iced tea to go with it?" She stood a hair too close to the man, then brushed a speck of something off his shoulder.

Blood rushed to my cheeks, but he took it in stride. "No, ma'am, this will do just fine. Thank you."

"You're welcome."

She stood there long enough that I spoke up between clenched teeth. "Could you please go check on Elma?" I whispered. "Make sure she's not robbing me blind."

"I can tell when I'm not wanted," she whispered back, one eye-brow cocked, but she turned and scooted inside.

He took a bite and closed his eyes for a moment before he spoke. "This is heaven."

I nodded. "It may not be world famous, but it's the best in Perry. Don't tell her I said that."

He laughed, and a little of his seriousness leaked away. "I think this is the best peach cobbler I've ever had." He scraped his spoon around the edge of the plate, slid the ice cream into his mouth, then gestured through the open front door with his spoon. "Mind if I look around?"

I held up my hands. "Be my guest. Let me know if you need any help."

As he wound around the display tables inside, I knelt and began pinching off spent blooms in an urn filled with petunias. I glanced inside at him as I worked.

He paused by the round oak table where I displayed small bou-quets of flowers and greenery. He reached out and touched a fern frond tucked into a handful of pale-yellow buttercups, then pulled out his phone and snapped a picture of the bouquet. Mama came up behind him and offered to take his plate.

"Oh, thank you." He dropped his phone back in his pocket. "If it's not world famous, it should be."

"Well, aren't you just the sweetest thing?" Mama said, her voice like syrup.

He took one last look at the bouquets, then walked back out onto the porch, stopping in the middle of a patch of sunshine. "You don't by any chance do flowers for weddings, do you?"

"Weddings?" I turned my head and spoke over my shoulder. "No. Sorry, I don't."

"Funny you should mention weddings," Mama called from inside the shop. "I've been telling her the wedding flower business is booming."

"Thank you, Mama," I called as I stood. I tossed the handful of wilted blooms in the trash can by the door and brushed my hands off on my shorts. Pinching back petunias always left a sticky residue on my fingertips. "I'm not a florist," I said to him.

"Hmm. That's a shame."

"Why's that?"

"Well, my daughter's getting married, and I think she wants something a little more"—he spread his arms out, taking in the shop, the trees, the land, and Mama and me in one swoop—"natural. She says she wants something Southern but not glitzy Southern. Whatever that means."

I smiled. "I'm not—"

"Do you mind if I sit a minute?" He gestured to the glider behind me. "I've been outside all morning and I'm roasting in these clothes."

"Oh, of course." I moved aside and sat in an adjacent rocking chair. I wondered what line of work he was in to have a meeting outside in the heat while wearing a suit.

"Forgive me." He stuck his hand out to me. "I'm Sumner Tate."

I tilted my head and studied him. His name sounded vaguely familiar, but at the moment I couldn't think of where I'd heard it. He raised his eyebrows, his hand still outstretched.

"I'm sorry. Jessie McBride."

"Nice to meet you, Jessie." He leaned forward and rested his elbows on his knees, wrinkling his knife-pressed slacks. "The wedding is in less than three months. Olivia, my daughter, sprang it on me just a few weeks ago. She wants everything to be perfect even though, in my mind, this is not much time to plan a perfect wedding."

I laughed. "No, it's definitely not."

"Thank you," he said with a sigh. "She keeps saying, 'It'll all be fine, Dad.' I don't think we're even in the realm of fine, but she knows what she wants. Starting with a wedding at my house Labor Day weekend." He rubbed a hand across his face. "Do you have kids?"

"One. A daughter. But nowhere near old enough to get married."

"I feel the same about Olivia, but she's not as young as I think. Twenty-five."

"Evan's fourteen."

"Ah. A teenager. Is she a good one?"

I shrugged. "Maybe . . . 97 percent of the time."

He laughed. The cool, intimidating presence he'd gotten out of the car with had backed down, and a comfortable ease took its place.

I checked my watch. Mr. Rainwater had called earlier, saying he needed to bring something around for Mama. I thought of him pulling his fragrant truck up alongside Sumner Tate's spotless, and decidedly unsmelly, Land Rover.

"Mr. Tate—"

"Oh, please. It's Sumner. I'm not that much older than you." His smile dimpled his cheek and crinkled his eyes. In the shop behind us, Mama puttered around, and I could just barely make out her humming Johnny and June's "It Ain't Me Babe."

I stood quickly, sending my rocking chair swaying back and forth. I grabbed the armrest to slow it. "Sumner, I'm not really . . . set up to do weddings."

"Okay. I get that. This is more of a nursery than a florist. But those arrangements inside?" He pointed through the window behind us to the table of bouquets—tussie-mussies in the loosest sense of the word.

They were extraordinarily simple. I bundled zinnias, poppies, sunflowers—whatever was blooming at the moment—along with a few daisies, ferns, or stems of goldenrod to lighten them up and then tied them all together with burlap and twine. Each one was different, and my customers loved them. In fact, they complained whenever I didn't have time to make them.

"Those already look like wedding bouquets," he said.

"Oh, those are just little nothings. They're not wedding material."

"I don't know. I think they're kind of nice. Olivia said she'd rather use someone off the beaten path than a traditional florist. Something about some barn wedding she saw on Pinterest? I don't know."

"I'm definitely off the beaten path, but I'm kind of a one-woman show here, and florists usually have several people working on events. My mom and daughter help out some, but it's mostly me." I shrugged. "We just don't have the time or staff to pull off a wedding."

Now, the money a wedding would bring in—I couldn't deny the allure of that. But surely it'd be too big a commitment for my small flower shop, right? Had Big Earl and his green thumb gotten into the wedding-flower business? Come to think of it, he'd probably already figured out how to do a BOGO deal on bridal bouquets.

"I see. So I guess you stay pretty busy around here."

"Well, today's pretty calm. But we do have busy times." I didn't mention that business in the summer tended to be slower since many of my customers were older than Mama and didn't like to be out in the heat.

As Sumner gazed out on our dirt parking lot—empty except for his car and Elma Dean's tiny Civic—a raucous serenade of cicadas swelled in the trees, then stopped as soon as it began. A hawk circling way up over the pines called out, high and lonesome. All of it seemed to put an exclamation point on our extreme non-busyness. In the still, quiet air, Mama's humming in the background reached a crescendo. She stopped and cleared her throat, then began again, this time in a lower octave.

"I guess that's your answer then." He stood and gestured toward the bouquets. "I'll take one of those home with me, if you don't mind. I owe you a purchase anyway since I've already enjoyed the cobbler and ice cream."

"Oh, it's fine, you don't have to . . ."

He shrugged. "How much are they?"

"Six dollars."

"I'll take two."

I plucked the two biggest ones out of their jars and walked to the back to grab a damp paper towel and a sheet of newspaper to wrap around the ends of the stems. When I handed them over, he reached out with a credit card. "Oh, I'm sorry. We're cash only right now. It's a problem with the computer . . ." I waved my hand toward the counter where the culprit sat. This man probably never had computer problems. Or if he did, he had "people" to fix them promptly.

"No problem." He fished around in his wallet—slim, shiny leather, a flash of small silver initials on the front—and handed me the cash. As he took the flowers from me, he passed me a business card. "If you change your mind about the wedding, give me a call."

"I will."

He smiled, his lips curling inward into a thin line. His cheek dimpled again. Then he started down the steps, pausing at the bottom. "I'm sorry about the phone earlier." He waved his hand toward his car. Heat radiated off the hood in waves. "The call was frustrating, and it got the best of me. I hope I didn't give you a bad impression."

"Oh no. I didn't think anything bad at all."

"Good." He opened his car door but stopped before he climbed in. "Olivia didn't seem to like any of the florists she called, but to be honest, I think she's being a little picky. I could probably find one who'd jump on board today, but something tells me she'd really like you." He glanced around, then back at me. "I hope you'll reconsider." He sat down, then closed the door behind him.

As he eased down the driveway, Mama appeared behind me, just as I knew she would.

"Well, if he isn't a tall drink of cool water." She took a deep breath and blew it out, stirring the hair falling out of my messy bun. "Come on up for lunch when you've recovered. Harvis is supposed to bring me some catfish. It remains to be seen if he'll come through. If he does, I suppose I'll have to ask him to stay and eat."

I heard Mama's words as if through a thick wall—audible but barely. I ran my thumb over the raised letters on his business card. His Land Rover was stopped at the end of the driveway, sun and shade dappling the windows. He stuck his arm out the window and waved, then pulled out onto the dirt road.

CHAPTER 8

*When grouping plants in a garden, take special care to select species
with similar needs. Consider the temperaments of each plant and
the relationships between them. Where plants are positioned in
a garden—and which plants they're next to—can spell happiness
or discontent, and it's often difficult to predict which it'll be.*
—LEIGH T. JACOB, HARMONY IN THE GARDEN

EVAN

I was spreading pine mulch under the new miniature gardenias we'd
just planted when a customer pulled up the drive in a fancy black
car. From my shady spot on the side of the shop, I listened as Mom
talked to the man about pie and flowers. When Gus started flirting
and Mom tried to dismiss her, I took my chance and sneaked down
the driveway toward the road. I hadn't finished with the mulch, but
it could wait.

I slowed down when I reached the fork in the driveway—the right
side meandered toward the shop and the other side wound around
toward our house. My favorite pecan tree stood guard at the fork. In
the fall it'd drop fat pecans by the bucketful. One of my favorite things
was to pick up pairs of pecans and crack them between the heels
of my hands. I stopped and tipped my face up toward the sunlight.

Above me, branches and green leaves reached for the pale-blue sky, and I squinted until the colors blurred together.

Sometimes the quiet of our road bugged me, but most of the time where we lived felt like a sort of paradise, like we were separated from the rest of the world by dark soil and trees and fields full of dandelions and clover. Most of the kids at school lived in regular neighborhoods with paved driveways and ice cream trucks, but we had it better out here. Fewer people, more room to breathe, more space to think.

I was thinking of ways to convince Mom to let me practice driving—I'd already told her I wanted to get my learner's permit the day I turned fifteen—when I heard a deep, quiet voice coming from the road. It was singing. And it wasn't just some random song, it was "Hallelujah," probably my favorite song in the world. I was sure it was the Jeff Buckley version, not Leonard Cohen's. But that may have just been wishful thinking.

I couldn't see him at first—he was behind the tall azalea bushes that grew next to the fence. I knew he was there because a dog on a leash trotted out in front of him. I saw his arm, then finally the rest of him came into view.

The face in the passenger window of the old Jeep flying down the road.

The guy at the gym when I picked up my student information packet. Earbuds, head bobbing to the invisible beat, black jeans, that last glance over his shoulder.

Nick.

The dog strained against his leash, pulling Nick to the side, toward the weathered wood fence separating the road from our front yard. Finally, the dog stopped and stuck his nose through the fence and panted. Nick pulled on the dog's leash, talked softly to him, then faced me. He didn't say anything at first, and since I didn't either, we stood there staring at each other for what felt like ten minutes but was probably only a couple seconds. Finally, unable to stand the awkward-ness, I spoke.

"I like your dog," I said. Inexplicably.

A half grin lifted one corner of his mouth. "I sort of do too." He gave a gentle tug on the leash, then he and the dog approached the end of the driveway. "Sit," Nick said. "Stay."

I forced one foot in front of the other and prayed I didn't look as nervous as I felt. Why was I nervous? I wasn't the get-nervous-around-guys type. A bead of sweat dripped down my chest into my bra. Gross.

He leaned down—he was very tall—and scratched the dog's ears. "This is Stanley." His voice was like melting butter, the kind Gus browned in the oven in her old cast-iron skillet so it turned deep and smoky. "I'm Nick."

"Evan."

"I remember you. From the school the other day. What kind of name is Evan?" He didn't ask it in a rude way, like some people did. He didn't quite smile, but the edges of his words weren't so sharp.

"It was my grandfather's name. His middle name. It's weird, I know." People let me know, in their own ways, that it was strange. I kind of liked my name though.

"No, I think it's cool." He gestured behind me. "So is this your . . . Do you live here?"

"Yeah. Well, in the yellow house." I pointed over to the left. "This is my mom's garden shop, Twig. I help her out some." I glanced down at my turquoise-and-black striped leggings and my favorite gray Village Records T-shirt, both flecked with dirt and a little damp from sweat and whatever else. "I'm working today."

"My dad could use some help with that. He's got this idea to start a vegetable garden in our backyard. I'm surprised he even knows vegetables don't always come wrapped in plastic with little stickers on them."

I laughed. "Send him down here. My mom can probably help."

Stanley stood and whined, then pushed against Nick's leg.

"Do you live around here?" I knew it was a stupid question, seeing as he was walking his dog and his dad was planting a garden in a backyard close by, but his presence confused me. No one like him had ever lived on Glory Road. I was sure of it.

He pointed his thumb back down the road. "My dad and I just moved in. It's my grandparents' house. They moved out, and my dad's fixing the place up."

"That's cool."

He nodded. "It's . . . quiet around here."

"It's always pretty quiet. Not much happens. But it's also kind of nice that way."

He tilted his head as if considering my words. "Yeah, I can see that. We moved from Atlanta. Midtown. Something was always happening there."

Stanley whined again and turned to Nick and panted.

"Okay, buddy." He smoothed the dog's ears. "I'll get you back home."

"Right. I need to get back too. We've got this computer thing going on and my mom's probably going ballistic by now."

"What's wrong with it?"

I shrugged. "It's just dead. I think she's getting it fixed, but it's going to be a while before the guy can get to it." As if he needed this much information.

"My dad works with computers. If it's not totally dead, he can fix it."

"Really?"

"Yeah. I could mention it to him. Maybe they could work out some sort of trade. Computer help for gardening advice."

"That'd be awesome."

"Okay then." He tugged on the leash and Stanley followed him. "See you around?"

I nodded. "See you."

"*Sit,*" I wanted to say. "*Stay. And please keep singing that song.*"

❧

For lunch Mr. Rainwater brought Gus a Ziploc of catfish fillets. I could hardly look at the bag. It was bulging and oozy and it made me want to gag, so Gus shooed me away so she could fry them up. As I left the kitchen she stopped me. "Who was that boy you were talking to?"

"Which one?"

She raised an eyebrow, expertly flipping a fillet in the hot oil. "The one out by the road."

I turned quickly to the den to see if Mom was there.

"So who was he?"

"A new neighbor." I tried to sound casual. "I was just welcoming him to the street."

"Well, aren't you a regular little welcome wagon. He was cute."

"Who was cute?" Mom breezed into the kitchen from the side door. Her cheeks were pink.

"No one—" I began, but Gus cut in loudly.

"Some boy Evan was talking to out by the street while you were chatting on the porch."

"Wait, what?"

I waited for more—the twenty questions I knew Mom wanted to unload—but she just looked at me with her eyebrows arched high.

"It's nothing," I said. "Really."

"It's been an interesting morning," Gus said from the stove. "Can't wait to see what happens this afternoon."

Now I was curious. What had I missed up on the porch? I remembered that black SUV sliding up the driveway and the man who climbed out of it.

I was about to ask Mom, but she pulled off her garden apron and tossed it in a chair. "We can talk later. Let's eat." She picked up a piece of catfish just out of the pan, blew on it, then popped it in her mouth. "I'm starving."

❧

That afternoon clouds pushed in and a breeze blew through the open doors of Twig. Mom and Mr. Rainwater were in the back organizing a shipment of ferns that had come in that morning from a grower nearby. Gus was directing them, pointing her red fingernails here and there as she saw fit. Mom mostly ignored her directions, but Mr. Rainwater tried as hard as he could to please Gus. Anyone with half a brain could see that.

A truck rumbled to a stop out front, but I didn't bother getting up. I was perched on the stool behind the counter, trying one last time to bring some flash of life back to the computer, when I heard footsteps on the front porch.

"Come on in." I didn't take my eyes from the screen. I thought I could see a faint logo behind the black. "Mom's out back if you need her. Ferns are 20 percent off today."

"How much are dead computers?"

I jerked my head up and the room spun a little. When everything evened out, there stood Nick in front of me, standing next to a man I assumed was his dad.

"What are you doing here? I mean—hey. What are you doing here?" I brushed my hair back from my face and mentally catalogued my appearance—hair falling down from the knot at the back of my head and leggings that bore the remnants of a bag of soil I'd ripped open too quickly.

"Your mom needs computer help, right?"

"Yeah . . . ?"

"I brought my dad. He wants some tomato plants anyway."

"Hi." The man smiled. Somewhere in his face—his eyes maybe, or his mouth—he was just an older version of Nick. But where Nick was tall and slim, his dad looked like he should have been chopping wood or leading a pack of dogs through the Alaskan wilderness. Like he'd be at home in plaid flannel and a hat with ear flaps. Maybe it was the beard. It was kind of nice though. "I'm Ben."

"Evan."

"Yeah, I've heard." Mr. Bradley glanced at Nick. Then my heart stopped.

I stood quickly and the stool tipped behind me. I grabbed it and righted it back on all four feet. "Let me run out and get my mom. She'll be so happy about the help." I turned toward the back of the shop and tripped over one of the legs of the stool. I grabbed it again, took a deep breath to calm myself. "She can definitely help you with the tomatoes. Or any other vegetables."

I slammed open the screen door and jumped down the steps in time to see Mr. Rainwater pushing his wheelbarrow around the back of the greenhouse toward Mom. She peeled up the corner of the tarp covering the plastic pool, and he dumped the load in.

"Mom, someone's here to fix your computer."

"What? Now?" She squinted in the sun and pushed her dark-brown bangs off her forehead with the back of her gardening glove.

I nodded. She said something to Mr. Rainwater, then started for the shop, pulling her gloves off as she walked.

"Did you call someone?" she asked as she walked toward me. "I think if I fool with it some more, I might be able to do something. This morning it started making these weird laser sounds. At least it was something new."

"Laser sounds?"

"Yeah, sort of like *Star Wars*?"

"Those are light sabers. And they probably won't do any good. Just come talk to him." I wanted her to hurry up and come on before the smell of Mr. Rainwater's fertilizer made it inside the shop to where I assumed Nick and Mr. Bradley were still waiting. But then I heard the screen door slam. I turned around when I heard Mr. Bradley's voice.

"Have you seen black lines across the screen?" He stood at the top of the steps, his mouth in a half grin. "Is it shutting down a lot?"

"It doesn't shut down," Gus said from the rocking chair tucked under the arbor. "It takes occasional afternoon naps."

"Hi, Mrs. McBride." Mr. Bradley smiled at Gus and my mind whirled. Mom was next to me now. "I can look at it," he said to her. "If you want. It's . . . That's what I do. Computers."

"Wait—y'all know each other?" The question was directed to all of them, but I was watching Mom. In a split second a whole universe of emotions skittered across her face before a pink flush spread across her cheeks. She tucked a strand of hair behind her ear and propped her other hand on her hip, then dropped it.

"Mom?"

She wiped her hands on her shorts, pointless since her shorts were covered in dirt too, and blew her bangs out of her eyes. "Hi, Ben." She put her hand on my back. "Looks like you've already met my daughter, Evan." I heard a squeak behind me, and Mom and I both turned. Mr. Rainwater was approaching with the empty wheelbarrow. "This is Harvis Rainwater. He lives down at the end of the road."

He tipped his cap at us. "I just have one more load, then I'll be out of your hair."

"You're fine," Mom said, her voice quiet.

"I'll head up front with Harvis," Gus called down as she stood from the rocking chair. "You go on and see about your computer."

I didn't understand the glance that passed between Mom and Gus, but Mr. Bradley seemed to. He retreated back into the shop.

"Mom?" I whispered. "How do you know him?"

With her hand still on my back, she gave me a gentle nudge. "We used to go to school together." Her voice was steady, but her eyes were darting around like she was taking stock of everything around us, which didn't make sense to me because everything was the same as always. "I . . . I guess he works on computers or something. How did he . . . Did you call him?" She shook her head. "But you didn't . . . This doesn't make sense."

"Well, I . . ." I knew I should say something, but all of a sudden admitting that I had anything to do with Nick and Mr. Bradley showing up here felt incredibly uncomfortable.

"It's fine. Let's go see what he has to say."

Inside, Mom stopped at the counter next to Mr. Bradley.

"It's been a long time, Jessie."

She bit her bottom lip. "It has."

"And you've been . . . ?" His gaze drifted over Mom's shoulder to where I stood. He cleared his throat and looked back at her.

"This is it." She patted the laptop. "And before you ask, yes, it's old."

"Nothing wrong with that."

"I bought it fourteen years ago."

"Oh." He chuckled. "That is old."

"I should have upgraded a long time ago, but . . ." She shrugged. "They're expensive."

"Not always. They're generally cheaper now than when you bought this thing. But maybe you won't need a new one. Let me try a few things." Mom backed up so he could slide around the counter and sit down. He punched a few keys, then tried another combination, then another. I watched them, but I also kept an eye on Nick. He stood at the rack of seeds, casually spinning it around.

As Mr. Bradley worked, Mom leaned against the other side of the counter and fiddled with a frayed spot on her shorts. "How'd you know about my computer?"

He pressed and held a button, and after a moment, the screen flashed and a green blinking line appeared in the top corner. "Nick and your daughter met this morning and she mentioned you could use some help." Mom's head snapped up and she cocked her head at me, brow furrowed.

Should have told her.

"Apparently Nick's trying to drum up some extra work for me."

"So this is what you do? I mean, for a living?"

"Sort of. I'm a consultant. I do cybersecurity for a bunch of firms, but I do some IT work on the side."

"He's a total computer geek," Nick called from the back.

Mr. Bradley laughed. "Thanks."

"He's also clueless about gardening, but he wants to grow his own vegetables. That's the real reason we're here. I figured if I could get him around an actual gardener, maybe something will rub off on him."

A corner of Mom's mouth tilted up, but her smile seemed more sad than happy. "I can give you a few pointers about vegetables. It's the least I can do if you can get this thing up and running."

"I'll see what I can do. May not be a quick fix though."

Mom watched as his fingers tapped on the keyboard. She bit her lip and crossed her arms, then uncrossed them. The silence between them was awkward, so I moved toward Nick at the spinner rack. As I slid around one display table of potted English ivy and another one of Gus's fried peach pies wrapped in waxed paper, I glanced back at Mom. I tried to gauge her tension level by the deepness of that little furrow between her eyebrows, but her head was turned too far. I did catch her smoothing her hair behind her ears though.

"Looking for seeds?" I asked Nick when I made it to the rack. I propped my hands on my hips and bumped my funny bone on the corner of the table behind me.

"Do tomatoes even come as seeds or do we buy them already grown?"

I massaged my elbow. "You can do either. But we have some already started. That'll be easier than starting them from seed. And anyway, you missed the time to plant tomato seeds."

"Of course we did. I was on board with this garden idea at first, but he's so set on it now. He's even marked out spots in the backyard where he wants different vegetables to go." He scratched the back of his neck. "I think he needs to direct his pent-up energy on something a little less . . . involved."

"Knitting? Cooking?"

He smiled and spun the rack with one finger. "Knitting. I like that. I could use a new . . . whatever you knit. Hats?"

It felt good to make him smile. "I have no idea. Let me show you the tomatoes outside." I turned toward the back door and he followed. I glanced up at Mom and Mr. Bradley as we walked out. He was focused on the screen, tapping out some sort of code onto the keyboard. Mom sat on the stool next to him.

"I could get into cooking," Nick was saying. "Dad's okay, honestly. But it's usually just the two of us and he doesn't feel the need to impress me much."

"It's just the three of us, but we do okay too." I led him down the steps, across the courtyard, and into the greenhouse. Through the open door in the back, I could see Gus and Mr. Rainwater standing by the plastic pool. "My mom can cook fine, but my grandmother Gus makes all the good stuff. Fried chicken, cornbread, fried green tomatoes . . ."

"Remind me to swing by at dinner next time." He leaned over to inspect a row of perfect orchids planted in ceramic pots, their stalks tied to thin metal stakes.

"She also makes the best desserts in town."

"Really?"

I couldn't tell if he was interested or not, but I was nervous and when that happened, I couldn't shut off my mouth.

"Yep. She likes to think her desserts make more money than the plants Mom sells. We let her think it. It keeps her happy."

Nick laughed and looked around the greenhouse. "Man, y'all have everything in here. From the front, it comes across as a little back-road nursery. This is the real deal."

I nodded. I was proud of Mom and her hard work. Then her expression when Mr. Bradley appeared on the back porch bubbled back to me.

I was dying to ask Nick about everything—about him, his dad, why in the world they moved to Perry of all places, and exactly what kind of connection did our parents have?—but I didn't want to hammer him with too many questions.

"So, uh, did you know your dad and my mom knew each other?"

He paused at the small water fountain on a table in the corner where water trickled over rocks into a small pool at the bottom. A tiny statue of St. Francis of Assisi stood in the shallow water, his arms held out as a perch for birds. Nick stuck his finger in a trail of water sliding down the rocks. "Yeah, he said they knew each other when they were younger. Dad grew up here."

"Here, as in Perry?"

"Here, as in right down the road."

"Huh." I'd heard stories of lots of my mom's childhood friends. I'd never heard of him.

"So which of these tomatoes are right for Dad?"

"That's sweet potato vine. Vegetables are over here."

I led him to the wooden tables where we kept potted tomatoes, bell peppers, and squashes. I was still telling him about the tomato's sun and water requirements when Mr. Bradley called Nick from the back porch of the shop.

"We gotta run, bud."

I could just barely make out his shape through the thick plastic wall of the greenhouse. He stood there a moment gazing out on the garden and field beyond. When he ducked back inside, he held the screen door so it wouldn't slam shut.

"I think you've got me set for a while here." Nick held a pallet with three tomato plants, cucumber, basil, and cabbage. Packets of zucchini, green beans, and sweet peppers were stuffed into his back pocket. On one arm he'd coiled a length of plastic netting to use as a cage for the tomatoes.

"For the hungry critters?" he asked.

"Birds, squirrels, rabbits. Once you get all this planted, they'll come out in droves. We also have deer that come out now and again. They love all this stuff."

He surveyed the stash in his arms. "We're never going to be able to get this up and running alone. Dad may need some—"

"Nick?" his dad called again. "Let's go and let these people close for the day."

Nick sighed. "Okay, second call. That's my cue."

I walked with him out of the greenhouse and back up the steps into the shop. On the way I reevaluated everything I'd said to Nick. This was the guy with the voice, the music, that dark hair, and all I'd talked about was garden pests, appropriate containers, and proper watering techniques.

But it was easier to talk about what I knew than focusing on the slippery feeling in my stomach.

Inside the shop Mom stood by the front window. Her lips were moving, but I couldn't tell if she was talking to Mr. Bradley or herself.

He stood a few paces away, staring out the window, the laptop tucked under his arm. They both turned when our feet hit the old wood floor.

"Wow," Mr. Bradley said. "That's . . . that's a lot." He pulled his wallet out of his back pocket.

"Yep, she loaded me down," Nick said. "Ask me anything—how much water they need, shade, sun, rabbits. I've got it all up here." He lifted a knee to hold the pallet, then took one hand off and tapped his forehead. When the pallet tipped precariously, he quickly grabbed it again.

"Okay, just don't drop it. Let's at least get the plants in the ground before we kill them." He turned to Mom. "What do we owe you?"

Mom hesitated, then stepped toward Nick to check labels and count seed packets. As she pulled her calculator from her front apron pocket, the screen door creaked open and Mr. Rainwater and Gus appeared behind us.

"Don't mind us," Gus said. "We're just going to wash off our hands real quick." She pointed Mr. Rainwater to the deep sink just inside the back door. Mom usually used it for rinsing dirt off flower stems before she arranged them in vases, not for washing Mr. Rainwater's "fertilizer" down the drain.

"Mama," Mom said, her voice low. "The hose outside would be a much better place to rinse your hands than the inside sink."

"That's what I said," Mr. Rainwater piped up.

"Well, we needed a drink too, so we came on in." Gus turned her head back to the sink and motioned for Mr. Rainwater to bring his hands closer to the faucet. The old man looked back and forth between Gus and Mom, unsure of what to do. Finally, he stuck his hands under the running water. "Augusta, you need to think about being more considerate."

"I'm always considerate. Now hush and let's wash up."

Mom rolled her eyes and turned back to Mr. Bradley, who struggled to keep a straight face. She gave him the total for the plants and he handed over the cash, then they walked toward the front door. Nick and I followed behind them.

"You've done well here on your own. I'm happy to see that." Mr. Bradley's voice was quiet.

"Thanks," Mom said. "It's not just me though. I have Evan and Mama . . . We're doing just fine."

"I can tell."

Mom smiled, but it was too bright. Something was off, but I couldn't put my finger on it. I glanced at Nick, but he was focused on the floor in front of him. He stepped carefully down each step, peering around the side of the pallet in his arms.

"If you have any trouble, just give us a call," Mom said. "One of us can run down and check things out. Make sure you haven't planted the tomatoes next to the peppers."

Mr. Bradley stopped halfway to his Jeep. "Wait, is that a bad thing?"

Mom gave a little smile, which was really more of an eye squint than anything else. "You'll figure it out."

He hung his head, then opened the liftgate before getting behind the wheel and cranking the engine. Nick slid the pallet into the back of the Jeep and slammed the hatch door. He waved at me before he climbed into the passenger seat and shut the door.

I waited until their car turned onto the street, then started to ask Mom . . . I didn't even know. Something. Anything. But by the time I turned to her, all I saw was the screen door closing with a quiet thud.

CHAPTER 9

*In gardening, how you begin sets the tone of the entire life cycle
of the plant. Start on shaky ground—the wrong light, soil, or
terrain—and your plant's life will likely be cut short. On the
other hand, ensuring correct conditions at the beginning of
the life cycle and encouraging companion plants to play well
together will help make your gardening experience a success.*
—GRACIE BROOKS, PROPER GROWING
CONDITIONS FOR GARDENING SUCCESS

JESSIE

Evan's friend Ruth came over late that afternoon, and Evan asked
if she could stay for dinner. Once the four of us were seated
around the table, we passed around a big white platter of pork chops.
A pot of butter beans sat on a hot pad in the center of the table next to
a green salad with cherry tomatoes from out back.

Ruth cut off a dainty bite of her pork chop and raised it to her
mouth. "Mmm." She chewed methodically and swallowed before
speaking. "This is delicious. My mom only makes plain chicken.
Usually with rice and green peas."

Mama patted Ruth's hand. "Sweetheart, you come eat dinner
with us anytime you want. We'll put some meat on your bones."

Ruth smiled, happy to be part of it all.

"I usually have dessert here too. I wanted to make a pound cake today, but I couldn't find my recipe."

I looked up at Mama. "Recipe? For pound cake? You could make that in your sleep."

"I know, I know." She pushed her food around the plate with her fork. "I got everything out to make it but then couldn't remember if I had it all together right. It was like I left my brain at home this morning." She laughed and took a sip of her water.

"You feeling okay?" I asked quietly. Evan and Ruth were already on to another subject, something about someone they'd run into at the Icebox. "You've been a little . . . forgetful lately."

"What else have I forgotten?" She smiled, but it was tighter than usual. "You worried I'm leaving my iron on or something? I don't wear much that requires the use of an iron."

"I don't know." Talking about Mama's increasing forgetfulness made me uncomfortable. I didn't like the feeling of the parent-child roles reversing, even if for just a moment. "You told me about Elma Dean coming into the shop when I'd been there to see her."

"It's just part of getting older. You'll know soon enough. Nothing a round of crosswords or Sudoku can't fix." With one hand she reached into her massive bag that dangled from the back of her chair and fumbled around for something. "Now, what do you say we talk about the visitor you had today?"

"Ben?" I glanced at Evan. She met my eyes as Ruth chatted on about her older sister's new secret crush. I'd explain Ben to her, but I wasn't ready to go there just yet. Thankfully, she didn't seem to want to talk about it either. At least not in front of Mama and Ruth.

"No, the other visitor. The one in that fancy black car. Ah, there it is." Mama pulled a magazine out of her bag, slapped it down on the table in front of me, and pointed at the front cover. "Mr. Moneybags himself."

Under the *Southern Living* logo was a photo of a majestic oak overlooking a river, Spanish moss swaying from the low branches, the sun setting in the background, sky a mess of pink and purple. "Good grief. Did they Photoshop that scene? It's gorgeous."

"Not Photoshopped. Straight out of the backyard of one Sumner Tate."

"What?" I scanned the page again. A caption to the side of the photo read, "Take a peek inside Oak House, one of the South's finest homes."

"He lives in Oak House?"

"What's that?" Evan peered over my arm. "Wow, that's so pretty."

I nodded. "Oak House is . . . Well, it's kind of well known."

"That's putting it lightly," Mama said. "It's a gorgeous spread out on Dog River. Seems every month it's featured in one magazine or another. They have events there all the time. Fund-raisers. Parties. *Weddings*."

I sighed. "Here we go again."

"I think you should try it. Twig needs the money. *You* need the money. It won't be that much work and you'll have plenty of extra help."

I knew we could use the money, but something about the man made me nervous, and in a different way than Ben made me nervous, which was considerable. Sumner was so polished and sophisticated, so out of place standing on Twig's front porch, listening to the sounds of Glory Road, sitting in the ancient rocking chair that probably left tiny pieces of peeling white paint stuck to his crisp pants.

I flipped through the magazine until I found the article on Oak House.

Sumner Tate, founder of the prestigious golf course design group Tate & Lane, moved into the charming but small Stinson-McDavid cottage on Dog River eight years ago. After a careful and tasteful two-year renovation, Oak House is a classic example of low-country style and down-home river house appeal . . .

I drummed my fingers on the table. "What's your agenda? Why do you want me to do his daughter's wedding so badly?"

"I don't give two hoots about the wedding itself," Mama said. "I'm suggesting you do it purely for financial reasons." She paused. "Plus, I think it's good for you to get out of your comfort zone every now and then."

"Out of my comfort zone?" I glanced at Evan to see if she was listening, then I lowered my voice. "What do you call marrying Chris? Or leaving him and moving back home? Or opening Twig? A large chunk of my adult life has been spent out of my comfort zone."

Mama held up her hands. "Okay. I hear you, and you're right. I just don't want you to give a quick no to something that could be a good thing for you. Allow a little—"

"I know, I know. Allow a little magic in my life. You tell me that at least four times a week."

"I'm just saying. Sometimes God puts things in our paths for a reason. Best to sit up and pay attention. Plus, Mr. Tate here would probably pay you a pretty penny to be the florist."

Florist. I shook my head. I was no such thing. Shrubs and fruit trees I knew. Annuals, perennials, what to plant in the shade or full sun. How to keep pests out of the garden. Containers and window boxes. That's what I knew. Boutonnieres? Wedding bouquets? How to please brides . . . and mothers of the bride? Not my thing. But an extra chunk of money for Twig? I'd be an idiot to turn it down, regardless of how I felt about lavish weddings.

"I'll think about it," I said finally.

Mama sat back in her chair, satisfied as a cat on a warm windowsill.

❧

Later, after dinner was over and the pots were clean and drip-drying on a dish towel by the sink, I sat alone on the porch and waited for rain. The storm was just a low rumble now, miles away. As I stared out at the muted purples and blues of the magic hour, thunder cracked, drowning out the sounds of Mama's and Evan's voices inside and silencing the cicadas screaming in the trees.

As I sat and listened, I remembered. I seemed to be doing a lot of that lately. Ben's reappearance had dredged up all kinds of old memories—not forgotten ones, but ones I'd left mostly untouched in deep recesses, like a chest buried in an attic, covered in dust, but with a few fingerprints here and there, betraying prying fingers and eyes over the years. And now all those little interactions—from the first time I saw Ben to the last—came flooding back, like the creek that fed the Icebox after a hard, fast rain.

It was almost hard to recognize myself as I was back then. Cheerleader. Popular. Flirty. Sometimes after a shower when the mirror was fogged up, I studied myself, searching for the girl I used to be in high school—the one with the perfectly curled blonde hair, who studied the cheers and knew the precise moment to kick my leg or jump into a split or raise my arms. The one who bought an extra tube of cheer captain–approved pink lip gloss, just in case I lost mine. Evan would go bonkers if she knew her mom had been one of those perky girls she loved to make fun of.

Back then I did anything I could do to be exactly as I thought I was supposed to be. There was no scary underlying reason. Nothing a therapist needed to uncover. I just wanted to be liked. To be desired. Loved, even. Who didn't want that? Especially when you're young, when everyone wants to fit in, to be connected, to not feel lonely. At Perry, the cool kids were cheerleaders and football players, so that's the personality I slid into, like a second skin.

I knew who Ben was, knew he lived somewhere down our road. I even knew he was cute. But he was different, and I didn't want different. I wanted to blend in, not stick out like he did. He was on the football team, but he was not the typical football player reveling in his glory days. He spent free periods in the library studying or in the courtyard after lunch. He'd sit in the sun and read instead of laughing and shoving with the rest of the team at the center table in the cafeteria.

I knew these things, because as "his" cheerleader, it was my job to make him posters, bake his favorite cookies, bring him balloons on game days, and I always had to track him down because he was never with the rest of the team. He was always polite and thanked me for whatever trinket or snack I brought him. He'd smile—he had a great smile—but he rarely said much more.

It wasn't until one Saturday afternoon in the spring of our sophomore year that the wall between us finally fell. I'd gone out to check the mailbox for Mama and saw Ben in the middle of the street pushing a huge monster of a car down the road toward his house. He had the driver side door open and he was walking just inside it, one hand on the open window ledge, the other hand on the steering wheel. He was pushing. Hard. I was so surprised, I just stood and stared.

"You busy?" he called when he saw me standing there, mouth open.

"I, uh . . ."

"I could use some help if you're not."

I held my hands up in question, but he'd already put his head back down, straining under the effort of pushing the car over the uneven spots in the dirt road. I tossed down the stack of catalogs and bills and jogged over to him. He was sweating in the spring warmth, and I could see the dip of his spine and the ridges of his shoulder blades through his white T-shirt. I looked away.

"What should I do?"

He pulled back so the car slid to a stop. "Hop in." He gestured to the driver's seat.

I raised my eyebrows. "You want me to drive?" I wouldn't turn sixteen for a few more months, but it wasn't the lack of a license that made me pause. The interior of the car—a Jeep Grand Wagoneer, as the nameplate on the side read in swirly silver script—was dirty. The leather on the seats was ripped, with stuffing poking out of each hole. The dash was covered in a layer of gray dust, and a dark stain—oil? paint? something worse?—was splattered against the passenger door and window.

"Don't worry, you won't be driving. All I need you to do is sit there and when I tell you, drop the clutch."

"Drop the . . . ?"

"You've never driven a stick." It wasn't a question, but I shook my head anyway.

"Okay. Sit down." He pointed to the seat. "Sorry for the mess. It'll look better soon."

I doubted the thing could ever look much better than it did right then, but I sat down anyway.

He reached across me and adjusted the gearshift by my right leg. "Okay, it's in second. Now press your foot down here." He pointed to one of three pedals. "When I give the word, pull your foot off it. With any luck, the engine will catch and we'll be in business."

"Wait, I . . ." But he'd already slid back out of the car and taken his place with a hand on the ledge and the other just inside the door.

"You've got this. Just hang on." He put his head down and pushed hard, muscles straining. When the Jeep started moving, he pushed harder, breaking into a slow run. After a few seconds, he grunted, "Okay, drop it."

I took my foot off the pedal and all of a sudden the engine sputtered, then roared to life. He whooped, a huge grin on his face, and slid into the seat right next to me. His arm pressed against mine, his leg hot through the cotton of my shorts. I quickly scooted over into the other seat, careful not to knock my knee into the gearshift as I moved.

"Awesome," he said, his fingers tapping on the steering wheel. "Thanks for the help."

"No problem." But there was one small problem. I hooked my thumb back toward my house, receding behind us. "Um . . ."

"Right." He dug his fingers through his thick brown hair. "Once it's going, I can't actually stop it until I'm back at my house. Otherwise we'll just have to do this whole thing over again."

He coasted down the bend in the road, then slowed as the Jeep approached the driveway of his house. He turned in, parked in the carport, and cut the engine. It spluttered, knocked a few times, then went silent.

I tried to open the passenger door, but it wouldn't budge.

"Oh, sorry. You have to come back out the way you got in. I gotta work on that door."

After scrambling back over the gearshift and finally climbing out of the Jeep, I brushed my hair back from my face and turned to him. "Good luck with your car. I'll just . . ." I nodded my head back up the road.

"I'll walk you."

"You don't have to."

"Without your help I'd still be out there pushing. I can at least walk you home."

We started up the road, the red dust still settling from the drive to his house. It felt strange walking alongside him. We'd known each other since the beginning of freshman year when I started cheering and he took his place on the offensive line, but we'd never had a real conversation. I always got the impression he didn't like cheerleaders much. Maybe not even football, even though he was really good.

Neither of us spoke for a few moments, but then we both tried to speak at the same time.

"You first," he said.

"How long have you had the Jeep?"

"Couple weeks. It's in rough shape, I know. But it's gonna be great."

I nodded.

"It was dirt cheap. My dad said he'd buy it for me as long as I fixed it up on my own. I'll probably still be out in the driveway working on it in the fall when you start hunting me down again with balloons and those little football cookies."

"Oh, I won't be your cheerleader next year. We change players every year."

"I gotcha." He kept his eyes on the road. Scuffed his shoe along the ground and kicked a rock out a few feet in front of us. I glanced sideways at him. He was big—muscular, broad shoulders, strong jawline. But the skin on his face looked soft, and he had a slight dimple in the middle of his chin. I already knew all this, of course, but being this close to him made it feel like I was seeing him for the first time.

When we arrived at my driveway a few minutes later, he shoved his hands in his pockets. "If you're ever free after school, I'll probably be out working on my car most days . . . like I said." He gazed back down the road, and I imagined him in his driveway peering under the raised hood of the Jeep, the familiar look of concentration on his face, tools scattered on the ground at his feet. He shrugged. "Company would be nice."

I was shocked. He wanted my company? Would I want his? I found myself nodding. "Okay. Maybe I'll come."

That maybe turned into a yes, which turned into me sitting under the dogwood tree at the end of his driveway most days after school working on homework while he did exactly as I had imagined—half his body hidden under the raised hood, tools everywhere, a can of Coke on the ground at his feet making wet rings on the concrete. Occasionally he'd ask me to jump in the front seat and crank the engine, but mostly I worked on geometry or French. And I watched him.

After the awkwardness wore off, I was pleasantly surprised to find we enjoyed each other's company. It was easy. Natural. I could let myself relax around him rather than always being so concerned about how I looked or how I appeared to my friends. I didn't have to worry about being popular or cool or pretty. I could stop pretending and just be me.

On days when he didn't work on his Jeep, we sat inside it—the AC or heat cranked, depending on the season—and listened to music from his huge collection of CDs. Or we walked to the Icebox and sat on "our" log, the one that spanned a deep crevice in the rocks, and talked while we dangled our legs into the water.

I let things out that I normally kept tucked away, like the fact that I enjoyed gardening in our huge backyard with my dad. That I secretly liked the wide-brimmed straw hat he wore to keep the sun off his fair skin, even though I once heard Carol Anne Davies—our cheer captain—say he looked like a scarecrow.

One afternoon at the Icebox, he asked me what I wanted to be when I grew up. I laughed and flicked water at him with my toe.

"I'm serious. What do you want to do with your life?"

I shrugged. "The usual. Go to college. Get a job I like. Make a little money. Have a family."

"Okay. Tell me about that job. What do you want that to be?"

I turned to him, expecting to see a grin on his face, but his eyes were serious. I knew what I wanted to do, what I hoped to do, but it was far-fetched and I'd never admitted it out loud before.

"I want to be a garden designer," I said quietly.

"Really?" He tilted his head as if pondering my career choice.

I nodded. "I know it's stupid . . ."

"No. It's not stupid at all, actually." He put his hands down flat on the log and bumped his shoulder to mine. "I think it's perfect for you."

I shrugged again. "I don't know. Maybe. If that doesn't work out, I've thought about being an English teacher. Though the people in my classes often make me rethink that."

He laughed. "If you did decide to be an English teacher, I have no doubt you'd whip those kids into shape in no time. You'd have them reading *The Great Gatsby* and *Lord of the Flies* and loving every minute of it."

No matter what I said, what secret hope or embarrassment I divulged to him, he never made me feel silly for saying it. He was always kind. Funny. But best of all, he was completely unself-conscious. I wanted some of that to soak into me.

The strange thing, though, was that we still rarely talked at school. It was like an unspoken rule that we both understood without saying it out loud. Our friendship existed on Glory Road. During school hours, at football games and parties afterward, at pep rallies and school assemblies, we were still separated by the invisible but almost tangible wall between us. Between my group and his.

Ben was quiet, encouraging, honest—not the kind of guy my friends and I usually hung out with. He spoke to some deeper part of me, but I had no idea how to handle it. So I ignored it.

Even if I didn't consciously recognize it, Mama did, of course. One afternoon on the back porch, watching as Daddy tried to finish cutting the grass before it rained, she told me to be careful with Ben.

"What do you mean?" I was only half listening as I flipped through a *People* magazine. I was meeting Ben at the Icebox in an hour if the rain held off.

"I see how that boy looks at you. You don't look at him in the same way."

That got my attention. I slapped the magazine closed. "And how does he look at me? Or how do I look at him?"

"He's a fool for you, Jessie Mae. And while I don't think you're purposefully leading him on, that may be what's happening."

"That's crazy. I'm not leading him on. I wouldn't do that. He's my friend."

"That's the problem." She shook her head. "I don't think he

thinks of you as a friend. I always worry about your heart—caring for it, protecting it—but in this case, it's Ben's heart I'm worried about."

Her words stayed in my mind that whole year as Ben and I continued our normal routine—homework, talking, laughing. It was different during football season, of course. We saw less of each other then, except while on the field, but at home, we spent most of our free hours together. I was happy hanging out with him—he made me happy—but thanks to Mama's words, now a measure of guilt was mixed in too.

Then our senior year wrapped up. We graduated, and everyone started making plans for their life after high school. Ben got an academic scholarship to the University of Alabama, and I was headed to Birmingham and a degree in English and horticulture. We still saw each other that summer, but it felt different, like someone had pushed fast-forward on the hours.

It was tradition for the outgoing senior class to have a big bonfire party at the end of the summer before everyone headed their separate ways. The party was held in a big, empty pasture supposedly owned by someone's uncle, although no one knew exactly whose uncle it was. We didn't care either. The police sometimes came, red and blue ricocheting off windshields and tailgates, tossing out warnings about hauling us off and calling parents, but they never did. Especially not on senior bonfire night. It was as if they allowed the outgoing class that last bit of freedom before they entered the world of adult rules and expectations.

When my friends and I arrived at the field, we tumbled out of our cars like dominoes, everyone laughing, freedom and the warm evening air making us feel alive and bigger than the universe. I noticed Ben's Jeep parked at the edge of the grassy field. By now it was a thing of beauty—the leather inside oiled to a shine, the seats repaired, the engine purring. When I saw it that night, a swell of happy pride crested in my chest, but then again, that night I was happy about everything. It felt like my real life was beginning.

Hours later, I sat in someone's abandoned plastic lawn chair as Dave Matthews Band's "Two Step" poured from a nearby truck's speakers. The fire had died down to a glow of embers and burned blocks of wood, and all around it people sat in pairs and small groups. Down the field a bit, a handful of people tossed a football around, their laughter bouncing through the trees, but it was quiet near the fire. That's where Ben found me.

"Having fun?" He sat on the ground next to my chair.

I shrugged. "I guess so."

He leaned back on his arms, then sat up and propped his elbows on his knees. It was unlike him to be so fidgety.

"Something wrong?"

He shook his head. "No. But I need to tell you something."

"Okay. Tell me." I leaned forward a bit, trying to see his face. The faint light from the dying fire cast an orange glow on his cheeks and the bridge of his nose, but I couldn't make out the emotion in his eyes.

Finally he spoke. "Jessie, I'm in love with you."

All the sounds around us—conversation, crickets in the night air, the pops and sizzles of the fire—died away, like the two of us were in a vacuum, a black hole that spit everything else out. All I heard was my heart thumping in my chest.

"You're what?"

"Sorry to just blurt it out like that. But I've loved you for so long." He said it like an exhale.

"Ben, I . . ."

He shook his head, his eyes still focused on the fire. "I just needed you to know. I'm leaving in a few days and . . ." That's when he turned to me. His eyes burned into mine, like he was trying to read the waves crashing in my brain.

But he was just my friend. Right? I couldn't . . .

But I did know. Deep down, I knew he loved me. I'd known it for years.

76

"You don't have to worry. I don't expect anything to happen. I just wanted to tell you before I left."

We stared at each other until someone called my name, startling me out of myself. I jumped up to my feet and searched the field. My friend waved her arms at me. "We're leaving," she yelled.

Next to me, Ben stood. He wiped his hands on his pants and took a step toward me. "Jessie, I know the real you. You're so much more than all this." His voice was low and by now sweetly familiar.

Then all of a sudden my friends were right next to me, laughing. One grabbed my arm. "Come on. James is pulling out and he's our ride." I let her drag me away—I'd left my purse in the Bronco and anyway, it was almost curfew—but I glanced back at Ben. He shoved his hands in his pockets and smiled.

I didn't see him again before he left for Tuscaloosa.

I went on to Birmingham and tried to live my life as I thought I was supposed to. He and I both made decisions—some good, some bad. Then Chris stormed in and blew me away, and the fallout had landed me here—on my own with my fiery mother and my incredible daughter, surrounded by the street and air and land that had cushioned me for most of my life. I knew there was more—Mama loved to remind me of that—but Glory Road was what I knew and loved.

It was just that somewhere along the days that stretched into months, that lengthened into years, I'd begun to feel restless. Like I had an itch somewhere I couldn't quite reach. It was relentless. I stayed quiet about it though, especially around Mama. I knew she'd start up with that "magic" speech again.

I didn't want to hear her speech, but echoes of her words came back to me as I sat in this spot on this porch, in the nest I'd made for myself. Inside, things were still. Evan and Mama were probably dozing on the couch, an empty bowl of popcorn between them. Next to me, the house sighed and settled, the seventy-year-old thing tired and weighted with the responsibility of sheltering all our hopes and dreams.

As the swing slowly moved back and forth, I tried to release some of the ache in my heart. It was the same ache—the same craving—I'd felt when I heard the music pouring from the windows of the Jeep flying down the road. The Jeep I hadn't realized was Ben's.

The ache was always there—pressing into me, pushing down on me—but I had a feeling the appearance of Ben and Sumner in one day was part of tonight's particular sting. If Mama's "magic" meant a man, she must have been pretty satisfied with the day. But I didn't know what to make of it. Only that the ache, the hunger, was still there—part pain, part something else. Hope? Desire? Fear? The potent mixture swirled in my heart like rich, fertile soil, all the parts meshed so completely it'd be impossible to tell one essential element from the rest.

CHAPTER 10

It can be tricky to keep an African violet content and thriving.
It doesn't like direct, all-day sun, and it prefers its leaves to be
dry. Keep the temperature even, and if possible, set it in an
east-facing window so it can receive nice, diffused light.
—ANNE P. SNIDER, FINICKY FLOWERS

EVAN

My mom used to have this bathing suit. I barely remember it. It floats around the edge of my memory like a red-and-white-flowered fog. It had delicate ruffles around the edges where it skimmed the skin of her freckled chest. Or maybe it was lace. The fog makes it all blurry. What I remember most is the brightness of the red against the soft white. It was a happy suit, a confident suit, even though it was only one piece. It covered everything from the midpoint of her chest to her hips, but it clung to her like silk and hugged every curve. I was only five and a half at the time, but I remember thinking I'd never be old enough to wear a suit like that.

I sat on the stool in the corner of the Parisian dressing room, my knees pressed together, my little Strawberry Shortcake purse in my lap. Mom did a twirl in the suit as if she were wearing a sequined cocktail dress instead of a strip of flowered nylon. I couldn't imagine anyone or anything being more beautiful. In my mind, she was a

79

princess, a fairy, and a magic ballerina all at once. I couldn't wait to
see her in that bathing suit at the pool, wowing everyone, making
them wish she were their mother instead of mine.

"I think this is the one," she said to me, giving her backside one
more glance. "What do you think?"

"It's perfect," I whispered, as if talking too loud would break the
spell she'd cast on the cramped dressing room.

"Okay then. I trust you." She smiled at me, and I felt my heart
settle into a comfortable place. "I think your daddy will like this one."

But that was a million years ago, and my dad didn't like it. Or
if he did, it wasn't enough to make him stay. Not that I would have
wanted him to.

A lot of girls my age hated their moms—thought they were dorky
or embarrassing—but I really kind of liked mine. I mean, I loved her,
but I also liked her, you know? She was smart and funny and she
didn't smother me too much. She was just there when I needed her
to be. And she was pretty. The kind of pretty I wouldn't mind being
when I got older. So if my dad could see her in that suit, see the
kindness in her eyes, the casual way she slung her beach bag over her
shoulder, and still leave us—and for someone named Tiffani *with an
i*—then I was glad he left.

I hadn't thought about that red-and-white bathing suit in years,
but that night, long after Gus had left and I told Mom good night, I
tiptoed back up to the front window just to stare at her. She seemed
so young in her sleeveless nightgown, one strap falling down off her
shoulder. She'd tucked one leg underneath her on the cushion and the
other pushed off the floor every few seconds. I couldn't stand seeing
her like that, all alone and exposed, so I opened the door and stuck
my head out.

"What are you doing up?" she asked. "I thought you were asleep."

I shook my head. "Not yet."

She patted the cushion next to her. "You can sit if you want."

I crossed the porch and sat on the swing. Lightning flashed, followed a moment later by thunder. The sound was both comforting and unsettling, and for a strange moment, I wanted to bury my face in her shoulder like I did when I was little.

"About eight miles, I'd say," Mom said.

"I think closer to six."

She raised an eyebrow. "We'll see."

It was something we always did—count the time between the lightning and the thunder to judge how far off a storm was. Although in the summer, it was hard to tell if the lightning was coming from a storm or if it was just from the heat of the day.

We rocked in silence for a bit before Mom spoke. "You and Nick seemed to get along well this afternoon. Do you want to tell me about him?"

"Do you want to tell me about Mr. Bradley?" I closed my eyes. I hadn't meant to ask such a personal question. Then again, maybe it'd get the focus off Nick. "I mean, you were totally flustered when he showed up."

She took a deep breath and exhaled, then held up her hands. "We . . . used to know each other in school. Well, a little at school, but more on the street. He grew up on Glory Road."

"That's what Nick said."

Mom smiled down at me.

"No way," I said. "This is about you, not me. From the way y'all acted, you were more than just neighbors way back when. Spill it."

I don't know what I expected—a bad date to prom? Something embarrassing like Gus asking Officer Kellan to take Mom out on a date? Whatever I thought it might be, it wasn't even close to the truth. Because Mom leaned her head back and sighed. Then she squinted one eye, as if the memory were too bright to look at full-on. "He was my first love."

I waited, wanting more. She rubbed her thumb up and down the swing chain. Lightning flashed, followed by thunder three seconds later. The first fat raindrops splattered on the front walk.

"Love?"

She nodded, her eyes unfocused, seeing something other than the porch, some other time, another history I wasn't a part of.

"What happened? Why didn't you stay together?"

"Well, that's the thing. We were never actually . . . together. I didn't realize until later that I actually loved him a little. Or a lot." She chewed on the edge of her bottom lip. "I don't know."

"But why didn't . . . Did he not love you back?" All I could think was, *Someone else? Someone else didn't love her enough?*

"Oh yes." This time her response was quick and sure. "He did."

I was relieved but then confused. "I don't get it. Why didn't it work? Why weren't you together?"

She shook her head, then patted me on the leg. "We just missed each other. Then later on we wanted different things. Or I thought I did. Then your dad came along and . . ." She sighed. "Sometimes things just happen. Or don't happen."

It was the vaguest answer she could have possibly given, but I didn't even know how to ask for specifics. "Why did you never tell me about him?"

"Honey, you're fourteen. There are things I haven't been able to tell you because you're too young. I know it doesn't feel that way. I know it feels like you have all the answers and know everything there is to know, but the world—and love itself—is complicated."

"Were you ever going to tell me about him?"

"I don't know. Maybe someday. If I needed to."

"Well, it would have been nice to know about him before meeting his hot son."

"He's hot?"

"Ugh, Mom, I don't know. Don't say that word."

"Well, you said . . ."

"Forget it. I just wish I'd known you and Mr. Bradley had such a steamy past—"

"Evan. It was not steamy."

"—before I went on to Nick about coming to Twig to get help with their vegetable garden. 'Sure, my mom would love to help your dad. She can really grow some tomatoes.'" I rolled my eyes.

"Sorry. Really, I am. I didn't mean to keep anything from you. If you want to ask me anything about Ben—Mr. Bradley—I'll answer as truthfully as I can. Shoot."

I laughed. "I don't know. Is it weird seeing him now? Today?"

She gave a slow nod. "A little."

"Do you ever wish things had turned out different? That it had worked out between the two of you?"

She tilted her head. "If anything had happened differently than it did, then I wouldn't have you. So, no. I'm satisfied with exactly how everything in my life has happened. Because of you." She kissed my forehead and wrapped her arm around my shoulder.

The thunder came on the heels of the lightning now, one after the other. The smell of wet dirt and grass floated up the steps and mingled with the jasmine climbing the porch rail. After a while, I peeked at Mom. Her eyes were closed. I thought of Mr. Bradley as he watched her from Twig's back porch. I thought of Nick, "Hallelujah," and the way he climbed into his dad's Jeep. I thought of Mom's red-and-white bathing suit, how excited she was to show it off to my dad. How soon that excitement turned to sadness.

"I'm glad it's just us," I whispered.

"Hmm?" Mom murmured, half in the here and now, half asleep.

"If it's just the three of us, no one leaves."

Her eyes opened and she stared at me hard. I thought she was going to laugh, correct me, something. Maybe tell me that was no way to go through life. But she closed her eyes again and pulled me closer to her. I let my head drop onto her shoulder and watched the rain fall.

CHAPTER 11

*Gardening is more than a hobby. It is a way of life for those
willing to accept the often-strenuous work, the disappointments,
and the impermanence of its beauty as part of the gift.*
—AARON IRVING, GRACE IN THE GARDEN

JESSIE

My dreams that night began with cheerleading—rising to the top
of a pyramid of thin, muscled arms and shoulders and doing a
perfect split before flipping all the way down. I landed on my feet, of
course. Ben came dashing out of the football huddle, helmet in hand,
to hug me and tell me he always knew I could do it.

Then there were wedding bells, but not for me. I stood at the back
of a huge gothic cathedral, waiting for the bride to make her entrance.
Then one by one, all the flowers I'd so painstakingly arranged at the
end of every pew began to wither. Pink blush roses, dinner plate–size
peonies, and peachy-pink ranunculus all turned black and drooped.
The bride, radiant in a shimmery dress, stared at me and cried.

The dream was still fresh in my mind when I woke, legs tangled
in sheets, fingers gripping the pillow. I sat up and pushed my messy
hair back from my face, then stretched my arms over my head. Both
Bens—the quietly determined one from years past and the more rugged and relaxed one of yesterday—remained with me, making my

stomach tighten with nerves. Or maybe it was just the dream. Even with sunlight streaming through my bedroom window, it clung to me like a spiderweb.

Then the scent of bacon and Mama's trembly early morning alto singing, *"And it burns, burns, burns . . ."* floated out of the kitchen, down the hall, and under my bedroom door. I inhaled and hoped she was singing about the ring of fire, not our breakfast.

I blinked, then threw on my work clothes. Today it was cargo shorts and a gray tank top with the shop's logo across the chest—"Twig" in a scrolled font, the tail of the g shaped into a thin twig with tiny red berries—and followed the scent and Mama's voice into the kitchen.

"Morning," Mama said to my back as I poured coffee into a mug and added half-and-half. "Hungry?"

"Always."

Evan trudged into the kitchen just as I sat at the table. I checked the clock on the microwave. "Seven fifteen and you're awake?"

"Who could sleep through all that warbling?" Evan pulled open the fridge and grabbed the bottle of orange juice. "She started with 'A Boy Named Sue.' Not exactly conducive to sleeping."

"I missed that one," I said. "Must have been sleeping too hard."

"Lucky you."

Mama reached over and tugged Evan's ponytail. "You've inherited my lovely singing voice, dear granddaughter. Don't deny it. I've heard you sing."

"It's true," I whispered in Evan's direction.

She rolled her eyes and tried to hide her smile.

I loved my daughter all the time, but I loved her so much in the mornings before she outfitted herself in her armor of the day— dark pants (shorts or leggings in the summer) and a T-shirt with some reference to music or the seventies or an obscure record shop on a forgotten alley in New York City. Anything to set herself apart. As if she even needed to try.

Mama set a plate of bacon—the real kind, no turkey bacon for Gus McBride—down in the center of the table next to a basket of fluffy biscuits and a plate of steaming scrambled eggs.

"Eat up," she said.

There were times when I felt guilty for allowing my mother to cook for my almost-forty-year-old self and my daughter, but then I reminded myself it was her choice. Not only that, but she loved it. She was always a good cook, but she started cooking and baking more after Dad died. When we left Birmingham and moved back home, one of the best parts of it for her was the fact that she had someone to cook for again. Plus, we probably took the edge off her loneliness.

When Evan and I moved back, she began spending most of her time at our house. Now hardly a day went by that I didn't return home at the end of the day and smell something delicious—sizzling chicken, simmering soup, or the sugared goodness of a fresh pie.

Mama turned to pour herself a cup of coffee. "Oh, Jessie, I was thinking," she said with her back to me. Across the table, Evan bit into a biscuit and a blob of grape jelly plopped onto the table. "You know, you're right about not needing to do the wedding for Mr. Tate. You're used to how things are, you're comfortable. Why go and mess that all up? You're making the right decision to just say no and stay away from any real challenges. Or opportunities."

Mama sat at the table and filled her plate. Her row of daily pills—beta blocker, three vitamins, and a baby aspirin—sat huddled on her placemat.

"Yeah, Mom. Familiar is good. Comfortable is good."

I heard Evan's words as her own truth, but Mama's smacked of snark even though she said them with a straight face. She gazed at me with wide, innocent eyes as she sipped her coffee. "Don't you think?"

Last night I'd lain awake in bed for what seemed like hours, unable to sleep. I kept thinking about how some extra money coming into Twig right about now would be such a help and how, truly, I could handle the extra workload. Why had I been so insistent on not doing the wedding? Staying in my comfort zone didn't pay me a dime, but for all I knew, Sumner had already called someone else and gotten an enthusiastic yes.

I pulled his business card out of the front pocket of my shorts.

"Oh, that's nice," Mama said. "You're keeping the card close just in case you need it."

"Mama, I can see straight through you."

She shrugged. "I have no idea what you're talking about."

I reached behind me and grabbed my cell off the counter, then punched the numbers into the phone. When I put the phone to my ear, Evan mouthed, *"Who are you calling?"*

It rang three times, then Sumner's deep voice filled the silence, asking me to leave a message and saying he'd get back to me as soon as possible.

"Hi, Mr. Tate—Sumner—this is Jessie McBride. We spoke yesterday about your daughter's wedding."

Next to me Mama whispered, "Trust me, honey, he remembers."

I shook my head. "I've . . ." I swallowed hard. "I've changed my mind. About the wedding. Could you please ask your daughter to call me when she can? I'd like to go over a few things with her."

I hung up and gently placed my cell on the table.

"The wedding is Labor Day weekend, so don't make any plans, either of you. I'll need all the help I can get."

"I can't believe you're doing it," Evan said.

I reached over and squeezed her hand. With my other hand I crammed a bite of now-cooled scrambled egg in my mouth.

"I'm surprised," Mama said. "Here I go telling you one thing and you do the exact opposite."

"Very funny. I knew what you were up to."

"I've never been able to make you change your mind. What did it?"

"The new computer we may need if Ben can't get mine up and running again. A new back fence from where Jay Clark's grandson ran through it with his riding lawn mower. I need more square footage in the greenhouse, new back steps. A new timing belt in the 4Runner." I counted the items off on my fingers. "What else? Oh, right. I'd like to take myself to the Grand Hotel for a long weekend. Maybe get one of those fancy spa treatments."

Evan and Mama stared at me, mouths hanging open a bit, "to catch flies," as Mama would have said if it'd been me.

"Good Lord, how much are you charging these people?" she asked. "While you're at it, I'd like a white Lexus and a pair of rhinestone-covered boots."

"Honestly, I'm not expecting to get any of that. Well, except the computer. I'm just making a point that I made the decision for purely business reasons. Nothing else."

Mama stood from the table and pushed her chair in. "My lips are sealed."

❧

I'd just hung the Open sign on the front door of Twig when the phone rang. I answered my cell as I walked through the front room, watering pots and straightening displays. Mama would be here in a few minutes to help me move the orchid display in the greenhouse to make room for new pepper plants.

"Mrs. McBride, I'm so sorry to just now be calling you back. This is Olivia Tate."

"Oh, it's fine." I checked my watch. I'd left the message for Sumner only twenty minutes ago.

"Well, I like to be prompt." Her tone was clipped and precise. "I would have called earlier, but I was stuck on the F train with no cell service. Something about a jam near Rockefeller Center. But I'm at my office now." She gave a quick sigh, then cleared her throat. "Okay, I'm ready. Fire away."

"I'm sorry?"

"Dad said you had some questions for me? About the wedding?"

"Yes, but . . . Rockefeller Center? You're in New York?"

"Manhattan, yes. Did he not tell you that?"

"No, he didn't mention it." So not only was she going to be a high-strung bride, but she was going to be a high-strung bride operating remotely. "I just assumed you lived in the area since your dad does."

"No, I haven't lived down there since I left for college. I went to law school here and I've been working at a firm in Midtown for the last two years." She shuffled some papers. I imagined her sitting at an immaculate desk in an equally immaculate office overlooking a classic downtown street scene. "I'm planning to fly home the week before the wedding. My dad mentioned that he thought you'd be a great person to do our flowers but that you were booked up. Is that still correct?"

I paused. *Last chance to back out.* "Actually I've had some time open up in my schedule and I may be able to make it work. I did want to ask—"

Olivia exhaled in a rush like she'd been holding her breath all morning. "That's wonderful, Mrs. McBride. Thank you so much."

"You're welcome. And it's Jessie. Not Mrs. anything."

"Okay. Jessie. Thanks for taking this on."

"Before you get too excited, I'm not sure how much your father told you, but I'm not a florist. I don't sell flowers by the stem. I sell azaleas, snapdragons, parsley. Plants people put in containers on their porches and in flower beds. My business isn't really set up to do weddings."

"But can't anyone with a business license order flowers wholesale?"

"Yes, that's true." She'd done her research. "If you got a business license, you could buy them yourself."

"Oh, I do not have time to do that. That's why I need you."

"Let me ask you this. Are you using a wedding coordinator? Because usually the coordinators take care of booking your vendors—florists, caterers, band, all the details. They're not cheap, but they're worth it. Especially with such a tight time frame."

"Oh, I'm not worried about money." From someone else, the comment may have come across as snobby, but she said it so matter-of-factly, I couldn't take any offense. "The sky's the limit with my dad."

I pushed open the back screen door and reached up to turn on the fan. As the blades swirled, tendrils of jasmine danced in the breeze. I inhaled deeply, as I did every morning. Heady midsummer scents—so different from the springtime sweetness—saturated the air.

"And believe me," she continued, "I called every wedding coordinator I could find in a forty-mile radius of Mobile."

"And they were all booked?"

"Oh no. They were all wide open. I got the sense that they were mentally canceling other events so they could focus solely on Sumner Tate's daughter's Oak House wedding."

"And . . . that's not a good thing?"

She paused. "How do I say this? They were pathetic. They could barely contain their excitement. Jessie, I'll be honest. I like efficiency and professionalism. I do not need some overly enthusiastic wedding planner gushing over me or my dad or the house. I definitely don't want anyone just trying to get her name in a magazine."

"You don't get the feeling that I'm trying to get my name in a magazine?"

"Not from how Dad described your place."

I tried to laugh, but it was more of a snort. "Well, that's . . ."

"What I mean is, it sounds perfect. And I think we can do this without a coordinator. A friend of my dad has a catering business and he's going to take care of the food. Some high school friends of mine have a band, and they're going to play during the rehearsal. My uncle is a pastor, so he'll officiate." I could hear the smile in her voice, but I imagined her trying to keep it tight. "That's all we need, right?"

"What about invitations?"

"Right." Another shuffle of papers. "I need to get on those."

I laughed. "I'll try to help as much as I can, but don't depend on me to remember all the details. Flowers, I can do, but that's about it. If you're not going to use a planner for everything, I'd suggest at least hiring someone to help you on the day of the wedding. That way you can enjoy your day and not have to think about whether your brides-maids are where they're supposed to be."

Back inside the shop, I sat behind the stool, kicked off my boots, and pulled out a notebook. "Now, your dad said you wanted the wedding to be Southern but not fancy. If you were in town, I'd say we could sit down together and you could give me an idea of what you want. Instead, maybe you could just email me some photos you like?"

"No need," Olivia said. "I put it all on a Pinterest board."

"Oh. Well, that's great."

"I've been saving photos there for two years. Ever since Jared and I started dating."

I was surprised at her display of romantic optimism. Although listening to her talk, I figured it may have just been part of her precise personality. Nail down all the important details early.

"They'll definitely help. I can see what types of flowers you want to work with and check with wholesalers around here to see if they carry them. If it's too exotic or rare, they might have to ship it in from somewhere else, and we probably wouldn't have time for that."

"Oh, nothing exotic for me. I want the arrangements to be loose and natural. Something to fit the setting. Inside Oak House it's pol-ished silver and expensive bourbon, but outside it's bare feet and beers on the dock."

Loose. Natural. Bare feet. I could imagine a wedding like that. Not mine, of course. My wedding was a grand ceremony. Two hundred guests—I only knew about forty of them—crammed shoulder to shoulder in the Cathedral of Saint Paul to see Chris marry his small-town bride. I wore a creamy Carolina Herrera, beaded heels, and flowers in my hair, trying so hard to be something else, *someone* else, anything other than what I was—a girl from a red-dirt road in a small country town. And I felt beautiful. A leading lady on the arm of her handsome, successful husband. It was exactly what I wanted. Then.

"I think it sounds lovely," I said to Olivia. And I meant it. "Have you and your dad set a budget for the flowers? That'll give me a good starting place."

"There's not really a set number. Just let me know how much everything is and we'll take care of it."

"Okay . . . It would probably help if I had some sort of guideline though. How many guests are you expecting?" The size of the wedding would give me an idea of how extensive the flower arrangements needed to be.

"We've just about finished up our list. Only close friends and family will be at the ceremony, but we're at about 250 for the reception."

I swallowed. "That's . . . quite a large wedding."

"Yes." She sighed. "It's gonna be big." That precise speaking voice—as if she'd been presenting her case before a judge—relaxed a little, exposing a twinge of her Alabama drawl. "But whatever your fee is, we can pay it. It'll be no problem."

Right. My fee. I hadn't thought of that.

"Also, it may help you to see my dad's house sometime soon. That way you'll get an idea of where flowers need to go and how to set everything up. I'm thinking the band will go under the big oak in the yard, but Dad thought that's where the food should go, to keep it in the shade."

I rubbed a hand across my forehead just as Mama walked carefully up the front steps of the shop, a tray of waxed paper–wrapped goodies in her hands. She nudged the front door open with her toe and exhaled. I pointed to a table near the window that had some open space. "Just keep in mind," I said to Olivia, "I'm here for the flowers. That's it."

Mama cleared her throat and pointed out the front window to where Mr. Rainwater was chugging up the driveway, the back of his truck loaded down.

"Right. I know. You're the florist."

I was about to correct her, but another phone rang in the background and a muffled voice called out. "I'm sorry, Mrs.—Jessie. I have a meeting starting in just a few minutes. I'll shoot you an email with a link to my Pinterest page. Just get back with me when you have a chance to look it over and we'll go from there. How does that sound?"

"Sounds perfect." I hung up and leaned back against the wall.

"A Bridezilla?" Mama asked, her gaze on Mr. Rainwater as he fumbled to unhook his wheelbarrow from the bed of his truck.

"Not exactly. But she is having a big old Southern wedding. Two hundred and fifty guests."

"My stars. You'll have your work cut out for you with that one."

"You too, remember?"

"Oh, I remember. And I've got just the thing for her Southern wedding. I've been watching that new girl on the food channel—the one who lives on the farm? I wrote down one of her recipes for a fried fig pie. Pair that with some cream cheese frosting and it'd be perfect for the dessert table."

I laughed, imagining Mama standing next to a dessert table full of her baked creations on the lawn of Sumner's fancy river house. "She didn't say anything about desserts, but if she mentions needing extra help, I'll let you know."

"In fact, maybe I'll go see if I can unearth that recipe. I wrote it down on the back of the obits. Plus . . ." She waved her hand toward Mr. Rainwater. "It's too early for all that." She took off out the back door. "I'll be back when the coast is clear," she called from the porch. The screen door slammed behind her.

Sumner's business card sat on the counter in front of me. I ran my fingers across the raised letters again. Images of his home, Oak House, sailed through my mind. A dock at sunset, a heron flying low over the water, an icy drink at my elbow. I shook my head. I wouldn't be relaxing there, I'd be working. I didn't know the man, hardly knew his daughter, but they were my job now, and from the sound of it, I'd be paid well for it. That'd go far toward helping with the computer issue and the repairs necessary around the place.

I stood and shoved my feet back into my dirty boots. I blew my bangs out of my eyes, tightened my ponytail at the back of my head, and headed out into the sunshine.

CHAPTER 12

Re: Moving plants from their natural habitat
Dear Ashley, If the roots are healthy, keep those babies where
they are and let them thrive. If they're thin and weak looking,
you could try moving them to another location. However, in
my experience, a plant with weak roots likely won't be satisfied
anywhere, no matter what kind of love or attention it gets.
—KATHERINE GRACE, YOUR DAILY DAISY

GUS

I knew Harvis Rainwater was in love with me. And I may have been
quick with a bad word about him, but I wasn't above admitting I
considered him from time to time. He always had dirt under his fingernails and Lord Almighty, there were days when he smelled three
kinds of bad from that load in the back of his truck, but he was a
sweet, patient man. He also had kind eyes, eyes that made me want
to lie down in them and take a catnap. Eyes that made me realize
just how long it had been since I'd sat on my own front porch with
a man who wasn't there to deliver my mail and enjoy a glass of cold
lemonade before heading next door. Eyes that made me think I may
have been approaching seventy, but I still had needs.

And that was just the thing. I was knocking on the door to my
senior years, willing to bet the earth, air, and holy Trinity I hadn't

used up all my shots at love, while Jessie, in the prime of her life, thought she was long past the possibility of it. It just broke my heart. She thought no one knew about her late nights on the porch when she'd sit with her hand over her heart, massaging it like she was hoping to tamp down those desires and longings flapping around in her chest like moths around a lightbulb.

But I saw her. I noticed. Underneath all her bravado, her insistence that she was fine on her own, there was a woman scared to admit she was lonely. I cast part of the blame on Glory Road itself. I'll tell you a story.

One Saturday afternoon when Jessie was about sixteen, Tom asked her to help him clean up the yard. We'd had a storm the night before and our property was covered in pinecones and small tree branches. Jessie moaned and groaned as teenagers are required by law to do, then yanked on her tennis shoes and went out to help him.

While I laid out ingredients for my Dolly—a peach-and-pear crumble with cinnamon-pecan streusel on top—and watched from the kitchen window, Tom and Jessie raked and swept the storm debris into piles all over the yard. When they finished, Tom climbed onto his ancient John Deere riding mower. He waved at Jessie and patted the seat in front of him, but she shook her head. He cranked it up, then patted it again and waved her over.

She mouthed a firm, "No," and stayed where she was, leaning against the upturned rake, as if the raking job had zapped all her energy. But Tom didn't stop, and I knew he wouldn't until he got a smile out of her. He inched the mower forward a bit in her direction. She shook her head. He raised his eyebrows, then hit the gas, steering straight toward her.

The thing was, this lawn mower was so ancient, its speed barely registered on the speedometer gauge. But Tom narrowed his eyes, hunched over like he was on the fastest motorcycle there ever was, and let it fly. Jessie showed off her perfect eye roll and hair flip, then

I saw it—the hint of a smile. Tom must have seen it too, because he whooped and hollered and kept the mower plodding in her direction.

She took off running, and their laughter trickled up to me in the kitchen. It was a sight to see—my lanky husband folded up on that slow-as-a-snail mower and our lovely, long-legged teenage daughter running around, acting like a carefree child.

But it didn't last long. When she stopped to catch her breath, she reached a hand out to steady herself against a walnut tree. I noticed the cotton candy–like swirls of webbing in the leaves at the same time I heard her shriek. She flew into the house, flailing her arms and wiping invisible bugs off her hands.

"Why do we have to live in a place where everything is crawling, moving, or buzzing? That tree was covered in worms! Covered!"

"Sugar, they're just caterpillars. It happens every fall. They don't bite, and you probably scared them more than they scared you."

She looked at me like I was crazy. "You say that like it's totally normal to have your trees covered in worms." She slid her hands up and down her arms. "Marcy and Carol Anne don't have to deal with things like this. They live in a normal neighborhood with houses and garage doors that open and close and a pest service that keeps bugs away."

She stomped out of the kitchen, still rubbing at the skin on her arms. "I can't wait to get out of here," she said just before she slammed her bedroom door.

I peered out the window at Tom. He'd parked the John Deere and was now shoving the piles of debris into a large black trash bag. His shoulders sagged.

I poured him a glass of tea and was about to bring it to him when Jessie entered the kitchen. Her eyes were softer now. "I don't hate it here."

"I know."

"It's home. But I do hate the bugs." Jessie took the glass of tea out of my hand and went out the back door toward her daddy.

Even then when she was caught up in the tangled web of teenage popularity, trying to figure out who she was and who she wanted to be, I knew a part of her felt more at ease here. When she was out with her friends, she was always dressing the part and trying to do and say the right things. Home was the place she could cast off that burden, even if she didn't realize the burden was there in the first place.

When she left for college, part of me thought she'd turn right back around and head home. Well, it took a little longer than that, but she did come back home. Glory Road had always been Jessie's landing place, her home base, and being Chris's wife for a few years didn't change that.

I understood—it was my home too, and you'd have to drag me by my fingernails to ever get me to leave. But the way this place had wound its way into her heart, mind, and soul made me hurt for her sometimes. Because to my eye, it seemed she thought this was all there was for her.

There I was, a sixty-nine-year-old widow forgetting my own name some days, and I was actually considering Harvis Rainwater as a man to love. If that was the case, how in the world could my lovely daughter possibly think she was past the age of wanting—of needing—love, companionship, the touch and heart of a man?

Something told me these two men appearing—or reappearing, as was the case with Ben Bradley—could be a harbinger of change in Jessie's life if she'd just allow it, but her inclination would be to see them as a sideshow to her real life, rather than the main act. This was in no way about me trying to marry her off. I didn't even know if these two men would amount to more than a hill of beans in the end. But the possibility of it—that's what I wanted her to see. To understand. That her life wasn't over just because she'd married the wrong man. That a fresh start could happen at any moment of any day.

CHAPTER 13

*If it looks like your garden is livelier after a good thunderstorm,
you're right, but it's not just the rain that causes the new lushness. In
a strange tale of chemistry and weather, it's the lightning that deposits
necessary nutrients into your soil through the rain. Yet another
reason to be thankful for those summertime thunderstorms.*
—AMANDA ANDERSON, *SOUTHERN GARDENS A TO Z*

EVAN

It got to where every time I walked to the end of the driveway for any reason, I looked down the road to see if Nick was there. To see if he was singing, walking Stanley, maybe walking home from the baseball field. I couldn't help it. I made up reasons to walk out there—check for mail (even though the mailman always stopped by our mailbox at two fifteen exactly), take out the trash (something I rarely did under normal circumstances), or walk Mrs. Birdie home (even though I knew perfectly well she could walk herself on home without any assistance).

I made myself available anytime an errand or a favor was needed, just so I could be within sight of the road. It was ridiculous. He was just a guy who moved in down the road, whose dad may or may not have broken my mom's heart, who had a voice from heaven and a really cute dog on an adorable plaid leash. Nothing more.

But still, when Mom asked me if I wanted to go with her on her evening run, I said, "Hang on, let me find my shoes." I knew she hadn't expected me to say yes—she was already out the door when she called over her shoulder—but she stopped and waited without asking any questions, which I so appreciated.

Mom often asked me to run with her, but I rarely took her up on it, even though I ran track at Perry Middle School. Summers were just so hot and sweat was so gross. I preferred walking to running, shade to sun, anything to keep from feeling like my skin would boil away. But today running sounded good. Great, actually.

I found my old track shoes—only a little too tight—under my bed and gathered my hair into a ponytail. Just inside the front door, I paused in front of the mirror. My cheeks were already flushed and my heart hammered in my chest. I took a deep breath and blew it out.

I'll be honest here. It wasn't just that Nick was nice to look at. Which he was. It's that he seemed like someone who might get me. Who wouldn't be boring or treat me like a girl just there to look cute, which was what it seemed like most guys wanted. He seemed less . . . simpleminded.

Outside, Mom was leaned over stretching her calves. When I closed the front door behind me, she straightened. "Ready?"

It had rained earlier that afternoon, a hard and fast downpour, the kind of storm that turned our road into an orange-red river. Luckily, the edge of the road had grass and leaves to give us firm footing and keep us from kicking too much red mud all over our legs. Thunder still rolled, but it was far off, the skeletal remains of what had already blown through, and it was a good ten degrees cooler than earlier in the day.

"I'm glad you came with me," Mom said after a minute. Her ponytail swung side to side as she ran.

Sometimes I could see what she must have looked like as a little girl. I'd seen pictures—Gus had photo albums all over her house—but seeing that youngness in her grown-up face was something different. It unsettled me a little—if you can still look like your little girl self when you're grown, do you still feel little? Like you're playing pretend and you really don't feel like the adult everyone thinks you are?

"Usually it's just me and the bugs out here."

"Bugs?" I swatted at a gnat by my ear. "Great."

"I used to hate the bugs too. Now I don't mind as much." She smiled. "It's just part of country life."

"I know, and I love it. I just don't love all the tiny details." I swatted at the gnat again. "Maybe I will once I've lived here as long as you have."

"I haven't been here forever. Neither have you." She paused. "Do you remember much from when we were in Birmingham?"

I remembered some—our huge brick house, the lawn-care service, the landscaper, the housekeeper who came three times a week—but I only had one solid memory of the place. I had a friend up the road, the only other young child on our block. We'd climb this massive magnolia tree in her front yard and pretend we were squirrels whenever anyone would walk by.

Well, I had one other memory, but I usually tried to block it out. It was the day Mom moved us out. Dad had followed us to the car, his eyes red, his shirt half buttoned. Behind him, a woman in bubblegum-pink scrubs—I think they had little hearts on them—jogged out of the house. She tossed Mom's bathing suit—the one with the flowers, the one she'd been so proud of only weeks before—into the back seat. "You forgot this."

Mom carefully picked it up, walked over to the trash can sitting by the side of the road, and dropped it in.

"I don't remember much," I said. "I was six when we moved here, right?"

"It was just a few days before your sixth birthday, actually. Mama

101

had everything planned, so when you came out of your room after quiet time that day, half the street was already crammed into her small kitchen. Everyone had balloons and party hats."

"I remember." The memory was hazy, but it was there. "Mr. Rainwater gave me a snow globe, didn't he?"

She nodded. "It was from Lake Lurleen, something he'd picked up at a souvenir shop years before."

"That's right. It had a man fishing in a tiny boat with a really big fish on the end of the line. I think I still have it somewhere."

"He was so sweet. He didn't know how to buy something for a little girl, so he probably just found it around his house and wrapped it up for you."

Thinking back on that party, which had previously been buried in my memory, made me look differently at the houses we jogged past. These people weren't just customers at our shop—grumpy, cheerful, or forgetful old folks. These people had welcomed us in when we could no longer stay in our home. When I was five, I had no idea what was happening—why Dad was crying but Mom wasn't, why that woman flung Mom's favorite bathing suit in the car, and why Mom casually threw it away. Now, at almost fifteen, I had ideas. But back then, we needed a new home and everyone on Glory Road offered it with open arms. As far as I knew, they never mentioned what may or may not have happened with Mom and Dad.

Now that I thought about it, Gus probably threatened them with death by cold shoulder—or maybe by withholding her baked treats from the church bake sale—if anyone spoke of my dad in front of us. Who would go against that?

Instead, they left little packages on our doorstep—a crocheted hat with plastic flowers around the brim from Elma Dean, a gallon of fresh strawberry iced tea from Ms. Rickers, a little wooden birdhouse complete with shutters on the windows from Mr. Rainwater.

"Someone left a copy of the book *Surprised by Singleness* on the kitchen counter after your party," Mom said. "I picked it up before Mama saw it. She would have been livid if she knew someone left it for me."

"Did you read it?"

"Lord, yes, every word. And every other self-help book I could find. For a while. I finally gave them up, thank goodness."

"Were you surprised by your singleness?" I said it lightly like a joke, but I was really curious. Did that day in the driveway come out of nowhere, or had she seen it coming? Could a person's hopes and dreams just blow up so quickly like that?

"Not really. I was a different person when I met your dad. The whole thing was partly my fault. Once you came and I fell in love with you, I fell out of love with the person I'd tried so hard to be—the person who wasn't the real me. Unfortunately, your dad wasn't too charmed by the real me."

"Well, he's an idiot."

"Maybe. Or maybe he just knew exactly what—and who—he wanted, and I wasn't her anymore."

"But he wanted that woman in the scrubs? I remember her. She looked ridiculous."

Mom inhaled sharply. "I didn't know you remembered that day."

I shrugged. "Just bits and pieces." No need to tell Mom the ordeal in the driveway was burned into my brain, etched into my memories. "She was so . . . perky. I wanted to throw something at her."

"Did you know why she was there?"

"You said she was one of Dad's hygienists."

She paused before answering. "That's right. She was."

It didn't make sense back then that his hygienist was there at our house. Why wasn't she at the office, flossing teeth and reminding people to brush twice a day? Why was she coming out of my parents' house like she owned the place? I understood more now, but this adult world—marriage, love, commitment—was murky.

We ran in silence. My thighs burned and sweat dripped down one side of my face, but the exertion felt good. I actually felt like I could keep running all evening, but Mom slowed down. I'd been watching the path in front of me, trying not to trip on the roots of a big oak tree, so I didn't see why she stopped. Then I heard the dog bark.

Ahead of us, Mr. Bradley stood at his mailbox flipping through a stack of mail, his back to us. When Stanley barked again, Mr. Bradley turned and his mouth pulled into a grin. I glanced at Mom. For a split second, her face mimicked his, but she wiped it away quickly.

"Hey, you two," he called. Stanley lunged for us, tongue already wagging, but Mr. Bradley was surprisingly quick. He grabbed Stanley's collar before he could jump up on us. "It's a good time for a run. Not too hot."

Why was it that people around here always started conversations with the weather? Everyone did it—even Mr. Bradley, and he'd only lived on the street for about five minutes. Well, his childhood and five minutes. It was as if the weather was a known icebreaker, like those silly games teachers made us play at the beginning of school years. Instead of "What's your favorite ice cream flavor?" it was, "Hey, how about this hot weather?"

But Mom went along with it, as everyone did. "It's great. We would have melted if we'd headed out earlier, but it's manageable now. I even got my partner to come out with me today." She put her hand on my back. Her heat radiated into my already-hot skin, but I liked the idea that we were partners.

"You got a good one. Nick would be impressed. He runs every morning for baseball. He's always trying to get me to run with him, but it's not really my thing."

"Not your thing?" Mom asked. "You used to get up at the crack of dawn to run too, didn't you?"

He laughed. "I did, but that was a long time ago. No more football, no more need to kill myself mile by mile. Now I'm just pouring my first cup of coffee by the time Nick finishes his morning run. I like it this way better."

"I'm with you on that." Mom wiped her forehead with the back of her wrist. "Mornings are for coffee and my front porch, rain or shine. I take them slow."

Mr. Bradley smiled softly out of one side of his mouth. They both grew quiet, and the silence was more than I could handle.

"Okay, so we'll get going." I both wanted to see Nick and didn't want to, but I couldn't stand there any longer with the awkwardness. Plus, it had started to rain again. Just drops now, but the sky was getting darker, and not from the approaching nightfall.

"Right." Mr. Bradley restacked the mail in his hands—a few magazines at the bottom, envelopes on top. "I take it you get a free pass on the parent meeting at school. You've been around here awhile, so you're not exactly 'new.' Honestly, I'd rather not go, but I don't want anyone to complain that the new dad's uninvolved."

"Parent meeting?" Mom stared at me. "I didn't know anything about it."

"Oops." Crap. The posters, the flyers—yeah, I'd totally forgotten. "So, there's an orientation meeting at seven thirty for new parents. I think it's a PTO thing. They told us about it at registration." I bit my lip. "Sorry."

Mom ran a hand over her hair and glanced down at her damp running clothes, ankles splattered with red mud. "I wish you'd mentioned it. I'd hate to miss any information we'll need later on."

"I'm sorry," I said again. "I was . . . distracted." There'd been a huge poster on the door to the gym, I remembered, and someone stuck a flyer in my hand, but who knew where that had gotten off to? I felt bad for Mom. She'd always been intimidated by the PTO moms. "You could still go. If we run back now, you can just hop in the car and take off. I'll clean up with Gus and make sure she gets home okay."

"No, I'd never make it." She checked her watch. "It's already ten after."

"You're welcome to come with me," Mr. Bradley said. "If you want. I can get you a towel too." He nodded at the dirt on her legs.

She tucked loose hair behind her ears. "I can't go like this."

"Mom, go. Go and come back and tell me how lovely and charming everyone was."

Lightning ripped across the sky and the raindrops fell faster. "Okay, not gonna happen," she said. "No way am I letting you run back home in this."

"Nick can take her. He's just inside watching TV." He pointed to the garage. "Let's get out of this rain."

Mom and I followed him up the driveway. The back wall of his garage was full of boxes, some still sealed with masking tape, others with the flaps open, revealing everything from shoes to books to tools.

Mr. Bradley stepped inside and called for Nick. When he returned, he gestured to the boxes. "Sorry about the mess. We're making slow progress." He shook water from his hair. His Jeep was sandwiched into the garage next to an old black muscle car. Nick's?

"So, meeting, yes or no?" Mr. Bradley raised his eyebrows. "I can run you both home, or Nick can take Evan if you want to come with me."

The door to the house opened and Nick stepped out. "Hey, I thought you were going— Oh, hey," he said when he saw me and Mom.

"I was about to leave, but I found some neighbors." He turned back to Mom. "So what's it gonna be?"

Mom groaned, then laughed. She looked at me. I shrugged.

"I get it," Mr. Bradley said. "If I had a daughter, I probably wouldn't let her anywhere near a teenage boy's car." He reached over and tried to ruffle Nick's hair, but Nick ducked out of the way. "But he's not so bad."

Something in Mom's eyes shifted. Her face softened. "Is it okay with you if Nick takes you home?"

"Yeah, it's fine, of course." I kept my eyes on Mom instead of Nick in the doorway.

"Text me when you get home," she said quietly. "I want to know when you're inside with Gus."

"Okay, I got it. Now go or you'll be late."

"She's right," Mr. Bradley said. "Nick, grab a towel out of the hall closet, will you?"

"Sure thing." He retreated into the house. I smoothed my hair into another knot, then fanned my damp top away from my skin. The shirt was one of my favorites—a vintage Allman Brothers tee with a red truck carrying a huge peach in the back. Same as the album cover. My too-small Reeboks screamed middle school though.

Mom kissed me on the cheek. "Don't forget to text me," she whispered. "Thanks, Nick. Take care of my girl."

"Mom," I groaned. "We live, like, ten feet up the road."

Mom climbed in the Jeep next to Mr. Bradley and waved as they backed out of the garage. Outside, the rain hid their faces from view.

"Our turn," Nick said.

We sat in his car and he cranked the engine, then turned to back down the driveway, his arm on the back of my seat. "All right, then. Here we go."

❧

"I can't believe this thing even runs." I glanced around the interior of his car. A 1971 Dodge Challenger, he'd informed me on the way to my house. It was just an old black car to me, but it was cool. A little run-down but clean. We'd made the thirty-second drive to our house and now sat in the driveway, the front seat lit by the glow of the porch light. We had to talk loud to hear each other over the rain beating on the roof.

"Hey, you should be impressed. I worked my butt off to get this thing in good shape." He ran his hand across the dash. Below, the dashboard held nothing but a couple of air vents, a cigarette lighter, and an ancient radio. It had two fat dials and a handful of huge AM and FM buttons. He leaned over and blew onto one of the air vents, then rubbed away a speck of dust.

"I am impressed. I mean, it's awesome. It's just so . . . old." I cringed and cleared my throat. "Where did you find it?"

"My dad found it at a junkyard for next to nothing, and we worked on it together back in Atlanta. If you think this looks old, you should have seen it when we started. Took two years to bring her back to life. Dad said if I worked on it with him, he'd give it to me when I turned sixteen. It was the same thing his dad did for him."

"Wow, that's kind of a great deal. A new car you don't have to pay for?"

"Oh, I paid for it. In long, hot hours after school and on the weekends. Dad and I used a friend's garage, since our condo didn't have one. As long as I wasn't on the baseball field, I was working on this car. I think it was partly my dad's way of keeping me in line."

"So you were a troublemaker?" It sounded dumb, but I wanted to know more about him.

"Nah, not really. At least not in the way my dad worried about."

That gave me exactly no real information, but I hardly knew him well enough to press for more. We sat in silence a moment while my brain whirred from subject to subject, trying to find something worthwhile to say. I came up blank.

My phone buzzed in my pocket and I pulled it out.

"Boyfriend?"

"Mom," I said, my cheeks hot.

"Good thing. I don't want some big guy to beat me up for sitting in the car with you." He grinned and I rolled my eyes. "Wait—how old are you?"

"I'll be fifteen in a few months." If seven months was "a few."

"My dad wouldn't let me even call a girl on the phone until I was fifteen, much less sit in a car with one. Your mom must be pretty cool."

"I don't sit in cars with guys very often. I think she just trusts you because she knows your dad."

"Guilty by association."

I sent a quick text back to Mom. Everything was fine and I'd make sure Gus got home soon. I quickly turned the screen off to hide the intrusion.

"So, tell me about yourself," he said. I looked up at him. "What?" he asked. "Isn't this what good neighbors do? Learn about each other? Tell me something interesting."

"Um . . . I like music."

"Okay," he said with a laugh. "Good start. I do too."

"I know. I mean, I've heard you. Sing. I heard you sing."

"When did you hear me?"

I swallowed. "A few days ago. When you walked Stanley near our house. You were singing 'Hallelujah.' It's a great song."

"The best. Which version?" He raised an eyebrow.

I paused. "Usually I'd say the original is best, but for this one, Jeff Buckley. He did it better."

"Amen. I agree on both counts." He leaned over the steering wheel and peered out the windshield. The porch light caught the falling rain and made the drops look like little diamonds falling through the air. He sat back in his seat and turned to me. "I didn't realize I was talking to a music aficionado."

"I don't know about that. I just know when I hear something good."

"Let's see, judging by your shirt, I'd say you like mostly old stuff—sixties and seventies. Dylan. Some Beatles, but the less poppy stuff. Led Zeppelin. As for the ladies—Janis, Joni, maybe a little Emmy Lou?"

"Have you been spying on me?"

"Nah, just a good guess."

"Well, you're right about most of it. Except Janis. I don't see what the big deal was about her. Her voice was like a garbage disposal."

"Ouch. But you're right. I gotta tell you, though, some good music has been made in, uh, more recent years. Ever heard of Shovels & Rope? Alabama Shakes? Florence and the Machine?"

I shrugged. "A little."

"Ah." He leaned to the side and pulled his phone out of his pocket. "I have something for you." He swiped the screen a few times, then handed me the phone with earbuds attached. I stuck one in my ear, and the sound of plucking strings filled my ear. After a moment, a woman's voice began to float. I smiled involuntarily.

"Right?" He grabbed the other end of the earbuds and listened.

When the song was over, I pulled the end of the cord and handed him the earbud. "Who is that? She's incredible."

"Florence and the Machine. They're unlike anyone else. See? The good stuff didn't stop with the seventies."

"Good to know," I said.

"So, give me more. What else do you like?"

"Nope. Your turn. Tell me something about you now." It was easy to talk to Nick. He may have just been wasting time until he could get me out of his car and get back home, but he sure made it easy to forget my usual awkwardness.

"Well, I like good music, as you know. I play baseball. I want to play ball in college, so I pretty much keep my head down and play as well as I can during the season. Off-season, I can have a little fun."

"Summertime too?"

"A little. The team at Perry is having practices this summer. The coach wants everyone to keep up their skills. Makes me a little worried that I'll be playing for some farm team, but we'll see."

"What position do you play?" I didn't know a thing about baseball, but I tried to cover it well.

"I'm the pitcher."

"Ever get hit?"

"Once. Ball bounced off my glove and broke my nose."

I laughed. "Sorry," I said when I saw his face. "Not funny."

"Not at the time, no." Then he laughed. "But later I guess it was. It swelled up pretty big."

"Okay, music, baseball, what else?"

He held up his hands. "I like to work on old cars. I'm trying to convince my dad to buy this old junked Camaro I found on Craigslist. It doesn't run, but it could be gorgeous. Oh, and we're going to have a killer vegetable garden in the backyard soon."

I laughed.

"Tell me about kids around here," he continued. "What am I going to find at Perry High School?"

"Your guess is as good as mine. This will be my first year too."

"Ah, that's right. Ninth grade?"

I nodded.

"We're both newbies then. We'll have to stick together. Navigate the halls of terror."

"Halls of terror?"

"I'm kidding," he said. "Mostly. I just know how people can be in school. But that was Atlanta. Maybe it's different here."

"Why did y'all leave Atlanta?" The question was out before I could filter it. "I mean . . ." I stumbled. "It's just, you were almost done with school. Seems like a hard time to move and start somewhere new."

He shrugged. "I didn't mind. I didn't love my school, and my mom . . . Well, Dad just needed a break. I think he wanted to revisit his roots a little, and I'm just along for the ride."

"And you're okay with that?"

"Maybe I needed the break too." He glanced out the window again and sighed. "So much for this being a quick rain."

"It's fine. I can just run for it. I need to check on Gus anyway.

She's probably on the phone with the police about the car in the driveway."

"Gus. Your grandmother with the . . ." He wiggled his fingers in the air.

"Yes, my grandmother with the horse manure on her hands. It's a long story."

"I won't even ask. She seemed . . . fun."

I laughed as my phone vibrated with a text. It was Mom again, of course. She assumed I was already inside, tucked into bed, but it was barely after eight o'clock. I texted her back, then slid my phone back into my pocket.

"They're almost done. I should probably be inside when she gets here."

"Good idea. I don't want your mom to think I didn't fulfill my chauffeur duties."

I cracked open the door, and Nick handed me the damp towel. "Here, you can hold this over your head or something."

"Oh, so I don't get my hair wet? I'm not worried about it."

"So, I'll see you around then."

I nodded and pushed open the door. It squeaked in protest.

"Sorry about that," Nick said. "I need to work on the door. Next time it'll be fixed."

I shut the door behind me and waited there in the driveway while he backed up and turned onto the street. Just before he drove away, he stuck his arm out the window and waved.

CHAPTER 14

When you see signs of decay—dropping petals, brown leaves,
refusal to bloom—don't be quick to rip out the plant. Take a step
closer and examine the stem. Even if the stem appears brown,
scratching your fingernail against it may reveal green life just under
the decay. And, my friends, in the garden, green equals hope.
—VIRGINIA PEARCE, THE WATCHFUL GARDENER

JESSIE

H it me." Ben drummed his fingers on the steering wheel. Rain pelted the windows as we drove the few miles to the school. "What are the parents around here like? As the new kid on the block, who do I need to watch out for?"

I laughed. "The PTO women run everything at the schools. The same group cycles through the board positions each year, and they head out like an army getting parents to sign up for their committees."

"Committees, huh? You mean like bake sales? I don't bake."

"Don't worry, it doesn't all involve baking. I'm sure if you have problems finding the right thing, someone will be more than happy to tell you when and how to contribute."

He exhaled. "All right. Consider me armed and ready. I'm glad I'm not doing this alone. You sound like you've got the hang of things."

"I don't know about that. I'm just used to it, I guess."

Rain streaked down the windows and blurred the world outside. Ben adjusted the AC and a chill blasted my face and made the hair on my arms stand up. Other than the persistent beat of the rain, silence filled the car and magnified the strangeness of the situation.

I'd often wondered what it would be like to be around Ben again. To hear his voice, see his familiar stance, soak up his calm presence. Sitting in his Jeep with him was almost too much—weird and uncomfortable, familiar and soothing, all at the same time. How was that possible? So much time had passed, yet it almost felt like it hadn't passed at all. But when I glanced at him—the beard, the faint web of lines at the corners of his eyes, the still-thick brown hair—it was a grown man sitting in the driver's seat, not the teenager I'd once spent so many idle hours with, like time outside of time. He was now a man with a twenty-year history I didn't know, except that it included a teenage son, computers, and, soon, a vegetable garden.

The rain slackened a little, and one of the windshield wipers scraped against the glass, giving off an irregular squeak.

"I don't know if Nick told you, but I met him a couple nights ago when I was out running. He was outside with Stanley."

"Ah, that was you. He told me he'd met a neighbor. He said Stanley about knocked you down."

"I think I held my own pretty well." I smiled. "It felt like worlds crashing together when I realized who he was. I saw the Jeep and . . ." I paused, felt his gaze on the side of my face. I reached up and tucked a stray hair behind my ear. "I can't believe you still have this thing."

He chuckled. "Sometimes I can't either. But I can't bring myself to get rid of it. I left blood, sweat, and tears in this thing. You remember?"

"I do. So what's going on with your parents? They moved out and you moved in?"

"That's the short answer, yeah. They got a call that space was available at this retirement village if they could move in right away, so they did. They basically gave me the house and said I could live in it, rent it, sell it, whatever. If I'm going to sell it though, it needs some work first. A lot of painting, new wood around some windows. I need to pull up the carpet in a couple of rooms. Nothing too big, but it needs to be taken care of."

"Couldn't you have hired someone to do that without having to move here to do it?"

He rubbed his cheek and opened his mouth but paused.

"I'm sorry. That didn't come out right. I just mean, it's a big thing to move when you have a kid in school. And to move to Perry, of all places." I let out a small laugh. "It just seems . . ."

"I know. I get it." He took a deep breath and let it out slowly. "Atlanta can be hectic and things were . . . complicated. So when my folks moved and I knew the house was just sitting here, I asked Nick what he thought about a little adventure."

"And he was up for it?"

"He and I are alike in a lot of ways. I think he needed a fresh start. He said as long as he could play baseball, he was game."

"It worked out well then. Have you started work on the house yet?"

"Nah. We're still trying to find all our stuff in boxes. I'll start soon though. How handy are you with a paintbrush?" He grinned.

"You know, it's funny—I've never minded painting. Turn on some music and open the windows, and I can paint all night."

"Okay then. I may take you up on that."

"Fix my computer and I'll paint whatever you want."

He laughed. "You're on."

Just up ahead, the school appeared in a swirl of watery lights. The gym was ablaze, light from the open double doors spilling out onto the wet concrete.

Ben didn't have an umbrella, so he parked as close to the doors as he could, then we ducked and ran into the gym. Just inside, we stopped to wipe water off our faces and arms. My bare legs were wet, and thin streams of water pooled at the top of my running shoes.

All around us, parents flowed in through the double doors and from other hallways. Most held damp umbrellas in their hands, their hair and clothes perfectly dry. Next to me, Ben shook droplets of water from his hair. "I should have grabbed an umbrella. Sorry about that."

"I was already damp. An umbrella wouldn't have helped much." From across the gym, I caught the watchful gaze of Carol Anne Davies, which did nothing to make me feel better about my appearance.

"Is that"—Ben squinted—"Carol Anne? Miss Head Cheerleader herself?"

"Yep. All these years later she's still the Perry Pirates' most devout cheerleader." I waved at her.

She held up a hand in greeting, then turned her eyes back down to the podium in front of her. She stood and cleared her throat into the microphone. It buzzed, then gave a high-pitched whine before settling down. "Hello, everyone. I'm Carol Anne Davies, PTO president for the upcoming school year. Thank you so much for coming out on this wet night. Please find your places and we'll begin the meeting." She eyed Ben and me. We hurried to the back of the gym where there was standing room only.

The principal spoke first, then Carol Anne and various committee members spoke about different areas of need. As they did, I pulled out my phone, carefully tilted the screen down, and tapped out a quick text to Evan.

At home?

Yes. All is well.

Great, I texted back, one eye on the screen and one in the general direction of the podium. Is Gus still there?

Yes. Will get her home soon.

Ben leaned over and whispered, "Everything okay?"

"Nick got her home fine."

"Were you worried?"

"No, I just like to know she's in safe."

"Yeah." He paused. "It's a little scary, isn't it?"

"What's scary?"

He shrugged. "Letting our kids out of sight. Giving them that little bit of leeway. Hoping they don't get hurt."

Our whispered conversation died when someone shushed us, but my mind remained tipsy, reeling from the surprising turn of events that landed me next to Ben at a parents' meeting at our children's school. It almost took my breath away to think what might have been if such small moments had gone another way. If I'd responded differently—if I'd responded at all—when he told me how he felt about me at the bonfire all those years ago. Or if I'd had the courage to speak up even earlier than that, to put into words what it meant for him to accept me so fully, to see who I was inside my polished and well-liked shell. If I'd let myself love him.

With just a few small twists of circumstance or intention, would we be raising our own children, running out to the parents' meeting together after having eaten dinner at home with our family? It seemed impossible, but such small twists had led us in opposite directions. Was it possible that similar small twists could have bound us together?

Before I realized Carol Anne had finished speaking, chairs were scraping across the floor as everyone stood and moved around. Conversation swelled, and parents migrated toward tables set up on the other side of the gym.

"What are we supposed to be doing?" I whispered to Ben.

He laughed.

"Sorry, I was . . ." I held up my phone and shrugged.

"I give you a D- for not paying attention." He bumped my shoulder with his. "We're supposed to pick up information at those tables over there." He pointed across the gym where parents were lined up behind various tables loaded with papers and clipboards. "So this is when I sign my life away. Think they'd notice if we skipped out?"

"Carol Anne would definitely notice. Come on."

He followed me as I waded through the tables in search of a place to sign up to bring food. I figured if I signed up to bring enough of Mama's baked treats that'd get Evan off the hook for going door-to-door selling wrapping paper or buckets of cookie dough. I knew she'd never go along with that.

"Hi, Jessie," Claire Brody said as we approached her table. "Good to see you." She glanced up at Ben. "Hi, I'm Claire, PTO party coordinator."

Claire had moved to Perry from Mississippi when her kids were in elementary school. If she'd been born and raised in Perry, like many parents at the meeting, she would have recognized Ben too.

"Ben Bradley," he said. "New kid."

"It's so nice to have you. And you two already know each other?"

I liked Claire, but I wondered if she was gathering tidbits of information to pass to Carol Anne. It was probably a requirement for all PTO members under Carol Anne's authority. I didn't give her much to go on. "We do."

"Oh. Well, I'm glad you're both here. Just sign your names up wherever you like. We have all kinds of needs, so I'm sure whatever you can bring will fit in somewhere."

"I'm going to respectfully decline to add my poor baking skills to the list here," Ben said. "I think I may find something over in the"—he waved his hand toward the tables on the other side of the room—"in that general direction." He patted me on the back. "Good luck," he whispered.

I wrote my name down to bring treats to a few different parties, then moved on to the next table. As I made my way through the gym, I picked up flyers in various colors, each proclaiming a different group or club Evan could get involved with. Knowing my daughter well, I bypassed the table advertising cheerleading tryouts but picked up a flyer about the school theater troupe and the science team.

I pulled out my phone and sent her another quick text.

All tucked in?

It's 8:15, Evan texted back a moment later.

I checked the time at the top of the screen. I could have sworn two hours had been sucked away by this meeting. Sorry. I should be home soon.

Don't worry about us. We're good.

I grabbed a few more flyers, then when my hands were full, I scanned the space for Ben. I finally saw him leaning over a clipboard, signing up for something with the baseball team. I headed toward him, but before I got there, Carol Anne stepped out from behind a group of parents next to Ben. Her voice rose above the buzz in the room.

"Ben Bradley, I heard you were back in town!" She reached out and hugged him. "Marissa told me the two of you are working things out, and I have to say I'm so glad. I know it means so much to have you and Nick in her life again."

The noise level in the room didn't change, but for a moment it felt like everything went silent. *Marissa? A girlfriend. Of course.* In a rush all the noise came back and filled the muffled silence in my head. I reached out for a clipboard on the table in front of me and hunched over, trying to make myself disappear in the scattered group of people around me. I kept my head down but turned my eyes so I could still see Ben and Carol Anne.

"Um . . . yeah. Things are . . . things are going okay." Ben's voice was tight.

She playfully hit him on the arm. "Better than okay, as she tells it. Although I don't see how with the two of you in different cities. I don't know why in the world you'd move back to little old Perry and give up the excitement of Atlanta."

He shuffled the papers in his hands. A little muscle at the base of his jaw worked back and forth. "Nick and I just had some things we needed to take care of around here."

"Well, I know it must be good for all three of you. I'm happy for you." She smiled at him and shook her head. "It must feel weird to be back at your old stomping grounds. Have you gone out to the field? I'll never forget the night you caught that pass in the end zone against Fairhope. And just as the clock ran out!"

He straightened up and cleared his throat. "Yeah, that was quite a night."

I didn't want him to see me, but before I could make my escape, Carol Anne called out to me. "Oh, Jessie! I didn't see you there." I cringed. I could feel Ben's gaze on my cheek as sure as if he'd touched me. "I hope you're signing up to bring some of your mama's lemon icebox cupcakes to the Fall Festival."

"Oh, yeah." I glanced down at the clipboard in my hand. "I'm writing them down now."

"That's great." She scooped a lock of bright-blonde hair over her shoulder with her manicured hand. "You know, your mama's cupcakes are the best in Perry."

I laughed a little. Perspiration pricked under my arms and at the back of my neck. "I'll tell her you said so."

"You do that. Oh and, Jessie, have you seen Ben is here? It's so great to have him back in town, isn't it?" She smiled at us both, then scurried over to another group of parents, her voice full of eager excitement.

Ben exhaled, then nodded toward the door. "You ready to call it a night?"

Outside, the lights from the gym cast a wet, shiny glow over the parking lot. Inside the car I crossed my hands in my lap, unsure of what to say, unsure if I wanted him to bring it up at all. He was dating someone. Why wouldn't he be? And more importantly, why did that fact make me feel like something had slipped out of my grasp?

The couple of minutes it took to drive back to my house were silent, making the single mile feel more like ten. We finally approached my house. Lights glowed in the windows, and from the driveway, I saw Mama on the couch watching TV.

He put the Jeep in Park and ran his hand through his hair, then turned to me. His dark eyebrows were pulled together, his mouth set in a thin line. Before he could speak, I did. "Do you still leave the car running so you don't have to deal with it not starting again?"

He hesitated a second—I'd caught him off guard, I could tell—then laughed. "You remember that?"

"Sure. I remember you used to lean your forehead on the steering wheel whenever it wouldn't start. You actually thought it would work."

"It always happened in the movies. Whenever someone's car wouldn't start, the forehead-against-the-steering-wheel trick made the engine turn over, without fail."

"Things are always a little easier in movies than in real life."

He sniffed. "That's the truth."

"I guess you don't have to leave it running anymore."

"Yeah, the engine is pretty dependable now. I fixed a few things."

It grew quiet again. I should have gotten out of the car as soon as he stopped in the driveway, thanked him for the ride, and waved good-bye. The evening had already been complicated, and now all of a sudden my throat felt thick, like I was about to cry. "I need to—"

"Look," he said at the same time. He nodded up to the front porch. Mama stood in the front window. She likely thought we couldn't see her since she'd turned off the porch light. The full moon blew her cover though.

I picked my bag up from the floor. As I pushed open the door, I kept my face turned away from him. "Let me know about the computer?"

"I will. Thanks for tagging along with me tonight."

"Anytime."

As the wet slurp of his tires retreated down the road, I stood rooted in the driveway, paused between my past and my present. A tap on the glass behind me brought me back to reality. I turned to see Mama in the front window holding her hands up in her classic, "What on God's green earth is going on with you?" stance. I took a deep, cleansing breath and shook my hair out of my face.

"Sorry," I said when I pushed the door open. "Come on, I'll take you home."

"I can walk just fine. I just wanted to wait 'til you got back before I left. Evan's in her room."

"Thanks for staying."

"Mm-hmm." She brushed past me and out the door. On the porch she stopped. "How's Ben doing?"

"He seems okay." I turned and craned my head to see if Evan's light was still on.

"Sometimes the past can be tempting."

I swung my head back to Mama and squinted. "Tempting?"

"You already know each other so you get to skip the uncomfortable 'who is this person?' phase. I'm just saying, it can seem easy."

"Well, I don't think Ben will be tempting. He has a girlfriend. And I don't know him anymore. Not like I did. It's been too long."

She studied me a moment, then smoothed her jacket over the crook of her elbow. "The heart can be a twisty little thing."

"Yes, it can."

"Good night, sweetheart." She trotted down the front steps and disappeared in the dark yard, a pocket flashlight her only guide.

Before shutting the door, I closed my eyes and listened. No sounds of tires on the road, no engine rumble. Ben was probably inside his house by now, chatting with Nick, winding down. I inhaled, expanding my lungs and throat until they protested. The post-rainstorm air was heavy with humidity and the scent of wisteria battered by the rain.

I knocked softly on Evan's door, then pushed it open. She sat up in bed, her damp hair piled on top of her head, a paperback balanced on her knees.

I sat down on the edge of the mattress. "Everything okay?"

"Just peachy."

"How was Nick? He seems nice."

"He is. And he was fine. Just brought me home and left like a gentleman." She straightened her legs out in front of her, dog-eared a page in her book, and closed it. "How was Mr. Bradley?"

"Fine too. A gentleman."

"Like father, like son?"

"I guess so. This evening has felt a little 'like mother, like daughter,' so I guess it fits."

"Huh?"

"Well, we both . . . Never mind."

"We both had unexpected dates," my daughter said. "Is that what you mean?"

I raised my eyebrows. "I suppose that is what I meant, but I'd hardly call them dates. And anyway, you're not quite old enough to date anyone."

"I'll be in high school in August. And fifteen soon after that."

"Yes, I'm aware of that. But when did I say fifteen and high school was the magic combination? I don't remember saying that."

Evan snorted. "You've never said anything about it at all."

"You're right. I've never had a reason to. Do I have a reason to now?"

Evan rolled her eyes but then glanced back at me. "No. I mean, I don't think so. So, no."

"Okay. Good."

"Do we have a reason to have this conversation about you?"

I opened my mouth, then exhaled. "No, we most definitely do not."

"Okay, good."

"Smart aleck. You must have gotten that from Mama." I leaned over and kissed her cheek. "Don't grow up too fast."

"Too late, Mom," she said, but she reached her arms up and hugged me.

I closed the door behind me and rested my head against the wall. I stayed there a minute, then remembered Mama. I walked the few steps to my bedroom and pulled back the curtain on my window. After a short moment, Mama's back porch light flicked on and off through the trees that separated our houses. All three of us, safe at home.

CHAPTER 15

Even with regular watering habits, your summer fern may lose its
bright-green color or stop growing altogether. If this happens, try
submerging the pot in water to saturate all the soil. A thorough
soaking should perk up your leaves even in midsummer.
—SARA BETH MCKAY, TIPS AND TRICKS IN THE GARDEN

JESSIE

Before I went to bed that night, I filled my bathtub with the hottest
water I could stand and eased myself down. Inch by inch, the
water covered my body until it stopped just below my chin, submerging everything else. As I soaked, I let my mind drift to those years
after Ben told me he loved me. After I let my friends lead me away.
When, unsure of what to do with such honest, unashamed love standing right in front of me, I responded with silence.

I'd often wished I could go back in time, back to that hot night in
a dry field on the outskirts of Perry. Back to the boy and girl we were,
but with the added benefit of years of wisdom and hindsight.

Over the next couple of years, we saw each other off and on
when we were home on school breaks. We both had jobs while we
were in school, so neither of us stayed in Perry long when we visited.
When we did see each other, it was awkward, something we'd never

experienced before in our friendship. The likely cause was that neither of us mentioned the night of the bonfire.

I wished he would, if only so we could move past the uncomfortable distance that had sprouted like ravenous weeds between us, but he acted like he'd never said anything. He wasn't the kind of guy to dwell on feelings or emotions—at least not out loud. And it felt too weighty, too sacred, for me to bring it up on my own.

In Birmingham I went on dates here and there with guys I'd met in classes or at parties, but Ben remained on the fringes of my mind, reminding me that he still had some kind of hold on me. Something I couldn't quite shake free.

Then I met Chris and everything changed.

During a late-night run to Waffle House one night with some friends at the beginning of my senior year, I took a bite and felt something crack in my tooth. The next day I called up the nearest dentist, a Dr. Chris Ashby, and made an appointment. Expecting someone older—maybe a nice grandfatherly type like my dentist back home—I was wholly unprepared for the young, handsome man who strode into the room. He sat on the swivel stool, his eyes focused on his clipboard.

As he scanned my chart, I took him in. Sandy hair, blue eyes, tan skin. His forearms were strong, thick with muscle, fuzzed with blond hair. Neat fingernails. No wedding ring.

Finally he lowered the clipboard. "Miss McBride, what . . . ?" As soon as he raised his eyes to me, he paused. He cleared his throat, then smiled. A wide, J.Crew smile. "What brings you to me today?"

An hour later I left with a new filling in my tooth and a card with my next appointment written down. On the back of the card, he'd written a note. "It would be my pleasure to take you out to dinner. I'll call you."

To this day I don't know how he got my phone number. Lord knows I hadn't given it to him. I didn't always obey Mama's teachings back then, but I knew not to offer my phone number to a stranger, even if he was completely charming and gazed at me like I was the most beautiful woman he'd ever seen. For all I knew, he got it from the paperwork I'd filled out and handed to the receptionist behind the front desk. That, of course, would have been unethical. Then again, Chris wasn't known for his high standard of ethics. But I didn't find out about that until later.

I came home from our first dinner together imagining what a life with him would be like. He was twenty-eight years old and had taken over his dental practice from his uncle, who was retiring early. Business was good. So good, in fact, that Chris only worked four days a week and owned a house on Lake Martin. I was twenty-two and hungry for life.

Ben's words the night of the bonfire came back to me. *"Jessie, you're so much more than all this."* I still had a pit in my stomach about how things were never resolved between the two of us. Unspoken explanations and confessions hung thick across the miles between us. But he'd said I was more than Glory Road. More than Perry. If that was true, Chris represented so much more. A life with him would be so much more.

That first date turned into a solid week of dinner dates, which morphed into me attending charity dances and fund-raising parties on Chris's arm during the holiday season. He made a lot of money, but he also gave a lot of it away, which I thought spoke to his kind and generous heart. People were always asking him to chair committees, speak at service-group lunches, and participate in auctions and tournaments. When we were out together, people constantly came up to him and shook his hand, thanked him for this or that contribution. But his attention was always on me. I felt treasured, desired. Like I'd finally become who I'd strived so hard to be.

When my friends met him, he charmed them just as he'd charmed me. Everyone was so excited for me, I let myself be carried off on the wave of hope and possibility. Deep in the quiet places of my heart though, I knew the me Chris had fallen for was different from the me Ben knew, different from the me I was when I was alone, staring at myself in the mirror.

One night in the spring of that year, I got all dressed up for a fund-raising gala. Chris picked me up and whisked me to The Club in time for a drink on the patio at sunset. The night felt magical—the air warm and fragrant, the breeze still a touch crisp, my pink dress shimmery, Chris's smile loose and directed at me. Guests filled the rooms and spilled out onto the patio. At one point in the evening, I left to search for the restroom. When I came back, I couldn't find him in the sea of people. In the dark, all the men in their dapper suits looked strangely similar. I stood by the glass doors and scanned the patio.

Finally I saw him speaking with an older gentleman by the bar. When Chris caught my eye, his face brightened and he excused himself. As he made his way toward me, a couple of people tried to pull him into conversation, but his eyes remained firmly locked on mine. When he finally waded through the crowd and reached me, he wrapped his arm around me. "You have no idea how glad I am that you walked into my office that day." His breath was warm in my ear, his hand a pleasant pressure on my lower back. "You'd make me the happiest man alive if you'd stay with me forever."

He kissed me then and led me to the dance floor inside. The band played Marvin Gaye and the lights were low. We danced until my legs felt watery and the band said good night. I waited for him to say something else about that "stay with me forever" bit, but he didn't. Still, I felt the conversation wasn't finished. What was to come both elated and terrified me.

Because even at night after Chris would drop me off at my apartment, my lips tingling from his kisses, my head swirling with his attention, his laugh, the giddy butterflies in my stomach, Ben was still there. In my mind, at the edges, in the silence. I still wondered what might have happened if I'd had the courage to tell him how his quiet acceptance of me and his steady, calming presence had given me sure footing, a solid ground under my feet. How his simple tenderness had made me feel secure and safe in a way that Chris, for all his bold charm and towering self-confidence, didn't.

I felt guilty for thinking of Ben when Chris was right there in front of me, beckoning me to a life that promised to be *more*. Whereas Ben had told his truth then backed away, Chris was only moving forward. Toward me, toward us.

On a rainy Sunday a couple months before graduation, when Chris was out of town and my apartment was empty, I made a choice. I felt in my bones Chris would be proposing soon—he'd already told me of his grandmother's engagement ring and his mother's dream to see her son get married in the Cathedral of Saint Paul downtown. Why would he let me in on these family details if he didn't plan to propose? I couldn't believe my luck at being chosen by this man, plucked out of my normal life and plunged into this new life of privilege and pleasure. But another part of me panicked at the thought of accepting his proposal without knowing if even a flicker of life remained in what Ben and I once had.

I hadn't called him in over a year, and as I did now, my fingers trembled. Then he answered, his voice low and so familiar. I squeezed my eyes closed, unsure of what I expected from him. How did he feel about me now? A part of me hoped he'd want to fight for me.

We chatted for a few minutes, catching up on trivial, superficial things—his parents and mine, finals, plans for after school. Finally he exhaled. Though I couldn't see him, I imagined him raking his hand through his thick hair, his brown eyes liquid and alive. "Jessie . . ."

"I met someone," I said.

"You . . . what?"

"I met a . . . a guy. A man. He's a dentist. He's . . . he's my dentist, actually." I was stammering, rambling, but I couldn't stop it. "We've been seeing each other for a while now. Since the fall. Things are . . . I think things are good." I swallowed and wished I could pull the details back in my mouth, like an avalanche in reverse. I closed my eyes and waited for his attempt. His fight. Waited and hoped.

Just when I thought he might not say anything at all, he spoke. "That's great, Jess. I'm happy for you. I want you to be happy."

I cried over Ben for the first and last time that night. Anger and embarrassment coursed through me, along with a fair measure of sadness. I told myself he must not have meant his words at the bonfire. That he'd tossed them to me with hardly a care. *"I'm in love with you. I've loved you for so long. I just needed you to know."* Maybe he'd been drinking. Maybe he didn't even remember it. I felt ridiculous for giving his words a second thought, much less years of it.

Chris proposed a few weeks later and I hesitated only a second before saying yes. He slipped his grandmother's ring on my finger and kissed the back of my hand, then my wrist, then the inside of my elbow. I closed my eyes and breathed it all in.

❧

The minute we returned from our honeymoon, I threw myself into the life I was supposed to lead. I hosted dinners and parties. I joined the Junior League. I bought golf skirts and strappy yoga tops and expensive wine, though I couldn't tell it apart from the cheap stuff. And I volunteered everywhere, from Children's Hospital to the Birmingham Botanical Gardens. This last volunteer post spoke to a deep part of me, tapping into my onetime desire to coax life out of dirt, seeds, water, and sunlight.

Sometime during my pregnancy with Evan, things changed. The flashy, well-heeled life I'd become used to lost its luster. Hosting dinners felt laborious. I was always nauseated, and my expanding middle didn't fit into the slim sheaths I generally wore to galas and parties. I had the urge to hole up and nest, to create a warm, soft space for this new little life.

Then Daddy died, a cruel surprise. He'd always been so capable, so dependable. His foot slipping was such a minor detail, but there at the top of the ladder, it was the one that mattered most.

I'd always wanted what my parents had—this one great love. They'd made me believe it was possible it would happen to me too, and I thought I'd found it in Chris. But Daddy's death changed my belief. Sure, a love may be great, but that didn't mean it would be forever. Where before I'd thought love was what sustained you, what carried you, I now knew it didn't last. Hurt would still come.

When Evan was born, I fell deep in love. She was so soft and sweet, her eyes so curious, her fingers tiny vises around mine. I didn't want to be away from her. She nursed frequently and refused a bottle, so it was nearly a year of sending Chris off to his functions while I stayed behind with Evan.

Meanwhile I soaked in my new role as a mother. I met moms for playdates, let Evan play in the sprinkler wearing nothing but a diaper, and pulled blankets out into the front yard and lay on the grass with her, pointing out shapes in the clouds. I was truly comfortable in my skin for the first time, and it completely changed me.

I loved my new life, but I knew Chris was bewildered by the change in me. Sometimes he'd come in late, the smell of bourbon on his breath, his hands fumbling for the edges of my nightgown. I knew something was off. Had been for a while, actually. It wasn't anything worth confronting him about, just a gut feeling I didn't know what to do with. Deep down I knew a woman should always trust her gut, but honestly, I didn't want to know if he was cheating. It was easier that way. Not to have to figure out what to do. Not to uproot Evan and cause her life to turn inside out.

Then one day I had a dental appointment. Just a regular cleaning. Evan was tucked away at preschool, and the spring air was fresh and green after an early morning rain shower. It was beautiful, really. The best kind of day.

I settled down in the chair and a new hygienist came in. My regular hygienist, Tiffani, was out for the day. The new girl began whispering to me the minute I lay back in the chair.

"I just admire you so much, Mrs. McBride."

Surprised, I managed to mumble an awkward "thank you" around the probe in my mouth.

"Some women would . . ." She pursed her lips together. "Well, I'll just say I think you're such a lady for letting everything roll off your back like you have. It shows true class."

I let that sit for a moment, then pulled her gloved hands from my mouth. I swallowed hard. "What are you talking about?"

Her eyes grew big and round. She shook her head. "You don't know?"

"Know what?" I sat up, fighting against the steep decline of the chair.

"He and Tiffani . . ." She took off her guard glasses and sat back in her chair. "I'm so sorry. I just figured you knew and you were . . . okay with it. I'll . . ." She yanked off her gloves and stood, then darted out of the room.

Sitting in that chair with the thin paper towel clipped around my neck, I realized with utter clarity that my whole world had crumbled around me. Not only was my dad gone, but my husband—the one who was supposed to love me enough to forsake all others—had instead forsaken me. I searched through memories and events and pulled out snatches of conversation, sideways glances, lingering hugs, sharp words. It all made sense.

I didn't need to know the details—how long it had been going on, who knew about it, whether he loved her—but of course, I learned them soon enough.

A year.

Everyone but me.

And yes, he did.

With nothing remaining but my baby girl, I packed our things and drove south, not stopping until we reached Perry. Mama was waiting on her front porch when we pulled up the driveway. A peach cobbler was in the oven, and her arms around me were strong.

CHAPTER 16

*The therapeutic use of gardens is a long-standing tradition. The
simple act of digging one's hands in soil, removing what's harmful,
and replacing it with what's beneficial and beautiful can add a
sense of purpose and peace to even the most distraught soul.*
—ELIZABETH MCLEOD, GARDENING IS GOOD FOR YOU

GUS

My daily routine didn't change much these days, and I was okay
with that. Most mornings I woke at six—no alarm clock, thank
you very much—poured a cup of coffee, and took it with me to my
back porch. From there, my gaze could roam across our deep property, filled with trees that had been rooted in place for generations.
That's part of what I loved most about our little swatch of land out
here—its permanence. It spoke of earth and time and dust and life. It
was here before I arrived, and it would be here long after I was gone.

Tom added the porch on to the back of our house when Jessie was
seven or eight, and it's been a respite ever since. It's where I've had
most of my morning coffees, where Tom helped Jessie with homework, where I talked to Jessie about boys. It's where I sat for hours
after leaving the hospital when Tom died. It's where we set up Evan's
dollhouse when Jessie moved in with me after escaping Birmingham
and Chris's wandering passions. The porch had been a silent family

member for most of the important events and decisions of our lives, but it had never seen me go crazy.

This morning I sat on my porch as usual. It was early, long before Evan would make her way to my house to borrow something or Jessie would call and ask me to bring her some sunscreen if she'd run out. It was just me, my coffee, and the sounds of the woods around my house waking up with the sun.

The chain on the swing had developed a new squeak overnight, and as I rocked, I tried to remember where I'd heard the sound before. Somewhere else in my memory, another swing chain squeaked as I rocked back and forth. As I searched, the carpet under my feet became dusty dirt and the beadboard ceiling above me became blue sky.

My parents' house in Poplarville appeared behind me, and Janey Riggins flew down the road in front of me on her shiny red bike, Santa's gift to her the year before. Other neighborhood kids raced past on bikes and bare feet, but I remained where I was. I was searching for someone I couldn't find.

Then the rain came. Long wet streams fell from the sky, soaking my legs and darkening the dirt on the road to an angry black. Janey and the other kids pedaled faster to escape the rising tide of swirling mud and sludge, but their pedals got stuck and they fell off.

I tried to get up to help, but I was rooted in place. When I yelled, no sound emerged. Someone tugged on my arm, and I turned to see Tom sitting on the swing next to me. He wasn't the fifty-five-year-old man he was when he died but the fresh-faced eighteen-year-old I fell in love with. His hands were on my face, my hair, my shoulders.

"Don't worry, Augusta Mae. I'll take care of you always."

I reached out to touch his face, but he trailed away from me. He grew smaller and smaller until he was no bigger than a squirrel. Then he disappeared in the rain.

Somewhere deep in my mind, my own voice told me this was ridiculous. Tom had been dead for fourteen years and I was sitting alone on my back porch. But Tom and Janey, the rain, the clouds, the bicycles—it all looked and felt so real. I had a hard time picking out what was true and what wasn't.

Finally reality came back to me, like it did when you woke from a dream and you could almost see it retreating. You reached out to hold on to it, but then your eyes opened, daylight streamed in, and—*poof!*—the dream was gone, and you couldn't remember even the first detail of what happened.

Except I still remembered. I patted the seat next to me, searched behind me, even leaned over the edge of the swing to peer underneath, but I had to straighten up before I fell off. Tom was nowhere. Instead, Jessie knelt in front of me, tears in her eyes, her hands grasping mine in a death grip.

"Mama? Are you okay?"

"Well, sure." I gently pulled my hands from hers and rubbed my sore fingers. "I'm fine. I just . . . I had a little daydream, is all."

"Who were you looking for?"

I knew if I said Tom, she'd worry. I scanned the porch, searching again. "No one. I just thought I lost something."

Her eyes were pleading and scared, and they ran across my face as if trying to detect either the truth or a lie. Internally, I was doing the same thing—feeling my way back into this solid reality, coming to grips with what must have been just a dream. But it couldn't have been a dream. A dream happened at night, in the safety of your own bed, under the cover of darkness. Not when you're wide awake with a mug of hot coffee in hand.

Jessie tugged on the hem of my nightgown. "Here. Let me help." I followed her gaze and saw my hem had gotten stuck on a bad place on one of the wood slats. I'd been meaning to sand it down, but I kept forgetting.

"When I got here, you were trying to stand up, but your nightgown kept you stuck to the swing. Probably a good thing though. You were so lost in that . . . dream, who knows where you would have ended up if you'd started walking around." She loosened the hem and smoothed the fabric across my knees. "You said Dad's name. You said Tom. Were you dreaming about him?"

I nodded, unable to speak. His face had been so clear and bold next to me. As if all the time between us falling in love and his topple off the ladder had drifted away. I glanced around my porch, my little respite, and saw it for what it was. A small room tacked onto the back of our house, full of knickknacks and plants secreted away from Twig when Jessie wasn't looking. It wasn't anything fancy, but the time and place were comforting rituals for me. Had I been sitting out here all these mornings, just waiting for Tom to find me? I shook my head. Tom never would have wanted to be a part of something so terrifying for me—this unnerving loss of reality.

I focused on Jessie to keep my mind from swirling through the possibilities of what the loss meant. "What are you doing over here anyway? It's early."

She checked her watch. "Not that early. It's seven thirty. You told Evan you'd be at our house at seven to make pancakes. Although I don't know why y'all settled on seven. She's never up that early."

Jessie was babbling. I hated that I'd made her nervous. No one wants to have to worry about her mother going crazy when she's young enough to still be right in her head.

But I was worried. I'd completely forgotten that I told Evan I'd be there. Those pancakes had disappeared from my brain, as if we hadn't talked about them twelve hours before. The pancakes weren't the big deal though. There were other, more important things.

A few days before, I had left my stove on. It was on low, so that teeny blue flame was hardly visible unless you looked right at it, but it was there. Luckily, I came back to my house to grab my recipe box before the shop opened. I had no reason to walk by the stove, but the Lord must have guided my feet there. I heard the flame flutter in the breeze when I walked past it. A yellow dish towel was lying on the counter next to the eye, a little too close for comfort.

And smaller things too—that I'd told Jessie a particular story three times already. That I'd tucked my backdoor key into my pants pocket, then panicked when I couldn't find it. That I'd set off on an errand, then forgotten where I was supposed to be going.

A few nights ago, I woke up to find myself sitting on the floor of my bedroom, pulling on an old pair of Tom's work boots. I'd rooted around in my sock drawer and somehow found my thickest socks in the dark, yanked them on and up to my knees, and pulled Tom's boots on over them. When I came to and turned on a lamp, I saw the mess. My heaviest winter coat lay on the floor next to me, coat hangers spilling out of the closet and onto the floor, and the sheets on my bed were a twisted pile of cotton and down. I vaguely remembered dreaming about a snowstorm and someone yelling out for help, but I couldn't pin down the dream.

I thought of my mother and her mother before that. How diseases passed from one generation to the next like a line of train cars, connected and steaming ahead. And here it was coming for me. I let myself feel the force of that truth—of my reality—then I buried it. I'd face it when I needed to—at some point I'd have to talk to Jessie about the inevitable—but until then, away it would go.

"Did you forget about the pancakes, Mama?"

I shook my head a little and focused on her.

"I don't care about them—Evan's still asleep anyway. It was just strange that you didn't answer your phone. That's why I came over."

"I'm fine, honey." I stood up on wobbly knees, then sat back down again. I'd give myself another moment. "Just feeling a little extra tired this morning. And I must not have heard the phone ring, out here all lost in memories. But I'll have the pancakes made before Evan wakes up. I have a new bottle of lavender maple syrup in the pantry that I wanted her to try." I stood again, and this time my legs didn't betray me. My head still felt a little swimmy, but I could handle that.

The creases in Jessie's forehead deepened. How did my baby get old enough to have those worry lines? "Listen to me, I'm fine. Right as rain."

She exhaled and stood. "Okay. But I'm waiting here until you get dressed. I'll walk back over with you. We're out of coffee anyway. I'll grab a cup while you get ready."

"Suit yourself. Half-and-half's in the fridge," I said before walking back to my bedroom. I only had to reach a hand out to the wall to steady myself once.

CHAPTER 17

Don't be afraid of pruning. Lack of sufficient pruning results in cramped conditions and impeded beauty in your garden. Check your timing, monitor your plants' growth patterns, and keep your tools sharp.
—R. D. MATTHEW, PRUNING BASICS

JESSIE

I tried to dismiss it, tried to ignore it, but it stayed there in my mind, poking me at random moments.

"Mama's forgetting things," it said. "She needs to see a doctor. What if something's wrong?"

But I had a business to run, complete with an absent computer, a thriving competitor right down the road, and a tropical storm in Florida that slowed my shipment of mandevillas, angering Ms. Rickers and an army of other neighbors vying for the brightest, perkiest front-porch flowers. Not to mention I had Olivia's wedding flowers to plan and design. I couldn't linger on Mama's forgetfulness or her frantic dream. I told myself if anything questionable happened again, I'd get her in to see a doctor.

But she was fine. She showed up at the house to make pancakes—hair sprayed, lips pinked, Reba concert shirt in place—as if nothing out of sorts had happened. She filled Twig's front table with pies and cobblers, helped a customer load two bags of pine mulch into the

140

back of her car, and swept up dirt and broken pottery from an orchid that toppled over during the night. If anything, she was more helpful than usual and doing it without even a single muttered complaint.

I was writing up a receipt for a customer when my cell rang. Olivia Tate. "Evan, can you finish writing up these flowers? I need to grab this."

"Sure." Evan hopped down off the stepladder and plunked a bottle of Windex on the counter a little too eagerly. She hated washing windows because she said newspaper on glass sounded like fingernails on a chalkboard. I agreed with her, but Mama said using newspaper instead of a paper towel made for cleaner glass. As usual, she was right.

I stepped out onto the front porch and answered just before the fourth ring. "Hi, Olivia."

"Jessie," she said, polished and businesslike. "How do you feel about driving to Dog River?"

"Right now?"

"Well, no, it doesn't have to be now, but soon. Today, if possible. My dad keeps reminding me we only have a couple of months to pull everything together, and I'll be honest—I'm starting to panic a little. I thought if you could get to his house, maybe we could talk through what the flowers should look like and where they should go."

I peered behind me into the shop. Evan was packing pots of geraniums into a cardboard box and Gus was sweeping. "I'm not sure I can leave the shop with my daughter and my mom. Could we do it—?"

"What about after you close? Later in the day might be better anyway. The ceremony will be on the dock at seven, so you'll be there roughly around the time the wedding will take place. That'll be helpful."

"I guess I could make that happen." Sunset wouldn't be until close to eight, and it took less than an hour to get to the river.

"Perfect. I have a meeting in four minutes, so I need to run. I'll let Dad know you're coming this evening. He'll leave the gate open for you."

❦

Evan assured me she and Mama would be fine without me, so once I hung the Closed sign in the window, I ran back to the house to freshen up. Remembering Sumner's neatly pressed pants and shiny shoes, I wanted to wear something other than the Twig T-shirt and shorts I'd had on all day. After a quick shower, I flipped through hangers in my closet, sizing up my options. I discarded the first few outfits I pulled out and finally landed on a maxi skirt and a white tank top. I added a long coral necklace Evan had given me for Mother's Day a couple of years ago and stood back to check myself in the mirror.

When I was married to Chris, I kept my hair chin length in a blunt cut with regrettable blonde highlights. Now my hair fell below my shoulders in its natural dark-brown shade with long bangs that softened my high forehead. I often pinned them to the side to keep them out of my eyes while I worked, but this evening I just brushed them to the side and tucked my hair behind my ear. I smiled at my reflection and added a little more blush to the apples of my cheeks. After a quick swipe of mascara—it always made my brown eyes look brighter—and a little lip gloss, I was ready.

Fifteen minutes later, Glory Road was in my rearview mirror. After a short jaunt on I-65, I headed west on I-10 and took the exit that would send me toward Sumner's part of Dog River.

The river formed a lazy C that cut into the western shore of Mobile Bay, with smaller creeks branching and bending away from it. Oak House was perched on one of those bends in the river, though I'd only seen it in magazine photos.

Following Google's directions, I turned onto his street and was surprised to find the area was less impressive than I'd imagined. I'd prepared myself for massive front lawns, expensive cars dotting the driveways, electronic gates protecting homes from unwanted visitors. Instead, I found a simple street lined with stately trees and thick underbrush. The evening sun streamed into my car, and a steady breeze stirred the tree branches.

I checked the note where I'd jotted down Sumner's house number. The farther I drove, the bigger and grander the houses got. At a mailbox bearing his name, I turned off the tree-covered road onto a smooth driveway lined with towering hydrangea bushes.

Oak House rose before me into the clear sky, white clapboard against the bright blue. Slate-gray shutters framed large windows, and along the front porch railing climbed perfect pink mandevilla blooms that would make the neighbors on Glory Road weep with envy. Next to the old wooden front door was an Alabama historical marker. Stinson-McDavid-Tate house, 1914. On the other side of the driveway was another cottage, smaller but no less charming. Guest quarters, perhaps.

I knocked on the front door of the main house, smoothing my hair with my other hand. I waited, but the house was silent. No feet crossing the floor, no turning of the door handle. I glanced around for a sign of life, but the gentle breeze rustling through the trees provided the only sound and movement. A small path—stepping stones with grass laced between them—traveled around the side of the house, so I descended the steps and followed the path. It ended at an ivy-covered gate that spanned the distance between the side of the house and a tall hedge of camellias.

Olivia had mentioned a gate, but she'd also said it would be open. This one didn't budge when I pushed on it. A peekaboo hole covered in elaborate iron scrollwork was cut into the door near the top, but it was too tall for me to see through. I spotted a bucket lying on its side under the azalea bushes at the edge of the porch. I hesitated, then

143

knelt down and pulled the bucket out, then turned it upside down and stood on top of it. It was a little unsteady, but it worked.

On the river side of the house, just beyond what I imagined were grand steps off the back porch, was a wide, deep expanse of manicured lawn ringed with hydrangeas. Abundant blooms cascaded in fluffy mounds of lilac, soft blue, and creamy white. Wrought iron chairs circled a few tables to the side of the lawn. Trays of candles in silver containers sat in the center of the tables, as if left over from a party. At the far end of the lawn, grass gave way to sand, and a dock stretched over the water leading to a large covered boathouse.

If that were all, the backyard would have been exquisite, the perfect setting for a wedding, but the main attraction stood to the side of the lawn opposite the tables. The oak tree must have been at least ten feet around. When I lifted my eyes from the low-hanging limbs sweeping across the lawn, the tree's canopy filled the sky. Moss floated from the branches, ethereal and ghostly even in the bright light. The ground below the tree—even the air around it—was sun dappled and shade kissed.

I jiggled the gate again from my perch on the bucket, then tried to see around the edge of the door. Maybe there was a trick to unlatching the lock. When that didn't work, I reached for my phone to call Olivia. Just as I stepped off the bucket, phone in one hand, the bucket tipped and my foot slipped.

A more graceful woman would have stepped gently down with no problem, but my landing was more of a sprawl than a gentle dismount. As soon as my knees hit the ground, a car pulled up to the front of the house. I turned my head just as the black Land Rover stopped and Sumner climbed out.

"Hey, what—are you okay?" he called as he approached. Embarrassment swam through me, pooling in my fingertips and cheeks. I picked myself up off the dirt and gravel, glad that at least I hadn't cracked my phone.

"So sorry." I blew a lock of hair out of my face. "I wasn't breaking in. I knocked but . . ." I trailed off when several pieces of gravel
fell from my knees to the ground. I brushed dirt off my skirt and
loosened a few more pieces of gravel from my sandal. When I
straightened up, he was smiling, but his eyes still held a measure
of surprise.

"Are you okay?" He held out a hand as if to steady me.

"Oh, I'm fine. I just stepped wrong off the . . . bucket." As if my
stupidity could be blamed on a chunk of blue plastic.

"Did you . . . Do you—can I help you with something?"

I rubbed my forehead. "I'm guessing Olivia didn't talk to you."

He shook his head. Worry lines etched his face. Behind him, his
car was still running and he was dressed as if he'd just left a business
meeting.

"She called this morning and asked if I could drive over after
work. I'm supposed to call her so we can talk about where flower
arrangements will go. She was . . . she was supposed to let you know
I was coming."

He ran a hand over his face, and the flood of embarrassment
in my cheeks kicked into overdrive. "But you're obviously just getting home from work and I'm . . . I'll call her and tell her we'll do it
another day." I started toward my car, but he stopped me.

"Wait, wait. You drove all the way out here, let's at least make sure
you get what you need. Hang on a second and I'll open up."

I followed him back to the front and waited by the porch steps.
He unloaded a small suitcase from the back of his car and led me to
the door. "Are you just getting back in town?" Olivia hadn't seemed
scatterbrained on the phone, but asking me to come by when her dad
was out of town led me to believe otherwise.

He nodded as he picked through keys on the key ring. "It was last
minute. Olivia didn't even know I was going. You came at the right
time though. I'd have felt terrible if you'd driven out here yesterday

when I was gone. Although by the looks of it, you may have figured out how to get in anyway." He smiled, but his eyes were weary.

"I'm sorry about that. She said the gate would be open. I thought maybe there was a trick to unlatching it."

"No, it's locked. My front lawn and the dock below have become somewhat of a hot spot for photographers around here." He pushed the door open with a creak. "There we go."

Cool air hit me with a rush, along with scents of polished hardwoods and well-appointed age. Dark wood beams crossed the span of whitewashed ceiling in the main room, outfitted with a pair of cream-colored couches dotted with tasteful silk pillows. Antiques were scattered throughout the space, from tables and lamps to a pair of copper seahorse bookends on the mantel. A freestanding fireplace separated the living room from a dining room beyond it.

Panels of rich wood gleamed under the last rays of sun pouring through the front wall of windows. Outside, the oak's limbs filled nearly every windowpane. As he tossed his keys on a table and grabbed a stack of mail, I stepped forward and ran a finger across an antique desk in the corner.

"Your home is beautiful." It was obviously aged, but in a pleasant, rambling, well-kept way. The space was immaculate, without a stray magazine, drinking glass, or shoe anywhere.

He slit open an envelope with his thumb. "Oh, thanks. I can't really take credit though. My decorator did a lot of it, especially in here. This isn't really my style, but she says it's right for the house and appropriate for someone like me."

"What does that mean?"

"I have no idea. Someone who doesn't like comfortable couches?"

I laughed. "Well, it's lovely, even if the couches aren't comfortable. It looks like a study or a library in one of those old houses in *Garden & Gun*."

"I'll tell Cheryl you said that. It's the exact image she was going for." He turned toward the other side of the house. "My favorite part's through here."

As I followed him through the kitchen that opened into a small den in the corner of the house, his phone rang. He checked the screen, then apologized. "I have to take this, but it'll be quick. Make yourself comfortable."

Half listening to his one-sided conversation, I gazed around the cozy space. A soft-as-butter leather couch and a cushy love seat upholstered in ticking stripes were scattered with down pillows in shades of blue and green. A wooden coffee table between them bore scratches and dings from years of foot-propping. There were books and magazines, a small ottoman covered in a red-and-orange kilim print, and a delicious cream blanket tossed across the back of the couch. It was comfortable, informal, and made me want to take off my shoes. Which was exactly what Sumner did when he walked back into the room and set his phone onto the kitchen counter.

"This is my space. I told Cheryl she could have the rest of the house as long as she didn't come within ten feet of this room. I can leave my drinks out and books on the table and she can't say anything about it." He loosened his tie and slid it off. "Can I get you something to drink?"

"Just some water, thanks. I should probably go ahead and call Olivia. She sounded nervous on the phone this morning. I think she's just now realized how short three months is. Or less than that now."

"I don't know how she's going to do it. She's refusing to hire a planner, and her job keeps her really busy. I told her I'd help out as much as I could, but I have no idea how to plan a wedding. When I got married, all I had to do was show up on time. This morning she was asking me about picking out fine china, and I had to give her Cheryl's number. Wedgwood, Limoges, Haviland . . . I know nothing."

"Does she want bone or porcelain?"

He raised his eyebrows. "No idea. I could ask."

"Porcelain is generally less expensive, so she might get more of it as gifts, but bone china is more durable. Won't crack as easily."

"You're an expert on fine china? I'm surprised."

"And why is that? Because I live on a dirt road?"

"No, I . . . You just seem a little more, I don't know, casual. I don't mean any offense."

"I'm teasing. Any fine china I still have is packed up in a box somewhere in my attic or my mother's. It's not my first choice for dining these days, that's for sure." I thought of the delicate band of gold that edged the cream dinner plates, the thin handles of our sterling silver serving spoons, the finely etched crystal wine and water glasses. All registered for with the utmost care and attention by me and my onetime mother-in-law. When our wedding gifts started rolling in, I couldn't believe the money perfect strangers paid for me to eat off such beautiful things. It was a stark contrast to the white Corelle dinner plates and mason jar glasses I'd grown up with.

My phone rang deep in my bag, and I was thankful for the interruption. I rummaged through blindly until my hand closed around it. I checked the screen. "Hi, Olivia. I was just about to call you. I'm inside and ready to talk."

"Perfect. I realized earlier I'd forgotten to call my dad and tell him you were coming. He was there to let you in okay?"

"Oh yes." I turned away from Sumner, as if he could hear Olivia's words. "Everything went just fine."

"Great. I thought we could start on the porch, then make our way down to the water. That's where the ceremony will be. The reception will be back up on the lawn. Under the tree, which I'm sure you've seen by now."

"I have. It's amazing."

"It is, isn't it? No one even knows how old it is, just that it's *old* old. Something about the way the house is situated in the bend in the river has protected it. Otherwise it could have been damaged by hurricanes over the years."

"I can't believe you could even consider getting married anywhere else when you have this in your backyard."

Behind me, Summer laughed, low and amused.

"If you knew how many times the tree has been photographed, you'd understand."

I had my doubts about that. This tree could have been in every photograph ever taken and I'd still jump at the chance to get married under it. If, that is, there was a chance of me ever getting married again.

"I even saw it up here in the city not too long ago," she continued. "In a magazine ad for air freshener. It's made it big-time if Glade has caught on."

She took a deep breath and let it out in a rush. "Now, I know I sent you my Pinterest page, but I was at a wedding last weekend on Long Island and it made me rethink some things . . ."

Listening to Olivia, I walked toward the back door. Sumner crossed in front of me and unlocked it, then held it open for me. As she dove into a detailed rundown of the flowers she'd seen at her friend's wedding, I took in the screened porch. It was obviously geared toward comfort, a bold change from the more sophisticated main living area of the house. Dark hardwood floors were covered in cozy, well-worn rugs. Instead of antique sideboards and sleek tabletops, the furniture was all wood and wicker, white canvas and sailcloth— everything made to withstand the humidity and heat. At the end of the porch was a hanging bed swing, complete with a fitted sheet and a striped quilt folded at the end. Ample pillows were propped up against the chains.

Olivia was talking about arrangements she wanted by the double-screened doors leading out into the yard. When she mentioned orchids, I stopped her.

"Orchids? You want to use them out here?"

"They're so delicate and pretty. Maybe in a small arrangement? I thought about having something on the wall on either side of the screen doors."

"That'd be lovely, but I'm not sure orchids would go with the natural look you've said you wanted. And your dad's porch is all white and wood—I can see using twig branches to loosen up some arrangements, maybe some magnolia leaves from the tree out front. Orchids could make things seem a little stark. Even though they are pretty."

"I like that idea. And you're the expert, so let's go with that. Now, about the food . . ."

As she switched gears to cakes and food and I moved from the porch to the lawn—which was even lovelier on this side of the locked gate—I realized that though Olivia had a lot of ideas, she needed someone to help her pull it all together in a cohesive way. Otherwise, it had the potential to turn into a hodgepodge of details rather than the elegant sunset wedding it could be.

"Olivia." I interrupted her one-sided conversation about a sushi-rolling station versus a meat-carving station. "I can tell you sushi at an outside wedding in September sounds like a trip to the ER, but you're going to need someone else to help you figure out the food." I felt competent to give her some advice, but I didn't want the success or flop of her wedding reception to fall on my shoulders.

"Right, right. I promise I won't overload you with extras. And I did take your advice and hired someone to help on the day of the wedding."

I exhaled a sigh. "Good for you. That'll help a lot."

She moved the discussion to the dance floor to be set up under the tree to protect the grass. Highboy tables would dot the edge of the dance floor so guests would have somewhere to set their drink while they kicked up their heels. She wanted arrangements on each of those tables, along with centerpieces on each of the food tables and the smaller tables where guests would sit and eat. Dollar signs flew through my mind. She hadn't given me a firm budget, which was good because I had a feeling she'd blow right past it.

After I'd walked through the lawn and given her an idea of how many arrangements she'd need, she said she had just a few minutes left to talk about the dock where the ceremony would take place.

"Let's head out there then." A short wrought iron gate enclosed the yard at the back, and from where I stood, it appeared to be locked. Not wanting to be embarrassed again, I looked behind me to where Sumner sat on the back porch steps, his collar open to catch what little breeze floated by. When I pointed to the gate, he stood and crossed the lawn, then unlocked the gate with a click.

"I'll head out with you," he whispered.

The boathouse at the end of the dock was rambling, with sections appearing to have been added over time. There were no walls, only thick posts and railings, but a massive fireplace stood in one corner, surrounded by comfortable chairs and a low coffee table. Lounge chairs were perched at the edge of the dock facing the river, with a metal ladder that disappeared into the water.

Down a few steps was another portion of the dock, but this part was older, basic, and no frills. Just two Adirondack chairs at the end and a pair of rubber water shoes. It was a calm evening, but the water made music, lapping against pilings, wood slats, and a canoe tied to one of the railings.

I could see why Olivia wanted the ceremony out here by the water. As we spoke, the sun was already sliding down toward the horizon. Passing clouds lit up like electric-blue-and-purple slashes across the sky. In minutes everything would be a blaze of orange and pink, an incredible backdrop to a wedding.

"Olivia, I'm not sure you need many flowers down here. Or decorations at all. The sky is going to be your biggest attraction. Next to you, of course." I walked to the edge. Next to me, Sumner dropped down into one of the Adirondack chairs, propping a leg up on the arm of the other one.

"I agree that we don't need much, but maybe something near where we'll be standing?"

I climbed back up the steps and focused on the rafter beams crisscrossing the ceiling. I imagined a big, rustic chandelier hanging from the beams, laced through with greenery and simple blossoms. "I think I can come up with something."

"Perfect. Oh, I almost forgot. Can you put my dad on? I need to ask him something."

"Sure." I glanced back to where Sumner still sat, comfortable in the Adirondack, one foot lazily bouncing up and down. I handed him the phone, then took a few steps back and sat on a bench. I didn't know him or her well enough to listen in on their conversation.

I did watch him though. The minute he said hi, his face grew animated and light. Even when he'd been sitting alone in the chair, the sun fading before him and his eyes half-closed, he'd had a deep crease between his eyebrows and a firm set to his mouth. But speaking to Olivia, his face lost all traces of concern. His genuine smile and laughter told me all I needed to know about their relationship.

Since we'd been on the dock, the sun had disappeared below the water and the sky gradually darkened by slow degrees. What had been a bright, almost neon color palette was now awash in cool pastels.

Sumner handed me the phone back a minute later, then held his hand out to help me up. I hesitated a fraction of a second, then took his hand and stood.

"Despite the fact that I'm just the father of the bride, I'd like to do more than just sign the checks. I know you have your daughter and your mother to help, but I'm available if you need me."

"Thanks. I'll probably need all the help I can get."

We walked back up the dock toward the house. Small lights

posted at regular intervals along the dock had clicked on since we'd been outside.

"Can you turn these lights off?" I asked.

"Sure. They're on a timer, but I could override it. Why?"

"Just thinking. Candles along the dock leading to the ceremony would be pretty."

"Sounds like you're really getting into this."

I shrugged. "Planning a wedding for someone else is kind of fun."

"Not as much fun to plan your own?"

"It's a lot more pressure when it's your own. Plus, I won't be the one who has to worry about not tripping or doing something else embarrassing in front of everyone I know."

All around us, nighttime sounds began in earnest—a steady thrum of crickets, shrill vibrations of cicadas, and somewhere close, a throaty tree frog croaking an evening lullaby. Ahead of us, Sumner's house was glowing from the few lamps he'd turned on before we walked out. The windows were warm and inviting, the huge oak lit from below with tiny spotlights. It made my breath catch in my throat. A light breeze from the water fluttered the leaves around us. Goose bumps crept up my arms.

"This is the best time of day, if you ask me," Sumner said. I moved to let him step around me and through the gate into the yard. "It's so peaceful—just nature and the breeze."

Back in the house, I picked up my bag in the kitchen. "Thanks for letting me interrupt your night like this. Especially when you weren't expecting it."

"It's nothing. I enjoyed it. It's all a little surreal to me, but bottom line, I'm thrilled my baby wants to get married here. And I really appreciate you helping to make it special for her. It means a lot to her. And me."

I smiled. "Weddings should be special. It's the beginning of a new life. Hopefully a good one."

I followed him to the front door, but he paused with his hand on the doorknob. I waited for him to open it and whisk me out into the night so he could get back to his evening, but he didn't.

"I hope this doesn't sound presumptuous since we've just met," he said after a moment, "but I'm going to run up the road and grab a quick bite to eat. Any chance you'd like to eat with me?"

"Right now?" I glanced down and noticed dirt under my right thumbnail that had somehow escaped my attention earlier. "Oh, I'm not dressed—"

"You look fine. And I know the perfect place. Honey's is about as casual as it gets. I usually stop there when I get back in town late and have nothing to eat in the house."

"I don't know. I've got Evan at home with my mom . . ." In the silence that followed, my stomach grumbled, loud and angry. I clamped my hand over it and we both laughed.

"How about this," he said, his smile creasing his right cheek. "Let me grab my keys and I'll follow you out. Honey's is on the way back out to I-10. You'll see it on your right. If you decide to come, just pull in. I'll be right behind you. If not, no problem. It was a spur-of-the-moment idea anyway."

I crossed the driveway to my car and opened the door. "I'll see how things are going at home. Maybe I'll see you there."

He climbed into his Land Rover and waited for me to back up and turn around. As I drove past him, my stomach turned in a quick flutter.

I took a deep breath to steady myself. He was essentially my customer, paying me for a job well done. I could handle that. Even still, another burst of nervous adrenaline shot through me, head to feet.

I fumbled with my phone as I pulled out of his driveway, ready to tell my little family I'd be home in an hour. I said a silent prayer Evan would answer instead of Mama.

No such luck.

"You must be having a fun evening," Mama said.

"I'm sorry I'm later than I thought I'd be. Are y'all okay?"

"You ask as if some catastrophe will befall us if you leave us alone for too long. You do remember that I've raised a child too, right? And you turned out just fine."

"I know. I'm just checking. I told Evan I'd be home by the time she went to bed, but I might not, unless she stays up late."

"We're just fine here. You interrupted our third game of gin rummy—this one is the tiebreaker. Loser scoops the ice cream."

Evan laughed in the background, and the sound of her voice, carefree and light, made my heart ache. I wanted to both be there with them and stay gone longer, enjoying some rare time away from home with someone who seemed to be decent company.

"If y'all are okay, I think I may stop and grab a bite to eat. I haven't eaten anything since lunch."

"And will you be dining alone?"

I could hear the smile in Mama's voice, and it made me hesitate. If I let her in on the fact that Sumner had asked me to dinner, she'd be sitting up waiting for me when I got back, like I was a teenager on a first date.

"Come on. What do you think?" I said instead.

"Well, okay then. Get yourself something to eat. I've got to get back to my game."

Ahead on the dark road in front of me, the glow of a restaurant lit up a portion of the street and I eased my foot off the gas. A sign out front pronounced it Honey's River Kitchen. People milled about as they waited for tables, and even with my windows up, music from a bluegrass band and the smell of fried seafood found its way into the car. My stomach protested again.

I checked my rearview mirror. From the headlights of another car, I could just make out the shape of Sumner's head and the angle of his shoulders. Dinner would be nice.

When the car in front of me slowed to turn into the parking lot, I thought about turning my blinker on, parking in the lot, and walking inside next to Sumner. In the small space of a moment, I was caught in the in-between, unsure of what to do.

At the last minute my indecision made my decision. I stayed straight on the road, passing Honey's and the promise of good food, good music, and very likely good conversation. After a few seconds, the restaurant was nothing more than a spot of light on the dark road behind me.

If I hurried, I could make it home in time for ice cream.

CHAPTER 18

Just as the color of the sky can foretell the weather, many flowers can predict changes in barometric pressure, weather patterns, even the arrival of a visitor. Keep a close eye on your blooms to stay a step ahead.
—CONNIE SUE, THE MYSTICAL GARDENER

JESSIE

A few days later, the sky was heavy, full of rain and anger. With the threatening weather, I hadn't had a customer since lunch, so I'd taken the afternoon to reorganize some of the shop displays. I did that sometimes when my mind felt uneasy, like something in me wanted to crawl out through my skin and move around before returning and settling back down.

With an almost cool breeze sifting through the open front door, I walked through the shop straightening tabletops and moving pots an inch this way, then an inch that way. Usually the organizing, prettying, and tidying up helped what felt out of place in my mind. Today it didn't. My mind remained restless, swirling with thoughts of Sumner's offer of dinner, Mama's continued memory lapses, and Evan's fast-approaching ninth-grade year.

As if that weren't enough, the space on my counter where my laptop usually sat yawned up at me, reminding me of Ben and his expression when Carol Anne asked him about *Marissa*.

I filled a glass with water and sat on the top porch step. A fine mist fell from the sky, so light I couldn't see it, but I could feel it. On another day I would have gone back inside, but the cool caress felt good on my bare arms and legs.

I'd only been there a moment, putting together a plan for the rest of the afternoon, when I heard a rumble, then Ben's Jeep appeared on the road. Stanley's head poked out of the back window. The sight was surprising yet, in some way, familiar too. As if I was used to seeing his car on the road. Which I most definitely wasn't. Not anymore.

He came to a slow stop in front of the shop, then climbed out and held up a hand in greeting. Before he realized what was happening, Stanley pushed his way between the front seats and leaped out of the open door with free abandon.

"Stanley, no!" Ben called.

The dog flew through the yard toward my house next door. When he noticed me on the porch of Twig, he changed directions and headed straight for me. I stood but not fast enough. Stanley bounded up the steps and stopped with one huge paw on each side of me, his face inches from mine. He finally stopped moving, panting and grinning at Ben as if to say, "Here she is! I found her!"

I brushed off my shirt, not sure if I wanted to laugh or curse. Ben grabbed Stanley's collar and pulled him down the steps. "Not exactly the way I planned to say hello."

"He seems extra boisterous today. Maybe it's the weather."

"Maybe so. He was running circles around the den. If I hadn't gotten him out of the house, he would have worn straight through the carpet."

"You might as well have a seat while he runs around."

"Actually . . ." He glanced around me into the shop. "If you're not too busy, I wanted to see if you'd take a ride with me."

I raised my eyebrows. "Oh. I don't know. I'm by myself in the shop this afternoon . . ."

"No, I get it. Totally. It's nothing."

I chewed on my thumbnail, thinking. It was *my* shop. And I was doing nothing productive today other than thinking myself into a frenzy. Plus, it was close to the end of the day. "On second thought, a ride would be nice. Let me just tell Evan." She'd been with me all morning, loading the table along the side of the shop with begonias, vincas, and geraniums, but she'd gone back to the house with Mama to help get dinner together.

I grabbed my phone and sent her a quick text. I'm running out for a little bit. Doubt anyone will be shopping in this weather, but please keep an eye out just in case.

K. Where are you going?

I paused, unsure of how much to tell her. I'll be back soon. Text me if there's a problem.

I dropped my phone in my bag before she had a chance to respond to my vague answer.

Ben corralled Stanley back into the car and I sat in the front seat. He turned around to back up, his hand on the back of my seat, his upper body close.

I shifted and turned toward the window. "How's the computer coming along? Any chance of it coming back to life?"

"I'm still trying to resuscitate it. It's taking some . . . creativity."

I groaned. "I hate computers."

"Don't give up on it yet. I may be able to bring it around."

As we talked, he drove up Glory to the highway, then turned on the next street, which snaked through a beautiful grove of oak and maple trees. Everything was familiar but somehow felt new at the same time. Sort of like Ben. A rock trail, just wide enough for one car, forked off the road. The end of the trail opened up to a wide pebble-bottomed creek. Trees and vines hung over the edges, and tiny fish darted here and there in the clear water. Even on a dreary day, this place seemed almost magical.

I smiled. "The Icebox."

"I haven't been here since high school. I was in the grocery store the other day and heard some kids talking about it. I can't believe they still hang out here."

"Oh yes, they still come. Evan's just recently started asking to go alone. I felt funny letting her go without me, but it really is so close. And we all did it with no problems. Probably younger than she is now."

"I walked up here once when I was nine," he said. "I had to give up my entire race car collection for a month, but I can still remember how cool I felt walking up here alone."

We climbed out of the Jeep and stood at the edge of the creek. The drizzle had stopped somewhere between leaving the shop and arriving at the Icebox, and gauzy rays of sun pushed through the cloud cover. To the left of us, a huge log lay suspended over the water, its ends long buried in the sand and rocks on the banks. Just under the center of the log was the deepest water in the Icebox, always a little colder than at the edges. I knew because that's where Ben and I always used to sit.

He leaned down and unclipped Stanley's leash but kept a tight hold on his collar. "Stay close," he said. Stanley whined, and as soon as Ben let go, he barked and ran off, nose to the wet, marshy ground.

Without the distraction of Stanley nearby, awkwardness crept between us. A dragonfly flitted low over the water, its wings a dull green rather than the usual iridescent.

"I guess tiptoeing to the center of the log is out of the question." He was smiling.

"Yeah, I don't think I'm as light on my feet as I used to be."

He chuckled. "You're not kidding. I think I'll stick close to the banks today." He sat on one of the large flat rocks that dotted the edge of the water and patted the space next to him. I slid my feet out of my boots and sat too, stretching my legs until my toes found the lukewarm water.

He leaned forward and picked up a smooth rock, then skipped it across the surface of the water. It bounced twice before plunking down into the depths.

"You used to be able to do four."

"I used to be able to do a lot of things." He picked up another rock and passed it back and forth between his hands. "Do you remember all those rocks we used to collect around here?"

I nodded. "You used to leave them in our mailbox."

"Only the best ones."

"Mama would get so mad when she'd reach her hand in the box and pull out wet rocks instead of her mail."

"I usually tried to dry them off before I put them in. Maybe I was in a hurry sometimes. Probably trying to go undetected."

One hot afternoon at the Icebox, I'd tromped through the shallow water, scanning the bottom for shiny rocks. Scattered among the regular brown and gray pebbles were what I now know were likely old pieces of glass—shattered Coke bottles, beer bottles, who knew what else that had been dropped and left over decades of people playing along the banks. All I knew then was that I liked the rocks that glimmered with a tumbled shine once I cleaned the mud off and held them up to the sun. I started collecting them, and Ben added to my collection. Then he added other rocks that caught his eye—some striped, some milky white, and others that appeared almost like marbles, with a thread of rich brown or red running through the center.

For much of high school, when I least expected it, Mama would come in from getting the mail and drop a little pile of rocks on the table in front of me. She was usually muttering under her breath, but I loved the treasures. I'd twist and turn them in the light, savoring the colors that bled into each other.

"What'd you do with them all? I must have left you hundreds of rocks."

"It wasn't quite that many."

"You probably tossed them out. No reason to keep a bunch of dirty rocks around."

I couldn't tell him I'd actually saved those rocks, dropping each one into a hand-carved box Daddy had bought for me at an arts and crafts show in Gulf Shores. I definitely couldn't tell him that box of rocks was still in my closet. That it had gone with me from Perry to Birmingham and back to Perry again. That I'd never had the heart to get rid of what felt like a box full of innocence and promise.

"I guess so."

He sighed and leaned back on his hands. Stanley darted around next to the water nearby, his feet wet and muddy.

"That meeting the other night." He shook his head. "Everything's exactly the same around here, isn't it? I guess I thought all these years later there'd be new faces. Or at least new gossip."

"As far as faces, there's some new mixed in with the old. But the gossip is the same—who's stopped going to church, who's had a baby, who's dating whom."

"And you're okay with it? Still being here, still hearing the same talk, seeing the same people?"

I shrugged. "My life is here. My work. My family." I brushed some dirt off the edge of my shorts. "I don't see many of those people all that often. Twig's open six days a week. That doesn't leave much time to get out and about."

"But you make time for exciting orientation meetings?" A half grin eased over his face.

"Yeah, when Evan decides to tell me about them." I laughed, just a puff of air. "If it's something for her, I go. She doesn't care one way or another if I don't show up at the pancake breakfast or sell popcorn at football games, but I like to know who people are—teachers, parents, kids. It's important to me."

He tossed another rock into the water, then tilted his face toward me. Twenty years slid away in that look. "You're a good mom."

I shrugged again. "I try. I feel like I have a lot to make up for. Things were . . . hard at the beginning. Before we moved back here. Even though she was too young to remember much." *She did remember some though*, a voice reminded me. She remembered the bathing suit. Tiffani in our driveway. Of every memory her young mind could have clung to, of course she remembered the most humiliating, gut-wrenching moment of my life.

"I can understand that. I feel the same with Nick." He sighed. "Talk about a difficult beginning."

I wanted to ask. I'd wondered for so long. But I felt too removed. Too separate from his life to ask personal questions like that.

"I'm trying to make things right now. I have no idea if I'm even in the vicinity of right, but I'm trying." He shifted and brushed the dirt from his palms. "I know you must have heard Carol Anne the other night at the meeting."

The words made my heart beat faster. I could hear it thumping in my ears. "I don't . . . I'm not sure."

"It's okay. I know you heard. About Marissa?" He turned toward me, his eyebrows bunched up. "If I didn't know better, I'd say Carol Anne was trying to talk as loud as possible. As if everyone in the gym needed to know about my personal life." He shook his head. "She and Marissa were roommates at Alabama, and apparently they still keep up with each other. Which is just perfect for me, as you can tell." He rubbed his eyes with his thumb and middle finger. "The last thing I wanted was to move back here and immediately become juicy gossip."

"So, Marissa. Is she . . . ?"

"Yeah." He ran his hand roughly through his hair and sat up, resting his elbows on his knees. "I guess she's my girlfriend, although that doesn't really even . . . cover it." He exhaled, as if the words had taken everything out of him.

"I'm not sure I really get it, but it's . . . it's okay."

"No, it's not . . . It's just kind of hard to explain." He paused. "Marissa is Nick's mother."

"Oh. Wow." If there was any time to play it cool, this was it, but I failed miserably. *Nick's mother.* This was no plain old girlfriend. This was a family. I passed a hand over my forehead, brushing my bangs away from my eyes. "So that's what you meant when you said you were trying to make things right."

He clasped his hands together, then picked at something on his thumbnail. "She's some of it." He didn't say anything else.

"I'm sorry. It's none of my business."

"No, I'm sorry. It's fine." He took a deep breath. "Okay, nutshell version. Marissa and I ran into each other at the Atlanta airport last year. She's a flight attendant now, and I was on my way back from a conference. I hadn't seen her in . . . Well, it had been a really long time. We didn't have much of a relationship back when we . . . Anyway, we were both shocked to see each other, and she wanted to get to know Nick. So here we are. A year later."

"Wow. You've been together a year. Things must be going well." The words *I'm happy for you* danced in my mouth, but I couldn't release them. They felt too loaded, too ironic.

"I guess so. I don't know."

"But you moved here. Won't that make things harder?"

"It's funny, even back in Atlanta, we didn't actually see that much of each other. She's gone all the time on flights—she often flies internationally and stays gone a week or more at a time. When she's in town, she usually catches up on sleep and exercise. We agreed that me moving here wouldn't change things all that much. She can change her destination to Mobile and visit us here, and I'll still have to take trips to Atlanta now and then for work."

"I get it."

He was silent a moment. "No, you don't. How can you? It's ridiculous. Even I can see that." He raked his hand through his hair again and sighed. "We're hanging on by a thread, but somehow we're still hanging on. That's got to count for something, right?"

"I guess so. I bet it does for Nick."

He watched Stanley on the other side of the creek pawing at minnows. "I'm not sure, honestly. He calls her Marissa. Not that I expected him to call an almost total stranger 'Mom,' but . . ." He shook his head. "Anyway, like I said, I think the break is good for both Nick and me. And who knows, maybe Marissa too. Maybe something good will come from it all."

Before either of us could say anything else, a car appeared behind us, heading toward the water. Stanley froze, ears perked up, then he bounded across the creek, spraying us with water and flecks of mud.

"Stanley, stop," Ben shouted. "Sorry about that." He scraped a splotch of mud from his shorts, then gestured to my left cheek. "Oh, you have some . . ."

I wiped my cheek with the back of my hand, but it came away clean. "Where?"

He reached up toward me and hesitated, then brushed a spot of mud away with his thumb.

"Ben? Jessie? Is that you?"

Ben's eyes widened at the sound of Carol Anne's excited voice. "That woman has incredible timing."

Laughter bubbled up from deep inside me and I clamped my hand over my mouth. I took a deep breath, then turned toward Carol Anne. Several kids poured from her car, making a beeline for the water. Stanley danced around in excitement.

"We were just leaving." Ben glanced at me.

"Yes, please," I whispered.

"What were y'all doing down here? Your kids aren't here?" Her eyes scanned the edges of the creek and Ben's Jeep a little way up the path.

"Just taking Stanley out for a swim," Ben answered. "He needed to let off some steam."

"I understand. That's the same thing I'm doing with these kids. Phillip lost his driving privileges for the week after an unfortunate curfew incident, so I'm stuck driving him around. I'm rethinking my discipline plan." She laughed. "I promised him I'd bring him here if he and my sister's kids gave me an hour to work on my PTO lists."

"Okay, well . . ." Ben waved. "Y'all have fun out here."

"We will! And, Ben, I'm looking forward to meeting Nick soon. Marissa says he's such a great kid. You've done well with him."

He tensed at Carol Anne's words. "She's right. He is a great kid." He opened my door, then crossed over to his side.

We were quiet on the way home, both of us absorbed in our own thoughts and memories. The day I found out about Ben and the baby was etched with such clarity in my mind. I'd been in a fog for days after hearing about it. Ben with someone else? Having a baby? I recognized my own hypocrisy—I was with Chris, after all. I knew I had no claim on Ben, but the thought of him finding a landing place with someone else made my chest ache and my fingers clench for months, even after I'd said yes to Chris.

I was still thinking of those hard days as we pulled in at Twig. Next door, my car was stopped in the middle of the driveway, engine on and doors closed. "Huh. Mama must have needed to run out for something."

Surprise turned to shock, then panic as I watched the driver's door open on my car and Evan stepped out. "What in the world?" I flew out of Ben's Jeep and jogged through the grass toward her. Ben was close behind me. "Evan? What are you doing?"

"I—"

Mama climbed out the other side. "Everything's fine," she called. "I realized I was out of Italian seasoning and needed it for dinner. Evan went with me up to the grocery and I decided to give her a quick driving lesson on the way home."

Behind Mama, Evan locked her eyes on mine and shook her head. Mama turned and headed up my front porch steps.

"Mama, wait."

"I just need to sprinkle this on the chicken. Be right back." But her movements as she unlocked the door were quick and harried. Something wasn't right.

I held up my hands, but Evan just shrugged. "I wanted another box of cereal so I went with her. On the way home she turned down the wrong street. When I asked her where she was going, she got all confused. She backed up, then stopped in the middle of the street!"

I put my hand up to my eyes, and Ben squeezed my shoulder, reminding me he was still there. I was grateful for the support.

"It was so weird, like she couldn't remember how to get home even though she's lived here for . . . forever. So I helped her around to the passenger side and I drove back. And did very well, I might add."

I gave her a small smile. "I'm glad you're safe. Glad both of you are safe."

"What's going on with her though?" Her voice grew quiet.

"She just . . ." I rubbed my fingers over my lips and shook my head.

"Don't say she's fine. She keeps forgetting things. We've both seen it."

"Sweetheart, people's minds aren't as sharp as they get older."

I knew she didn't believe me. *I* didn't believe me.

"Dinner'll be ready in fifteen," Mama called out the front door before disappearing back into the house.

"I guess I'll go see if she needs any help," Evan said.

As she ran up the steps and entered the house, I exhaled.

"I'm sorry." Ben's voice behind me was low. "Has she been . . . ?"

"Yeah. It's . . . I don't know."

"Okay. I'm sorry," he said again. "I should probably get back and check on Nick."

"Sure. Of course."

He turned toward his Jeep but paused. "Jessie, you know you can talk to me if you need to. I'm still . . ." He held his hands up. "Well, I'm here."

CHAPTER 19

Studies show a fascinating relationship exists between plants and sound, specifically music. In fact, one scientist in Maine observed a 55 percent increase in his greenhouse corn harvest when he played Gershwin's "Rhapsody in Blue" in the greenhouse at a soft volume for at least twenty hours a day.
—WARREN ELLIOTT, THE SECRET LIFE OF FLOWERS

EVAN

I'd always loved a good stormy day, and this afternoon I was on the couch waiting for the sky to do something more than tease me with dark clouds and occasional raindrops. I'd been lying here trying to read for half an hour, but my eyes wouldn't stop straying out the front window. I told myself I was just watching for rain.

I'd just about given up when Nick appeared between the trees out in front of our house. He wore gray pants and a backward cap, and he tossed a baseball up in the air. He glanced up at our house a couple of times, so I grabbed my rain jacket and ran outside toward him.

"Hey, kid," he called when he saw me.

"Kid?" I asked when I reached the edge of the driveway.

"You know—kid. I feel like I should ruffle your hair or something."

I wasn't sure if he was joking or not, so I laughed along with him.

"How are things?" he asked.

"Good. Mom's working and Gus is inside baking something."

"And you're just hanging out?"

I shrugged. "I need to be over at the shop with Mom soon. But I thought I'd take a walk."

"Well, come on then." He tossed his ball in the air and caught it, then resumed walking. I fell into step next to him, trying to match his strides. Then I heard the other voices on the road. I turned around. Two guys were walking several yards behind us, each carrying baseball gloves and laughing and jabbing each other in that obvious way guys have when they're making fun of something. It only took a few seconds to realize they were laughing at Nick. Or was it me?

My stomach dropped and I turned around quickly. "Were they with you?"

Nick peered over his shoulder and threw his baseball at one of the guys. Hard. The other guy caught it easily in his glove, then he threw it back. Nick laughed. "No, I'm not with them. Well, we were all up at the field together, but we quit when the lightning started. Some of the guys were going to Carter's house to hang out. Those two bozos behind us are going to Scott's grandmother's house. She lives down near me. I think she has cookies or something."

"You're not going with them?"

"I don't know. I might. But I kind of thought I might run into you. And I want you to see our vegetable garden. We got everything planted. It's crazy—we can already see some shoots coming out of the ground."

"That's what happens when you plant things. They grow."

He punched me lightly on the arm.

"I'll tell Mom. She'll be happy we steered you in the right direction."

Nick's house came into view up on the right. I didn't see his dad's Jeep in the driveway, which made me wonder if Nick had rules about having girls at his house when his dad wasn't home. But it didn't matter. He was a senior and I was a freshman. Or would be soon. Obviously we were just friends.

"There's something else I want to show you too." He fished his key out of his pocket. "Considering your great love of music and all." He pushed the door open and we stepped inside. The house smelled so different from ours—earthy and musky, but something flowery too. I sniffed and glanced around.

"It's potpourri. My grandparents had it everywhere. We've tried to find it all, but I think we've missed some."

On the other side of the living room, several cardboard boxes were pushed against the wall, including an open box full of records. A small turntable sat on the floor next to the box. I peeled my rain jacket off and knelt in front of the records. Tom Petty. Van Morrison. Neil Young.

"Wait," Nick said. "I want to show you the garden first."

"Are you kidding? This is vintage vinyl. Trust me, I know what a garden looks like."

He smiled. "True."

We spent the next hour on the floor listening to record after record on the scratchy player. Every time he set the needle down on a record and it began to spin, it felt like time stopped and only the music existed.

"I've never actually listened to a record player before." I leaned down so I could watch the needle at eye level as it bumped and slid over the grooves in the record. "Just seen them on movies and TV and stuff."

"Sounds good, doesn't it?"

"Oh yeah. All the scratches and pops make it sound so much more real than a CD."

"It's not actually supposed to sound scratchy. That's just because the records—and the turntable—are old. Dad said he went on a vinyl kick in college. Bought them all at a used-record store in Tuscaloosa just before it went out of business."

"Your dad likes good music."

Nick nodded. "His music is all mixed up with my early memories. He used to play records for me when I had trouble sleeping."

"How old were you?"

He shrugged. "I don't know. Six, maybe? I had nightmares."

I waited for him to say more, but he moved right past it.

"Let's try this." He reached around me toward the stack of records. As he leaned, it was stupid, but I breathed in. He was so close, I couldn't help it. I smelled sweat—he'd been playing baseball, after all—but he also smelled like the air outside when it was about to rain. "Here it is." He pulled a record from the middle of the pile.

I exhaled. "'Hallelujah.'"

"Mr. Buckley himself." He slid the record onto the turntable.

When the first strains of the song came over the speaker, I closed my eyes and leaned back against the wall. Nick leaned back too. When Jeff began to sing, "Now, I heard there was a secret chord," I couldn't help myself. I sang too. I'd never sung in front of anyone before—only Mom and Gus, but they didn't count. Nick counted. And he sang with me. I kept my eyes shut tight and concentrated on the sound flowing from the speaker and my heart that felt like it was trying to pour out of my body.

We sang the last Hallelujah, the word gradually becoming lower and softer until it disappeared. The music ended but the record spun on, the needle bumping and skipping over the ridges. I was thankful for the noise so it wasn't just me and Nick and the memory of us singing.

Then Stanley barked, followed by Nick's dad's voice. It's not like we were doing anything wrong, but we jumped anyway. Nick pulled the record off the turntable, and I stood and straightened the records on the floor, anything to make us look totally normal.

Mr. Bradley opened the back door. "Evan." He tried but couldn't quite hide his surprise. "How are you?"

I smiled. "I'm fine."

"Hey, Dad." Nick grabbed Stanley and tugged him through the kitchen to the back door and pushed him outside. He was still whining when Nick returned to the living room.

"What are y'all up to?" Mr. Bradley dropped his keys on a side table and draped his rain jacket over the back of a dining chair, where it dripped puddles onto the floor. Gus would have had a cow.

"Nothing. We were just listening to some music." Nick gestured to the floor and the turntable. My stomach was already flipping around like a fish after singing *that* song with *that* boy, but Mr. Bradley's face made it worse. It was like he knew something had happened, even though nothing had actually happened.

"Come on, Evan." He picked up his keys again. "I'll take you home."

"Wait, Dad."

"It's fine," Mr. Bradley said. "I don't mind. We need to figure out what we're doing for dinner anyway." He looked at me. "Sorry, but I'm not quite ready to try my cooking skills out on someone new." He opened the back door, and I walked out behind him.

"Hey, Evan." Nick walked to the door. I waited. "You should sing more often."

"Let her go, Nick," Mr. Bradley called from the carport.

Nick grinned. "I'll see you around."

CHAPTER 20

Re: I planted the wrong seed!
Dear Ellis, Trust me, I understand your panic. I once planted three
rows of dianthus seeds thinking they were delphiniums. Instead of
ethereal blue stalks, I got short pink clusters. However, my advice
is to keep what you planted. It may not be what you expected,
but if it showed up in your garden, it's there for a reason.
—KATHERINE GRACE, YOUR DAILY DAISY

JESSIE

Sumner called a couple of days later. He was in the area and asked if he could stop in for a slice of Mama's pie.

"You just happen to be in the area?" I wiped my forehead with my wrist. With the humidity, the eighty-five showing on my outside thermometer felt more like ninety-five. My shipment of pink mandevillas finally showed up, and neighbors had been coming in all afternoon, squabbling over which had the most promising buds and the shiniest leaves. The day's constant motion had been a good distraction from that afternoon at the Icebox. From thoughts of Ben and Marissa. Of Mama.

"You got me," Sumner said. "I'm not anywhere close to you. But I can be soon. What time do you close?"

"I can always take a break, but the boss usually lets me off around six."

"Think the boss will accept a customer right at closing time?"

"I think she'll be fine with it as long as he helps clean up."

He laughed. "I can manage that."

As I closed out the rest of the afternoon—divvying up plants, showing Evan how to root an oakleaf hydrangea, keeping an eye on Elma Dean as she sampled Mama's sugared pecans—I anticipated seeing Sumner. We hadn't spoken since he'd left it up to me whether to turn into Honey's and have dinner with him. I didn't regret not going, but now I both worried and hoped he'd ask me again.

And I'd made the mistake of telling Mama he was coming.

"Oh, for crying out loud," she sputtered. "I wish I'd known earlier. I'm making chicken piccata and green beans. It's not my best dinner for company."

"Your chicken piccata is delicious, Mama, but he didn't say a thing about dinner. He just wants a slice of pie."

"And he can have it. Right after he eats his dinner."

I tried to say no, but she held up her hand. "No Southern woman lets a guest come over at dinnertime without offering him a plate. It's just good manners."

On her way out of the shop, she'd grabbed Evan. "Come on. You can pound the chicken. I'll whip up some mac and cheese."

A few minutes after six, a text message arrived on my phone. Expecting it to be Sumner, I grabbed it off the counter and opened the message without checking the screen.

I've made some progress with the computer. Better get your paintbrush ready.

I laughed at Ben's text and tapped out a quick reply. I'm not making any promises. Show me the computer first.

You already promised. I have a roller with your name on it.

Just then I heard the purr of Sumner's Land Rover in the driveway. I left my phone on the counter and walked outside. He slammed his car door and grinned. "I didn't know a woman covered in dirt could look so lovely."

I hoped the pink in my cheeks came across as sun rather than a nervous blush. "Are you often around women covered in dirt?"

"Actually, no. Never. You get that distinction."

I showed him to the strawberry patch along the back fence where the netting protecting the berries from hungry birds had fallen loose. I wanted to stake it back up before any more disappeared, and four hands and arms made it easier work than just two.

Before we finished, I heard the *chug-chug-chug* of Mr. Rainwater's truck coming up the road. I froze, then groaned.

"What is it?" Sumner's salt-and-pepper hair was ruffled in front and his short-sleeved button-down was wrinkled, but he still looked sharp. Almost regal. Unaccustomed to our informal way of life.

I bit my lip. "It's nothing. I'll be right back."

I met Mr. Rainwater around front as he rolled his truck to a stop. "Hi there, Miss Jessie. I've got another small load for you. I have a doctor's appointment in the morning, and I didn't want this bit to go bad before I could get it to you."

"Oh, it's okay. Actually, I don't—"

"Well now, who's this?" His eyes lifted just past my left shoulder.

I followed his gaze to see Sumner coming around the side of the shop. I introduced the two men and they shook hands.

"It won't take me long to unload this." Mr. Rainwater patted the side of his truck bed. "I'll be out of your hair in a jiff."

He retrieved his wheelbarrow from the back of the truck and set the plastic tub of manure inside it. When he grasped the handles of the wheelbarrow, he winced and let go, shaking his right hand. "Old Arthur gets my hands all worked up sometimes."

"Here, let me," Sumner said.

"Son, I don't think you're quite dressed—"

"I don't mind at all." Sumner easily lifted the handles of the wheelbarrow. "Just point me in the right direction."

I pointed around the side of the shop, then fell in step beside him. Mr. Rainwater followed behind, massaging his right hand with the thumb of his left hand.

"This isn't . . . ?" Sumner sniffed and nodded to the small mound he was dutifully pushing.

"Yes. It's exactly what you're thinking." I shrugged. "What can I say? It makes for healthy plants."

After dumping the load in my plastic pool and smoothing it out with a shovel, Sumner pushed the wheelbarrow back around front and loaded it into Mr. Rainwater's truck for him. I watched from Twig's porch as they chatted a moment, then Mr. Rainwater waved good-bye.

Sumner's crisp white shirt was streaked with dirt from the handles of the wheelbarrow, and the rest of him was covered in a smattering of soil.

"Sorry about that."

"A little dirt never hurt anyone, right?" He smiled. "I like it out here. It's . . . I don't know, it's nice. It's like an escape from real life."

"For you, maybe. For us, this is as real as it gets. Although it doesn't always smell this bad." He laughed. "Let me lock up. You can wash up at the sink in the back."

While he washed his hands, I grabbed my phone off the counter. Ben had sent another text while Sumner and I were outside.

Also wanted to check on your mom. Is she doing okay?

I sighed. I'd done the research—I searched for things like "memory loss" and "age-related forgetfulness" months ago when I first sensed something with Mama wasn't quite right—but all Google did was scare me. What loomed ahead of us had the potential to be life changing, and to be honest, I wanted to hide from it. But of all people, Ben would probably be a good person to talk to about it. Not much fazed him, whereas my mind could tie itself into knots if I let it.

Back in high school, during our junior year, we'd had precalculus together. Better with words than numbers, I had no business being in the class, and I had a meltdown one night over parabolas and hyperbolas. He sat at our kitchen table with me that night long after Mama and Daddy had gone to bed, painstakingly reteaching me everything the teacher had gone over, but with Ben's slow, methodical approach, I understood it far better. His temperament—his whole way of life, really—had been like a steady hand at my back. Calm and comforting.

In the back room Sumner turned off the water and I heard him pull a paper towel off the roll. I quickly sent Ben my reply.

She has an appointment with a doctor in Mobile, but I couldn't get her in for a few weeks. Thanks for checking. I'll try to fill you in at some point.

Anytime.

Sumner entered the room, his hands and forearms fresh and clean, and all traces of dirt gone from his clothes. He held up his hands. "Spick-and-span."

I returned the smile, but it faltered on my face.

"Everything okay?" His gaze dropped to the phone in my hand.

What about Sumner? Ben's parents were strolling through a retirement resort, probably with a fruity drink in their hands, but Sumner's parents had to be a good bit older than Gus. Maybe he had experience with these sorts of changes and fears. Maybe he'd done the late-night research too.

But talking about it—to anyone—made it real, and I wasn't sure I was ready for that. Instead, I dropped the phone in my pocket and grabbed my keys to lock up. "Yep. Everything's fine. Let's head next door." I led him across the yard to my house. Through the window I could see Mama flitting around the dining room. "Right. I forgot to mention something to you."

"Something other than me spending the evening shoveling manure?"

"Well, this may be a little more appetizing, depending on how hungry you are. My mother has made dinner."

"Perfect. I'm starving."

Inside, the dining room appeared normal at first glance. Then I noticed the extra touches. Instead of the usual paper napkin, a cream linen napkin sat next to each plate. Each tea glass had a small lemon wedge on the lip, and a pair of silver candle holders—where she'd dug them up, I had no idea—held slim tapers.

Evan rolled her eyes at me when I came through the door. "Gus is on a rampage," she whispered.

"Evan, this is Mr. Tate," I said pointedly.

She gave a polite smile and he said hello.

We washed up and Mama ushered us to the table. In the center she had set out the chicken, mac and cheese, and green beans. Corn-bread biscuits sat in a basket lined with a checked dish towel.

"This looks wonderful. Do you eat like this every night?" Sumner asked.

I passed the basket of cornbread to him. "It's Mama's payment for all the plants she lets her friends walk away with." I winked at Evan.

"It's what you do for friends," Mama said, unapologetic. "I'd cook them a meal if I could, but I can't feed them all. Instead, I give them a small token—a petunia here, a snapdragon there. You can't blame me, can you?" She smiled sweetly at Sumner, then glanced at his plate. "Sugar, you didn't get near enough mac and cheese. Here, have some more. It's considered a vegetable, you know."

❧

By the time we brought out Mama's apple pie, Sumner was min-ing her for information about me. Mama told him everything, from how old I was when I lost my first tooth, to how I broke my arm leaping from the top of a ladder thinking I could fly, to the time I jumped off the front of a boat and ended up hanging from the back of my shorts.

"Why were you jumping off the front of a boat?" Sumner asked. "Was it moving?"

I shook my head. "It wasn't a big deal. It was just—"

"No, no." Mama pushed her hair back from her face and leaned forward on her elbows. "Tom had beached the boat on an island down near Gulf Shores. When we stopped, Jessie hopped down off the front, intending to land in the shallow water. Unbeknownst to her, her shorts got hung up on that little rope cleat right at the edge of the boat, so when she jumped, she just sort of hung there, suspended from the back of her shorts until Tom noticed and unhooked her."

"Mom!" Evan gasped. "That's terrible. Did you just want to die?"

"I did, in fact, but I couldn't do anything, hanging there like that. But, Mama, you left out an important detail. If you saw the whole thing, why couldn't you come rescue me yourself?"

"Well, I may have been laughing a bit. Wouldn't you be?"

"I can't honestly say what I would have done in that situation." Sumner turned to me. "Of course I would have helped you. But I do see the humor."

"Thank you," Mama said.

I enjoyed watching Sumner and my mother banter back and forth, even if it was about my most embarrassing moments. In a strange way he fit right in—from asking for second helpings of everything on the table to listening intently to Mama talking about Johnny and June as if they were old friends. Evan seemed to enjoy herself too, and that was before Sumner commented on the T-shirt she was wearing.

"Laser's Edge." He gestured to the logo on her shirt. "That was a great old music store. I went there once when I was in Birmingham on business."

"Are you serious? That's incredible. They used to have all these bands play there in the store when they were in town for concerts."

"You're right, they did. The day I was there, a band was setting up for an in-store show later that evening. This was before you were born though. How'd you even know about it?"

"I read about it in a Rainbow Rowell book."

"Rainbow what?"

Evan shook her head. "It's . . . nothing. What kind of music do you listen to?"

"Well, let's see. Probably no one that'll make you happy." He tipped his head toward Mama. "Not much country music, I'm sorry to say."

Mama pursed her lips and cleared her throat.

"I'd have to say my favorite is probably Neil Diamond. I know he's a bit of a throwback, but 'Sweet Caroline'? 'Forever in Blue Jeans'?" His grin faded when he noticed the silence around the table.

I let out one laugh, then covered my mouth with my hand. Evan raised one skeptical eyebrow.

"I'm guessing that was the wrong answer," he said.

"Have some more tea, why don't you?" Mama's smile was tight as she reached over and filled his empty glass.

❦

After dessert, Sumner all but ordered Mama to go relax in the den so the three of us could clean up.

"I always clean up," Mama said, "and I'm perfectly relaxed."

Sumner laughed. "I can see that. I'd just like to do the honors in your place tonight."

"If you insist." She settled on the couch with the remote. "I'll see if I can find Chip and Joanna."

As Sumner washed the skillets and pots, I dried and Evan wiped off the table and counters.

"You know, I do like more than just Neil Diamond," Sumner said to Evan when she brought our stack of plates to the sink. "I've always been a big Rolling Stones fan."

Evan nodded. "Most people are. Let me guess—your favorite Stones song is 'You Can't Always Get What You Want.'"

Sumner looked at me with raised eyebrows. "That one's a no-brainer," he said. "I think I prefer 'Wild Horses' though. Maybe 'Moonlight Mile.'"

Evan watched him a moment, then wiped her hands on the dish towel hanging from the stove. She paused on her way out of the kitchen. "'Wild Horses' is all right. Did you know it was recorded in Alabama?"

"Sure. Up in Muscle Shoals."

She flashed him a quick smile, then left and joined Mama on the couch.

"She's smart," Sumner said when she was out of earshot. "And funny, although I was a little afraid to laugh."

"You'll have to excuse the sass. She's actually not like that very much."

"Oh, I'm not offended. I know what teenagers are like. And I hate to break it to you, but the sass will probably only increase." He turned the water off and grabbed the dry skillet.

"That's what I hear." I pointed to the pot rack above the counter, and Sumner hung the skillet by the end of the handle. "But right now she's . . . well, she's pretty great." It made me happy to see Mama and Evan watching TV together, even though I could only see the backs of their heads from where I stood in the kitchen. How many fourteen-year-olds actually wanted to spend that much time with their grandmother?

Sumner leaned against the counter and placed his hands on the edge behind him. "You know . . ." He stopped and gave a small laugh. "It's kind of weird that I'm here in your house, having just eaten dinner with your family. I wasn't even sure I'd see you again after I shoved my business card in your hand."

I laughed. "I wouldn't say you shoved it."

"Well, maybe it wasn't that aggressive. I just . . ."

"I know. You wanted the flowers. I'm 'off the beaten path,' like Olivia wants."

His face was thoughtful. "That's part of it."

"And the other part?"

He shrugged, then gazed at me full in the face. "I didn't want to leave without the chance to see you again."

I opened my mouth but had no idea what to say. The only light in the kitchen was the one on the hood above the stove and the glow that trickled in from the den. On the table by the back door, my phone dinged with another text, but his gaze didn't leave my face. He reached over and smoothed down the hem of my shirt where it had folded up. The skin at my hip tingled even though his fingers never touched me.

"You're smart and funny and hardworking." One corner of his mouth pulled up, smooth and slow. "You intrigue me."

Neither of us moved, but the space between us—at least a couple of feet—seemed much smaller than it had a moment before. I swallowed hard. Then from the den, a toothpaste commercial came on the TV, the volume several notches higher than it had been. I blinked as if a light had blinded me.

"I should get back home." He called good-bye to Evan and Mama, who didn't let him escape without an extra slice of pie on a paper plate, and I walked him outside to his car.

"I appreciate the dinner." He opened his door and faced me, one hand on top of the doorframe. "And the pie."

"Don't thank me. It was all my mother."

"Ah. That is true, isn't it?"

"No, I don't—I didn't mean . . ."

"It's okay. I totally crashed your evening." He laughed. "And I'm overstaying my welcome. After all, I only came for the pie."

"Really?" I raised an eyebrow. All of a sudden I felt bold. I was intriguing.

"Well, no, that's not true at all."

"Tonight was . . . nice. Very nice, actually."

"I'm glad. Would you like to have a nice time with me again? Because I'd love to take you out to a real dinner. Not that this wasn't real, and not to slight your mother or daughter at all, but I'd love to have you to myself for an evening. Get to know you more."

I found myself nodding before I even had a chance to think it through. But sometimes not thinking was a whole lot easier. "I'd like that."

"Good." He sat and closed the door behind him, then rolled down the window. "I like that answer."

I was still standing in the driveway when he disappeared around the curve in the road.

CHAPTER 21

*Some people consider creeping Jenny to be a plant-strangling nuisance.
If you find yourself in this category, by all means, keep it out of your
garden. However, if you want a quick shot of electric color, this lime-
green ground cover may be for you. You can contain it or, if you don't
have other plants nearby, let it grow freely for a bright swath of beauty.*
—SUSAN K. SEALE, WEEDS FOR LIFE

EVAN

I didn't know what was going on with Gus. One minute she was
fine, then the next she'd be patting the table and her hair, fumbling around her chair like she was feeling for her glasses or sewing
scissors or something.

"Gus," I'd say. "What are you looking for? What do you need?"

When she got like that, she could never tell me what was wrong.
It was like she didn't even hear me. But then she'd just snap out of
it. Her eyes would lose the glassy stare, she'd focus, smooth her hair
back, and go right on with whatever she was doing.

Sometimes it happened two days in a row, or even twice in
one day, but then she might be fine for a week or more. It was nuts.
Sometimes it made me want to laugh, but most of the time it just
made me sad. Nothing could happen to Gus. She was a constant—
like the water that always flowed through the Icebox. Or like the huge

pecan tree standing in the fork of the driveway. Always there, never changing. I liked that.

I had to admit this though: the only good thing about Gus freaking out the other day in the car was that I got to drive. I'd never even driven down the driveway before, but somehow I knew just what to do. It was a little jerky maybe. A lot jerky, actually. But still. I was in the driver's seat and it felt good.

Later that night before Mom went to bed, she came in my room and asked for all the details. Again. I'd already explained everything in the driveway when Mr. Bradley was still there, then a second time after she made it back into the house. But I guess she needed to hear it again.

"Mom. The story isn't going to change. I'm not hiding anything from you. She got confused, stopped in the middle of the road, and I drove home. End of story."

She rubbed her hand over her face. She'd pulled her hair up in a bun and was wearing the tortoiseshell glasses she wore at night after she took her contacts out. Sometimes I thought she looked like a model. But not the usual kind, all pouty lips and hip bones.

"Is Gus going to be okay?" I shifted my legs on the bed and she put her hand on my knee.

She nodded slowly. "I think she'll be fine. I just need to find out from a doctor how I can best help her." She stood. "Good night, sweetheart."

"Wait, Mom?" I asked just before she closed my bedroom door. "About the driving . . ."

"Honey, you're fourteen."

"I know, I know. But if you're in the car with me?"

"I'll think about it."

"So . . . that's not a no?"

She smiled. "Not a yes either."

❧

So maybe she didn't say yes, but she didn't exactly say no. I told myself that any careful, licensed driver would work if she wasn't available. I did this because when Nick asked if I wanted a driving lesson, I said yes.

He didn't tell me a driving lesson would be involved when he stopped by on Sunday afternoon. All he did was ask if I wanted to go with him to get a slushie at the Gas-N-Go.

"Now?"

"You doing anything else?" He peered past me into the house. Gus was at her own house, and Mom was taking a nap. Sunday was the only day Twig was closed, and she was good at relaxing on her day off.

"Not a thing. Let me just . . ." I was going to say I'd tell Mom where I was going, but wouldn't a note be better? No chance to ask questions.

Nick raised his eyebrows and tossed his keys up in the air, then caught them in his other hand.

"Be right back." I scribbled out a quick note on a Post-it and left it on the kitchen counter, then grabbed my phone just in case she missed the note. I hated the phone, but if she couldn't find me, she'd call. I didn't want her worrying about me too.

Outside, the sky was so bright, it had lost any hint of blue—just a white expanse broken up by a few high wisps of clouds. Inside Nick's car, it was just as neat as it had been the night he drove me home. It still had the same scent—leather and Windex.

He cranked the engine and backed up, then headed down the driveway. Before pulling out onto the road, he stopped and flipped his sun visor down. A CD fell into his hand and he slid it into a slot just underneath the radio.

"I didn't know old cars had CD players."

"They don't. I had to add it. Can't use Bluetooth in something this old, so I stick with CDs while I'm driving."

"Who are we listening to?" He pressed the scan button and stopped at track eight.

"I'm continuing your musical education. This, my dear Evan, is Josh Ritter. He will change your world."

I turned to face out the window. "We'll see."

Out on the road, he rolled the windows down, and a voice streamed from the speakers, soft and melodic at first, then stronger until the voice filled the car and poured out of the open windows. There was acoustic guitar, then drums, then a strong bass line. It was so full and so close, I felt like I could reach out and touch it.

Nick said something to me, but I couldn't hear him. He'd passed the Gas-N-Go, but I didn't care. I didn't really want a slushie anyway.

"What?" My hair whipped around my face and I pulled it away from my mouth.

"I said you're smiling."

I tried to wipe it away, but I couldn't. It was the music and the breeze. It was the air, all light and feathery. It was Nick.

He turned off the highway onto the next road, the one that went past the Icebox. At the end of the road—desolate except for straight rows of pecan trees off to the left and a few horses in the distance behind a fence—he pulled over to the side of the road and climbed out.

"What are you doing?"

He walked in front of the car and opened my door. "Time to switch."

"Switch what?" I asked, but my fingers were already unbuckling my seat belt.

"You want to drive?"

I stood next to him and smoothed my hands down the front of my T-shirt. No one else was around. No questions, no one to worry.

"Yes."

He tossed me the keys. I caught them and crossed behind the car and sat down.

"Okay, this is a lesson. Got it?"

"Got it."

"Rule number one?"

I stretched the seat belt across my chest and buckled it. "Check."

"See? You're already a pro. This'll be a piece of cake."

He grinned, but I didn't. All of a sudden the courage and boldness I'd felt seconds before scattered, leaving me terrified. I was sitting in the driver's seat of Nick's car, next to him, and I had no idea what to do. It hadn't felt like this when I was driving with Gus.

"You okay?" I knew he was watching me, but I couldn't turn and face him. "It's fine. You'll do great. I'll talk you through it."

My fingers were tight around the steering wheel.

"Evan. Look at me." I turned to him. "You're fine. I'm here."

"Okay." I relaxed my fingers one by one, wiggling them a little before gripping the wheel again, but this time not as tightly. "I can do this."

"Yeah, you can." He laughed. He was way too chipper about this. "It'll be fun. You'll see. Okay, foot on the break. No, your right foot. Tuck your left one away—you're not going to use that one at all."

"What? Why not use one foot for each pedal. Two feet, two pedals."

"It's just . . . that's not how you do it. Trust me. You'll wear out your brake pads if you do that. Just pretend your left foot doesn't exist."

"Whatever," I muttered under my breath, but I pulled my left foot away from the pedal.

"Now, gearshift." He pointed. "Slide it into Drive. There you go. Now you're in business." He sat back in his seat and flopped one arm out the window. "Let's fly. Well, maybe don't fly. Just give her a little gas."

The car crept down the road at a sloth's pace, but we were moving.

"It's okay to go a little faster."

I pressed my foot harder on the gas and the car responded. After a moment, we were cruising at twenty miles per hour.

"You're doing great. You should've seen me at my first driving lesson. Dad took me to the back of the IKEA parking lot at eight o'clock on a Saturday morning. It was deserted, or so I thought . . ."

As he told the story of his first driving experience, my nerves leaked away and I felt that hint of freedom again. I didn't even mind the heat blazing in the windows. After a moment, I took my left hand off the steering wheel and hung my arm out the window. The wind flowed between my fingers and across my skin. It was delicious.

Nick's head was leaned back against the seat and his eyes were closed.

"Um, shouldn't you be watching the road?"

He shook his head. "I'm not the one driving. And you're doing fine. Nothing ahead of you but the road."

It was true. The road was empty, and it stretched ahead until it disappeared around a curve. The trees were closer to the road now, creating a sort of canopy above.

He sighed. "This is so great."

They were just words—four simple little words—but they made my stomach do that funny fluttery thing. I bit my lip to keep from smiling too big. It *was* great. It was more than great—it was amazing. And he knew it too.

"Yeah," I said. "It is."

"Everything's just been so messed up lately. At my old school, with my mom, with . . ." He ran his hand through his dark hair. "I feel like I can relax here. It's nice."

Up ahead, a car rounded a curve and headed toward us. It was in its own lane, but it felt way too close to me. I instinctively slowed down and inched the car closer to the edge of the road.

"Keep it in the middle," he murmured.

The car zoomed past me without incident and I let out the breath I'd been holding.

"Everyone was just asking me so many questions all the time," he continued. "'What are your plans? What do you want to do with your life? Where are we headed?'" His knee bobbed up and down. "I mean, just . . . let me be, you know?"

I nodded like I had a clue what he was talking about. Then his phone, sitting in the cup holder between us, buzzed with a text. He grabbed it and checked the screen. I didn't mean to look, but it was right there, glowing and visible, and my eyes slid to the right involuntarily.

The name at the top said *Cassidy.*

I'm sorry about all the drama. I miss you. At least let me know you're alive and well in Alabama. xoxo.

Cassidy? xoxo? I wasn't stupid. I knew what that meant.

He sighed, exhaling air out in a thin stream. "Anyway, when Dad told me about Perry, I couldn't think of anything better than to just get out of town. Get away from it all." He laughed, but it sounded tired. "You're pretty easy to relax with, kid. You don't ask me so many questions."

Something in my chest felt both hard and soft at the same time. I was mad—here I was, driving this car with this boy, feeling a freedom I'd never experienced, yet here he was, getting a flirty text from someone named Cassidy. Then again, he turned the screen off and dropped the phone back in the cup holder. His only response to her was a heavy sigh. That was something.

"You have to quit it with this kid business, you know."

He laughed and this time it was lighter. Maybe I really did help him relax. Forget. "You got it."

❧

When we got home, Mom was pulling weeds out of the front flower bed. She always said she didn't mind pulling weeds because she liked to see the immediate results—clean, clear space instead of uninvited intruders. When she turned around and saw me in the driver's seat of Nick's car, I felt like the uninvited intruder.

Nick cursed under his breath. "We should have stopped and switched places. I don't know what I was thinking."

"It's fine, it's . . ." But it wasn't. Mom was walking toward the car, her mouth a firm line. I unbuckled my seat belt and opened the door. Nick did the same.

"Ms. McBride, it was my fault," he said before I could speak. "I asked her if she wanted—"

"Thank you, Nick. You can go now."

"I—"

"Why don't you head on back to your house. I'll talk with your dad later."

"Yes, ma'am." He walked in front of the car to the driver's side. "Sorry," he whispered when he was next to me.

"It's okay," I whispered back. "It was fun." Understatement of the year.

He flashed a quick smile, then climbed in the car and backed out of the driveway.

Mom stared at me, one eyebrow raised. I wanted her to say something, but she didn't.

"I know, I know. It's bad."

Still nothing.

"I'm sorry?"

"Did we not just have a conversation about driving? 'I'll think about it' does not mean yes. You are not old enough to make the decision to get behind the wheel of a car and drive. Do you understand that?"

"Yes. I do. Really, I'm sorry. It's just . . ."

"Just what?" Her eyes were wide, her voice pleading, like she really wanted to understand.

I took a deep breath, held it a moment, then let it out without speaking. I was stuck in that place again, feeling like I couldn't talk to her about something as mystifying as my heart.

"Oh, honey." She put her arm around my shoulder and turned me back toward the house. "Being young is weird. It's hard and confusing, but at the same time it's . . . spectacular. Does that sound about right?"

"Spectacular might be a stretch, but yeah, something like that."

She gave a small half smile. "I remember."

At the top of the porch steps, she held the screen door open for me. I took a step away, then paused and turned back to her. "So . . . does this mean I'm not in trouble?"

"Oh, you are, don't worry. I'll have a list of chores ready for you before bed. And that'll be on top of your regular duties at the shop." She crossed the hall into the kitchen and filled a glass with water. "You might as well rest up. You have a big week ahead of you."

In my bedroom the late-afternoon sun slashed long beams of light across the hardwood floor. My bed seemed more inviting than ever. I stretched myself across it and rolled over onto my back. The ceiling was crisscrossed with shifting shadows from the crepe myrtle outside my window and the fan swirled on high. Despite the chores, I was looking forward to the week. I may not see Nick—Mom would probably make sure of that—but inside, my heart was feeling pretty spectacular.

CHAPTER 22

One current gardening trend is to design modern, stylistic gardens with
austere lines and hyper-defined borders. This is all fine and good, but
remember that gardening is meant to be relaxing, regardless of how
loose or rigid your space is. The best gardens leave room for surprises.
—DR. JULIUS GRISSOM, THE GRISSOM GUIDE

GUS

I'd already been watching myself carefully when the grocery store debacle happened. Oh, I made it through the store just fine. It was the trip home that got me. And to make matters worse, I lied to Jessie about it—told her I was just in a hurry to season the chicken—but I knew she saw right through it. I was trying so hard not to slip up, but sometimes I just couldn't manage to hold it together. What was happening was bigger than me.

The day before the grocery store, I found Jessie gathering the recipe cards I'd left strewn all over her kitchen table. Why I'd taken them out of their box, I had no idea, but she gently stacked them and slid them back in the box within their appropriate tabs—soups, poultry, desserts, and the like. She didn't say a word about it. I almost wanted her to, wanted to unburden myself of the weight of truth I'd come to understand, but it would have been too much. I kept quiet instead, waiting for the right time to let her know.

And that was my plan until the water almost pulled me under. I'd gone back over to my house to lie down for a little while. I tried to nap, but the sleep was fitful and unsatisfying. Something kept knocking on the door to my mind, an insistent *tap-tap-tap* that kept jerking me awake.

Finally I sat up, damp hair plastered to my forehead and the back of my neck. It was when I swiveled my hips to set my feet on the floor that I noticed the water. It rushed around the bottom of the couch and the legs of my kitchen chairs. Fear clawed across my skin. I tried to yell, but if any sound escaped, I couldn't hear it for the loud pounding of water, like a huge waterfall had somehow materialized in one of my back bedrooms during the last hour. The couch was an island, the only dry surface in the whole house.

Some rational part of my brain told me this was a dream, that it was part of the burden I carried, but another part of me—the part that didn't want to drown in my own house—broke into pieces. I tucked my legs under my chin, made myself into the tightest ball I could without wrenching my back, and I sat, rocking, waiting for the water to recede.

Sometime later—could have been hours, may have only been minutes—a knocking made its way to my ears over the sound of the water. After a few knocks, it became a pounding, more demanding than the *tap-tap-tap* that continued to stab my brain. The pounding was close by, almost sounded like it was inside me, but then the front door opened a crack and someone called my name.

"Gus, it's me. Harvis. I'm coming in, okay?"

"No! Wait—the water . . ." I tried to warn him, to keep him from being swept under the waves as they rushed out the front door, but when he pushed the door open wider, nothing happened. The floor was dry as a bone.

He crossed the room in quick strides and sat next to me on the couch. I wrapped my arms around him, pressing my face into his chest. "Please don't leave me." My voice was a strangled whisper, startling me with its desperation.

He tightened his arms around me. "I'm not going anywhere."

"But the water . . . ," I managed.

He leaned back to look at me full in the face. "What water?"

I checked the floor again. "It was . . . it was everywhere."

"There's no water. It's all dry. Everything's fine."

I didn't quite believe him, but his eyes were so clear and soft, I kept my gaze there, using them as a lifeline to pull me back to what I took for actual reality. When I peeked at the floor a moment, it was still dry.

He unclenched my white-knuckled fingers from around his arm. "I'll be right back."

He fiddled around in the kitchen, opening cabinets, and turned the water faucet on. While he did whatever he was doing, he talked— just idle chat about Loretta and something stuck in her hoof. By now I was clearheaded enough to know he was talking only to calm me down. Well, that and possibly to distract us both from the fact that mere seconds before we'd been locked in an embrace that might make a teenager blush. But rather than feeling racy, his arms around me had felt like protection.

When he sat back down next to me, he held a damp, cool dish-cloth to my cheek. I took it from him and pressed it to my forehead, then my neck. In my chest my heart slowly returned to its normal speed.

He reached over to the coffee table and opened a Ziploc bag with four fluffy biscuits in it. He broke off a piece and handed it to me.

"How'd you get ahold of those?" I'd recognize my own biscuits anywhere. They were taller and fluffier than anyone else's and flecked with a smattering of black pepper across the top.

"I stopped by Jessie's to get some details about this chandelier contraption she's asked me to build for the gal getting married. She wrapped these up for me and said if I stopped by your house, you might give me some of your fresh apple jelly to go with them." His right eye twitched. It may have been an attempt at a wink, or possibly just a speck of dust.

"Oh, she did, did she?"

"She did. I saw the jar on your kitchen counter, and if you don't mind, I'll help myself to some as soon as I make sure you're okay."

I waved my hand in front of my face, swiping away the memory of my bungled-up reality, although my hands were still shaking. I clasped them together to keep him from noticing. "It was nothing. I'm completely fine, although that doesn't mean I'm parting with any of my apple jelly."

He laid his hand on top of mine. "Augusta," he said quietly. "No more joking. Is it what I think it is?"

"Depends on what you're thinking." I pulled my hand away and reached for another chunk of biscuit. "But probably. Alzheimer's, dementia, losing my marbles, coming unglued." My voice caught on that last word and I swallowed hard. It was the first time I'd admitted to another person what I already knew to be true. Could he handle it?

I turned the biscuit over in my hands. Tom had known about my mother, of course, and about my grandmother, but he never liked to talk about it. I knew it pained him to think about the disease that would more than likely infiltrate my mind as well, and to be honest, I always worried a bit that the force of it would cause him to buckle. We never got the chance to see though. He died before any of it came to pass, and I'd carried the weight of my bad odds on my own in the years since. I admit it felt good to pass a small part of that weight to someone else.

I took a deep breath and dropped the crumbs back onto the plate. "Does Jessie know?"

"No, and I don't plan on telling her. Not until I have to, anyway. And I don't want you to tell her either."

"She's your daughter. And she's a grown woman. She can handle it."

"I don't need anyone worrying about me. Especially not my child."

He stared hard at me. "You are the toughest woman I've ever met. I have no doubt some of that toughness trickled down to Jessie. You need to tell her. Have you been to see a doctor?"

I shook my head. "All they'll tell me is that it'll keep happening, it'll get worse, and I'll end up in a home somewhere. I know how to Google."

"Tell Jessie and see a doctor. There could be treatment. Medicine. Something to slow this train down or at least keep it from derailing. Do it for me?"

I'd been looking down to the floor—partly to check for streams of water trailing out from under the furniture and partly to keep him from seeing the embarrassment on my cheeks—but when he said that, I raised my head. "For you? Why would I do it for you?"

He sighed, long and deep, heaving the air out of his nose. I'd seen this man nearly every day since Tom died. He'd been a faithful presence all these years—helping Jessie out with her plants, doing odd tasks around the house when I needed the help, offering up his services in any way he could. His truck, his overalls, his thick gray hair, his weathered skin were almost as familiar to me as my own shadow, yet the look he gave me—the determination in his eyes, the set of his mouth—it was as if a different man sat next to me on the couch. Not just Old Harvis from down the road, but Harvis, the man who rescued me, who very well could continue to rescue me if I let him. A man who wouldn't buckle.

"Okay," I said. "Okay. Let me think about it."

He nodded. "You sure you're feeling okay? I could stay—"

"No, it's fine." I swallowed. "I need to get back over to Jessie's for dinner. She'll wonder where I am if I'm not there soon."

At the door he paused, then turned back to me with those soft green eyes that could carry me for days. "I know we haven't . . . You probably don't . . ."

"What is it, Harvis?" I probably could have been a little gentler, but I wanted him to be direct. At our age, there was no need to beat around the bush.

He tapped the door with his index finger, as if judging its strength or hardness. "I'm here for you if you need me. If you want me. That's all."

And just like that, something snapped into place, like in baking when I added a little of this and a little of that and it was not quite right, but then one more dash of salt or cinnamon or nutmeg did the trick and I tasted it and it was perfect goodness. As if the right combination of spices had been there all along, waiting for me to stumble on it.

CHAPTER 23

Four-o'clocks were originally grown for their medicinal properties. It's possible a nibble on these sweet flowers could cure what ails you, but I don't recommend you try it. Instead, enjoy the tender blooms that open, as their name suggests, in the late afternoon and last through the sultry evening hours.
—WENDELL BANCROFT SR., *LATE BLOOMERS*

JESSIE

I want it big and loose, with flowers and vines and those twirly little sticks tucked all around the lights."

Olivia was on a roll. I'd called her to talk about the chandelier I'd asked Harvis to build to hang from the rafters of the boathouse where the ceremony would take place. Up until this point, I'd thought the chandelier would be purely decorative—a way to add some greenery to the space and make the most of the tall ceiling and gorgeous rafters. Now I wasn't sure.

"Lights?" I asked.

"It shouldn't be too hard to run electricity to it, right? Just run a line from the plug on one of the posts—I know there's at least one because we used to have a radio out there that we had to plug in. Or— ooh! What if we used candles instead?"

She'd taken to calling me on her morning treks to the subway.

There was always a lot of background noise—voices, engines, horns, screeches, squeals—but she was never short on ideas, and her voice rang clear and crisp over the din.

"What do you think? Candles would be romantic, right? Much more so than lightbulbs, even if we did use those cool Edison bulbs."

"Romantic, yes, although I don't know how safe it'd be to have open flames near a bunch of combustible greenery." Not to mention I had my doubts about whether Mr. Rainwater could construct the thing at all, much less outfit it with candles. I thought it was probably best not to mention the fact that I'd asked the elderly gentleman from down the road to build her chandelier.

"Hmm. Good point."

"Unless . . ." As my gaze landed on the grapevine wreath hanging on the inside of Twig's front door, a loose vision began to clarify itself in my mind—lengths of grapevine twisted together to form a large oval suspended parallel from the rafters. Eucalyptus leaves, dried seed pods, and simple flowers tucked in here and there. Tea-light candles suspended in mini glass jars hanging from the chandelier but well below the greenery. She'd have her natural look and the romantic glow of candles but without the risk of burning the place down. "Let me think on it a bit. I may have an idea."

❦

I texted Sumner after lunch: If you don't mind, I'd like to come by again to measure some spaces in the boathouse. We're working on a chandelier.

Less than half a minute later, he responded: What about tonight?

Then a moment later: Maybe we could have dinner too, if you don't have plans.

My thumbs hovered over the screen. A few days before, I'd so boldly—so quickly—said yes to his offer of a "real date," but now I was second-guessing my spontaneity.

I'd call and ask you like a proper gentleman, but I'm in a meeting that isn't anywhere near over. A bunch of suits sitting around talking money and turf grass. You'd hate it.

You assume I don't know anything about grass. I do have a horticulture degree.

A few seconds ticked by, then: I stand corrected. How about my house, 7:00. Bring your tape measure, then I'll take you out and you can astound me with your horticultural insights.

I bit my lip. See you then.

❧

A few hours later, Evan entered the shop through the back door, her face pink and damp, her knees covered in dirt smudges. She went straight to the sink at the back and dunked her arms under the cold water, then cupped water in her hands and poured it over the back of her neck. I could hear her sigh of relief all the way in the front of the shop.

Once I made the decision to fill her week with chores after her little jaunt down the road with Nick, it hadn't been hard to find extra work for her to do. Weeding near the back fence as she'd been doing today, unloading shipments, watering, loading customers' cars, helping with home deliveries—it was everything she normally did, just more of it. I even tasked her with making up some of the small arrangements I kept on the front table. She actually seemed to enjoy those, and I made a mental note to give her that responsibility more often.

It wasn't that I didn't like Nick—he was a likable kid, and with Ben as his father, he no doubt had a decent amount of goodness deep inside. It was more that I feared what he represented: Evan was growing up. Along with that would come the desire to experiment, to push against her boundaries, to figure out who she was and who she wanted to become. I'd gone so haywire in my pursuit of who I'd mistakenly thought I wanted to be, it made my head and heart pound to think of her making the same mistakes—or worse—in her quest to become her own woman. I couldn't force her down a certain path, but it was so hard to let her make her own way. Learning to walk on her own feet was a necessary part of growing up, but that didn't mean I couldn't rein her in when necessary.

"You okay?" I called to her once she turned off the water and held a towel up to her face. "Late afternoon's pretty hot for weeding. Why don't you work on something else and hold off on the rest of that until the morning?"

She shook her head. "I'm almost finished. I don't want to have to do it again tomorrow."

"Okay, then what about using my stool? If you sit on that, your knees won't hurt as bad."

"The little old lady stool? No thanks. My knees are fine."

"Suit yourself." I would have corrected her for her jab about the stool, but the truth was if I didn't use the stool, an hour or two of kneeling in the garden made my knees feel creaky. I was thankful for the little old lady stool.

She pulled a can of Sprite from the fridge and took a long swig.

"I'm headed back out to the river after we close up here today. Will you be okay with Gus?"

"Sure." She turned but then paused with her hand on the door. "Can I come? I kind of want to see this guy's fancy house."

I hesitated. Any other time I'd jump at the chance to spend nearly an hour of uninterrupted time in the car with my daughter. Especially if she was the one to suggest it. But the dinner. What would he say if I showed up with Evan and bailed on our date? He didn't seem to be the kind of man who'd get upset over something like that—after all, he had a daughter. Surely he'd understand me wanting to spend time with mine.

"You know what? Don't worry about it. It was just a thought."

"Oh no, honey, it's fine. Let me just—"

"It's okay. It's better that I stay here anyway. Gus just discovered *The Gilmore Girls* on Netflix and loves it. She needs me around so I can translate Lorelai and Rory's conversations." Evan pushed open the screen door and breezed out. As the door thudded closed behind her, something in me splintered. My throat was tight and pinpricks jabbed behind my eyes, but I blinked them away.

❦

Sunset on Sumner's dock was just as beautiful as it had been the first time I showed up at his house. At least this time I managed to stay on my feet and act like a mature adult. I was thankful, however, that he couldn't hear the hammering in my heart.

To be honest, I hadn't decided what exactly I thought about him. I was completely bewildered by his attention and captivated by his charm, his polish, his confidence. But occasionally, a quiet, annoying voice said, *Watch out,* and I knew it was in no small part because of my ex-husband.

Chris had appeared in my life in a similarly random way, and he had been equally as attractive and captivating. It was him, his life, his prominence. He was seductive, just as Sumner was. Was I letting myself head down the same wrong road again, or was Sumner different? He certainly felt different. Not that I was necessarily looking for different. I wasn't looking for anyone at all.

As a single mother who worked in the dirt, had failed at marriage, and practically lived with my mother, I was not the prime candidate to date anyone, much less someone like Sumner, but he was here and he was asking. He thought I was intriguing. Standing on his dock in my loose summery dress with my hair pulled up and gloss on my lips, I felt leagues out of my comfort zone, which would make Mama happy. It felt vaguely like I was taking a nosedive off a high cliff, but it felt good too. I'd said no a lot. Maybe it was time to say yes.

It didn't take long to decide where the chandelier should hang and to measure out the necessary space. I snapped a few photos and drew a quick sketch of my plan. Before long, we were in his Land Rover headed east as the sky faded to a pastel sunset.

About a mile past the Dog River bridge, Sumner slowed at a small house. A wooden sign out front pronounced it Donny's. With a name like that, I'd expected another casual restaurant much like Honey's River Kitchen with its neon signs in the windows and crowds milling outside, not this charming cottage nestled in the trees. A wide porch on two sides offered outside seating, and tables inside were lit with candles.

Sumner opened my door and held out his arm. He wore another white button-down shirt, open at the neck, well-fitting khaki pants, and brown Sperry boat shoes, the picture of coastal elegance. We fell into step together on the way to the front door. Around us, a tropical breeze swirled my dress around my thighs and lifted tendrils of hair around my face.

Inside, the hostess showed us to a small table in the corner. Three candles sat in the center where wax dripped lazily down the sides and hardened in place at the bottom of the mercury glass holder. The window next to our table was raised, and the breeze made the flames jump and dart.

"The name Donny's doesn't exactly sound Italian," I said.

"The owner is first-generation Italian. From Naples."

"Donny?"

"Donatella Marchetti," he said with a smile. "Donny for short."

"Ah. I see. And you know her well?"

"Donny knows everyone well. She greets all her guests and she never forgets a name. Here she comes now." He nodded over my shoulder.

I turned to see a very small, very old woman walking toward us. Her gray hair was piled atop her head, and she wore a beautiful silk dress in a deep burnt orange. Her eyes crinkled as she leaned down and kissed Sumner on one cheek, then the other. "You haven't been in to see me in a while."

"I'm sorry," Sumner said. "I've been busy. Out of town a lot. And my daughter is getting married."

"Ah, *bella*. Please send her my love. She will always be the little one riding her bicycle on my front porch."

He laughed. "I'll tell her that. She probably hasn't ridden a bicycle in—well, at least not since she moved to New York."

As if just noticing he wasn't alone, Donny glanced at me, then back at Sumner. She winked. "Another pretty lady." Sumner's smile faded and he shifted in his seat. Donny looked back at me expectantly, but I didn't know what to say.

"Donny, this is Jessie. She's—"

"I'm doing the flowers for his daughter's wedding."

I felt Sumner's eyes on me, but I kept mine on Donny. She patted me on the shoulder. "Thank you for taking care of things for him. He needs all the help he can get."

"Well, I don't know anything about that, but I'm happy to help."

She shuffled away as another couple came through the door, ushering in a fresh warm breeze from outside.

"That was awkward." He gazed at me as if to measure my discomfort level.

I shrugged and shook my head. "It's fine. She seems sweet."

"She is. She's deceptively sharp too. A quick mind in that little body."

"She seems to know you well. This must be where you bring all the girls." I said it jokingly, but to my horror, it came out sounding petty. "I'm sorry. I really didn't mean that. She just said the thing about the ladies . . ." Embarrassed, I took a sip of water to hide the heat blazing from my cheeks.

He propped his elbows on the table and rubbed a hand across his forehead. "The last time I was here, I was with a woman," he said matter-of-factly. "It was a few months ago. Donny obviously doesn't forget anything." He straightened when a waitress brought two glasses of red wine. "Oh, we haven't—"

"They're on the house." She pointed her chin across the room. Donny stood near the front door and winked at us.

"While I'm here, let me tell you about our specials." With hands clasped behind her back, the waitress rattled off an impressive list of seafood and pasta dishes. "Our desserts for this evening are fresh peach galette and chocolate bourbon bread pudding."

I moaned and Sumner laughed. "You must have a sweet tooth."

"A small one, yes. Bread pudding is my weakness."

He glanced up at the waitress. "We'll take a minute on the menu, but go ahead and put us down for a bread pudding."

"No problem."

As the candle flickered and conversation around us dipped and swelled, I sipped my wine and skimmed the menu. The shrimp and angel hair pasta was my choice, as was the Caesar salad. Sumner ordered a steak.

With the menus out of the way, nothing was between us except the candles and a few feet of rustic, gnarled oak. Everyone around us was relaxed. Wineglasses and forks clinked and laughter rippled from across the room, but my nerves returned. Thankfully he broke the silence.

"When I was in college, I planted a flower bed in front of my house to impress a girl."

"Did it work?"

He shook his head. "She had to cancel our date—she had a cold or something—and by the time we went out a couple weeks later, all the plants had died."

"All of them?"

"Every single one. Turned out the nursery where I'd bought them had unknowingly sold a bunch of plants infested with bugs in the roots. Some kind of weevil?"

I nodded. "They're a killer."

"Yes, they were. Another customer found them when he was planting the ones he'd bought and threatened to sue."

I laughed. "Oh no!"

"Yep. I wasn't quite that mad, but I was sure I would've gotten a second date with Elizabeth if my flower bed had survived. I didn't know it yet, but she had quite a green thumb."

"So you must've gotten another date with her at some point."

"Oh yes." He looked down at his lap for a moment, then back up at me. "I married her."

I widened my eyes. "Oh. Then you got more than just a second date."

"I got her for twenty-four years." He took a drink of water. "She died eight years ago. Olivia was eighteen."

"Oh, Sumner."

He leaned back in his chair and fiddled with the edge of his white linen napkin. "It was really sudden—a blood clot that the doctors thought started somewhere in her leg. We were on vacation and she had some pain in her right leg, but we didn't think much of it. She got up one night, to go to the bathroom, I assume . . . She was on the floor before I was even fully awake."

I closed my eyes. "I'm so sorry."

He wrinkled his nose and glanced around the room. "It's weird, it's . . . different now. I still miss her, but I'm not as . . . gutted as I was back then."

Gutted. It was the same word I'd used to describe to a friend how I felt after learning about Chris's infidelities. I was humiliated, angry, heartbroken—I was gutted. Yet this man across from me—the man with the fancy car, the enviable house, the Gregory Peck good looks—he was acquainted with a level of pain that far surpassed my own. In that respect, he and Mama were on equal footing. Two spouses, two sudden, shocking deaths. I still felt Daddy's absence as a dull throb in my chest, but for Mama, I wondered if after all these years, his death was still sharp as a razor.

When it came down to it, no amount of money or influence, kindness or spunk could protect you from death, whether the death of your other half or the death of a marriage. Love hurt when it ended, and my experience—and that of so many other people—was that love usually ended. Some way, somehow.

Without thinking I reached across the table and squeezed his hand. He looked up at me and smiled. Hooked his thumb over mine for a moment.

The waitress appeared then with a tray of food. I pulled my hand away to make room for the dishes she set down. Sumner chatted with her a moment, then she moved to the next table and we dug into our food.

It was exquisite, of course. The pasta was lemony and creamy, the shrimp plump, the salad crisp and tangy. Across the table Sumner's steak was red and marbled, and it smelled heavenly. When he noticed me eyeing it, he cut off a bite and held it out to me on his fork. "Want to try it?"

I looked down at my fork, unsure of how to transfer the bite from his to mine.

"It's okay. No germs here."

I smiled and leaned over the table. He lifted the bite a little higher and I took it in my mouth. It was warm and juicy, and I tasted cracked peppercorn and a little garlic.

"Mmm." The throaty sound escaped before I had a chance to bite it back.

"Good?"

I nodded, a little embarrassed by what felt like more than just a simple act of sharing food.

He cleared his throat. Maybe he'd noticed it too. "So tell me about your . . . ex, I presume? Although by now, I should know not to presume someone is divorced. I've found not many people advertise their widowed status."

I took a sip of water. "I can see that. But yes, he is my ex. We've been divorced almost ten years now."

"Does he live close by?"

"He's in Birmingham. We haven't seen him in . . . I guess it's been two years. He was in Mobile for a dental conference and he came by to see Evan."

"Two years? I can't imagine staying away from my daughter for anywhere close to that long. Especially when she was young."

I gave a half shrug. "He has other kids now—they're a lot younger than Evan, so I think he stays pretty busy."

"Wow. And Evan's okay with not seeing him much?"

"Oh yeah. She sulks for days when she knows he's coming. It's not pretty."

He laughed. "You seem very accepting of the situation."

"Well, it is what it is, you know? I think it's probably easier for him to focus on what he has now rather than what we used to have. It got . . . Well, it was ugly for a while. I'm much happier without him, and the only memories Evan has of him aren't particularly good. Life is better this way, I think."

It was a simple answer, but was it true? I'd long ago developed a script to explain away the dissolution of our marriage, and though I hadn't had to use it in a while, it rolled off my tongue now as easy as ever. The words didn't quite sit as well with me as they used to, however. Yes, deep down my life was better without him in it—more truthful, in some way—but that didn't mean it felt wholly complete. It always felt like there was some small part, some missing puzzle piece I couldn't get my fingers on, as much as I tried to grasp it.

He watched me over the top of his water glass. It was obvious he knew I wasn't giving him the whole picture. There was so much more I could say, but how did you tell someone your husband cheated on you—had a whole other private life you weren't aware of—without coming off as completely naive and pathetic? In the face of Sumner's true tragedy and loss, no way was I ready to let him in on the soap opera that had been my life, the one that had starred a cheating husband and the family he left behind.

I caught the eye of the waitress and gave a small wave. "How about that bread pudding?"

Over dessert, the conversation was easier. He asked me about getting Twig up and running, and I asked him about his work.

"I saw the article in last month's *Southern Living*. It said you're in golf course design. What does that mean? Do you lay out the holes?"

He nodded. "We do everything from designing whole courses to remodeling existing ones. Sometimes it's as small as laying out a new fairway, and other times it's working with clients to scout new locations for entire golf communities and using GPS to build the courses."

"So it's more than deciding how to keep the sun out of golfers' faces when they're playing?"

"You joke, but that's part of it. We have this software that lets us see whether a particular hole will have the sun in your face at 4:00 p.m. in March or at 9:00 a.m. in August."

"Wow."

"I can see you're completely fascinated."

"No, it's just—it's a career I didn't even know existed, but I can see you're passionate about it."

He twirled the stem of his wineglass back and forth. "I am. I've always enjoyed golf, and I grew to love architecture and design in college. This was a way for me to build on all that. I like knowing that

I'm making it more enjoyable for others to play the sport that makes them happy and helps them relax. It's my way of adding a little beauty to the world. You do the same thing, right? You cultivate beauty and make it so other people can enjoy it at their own homes."

"I guess so. I do like the idea of spreading beauty and helping other people enjoy it." I was quiet a moment. There was more to it for me, though it was hard to put into words. "I think the part I like best is that I can take this seemingly dead—or at least empty—patch of dirt and nurture it and feed it until it becomes something new. Something alive."

He took a sip of wine. "You're very poetic."

"Only on my good days."

When we'd scraped the last bit out of the dish of pudding, we both sat back in our seats. The waning candlelight made his eyes sparkle, a deep chocolate brown that seemed even darker there in the dim corner of the room.

I'd begun the evening with my guard partially up, worried about the similarities between Sumner and Chris, but the truth was Sumner's charm, thoughtfulness, and humor had whittled it down. I'd let myself enjoy his attention, which was copious and focused only on me. His gaze, which had made me feel tight and nervous at the beginning of the evening, now made my smile loose and my shoulders relaxed.

When the waitress slid the check onto our table, he checked his watch. "It's getting late. You still have a drive ahead of you."

On the way out, he stopped at the front counter to pay the bill. Though I was no longer in the dating scene, even I knew not to protest if a man offered to pay for dinner. It was one of the first things Mama taught me years ago when she talked to me about dating. In hindsight, I should have been less concerned about Southern-style manners and more attentive to the kinds of men to stay away from. Men like Chris who saw their wealth and importance as a permission slip to do whatever they pleased, no matter who they hurt in the process.

As Sumner waited for his receipt to print, he chatted easily with Donny and the hostess. He carried himself confidently, as if he expected those around him to laugh and participate in the conversation with him, just as Chris had done. But Sumner wasn't like Chris. They were vastly different men. When we talked, his attention never once strayed. He made me feel like I was the only person in the room. He didn't showcase his wealth like a badge of honor. Plus, he was a total goner for his daughter, something I'd never sensed in Chris.

Sumner walked toward me now, calling good-byes over his shoulder. When he reached me, he extended his elbow. I slipped my arm though his and we walked across the lot to his car. I was mostly silent on the short drive to his house, my mind muddied by the food, the warm air, and the competing thoughts swirling in my mind.

Back in his driveway, I climbed out and unlocked my car. Finally I turned and faced him.

"I'm glad you said yes to tonight," he said.

"I am too."

"Now it'll be less awkward the next time I find you trying to break into my back gate."

I laughed in spite of myself. "Won't happen again. I promise."

"I don't mind if it does. Oh, I almost forgot." He turned back to his car and grabbed a small brown box off the passenger seat. *Donny's* was stamped across the top in a swirly script. "I asked them to box you up an extra bread pudding. You can share it with Evan and your mom." He grinned. "Or not."

"Thank you. Tonight was such a treat."

"I have to admit, I wanted to impress you."

"Well, you did that, but I would have been impressed with much less. I live in Perry, remember? Our nicest restaurant is Berta's BBQ."

I expected a laugh, but instead he leaned toward me and softly kissed my cheek. "Don't sell yourself short. I think you're enchanting. I don't know what happened with your ex-husband or what made the situation ugly, but I know he's an idiot. He'd have to be to let you go."

I stood frozen still, unable to unclench my fingers. My cheek throbbed where his lips had touched it.

"I'd like to see you again. Soon, if that's okay with you."

"Sure," I said, forcing my mouth to work. "I'll be working with Mr.—with a friend to make Olivia's chandelier, then I'll need to make some phone calls and see if I can get her flowers in the right quantities. I can—"

I stopped when he laughed softly. "I don't mean about the wedding. I just want to see you. Flowers or no flowers."

The light above his garage was behind him, casting his face in deep shadow. I could just make out the slight dimple in his cheek and the angle of his jaw. He reached out and touched my arm. I nodded.

"Okay then," he said. "I'll make sure it happens."

A moment later, safe inside the cocoon of my car, I exhaled, long and deep. I closed my eyes for a second, then turned down the driveway. The tunnel of trees was ghostlike against the dark, and above, a universe of stars spilled across the sky. It was a night for air, so I left the window down and let the breeze carry me back home.

CHAPTER 24

*If critters get to your tomatoes before you can pick and enjoy
them, try picking them earlier—as soon as you see a little pink
on the skin—and let them ripen inside on a windowsill.*
—EDWIN NICKERBOCKER, *1916 TREATISE ON TOMATOES*

JESSIE

The next morning I slept in. I usually woke to an internal alarm clock around six thirty, but after my date with Sumner, I managed to stay blissfully asleep an extra two hours. I only woke then because a crow had decided to land on a tree branch outside my window and *caw, caw* at every other crow in Perry, resulting in a cacophony of crows serenading me awake. Not exactly the soft wake-up process I'd prefer.

I'd lain awake in bed the previous night until well past midnight, despite the fact that I'd arrived home at ten. I tried to sneak in but it was to no avail. Mama stuck her head out of the kitchen and into the darkened hall as I tiptoed toward my bedroom.

"How was your date?"

"How'd you know it was a date?" I'd escaped earlier in the evening without giving her any details.

"Evan said you were going back over to Sumner's. In my book if a man invites a woman anywhere in the evening, it's considered a date."

"What if—?" I stopped. No use arguing. "It was nice."

"Nice." She pondered the word a moment, then shouldered her bag. "I guess it's time for me to get going." Instead of a more typical barrage of questions, she just gathered her books and shuffled toward the door.

"Everything okay?"

"Oh, I'm fine. Just a little tired. I think I'll see if I can find *The Golden Girls* on TV, then call it a night."

Mama had always loved *The Golden Girls*. She fancied herself a Blanche, and in some ways she was. She could give a powerful stink-eye and wouldn't dream of going out in public without her hair combed and fluffed. But in personality, she was Sophia through and through—wisecracking and honest to a fault.

As I turned off the lights in the kitchen, I saw the small dry-erase board tacked to the front of the fridge.

Cheese
Raisins
Milk
Pine mulch coming Tuesday
Mama—Dr. Dudley Aug. 9

Dr. Dudley was supposed to be one of the best neurologists in Mobile, as evidenced by the long wait to get in to see him. I just hoped he'd tell us her memory lapses and confusion were normal parts of the aging process and nothing more.

Between thoughts of her and my fluctuating, indecipherable feelings about Sumner and my nagging disappointment about Ben and Marissa, as ridiculous and unjustified as that disappointment was, I was awake for hours after I turned off my light. I knew I'd be a tired mess the next day, but turning my brain off proved difficult. Finally, after cycling through my go-to methods of falling asleep, my brain gave up the fight.

I lay in bed the next morning until the crows all flew away in tandem, taking their cackling ruckus with them. The silence left behind was nearly as loud as the crows had been. Strange how the absence of something could sometimes be louder than the presence of it.

❧

Whenever a business in Perry asked me to plant their flower beds, I included a midseason upkeep, where I returned and deadheaded as necessary, pinching off spent leaves or blooms, and pulled stray weeds that poked up through the mulch. Today's list included Kim's Café, Jack & Mack's, and Cliff's Computer World. Since Cliff's was on the shady side of the street, I started with his beds.

Twenty minutes passed before Cliff came out to say hi. "Ms. McBride, I've just finished up with the fire department's computers, so I can take a look at yours if you're still having trouble."

I sat back on my heels and peered up at him from under Evan's olive-green military cap. It was the only hat I could find this morning as I rushed out the door.

"Well . . . ," I began, but another voice spoke over me.

"Already got her covered."

Ben walked down the street toward us, a to-go cup from Kim's Café in his hand and a beat-up leather messenger bag slung across his chest. The sight of him was so clear, so reassuring, it was as if I'd half expected to see him. As if after a night with Sumner—surprising, invigorating, refreshingly new—of course Ben would appear with his thick, wavy hair, his beard, his broad shoulders, and his soft brown eyes.

When he reached us, he smiled down at me and reached out a hand to pull me up. When I was on my feet, he turned to Cliff and extended his hand. "Ben Bradley."

"Cliff Baker. You stealing my customers?" Cliff laughed, but there was an edge to it.

"Wouldn't dream of it. Just doing a favor for a friend." Ben turned to me. "You have plans tonight?"

"Um, I . . . No, I don't think so. Why?"

"You do now. My house, seven o'clock." He paused. "We're painting."

"You fixed it? Are you serious?"

"Wait one minute." Cliff held his hand up. "Jessie, do you know this fella?" He took a step closer to me and lowered his voice. "Does he have any credentials for this kind of job?"

I glanced up at Ben, trying to keep a straight face. "I'm not actually sure about his credentials, but I think he's fine. I'll tell you what though. If I have any problems with it, I'll let you know."

"You do that." He nodded at Ben, then turned back to his shop. "The flowers are great, by the way. As usual."

When the door jangled closed, Ben laughed. "So that's my competition in Perry, huh?"

"I don't think you have to worry about him."

"Good." He adjusted the strap across his chest and checked his watch, then muttered under his breath. "I have to get home. I've got a conference call with a tech company in Denver in five minutes. But I'll see you at seven."

"I'll be there."

He headed back down the sidewalk. Before he turned the corner, he called back to me, "Wear your painting clothes. And come hungry."

❧

I walked the half mile to Ben's that night. When I arrived, Nick was backing out of the driveway. He slowed next to me and rolled down his window. "Hi, Ms. McBride."

"Hey, Nick. You're not sticking around to help us paint?"

He shook his head and dragged his fingers through his hair, a pure Ben gesture. "I've been working all day in there, ripping up carpet and pulling adhesive off the floor. I'm taking a break. Some of the guys from the team are getting together to watch the Braves game."

"Good for you. I'm glad you're making friends."

He tapped a beat on the steering wheel with his thumbs, then glanced back up at me. "I'm sorry again for the other day with Evan. I just thought if we were on an empty road . . ."

"I know. Just remember she's only fourteen."

"Yes, ma'am."

So much of Nick reminded me of Ben at that age. Arm out the window, freedom in his eyes, the whole world ahead of him. We thought we owned our destinies, but we were such babies, so unaware of all life would throw at us.

"She'd hate me for saying this, but even at fourteen, she's still my little girl."

"You don't have to worry. It won't happen again."

"All right. Get out of here then. When you get back, things will look different in your house."

He jerked the gearshift into Drive. "Good. Anything's better than the bright green my grandmother liked."

Inside, I found Ben stretching blue painter's tape in the sunroom at the back of the house. I smoothed my hand over the wall as green as mint ice cream. "You've got a big job ahead of you."

He peered at me over his shoulder. "We have a big job ahead of us." He climbed down off the stepladder, pulling a stray piece of tape off his forearm. "I didn't hear you come in."

"I'm here. And I'm ready to work, although I have to say, whatever you have cooking in the kitchen smells amazing."

He grinned. "Pizza. And I'm starving. Let's eat first, then we can paint."

I followed him to the kitchen. He opened the fridge and gestured over his shoulder to the desk by the back door. "Check out your computer."

I inhaled. "You're a lifesaver. Truly." I opened the top and was greeted with a familiar screen and a box asking for my password. When I entered it, the screen blinked to life. All my file folders stood in a row, as they always did: Invoices, Shipments, Requests, Deliveries.

"I'll be honest." He held out a Blue Moon he'd pulled from the fridge. He raised his eyebrows. I nodded and took it from him. "You'll want to think about replacing it soon. You've gotten more life out of that laptop than most people do."

He grabbed a beer for himself, then handed me a package of paper plates. "Hope you don't mind paper."

"Not at all. Less to clean up later."

"My parents' dishwasher broke years ago and they never fixed it. Mom didn't mind washing dishes by hand, but if I'm going to sell this place, it'll need a working dishwasher."

"Is that your plan? To sell the house?"

He grabbed a dish towel and pulled a pizza stone from the oven. On top was a bubbling thin-crust pizza covered in fluffy mounds of mozzarella, greens, and thinly sliced tomatoes. "I don't know yet." He set the stone on top of the oven. "Probably. It feels weird being back in this house again. Not bad, just . . . not me anymore. Then again, everything's pretty up in the air these days. It's hard to say anything definite right now."

Something in his voice shifted. He almost sounded annoyed. I was curious but didn't press.

After cutting the pizza and sliding slices onto our plates, we sat at the small kitchen table. Ben twisted the caps off our beers, then held his out to me. "To fixing broken things."

I smiled and clinked my bottle to his.

While we ate, we talked about Mama's upcoming appointment with the doctor and about Nick and Evan's afternoon drive.

He shook his head. "I let him have it for that. I think he just got a little bored, and honestly, I think he's found a friend in Evan." He shrugged. "They seem to be cut from the same cloth."

"I can see that. She thinks a lot of him. But then again, of course she does. He's a cute boy and he's older, therefore *way* cooler. I remember pretty clearly what seventeen-year-old boys were thinking about."

"Yeah, I bet you do. You had the entire football team at your beck and call back then."

I laughed. "How can you even say that? I was sitting out on that driveway almost every day, watching you mess around under the hood of your Jeep."

"I guess you're right. But I don't think Nick's like most teenage guys. He really has a good head on his shoulders. He'll look out for Evan when school starts."

When we finished eating, I grabbed our plates and tossed them in the trash. "Okay, boss, I'm ready to pay off my debt. Put me to work."

"Gladly." He led me to his old bedroom at the end of the hall. "I've almost finished taping in here, but I didn't get to that one window and around the baseboards. Why don't you finish that up and I'll go grab the paint from the garage?"

His footsteps receded down the hall and the back door opened and then closed. I took a step toward the dresser to grab the roll of painter's tape, and as I did, I noticed a partially unrolled poster sticking out of one of the drawers. Red and gold, along with a smidge of bright-green turf, peeked out from the roll, and I instantly knew what it was. I unrolled the poster, then sat back on my heels and took a deep breath.

Scowling up from the poster was the entire Perry High School football team, circa 1997. Just in front of the team were the cheerleaders, our smiles bright and open, our hair smoothed and sprayed, the sequins on our uniforms sparkling in the sunshine.

I remembered the moment like it was yesterday. The photographer took the photo in the morning, before first period. The turf was still damp with dew and most of the girls complained that their legs were getting wet. Each of us knelt in front of "our" football player, our pom-poms held at waist level, Carol Anne yelling at us to smile like we meant it. Behind me, Ben was singing under his breath, making me laugh, resulting in my eyes closed in laughter and Ben being captured with his mouth open, in mid-verse. It was such a picture of how we were with each other, it made my chest ache. Without thinking, I leaned down and touched my fingers to his face in the photo.

"See anyone familiar?" I hadn't heard him return and his voice startled me.

"A whole bunch of kids is all I see." I rolled up the poster, tighter this time, and stuck it back in the drawer.

Ben poured paint—a creamy neutral khaki—into two trays and handed me a roller. We got to work, Ben on one wall, me on the other. All the furniture was lumped together in the center away from the walls, so all I could see of him was his head over the clutter between us.

After just a few minutes, he stopped. "We need music." He left the room and returned a moment later with an almost suitcase-sized stereo and something black tucked under his arm. He set the stereo down on the floor and plugged it in.

I ran my hand across its dusty top. "I haven't seen one of these in so long. Was it yours?"

"Yeah. I can't believe my parents kept it. It was out in the garage. But it's perfect for these." He set the black zippered case down.

When he pulled his hand away, I saw the familiar black-and-white Case Logic logo at the bottom. "You still have it."

"Yep." He zipped it open and handed it to me.

I took it and rested my hand on the top. "What is it with all these old things? Your Jeep, the stereo, a case full of CDs. It's like nothing's changed with you."

I said it as a joke, but he only smiled, one side of his mouth pulling up slowly. "Maybe it hasn't. Maybe I just found what I liked early on and stuck with it." He nodded toward the case. "Go ahead. It's a great trip down memory lane."

I flipped through the pages and breathed in all our old favorites. Blues Traveler, the Black Crowes, R.E.M., U2, Dave Matthews Band. I pulled out the liner notes of *Remember Two Things* and held them in front of my face. I tried to let my eyes slide out of focus. "Remember how we'd spend afternoons trying to see the 3-D image on the cover?"

"I remember *you* trying. I had no problem. You were the one who could never see it. What about now?"

I shook my head. "Still nothing."

I replaced it and flipped another page, then gasped. "*August and Everything After*. I thought you didn't like Counting Crows." I looked up at him. "You always made fun of my crush on Adam Duritz."

He shrugged. "Maybe I was jealous."

I reached over and punched his leg lightly. "Whatever."

"It's a good thing you made me listen to them on repeat. I decided later on that they weren't so bad."

"Not so bad?" I clutched my chest in mock horror, then pulled the CD out and handed it to him. "Play it straight through, please."

"Yes, ma'am."

We picked up our brushes again. The familiar verses and choruses swirled around me, mixing with the breeze from the fan above, the lingering scents of mozzarella and spicy tomato sauce, and the evening serenade of nighttime sounds outside the open window. As my arm reached and dipped, leaving clean swaths of fresh paint behind, I was finally able to let my mind relax. Being in Ben's presence was comforting. Relaxing. It was the same way I felt on all those afternoons we spent together. It still felt good.

Then I remembered Marissa. Did she feel a similar rush of calm when she was with Ben? I pushed the thought away. How they were together didn't matter. In a way, knowing he was in a relationship with someone so important freed me to enjoy my time with him with no pressure or expectation.

We finished the first coat quickly and moved into the master bedroom, where the mint green was in full effect.

Before he dipped his roller in paint, he ducked out of the room and returned with two more bottles of beer. When he held one out to me, I hesitated but then took it. By my estimation we'd still be working for a while, and anyway, I'd walked to his house. The walk home would clear any fuzziness. We picked up our rollers again.

An hour and a half later, we were back in Ben's bedroom, sitting on the floor with our backs against the dresser. While finishing the second coats on both rooms, we'd gone from Counting Crows to Tom Petty's *Wildflowers* to Smashing Pumpkins and now were listening to U2's *The Joshua Tree*.

I settled against the dresser. "I'm so glad you still have all this music. It's like a portal to high school."

"Back in your glory days?"

I turned my head to face him. "Glory days? Funny. Not quite."

"Really? I would have figured those were your best years."

I let out a snort of laughter. The two beers had loosened me.

"I'm sorry. That was . . . I didn't mean that." He rubbed the side of his face. "I just mean you seemed happy. You saw your face in that poster. You couldn't hide that big, beaming smile if you tried."

"That was because you were singing like a goof behind me."

He smiled and stretched his legs out straight in front of him. He was wearing a dark-green T-shirt that clung to his chest. His blue jeans were frayed at the bottom edges and his feet were bare.

"I think I'm happier than I used to be," I continued. "I know more now."

"There's something good about being blissfully ignorant though, right? For a little while, at least."

I thought about that a moment. There was plenty I wish I didn't know, hadn't experienced.

When he spoke again, his voice was much quieter. "What happened with you and Chris? If you don't mind me asking. I thought life with him was great."

"Who told you that?"

He caught the hard edge in my voice and looked at me, then shrugged. "I guess I just assumed. Rich dentist, successful family. What's not to love?"

"Yep. That's all you need. Money and influence, then it's smooth sailing, right? Things just fall into place."

Thankfully he ignored my sarcasm. "So what went wrong?"

I tilted my head to the side and sighed. "He got bored with me. So he moved on."

Ben exhaled and cursed quietly.

I leaned my head back and closed my eyes. The details weren't hard to dredge up. They were always there, just under the surface, ready to knock me back down anytime I thought I'd finally gotten past it.

I took a deep breath. I hadn't told anyone, not even Mama, all the details of the day I found out everything. It was so ugly and hurtful, I usually just gave the bare minimum, enough to get the point across, and left it at that. But the hushed privacy of the room, the dark night outside, and Ben's steady warmth next to me made the words spill out. I told him everything—the hygienist with her hands in my mouth, her whispers, the realization that my marriage was broken and I was the last to know.

When I finished, a beat of silence ticked by. I reached for the tray next to me, where paint had dried in little rivulets along the edges. I picked at the dried bits with my thumbnail. "It sounds bad, what he did. And it was. But I was to blame for part of it."

Ben ran his hand roughly through his hair. "How can you say that?"

I flicked the dried paint onto the drop cloth. "I pretended to be someone I wasn't." I shrugged. "He liked *that* Jessie. She just wasn't me. I guess I kind of set myself up for it all."

I was about to gather our supplies when he spoke again. "Jessie, I'm so sorry that happened to you. But nothing you did could possibly make his actions your fault. That's on *him*, not you."

I shrugged again. "I was good at pretending though. You know that."

He bent his legs and leaned forward on his knees. "But you never pretended with me. From day one, when I made you drive my Jeep down the road, you were always different with me than you were at school." He closed his eyes a moment. "It was like you let that other Jessie slide off your back and the real you came out."

"That's how it felt to me too."

"Why did you let me in?"

"I don't know. You were . . ." I took a deep breath. "You were always the same." I picked at a smudge of tan paint on my wrist and tried to explain. "My dad was infuriatingly consistent. It used to drive Mama crazy how he'd follow his same routines day after day: wake up, sing in the shower, shave in her sink, make a cup of instant coffee that she said smelled up her kitchen. At night, he'd shower again, put on his striped pajamas, and watch *Law & Order*. Always the same."

I smiled, remembering Daddy's skinny ankles sticking out of those striped pajama pants. "But it was comforting that he never changed. It was the same with you. I always knew exactly what I'd get with you, and it was always something good. It made you feel . . . safe."

Ben was silent, and I had the distinct and sharp realization that I'd said too much. All of it, all evening. I sat up and leaned my arms over my knees to avoid his eyes. "Or maybe these two beers have just messed with my memories."

I gathered our paintbrushes and stood. He hesitated, then did the same, collecting buckets and rollers. By no spoken word, the evening had ended. It was time for me to go home.

"I have a plastic sheet outside." He pushed open the back door. "Just leave the brushes there and I'll clean them off later."

We laid our brushes side by side, then he walked me around the side of the house to the front. The night air was still and warm but not uncomfortable. Down the road, an owl hooted, calling to a friend or maybe a mate.

At the end of the driveway, we stopped. "Thank you for dinner. And the music. It was fun."

He started to say something but then stopped.

"What is it?" I asked. The garage light behind him shone down the driveway but didn't quite make it to the street. He was mostly a dark form in front of me, the curves of his shoulders just edges in the darkness.

He crossed his arms in front of his chest and stared down at his feet. "I wished for so long that I could've been the one to go through it all with you. Marriage, kids, figuring out life together. I tried. I wanted to be the one."

A fist clenched in my chest, squeezing out all my air. I opened my mouth, but he went on. "It sounds crazy now, especially knowing everything that happened with the two of you, but back then, I was . . . It broke my heart to hear about you and Chris getting engaged."

He clamped both hands on the back of his neck, then let them fall. "You basically told me on the phone you were going to marry him, but I guess I'd still been holding out hope." He crossed his arms again. "Stupid me, I'd been holding out hope since high school. Hearing it had actually happened just about killed me."

"But . . . you and Marissa . . ." I held up my hand, as if it were an antenna that would make everything clearer. "I heard about the two of you so soon after Chris proposed. You must have been together when—"

He shook his head. "No, Marissa and I weren't . . . . We weren't anything. We were just two hurting people who shared our hurts for a night."

"You were never together?"

The crease between his eyes was deep and sad. "I met her at a party a few days after I heard your happy news. She was in a bad place in her life. I think she'd just broken up with someone and wanted a way to forget. Just like me." He sighed. "I still hate that Nick's life came out of that pain. Especially when she and I had no business being together in the first place. I'd never done anything like that before."

"So . . . ," I began, trying to understand, then stopped. I put my fingers up to my lips.

"I saw you and Nick outside talking tonight before you came in. Seeing the two of you together . . ." He looked up at the sky. "I couldn't help but wonder what it would have been like if it had been you and me. If he were . . ."

I swallowed hard. It felt like the ground beneath me had heaved, spitting me out in a place where I didn't understand the language. "If you were still so . . . If you still wanted . . ." I held my hands up to the sides of my face, then let them drop. "I gave you a chance to tell me, but you didn't. You told me you were *happy* for me." My voice broke at the end, and I silently cursed myself for not holding it together.

All this happened so long ago, it shouldn't even matter, but standing there in the darkened street with Ben right in front of me—my Ben, although that was crazy because he was never truly my Ben—it did matter. It mattered almost more than anything, and my heart was on the verge of breaking all over again.

"You—what are you talking about?"

"When I called you, about me and Chris . . ."

His eyebrows rose. "You mean when you told me you were dating him? That things were going great? You think that was a *chance*?

Jessie, that was a joke. You made me and my feelings for you into a joke."

"What?" The word rang out across the silent street. "That is not what I was doing. You were never a joke. I called because I wanted . . ." His hurt was an almost tangible force in the air and my chest prickled with heat. He raised his eyebrows, but I couldn't force the truth out. My hands trembled and I tightened my hands into balls.

"What did you want?" he asked, each word a slow press.

I took a step backward, then turned and paced a few feet. When I came back to him, his eyes were pleading. Tears stung at the back of my eyes, but I refused to let them fall. "I wanted you. I wanted you to still want me. To tell me not to marry Chris." There. The words were out.

"But you wanted to marry him, right? You sounded happy. Like you were just telling me the good news."

I shook my head. "I was happy, at first. Chris was exciting and came from this life I still thought I wanted to be a part of. It all happened so quickly and I . . . I lost myself in it."

My cheeks grew warm as I remembered Chris's hand on my lower back as he led me through a sea of people at that party on the patio, my dress swishing around my calves, my feeling of belonging.

To think that all I'd wanted was a love that swept me away like Daddy had done with Mama. A love that made all the others seem like dim, faraway stars. I thought I'd found it in Chris, and I let myself be swept away by him and the life he offered, not realizing that the one who may have represented what I truly needed had been calmly waiting in the wings.

"When I knew the proposal was coming, I panicked. I needed to know if you still had the same feelings you did on the night of the bonfire. When you told me you loved me."

I wiped away the tear that tickled at the edge of my eyelashes. "But when you said you were happy for me, what else was I supposed to think except that you'd moved on?" I sighed and held my hands up. "Chris proposed two weeks later."

Ben closed his eyes and ran his hand up and down the side of his bearded cheek, then across his eyes. "All that time—"

"But you and Marissa—" I said at the same time.

Our words were cut off by the deep throb of an engine rumbling up the road. I glanced over my shoulder as headlights roamed across Ben's front yard. Nick. Ben and I both took a step away from each other. I quickly passed a finger under my eyes and ran my hands across my hair. He shoved a hand in his front pocket and held up the other in a wave.

Nick stopped and rolled his window down at the foot of the driveway. "How'd the painting go?" If he saw the unease on our faces or sensed any tension, it didn't show.

"Two coats on both bedrooms," Ben replied. "How was the game?"

Nick shrugged. "Braves lost by two runs."

Ben nodded. "I'll be back up in a sec."

Nick waved to me and parked farther up the driveway, then headed into the house. The door slamming behind him shook me out of my fog.

"It's late. I need to get back home."

Ben reached out and tugged on my shirtsleeve. "Jess, I can't . . . I didn't . . ." His stammering echoed what was happening in my mind. The shock of such a years-long miscommunication was hard to wrap my brain around.

"I know." I took a step back from him, then another.

"I'll bring your computer to you tomorrow."

"Thanks." I turned and started walking. After a few paces, the glow from his garage light faded and I savored the dark as it wrapped around me. The farther I walked from his house, the easier it was to let the tears fall.

"*To fixing broken things*." When he'd said it earlier in the night, it felt so true, so fitting for the two of us. We fixed broken, lifeless things—cars, computers, barren dirt, a tender heart. But maybe our repair skills didn't extend to the brokenness that existed between the two of us.

Nothing was the same as it used to be, and there was no way to go back. I shouldn't want to go back, anyway. The past was just that—in the past.

Just ahead, the glow from my little yellow house beckoned. I'd always loved the way houses looked at night when darkness surrounded them, yet inside everything was bright and clear. That was how my house appeared as I approached it. Everything inside it ablaze with life. I took a deep breath, shaking off thoughts of what might have been, and crossed the yard toward home.

CHAPTER 25

*The spirit of a gardener is both tenacious and yielding. The best
caretakers of natural beauty can persevere in seemingly hopeless
situations but will yield to nature's authority when necessary.*
—SELA RUTH McGOVERN, THE WISDOM OF GARDENING

EVAN

Mom stuck to her plan of making me work off my "lapse in
judgment," but I was surprised to discover I didn't mind the
increased workload like I thought I would. In fact, I kind of liked
it. I could've done without being so up close and personal with Mr.
Rainwater's drop-offs, but the rest of it—spreading mulch in the far
beds, breaking up the hard-packed dirt where Mom wanted to plant a
row of lemon trees, moving the ladder around to hang Kimberly ferns
along the front porch and under the arbor in the back—wasn't too
bad. If I let my mind drift and ignored how hot and sweaty I was, the
hard work actually felt good.

I was pulling a wagon full of big blue liriope—a fancy name
for monkey grass—to Ms. Rickers's tiny Smart car when Nick's
Challenger rounded the curve in the driveway and coasted to a stop
right next to me.

"Looks like you have another customer," Ms. Rickers said as I
pushed one tray of monkey grass under the seat to make room for

another one. A Smart car definitely wasn't ideal for hauling what must've been fifty pots of monkey grass—enough to line both sides of her new front walk.

Nick climbed out of his car and leaned against the side of it, arms crossed, sly half grin on his face. My stomach twisted into the hard knot of nerves I now expected anytime he came around. "Working hard?"

I held my hands out to encompass the wagon, the monkey grass, and the other cars in the lot. "Yep. Stand there too long and I'll put you to work."

The grin disappeared, and he shoved his hands in his pockets. "Yeah, that's kind of why I'm here. Dad told me you'd gotten in some trouble over the driving thing."

As soon as she heard the word *trouble*, Ms. Rickers stiffened next to me. She was always first in line—well, after Gus of course—to receive or deliver juicy Glory Road gossip. I could practically hear her wishing she could turn up her hearing aid just a smidge more.

Nick took a step toward me and lowered his voice. "Since it was pretty much my fault that you're in this mess, I thought I'd come by and help you work."

"You want to work?"

He shrugged. "Well, my dad kind of told me I had to." I laughed and red splotches rose on his cheeks. "I wanted to anyway though. It's the least I can do. So . . ." He held out his arms. "Tell me what I need to do."

I closed Ms. Rickers's trunk and motioned for him to follow me to the passenger side of her car. "You can start by figuring out how to fit the rest of these pots in here."

"You got it."

After ten minutes of pulling, shoving, and creative maneuvering, Nick managed to fit all the monkey grass into the tiny car.

"Son, I wasn't sure it was all going to make it in, but you did just fine." She reached into her purse and pulled out a small wad of bills. "Here's just a little something. Maybe treat yourself on your way home." She smiled, and I could have sworn she batted her eyelashes at him.

"Unbelievable," I said as she drove away. "She's never tipped me and I help her every time she comes in here."

"Maybe she just thought I deserved a treat."

I shoved his shoulder and he laughed. "It's only three dollars. I'll buy you some ice cream or something."

Inside the shop Mom was ringing up a customer and another couple waited in line, so I just pointed to Nick and mouthed, *"He's here to work."*

Her face brightened and she held up a finger so I'd wait. When she finished with the customer, she pulled me over to the back door. "I found a beetle on one of the hydrangeas this morning." Her eyes were wide and a little frantic.

"Okay," I said slowly. I tilted my head to the side. "That's a problem?"

"It's a Japanese beetle. They'll eat through the leaves until they're skeletons if we don't get them off. I need you to check all the hydrangeas and . . . why don't you just check everything? If it's an invasion, we're in a world of trouble. If it's just a few, you'll have to pick them off."

"With my fingers?" I wrinkled my nose.

"Just get a bucket from the back and fill it with soapy water. Pick them off—yes, with your fingers—and drop them in the water. Let me know what you find." Before I could ask anything else, she headed back to the counter and a customer balancing four birdhouses in her arms. "Oh and, Nick," she called. "Thanks for the help."

❦

An hour and a half later, we'd finished going through the hydrangeas and azaleas practically leaf by leaf and moved on to the small potted fruit trees. We each carried a bucket of soapy water with a couple dozen dead beetles floating on top. It was gross, but having Nick as a partner made it slightly better. We didn't talk a whole lot, but I liked having him there. He sang a little—he cracked me up belting out "Cotton-Eyed Joe"—and tried to get me to sing a few verses of Johnny and June's "Jackson," but I politely declined.

When the trees were cleared with minimal picking necessary, we dumped the soapy water and drowned beetles way out back past the fence. Next on my list was planting Mom's gardenia shoots into pots. Earlier in the summer we'd taken cuttings off branches of the largest gardenia bushes and stuck the ends in jars of water. Over a few weeks, they sprouted delicate white roots and the beginnings of new leaves. A few customers had been in asking when the pots would be ready, and Mom and I had both been meaning to transplant the shoots for several days. Now it was time.

After dropping off the buckets at the back of the shop under the sink, I grabbed a tray of empty plastic pots—Mom rarely threw empty ones away because there was always another use for them—and directed Nick to the potting shed next to the shop. I pushed open the faded green shutters that served as doors to the shed and breathed in. Twig always smelled nice—a mixture of scented candles, potting soil, and whatever Gus had baked that morning—but the potting shed smelled like heaven to me. Soil and moss and damp pea gravel and sun-warmed wood.

It's how I imagined a deep forest would smell. Or maybe Narnia. It was always warm inside, but a different warmth than the heat outside. Usually the windows were cranked open and the shuttered doors never closed all the way, so there was always some airflow, making the heat feel good, somehow, no matter what time of year it was.

Inside, Nick ran his hand over the wall. Over the years Mom had tacked up so many random bits of paper and torn-out magazine pages that they almost formed wallpaper in the small shed. Anything she ran across that she thought was important or that caught her eye—photos of gardens, charts of sunrises and sunsets, flower names and their meanings, gardening quotes or bits of wisdom—she'd stick it to the wall with a thumbtack. Many of the pieces of paper were yellowed with age and softened by time.

A long farm table under the big, south-facing window held two rows of gardenia sprout jars. I showed Nick how much potting soil to add to each pot and how to nestle the cutting into the soil, then we settled into an easy routine. I scooped soil from a bag and poured it into the pot. He pulled the cutting out of the jar and placed it in the soil. I covered it and set the pot back in the window. Rinse, repeat.

As we worked in front of the wide bay window, Mr. Rainwater trundled toward the plastic pool behind the greenhouse. The tire of the wheelbarrow bounced a little over the stone and grass path. When he paused to wipe his forehead with his bandanna, Mom hurried out the back door and tried to take the handles from him. He shook his head. Behind them, Gus stood on the back porch, her nose wrinkled.

"So it's just the three of you?" Nick tilted his chin toward the window. "You, your mom, and your grandmother?"

"Pretty much."

"What about your dad? Does he ever come around?"

I shrugged one shoulder. "Not much. He lives in Birmingham. And he's kind of a jerk."

"Really?"

"Yeah. He wasn't that great to my mom, I don't think." I dropped the scoop into the bag and a little plume of soil burst out. I wiped my cheek with my wrist. "There was this other woman . . ."

"Geez." He paused with a plant in his hands. "That sucks."

"Yeah." I pulled the scoop out again and poured soil into the next pot. "I'm pretty glad he's not around much. I don't have to go through the whole pretending-I-like-you stuff."

"I know what you mean. I see my mom a good bit. These days, at least. It's weird though."

"Weird how?"

He ran his free hand over the top of his head. His hair wasn't long, but it wasn't cut short like most guys' either. It was somewhere in between.

"She and my dad had a . . . a thing a long time ago, then I came along and she split."

"Split? Like—she left you?"

"Well, not alone, but yeah. She decided she couldn't do—I don't know, the mom thing. She dropped me off at my dad's with a bag of clothes and this Mr. Potato Head that apparently I loved." He chuckled. "I think my dad still has it somewhere."

"So your parents are divorced?"

He shook his head. "No, they were never really together at all. They just had me, and I lived with her until I was three. That's when she took me to my dad's and left. I didn't see her again until my dad randomly bumped into her at the airport last year in Atlanta. A few days later she came over for dinner. *That* was weird."

"Yeah, I can see how it would be." And there I was, thinking my parental situation was strange—cheater dad who married his mistress and twin eight-year-old stepbrothers I'd only met once in my life— but not seeing your mom for thirteen years? I couldn't even begin to imagine that.

"So your mom and dad—are they . . . ?" My heart began to thump and my hands felt clammy. I thought of Mom and Mr. Bradley and the unspoken things that seemed to fly between them anytime they were together. "They're not married now, are they?"

"No! No, no. Not married."

I exhaled. "Good." When he looked up at me, I pointed to the next jar. "Hand me that one, will you?"

He reached and handed me the jar. "It is good, actually. I mean, they're dating . . . sort of." He sighed. "It's stupid, really. They're only together because of me. In some warped way they think I need them

237

to be together. A unified front. Like I'm not . . . whole or something without a mom around." He brushed a dusting of spilled soil off the table. "She wants me to call her Mom. But I can't. She's just Marissa. Like a babysitter or something. As if I need one. And he doesn't love her. I'm not even sure he likes her all that much."

I worked quietly. That was the most words he'd said at one time since I'd met him.

He grinned. "So now you know all there is to know about me."

I thought of the one thing I was still so curious about, and it popped out before I could stop myself. "Who's Cassidy?"

His smile faded. "How'd you know about her?"

I shrugged. "I just—I saw her text in the car. I mean . . ." *Ugh.* I shouldn't have said anything at all. "I wasn't looking, it just . . . It was right there."

"It's all right." He took a deep breath and leaned his hip against the worktable, then let his air out slowly. His fingers were coated with soil. "It doesn't even matter. Right now she's no one." His gaze was far-away, unfocused, trailing out the back window toward the far orchard and the fields beyond. He seemed so calm, so peaceful, I didn't want to press further. It wasn't my business anyway, but I still wondered about that *xoxo.*

"Nick? You hungry for meatloaf?" Gus propped open the screen door on our house with her foot. "We'll have plenty."

Nick and I had finished the gardenias and almost everything else on Mom's list for the day. We were about to haul the last of the trash to the street while Mom swept the front porch. I looked back up at her and raised my eyebrows. "Maybe you could ask Mr. Bradley to come eat too. You know Gus always makes enough to feed the neighborhood."

Mom stopped and leaned against her broom. "Oh. I don't know."

Just then we heard the grumble of Mr. Bradley's Jeep. A moment later, he pulled in the driveway, like mentioning his name had summoned him here.

"How's the work going?" he called through his lowered window.

"Great," Nick said. "We just finished."

"My grandmother is asking if y'all want to eat dinner with us," I said.

Behind me, the broom handle bumped against the wall and Mom trotted down the porch steps. "Evan, I don't . . ."

"No, I . . . ," Mr. Bradley stammered with the same hesitation. Why were they being so weird? "Nick, we need to get on back. I have dinner planned."

Nick laughed. "Since when do you plan dinner?"

"Since today. I just came by to drop off Jessie's computer, then I need to run by the store for a couple of last-minute things." He reached over to the passenger seat and grabbed the laptop, then held it out to Mom. "Sorry I didn't get it by earlier. I got tied up and . . ."

She took it from him and smoothed her hand across the top. "Thank you. I mean it."

"It's nothing. Let me know if it gives you any more trouble, but I think it'll be fine."

They both fell silent. Nick and I just stood there, waiting for them to say something else, but watching them was unbearable. No way would I be that awkward when I was an adult.

"Okay then," I said in an attempt to bring things back to normal, then turned to Nick. "Thanks for the help today."

"Yes, Nick." Mom finally pulled her gaze away from Mr. Bradley. "You were a huge help to Evan. I think she's just about worked off her—"

"Lapse in judgment, yeah, yeah." I rolled my eyes at Nick.

He laughed and gave me a high five. "Anytime, kid. Sorry."

A minute later, he and Mr. Bradley were both backing up and turning around, one after the other. Mr. Bradley left without waving, but Nick held his hand out the window before driving off. My skin still stung—pleasantly—from where his hand slapped against mine.

Gus stuck her head out of the door again. "Where'd everybody go? I thought we were about to have a full house."

I turned to Mom, but she'd already begun walking toward the house. "No, Mama. It's just the three of us."

I glanced back toward the road one more time, but nothing remained. Even the sound of the engines was gone.

CHAPTER 26

The best gardens aren't "plant-and-go" varieties. Gardens will bring you the most pleasure and peace if you do a daily walk-through. Appreciate the beauty, check for bugs, make corrections as needed. In short, be present in the world you've created.
—ELIZABETH MCLEOD, GARDENING IS GOOD FOR YOU

JESSIE

In the days since my dinner with Sumner at Donny's, he'd sent me texts every day—sometimes just to say hi, other times to give me some random bit of trivia about golf or tell me something funny he'd heard on the radio. Then he found reasons to come see me at the shop. He was developing a new golf course about twenty miles north of Perry, so stopping by wasn't as far out of his way as I originally thought it was, but it still wasn't exactly on his way anywhere.

Some of his visits were necessary, such as getting a sneak peek at the arbor Mr. Rainwater was building for Olivia and Jared to stand under during the ceremony. Sumner was having it made as a surprise for Olivia. I'd asked Mr. Rainwater to construct it with the same twisted grapevines as the chandelier that would hang from the center of the boathouse ceiling.

Other visits were less necessary: He'd taken a picture of a plant at the new development he couldn't identify and thought I might be able to help. Then one afternoon he stopped by because he'd been "out our way" and realized he hadn't paid me a deposit to secure me as the wedding florist.

I laughed. "You don't have to secure me. Olivia's is the only wedding I'm working on."

"For now, maybe. Who knows where this will lead?"

"Your lips to God's ears," Mama called from the glider on the front porch. "If there's anything I've learned, it's that one thing always leads to another."

Why he couldn't have just texted me the photo of the flower or mailed me a check, I didn't know, but I had to admit I enjoyed being the recipient of his lavish attention. He brought gifts too, for all of us. It felt extravagant, although slightly misplaced. A dog-eared copy of *On the Road* for Evan—"I found it at a used bookstore in New Orleans. Thought you might like it." A new, remastered CD of Johnny and June singing their favorite hymns, a disc missing from Mama's collection. A shiny new pair of garden shears for me, to replace my old pair that had dulled with time.

Then came a lush bouquet of pale-pink peonies and blush roses with a card tucked inside. "If you're free Friday, meet me on the dock at 7."

❧

On Friday, an hour before I was supposed to leave for Dog River, I rounded the corner from my bedroom out into the kitchen where Mama and Evan were making dinner.

"How do I look?"

Mama turned around, one hand still stirring the pot of rice on the stove. She sighed when she saw me. "Prettier than a sunset."

Evan wrinkled her nose. "You don't look like yourself."

"Isn't that the point?" Mama stirred the rice with a little extra vigor than necessary.

"Thanks, Mama," I said.

"You could wear a potato sack and still be beautiful. I just think it's not a bad thing anytime you have an excuse to peel yourself out of those rubber boots and old T-shirts."

My new blue-and-white dress grazed the tops of my knees, not too tight, but not loose either. I'd found it at Perry's only boutique, specializing in squeezing country girls into hip-hugging blue jeans and midriff-bearing tops. Thankfully, they'd had a few other options. I also bought a long necklace with a delicate silver-and-gold feather tassel and a pair of strappy sandals. When I tried it all on in the privacy of my bedroom, I was unexpectedly pleased at my reflection staring back at me. Until I saw Evan's wrinkled nose.

"Maybe it's too much." I turned sideways and peered at my rear end where the fabric hugged.

"You look just fine." Mama checked the clock on the stove. "Anyway, it's too late to change. You need to get going."

Evan raised an eyebrow, then headed back to her room.

"Hey, where are you going?" I called. "I need your opinion."

"I already gave it. And Nick asked me to come up and help him restake the cages around their tomato plants. He did it wrong and they fell over." She stuck her head back into the kitchen, her hand on the doorframe. "Is that okay?" she asked, her eyes pleading. "I'll walk up there and Mr. Bradley can drive me home. I won't stay long, I promise."

"I don't know if I want you out while I'm not here. What if something happens?"

Mama caught my eye. "I can stay here while you're gone."

"And Mr. Bradley will be home. Nick already said they're replacing some wood around a window or something."

"You and Nick have been talking a lot."

Evan rolled her eyes so hard I thought they might not return to normal. "We're just texting."

"I thought you didn't like texting. Or your phone."

"It's just . . ." She exhaled, a quick, hard burst of breath. "I don't know, he's someone to talk to. Ruth doesn't have a phone and there's no one else."

I smoothed my hand down her long braid. "Okay, baby. Show him how to stake the cages. Although it's pretty hard to mess them up."

"I know. It's kind of funny that he can't figure it out." Evan turned to head back to her room. "And you actually do look kind of nice."

I watched her retreating figure in the dark hallway. "I guess I should take that as a compliment."

"Take it however you want." Mama dropped an extra pat of butter in the rice and checked the clock again.

"You sure you'll be okay?"

"Honey, I'll be just fine. Now, get out of here or you'll make me miss the beginning of the *Gilmore Girls* marathon. Harvis may pop down a little later for a cup of tea. You go have fun and I'll be all ears when you get home."

❧

I was almost to Sumner's house when Olivia called me.

"Jessie, I'm freaking out," she said as soon as I answered. "We have less than four weeks until the wedding, people aren't sending in their RSVPs so I have no idea how many people we'll have, the caterer nixed the sushi, and my dress is too loose. And it's strapless, which makes it worse."

I paused, deciding which fire to address first, but she continued. "Anytime I raise my arms, the dress slides three inches down my cleavage. My dad will have a heart attack!"

"Okay, let's take it one at a time. People never RSVP the way you want them to. Just plan for half the number you invited. That'll at least be in the right ballpark. And about the sushi, what if you take some of the ingredients you like in sushi, other than the raw bits, and make a sort of vegetable platter with it? Or forget it completely and do something like shrimp and grits? Serve it in martini glasses or little glass jars."

I shook my head, hearing myself spout out ideas like I was used to helping people work out kinks in their wedding planning. So much for my plan to just deal with the flowers. Since Olivia had no one else to give her advice, it had fallen on my inexperienced shoulders. Though right now it sounded like she needed a therapist more than anything.

"Hmm. I'm liking that idea."

"As for your dress, it sounds like you need to either put on some weight or have a seamstress take it in."

"I know. It fit perfectly a few weeks ago, but that was before the nerves kicked in and my weight started dropping."

"Why the nerves? You seemed calm when we last talked."

"I don't know, I just . . . Argh, I'm getting married! I'll be with this man forever. Attaching myself to him for the rest of my life."

"Yes, that is the idea."

"It's just . . . It's a little nerve-racking. How do you know if it's right? If getting married is what we're supposed to do?"

"Well, you don't."

She laughed. "Gee, thanks. That makes me feel tons better."

"It's true though. There's no way to know every single thing about a person, even the person you marry. To some extent, we're all kind of a mystery."

Some more than others, I thought. My marriage to Chris showed me exactly how much you can *not* know about another person. In that regard I didn't blame Olivia for worrying. "Have you talked to Jared at all about this? Have you let him know you're nervous?"

"We've talked about marriage exhaustively, but no, I haven't told him I'm nervous. It'd crush him. He's like . . . He's the best person I know."

"And you're still worried?"

She sighed. "I hate to even say something like this, but what if I meet someone else later—even years from now—and I wonder if *he's* the one I should have married?"

"Easy. He won't be. Because you'll already be married to Jared, which means *he's* the right one for you. Love is . . . Well, a lot of it is a choice. A choice to love the person you're with."

I propped my elbow on the window ledge and rubbed my forehead. I wasn't making marriage sound very romantic.

"A choice," Olivia said slowly, as if pondering the word. "Like a plan that you carry out."

By this time I knew enough of Olivia's personality to imagine her working that out in her head, seeing *Love* written on an efficient checklist where she could cross off items as she accomplished them.

1. Be a successful lawyer.
2. Get married.
3. Love my husband.

Check, check, check.

"Well, it's—not exactly."

"No, I like that. I like a plan. I'm good with those."

When we hung up a moment later, she sounded better, not as frantic. My phone, however, showed a red bar at the top, indicating I only had 5 percent battery life left. I dug through my console for my spare phone charger. Coming up with nothing, I made a mental note to ask Sumner if I could use his charger for a bit, just to get enough charge to finish out the evening.

Parked in his driveway, I checked my hair in the rearview mirror, then hopped out. Sumner opened the front door as I reached the top porch step.

"You're late," he said with a smile.

"Sorry. I was on the phone with Olivia."

"Ah. It's no wonder you're late then. Did she have a million things to go over with you?"

He held the door open for me and I slid past him. Inside smelled musky and delicious. The evening sun rays were sharp, turning the hardwoods a bright caramel color. "Not quite that many, although she did seem to have a touch of nerves."

"I got that from our last call. I tried to calm her, tried to think of things Elizabeth would've said, but as usual, I don't think my advice was all that great."

"Don't be so sure. Grown-up girls tend to listen to their daddies. I know I did."

He shook his head. "Grown-up girl. Hard to believe she got there so fast."

In the kitchen he handed me a chilled glass of wine. He wore a white polo shirt, unbuttoned at the top, and had bare feet. "How's the arbor going?"

"It's looking good. Mr. Rainwater is really enjoying the process, I think. It gives him something to work on during the day when he's not up at the shop helping me. I have some photos to show you . . ." I reached into my bag for my phone. "Oh, that reminds me. Do you mind if I plug my phone in? I didn't realize until I got here that I'm almost out of battery."

"Sure." He pulled a charger from a drawer under the counter and handed it to me.

I tried to plug it into my phone but the end was the wrong size. "Oh well. I'll just have to hope that 5 percent gets me home tonight."

"We could run out and buy you a charger. It won't take long."

I shook my head. "It's fine. Anyway, we'd miss the sunset."

"Speaking of . . ." He held his arm out toward the back porch. "Shall we?"

He grabbed a soft-sided cooler and the bottle of wine and I followed him through his vast grassy lawn with the majestic oak in the corner and down to the dock. The water just barely lapped against the pilings of the boathouse. A small, sleek boat was tied up next to the steps that led down to the water. All black paint, chrome, and rich mahogany wood, it bumped gently against the dock.

"Is that yours?" I felt silly for asking—whose else would it be?—but he hadn't mentioned anything about a boat, and it wasn't there the last time we were down at the dock.

"Oh no. It belongs to a friend. He's just letting me borrow it for the evening." I exhaled and he laughed. "I do have a boat though. It's docked down in the Bahamas at the moment." He winked at me, then took my hand and helped me step onto the boat.

We spent the next half hour before sunset zipping up and down the river, exploring small creeks and inlets as they appeared along the edges. When the sun dipped low toward the horizon, Sumner dropped the anchor and we floated, bobbing gently in the small swells that rippled under the boat. He pulled a wedge of soft cheese, a bowl of bright-green grapes, and a box of crackers from the cooler, and I chose a spot at the front of the boat.

After a few minutes, the lull of the water and the sound of birds singing in trees along the shore made my eyelids heavy. Closing them felt luxurious.

"I have to say, you look good on the front of a boat," Sumner said.

I opened one eye. "We're lounging on a beautiful boat in the middle of the river at sunset. Anyone would look good in this setting."

Sumner laughed. "Maybe you're right."

"If this were a movie, Evan would have already gagged and thrown popcorn at me."

"Good thing she's not here then. Flying popcorn would definitely ruin the mood." He reached over and took my hand. The fading sunlight cast every surface—the water, the boat, our skin—in a faint golden glow.

❦

It was nearly ten thirty when I got home, and I wasn't prepared for what I saw in the driveway—Ben's Jeep parked next to Harvis's truck. I threw my car in Park, then ran inside to find Ben, Nick, and Evan at the kitchen table. As soon as I opened the front door, Evan ran to me and wrapped her arms around me. "I didn't know what else to do. I couldn't get you on the phone, so I called Mr. Bradley. Well, I called Nick, and he got his dad."

I pulled back and put my hands on the sides of her face. "Tell me what happened." Her eyes were dry, but I could tell she'd been crying. A hard rock formed in my stomach. I glanced at Ben.

"When Mr. Bradley dropped me off tonight, I opened the door and called to Gus that I was home," Evan was saying. "I went over to the shop to get my book I'd left there this afternoon. When I came back here, she wasn't in the house. I checked her house and looked everywhere, but I couldn't find her. I still don't know if she was in the house when I first called to her. I'd just assumed she was. Finally I called Nick and he and his dad came to help me search."

Ben stood and was by my side in an instant. "Your mom's okay. We found her up the road, toward the highway. She was pretty confused and couldn't tell us where she'd been going. We brought her back here and laid her down. She's in there resting." He gestured to the den.

I nodded absently, my mind spinning. "And Mr. Rainwater—why's he here?"

"She asked me to get him. She didn't calm down until he got here. He's sitting with her now."

"Mom, where were you? I kept calling you."

My phone. Under the spell of the sunset and the wine—and Sumner himself—I'd totally forgotten about the phone and its low battery. When I finally got back in my car to leave, the battery was dead.

"Oh, baby." I smoothed my hand down the back of her head. "My battery died and I didn't have the right charger . . ." My voice trailed off. It didn't matter what happened or where I was. The fact was I wasn't where I was needed. "I'm so sorry." I pulled her to me in a tight hug. The top of her head fit snugly under my chin. She tightened beneath my touch, but she didn't pull away. In my peripheral vision I saw Ben plug my phone into the charger that sat on top of my desk.

"*Thank you*," I mouthed to him over the top of her head.

He tapped Nick on the shoulder. "Time to go."

When the door closed behind them, Evan turned toward her bedroom and I approached Mr. Rainwater in the den. He'd pulled a chair next to the couch where Mama was asleep. She was almost angelic, like nothing in the world could make her upset, like she hadn't been walking down the road alone and confused just a couple of hours before.

"Mr. Rainwater?" I whispered. He jerked as if he'd been asleep.

"Hey there, Jessie." He rubbed his eye with the heel of his hand. "I suppose I should get on back home. I just wanted to make sure Augusta was okay."

"Thank you for looking after her. Your friendship with her means a lot to me."

He nodded and made his way to the door. After one last glance over his shoulder at Mama, he paused at the threshold. "She didn't want me to say anything to you, and I didn't out of respect for her, but I'm glad you know now."

The rock in my stomach shifted and tumbled, finally settling back down but in the wrong position. "How did you know? And what do you know?"

"She had a . . . an episode a little while ago. Couple weeks maybe. She just got confused, thought there was water . . ." He shook his head again. "Your mama is a special woman. I'm lucky she even wants me around."

"Tonight she more than wanted you around, Mr. Rainwater. It sounds like you're the only one who could calm her down."

His lips pulled in and he chewed his lip a moment, as if searching for words. Or trying to hold himself together. "Jessie . . ." He stopped and patted my shoulder. "Sweetheart, I think it's time you called me by my first name. Just Harvis. That'll do."

I smiled. Tears building up behind my eyes made them prickle and burn.

Once he left, I tiptoed back into the den and sat in the chair Mr.—Harvis had just vacated. Someone—probably him—had covered her with a quilt up to her chest. Her arms lay on top of it. I lifted her hand closest to me and gently wrapped my hand around it.

Seeing her every day, week in and week out, I didn't notice physical changes all that much. But now as I watched her sleep, I noticed more than ever how she'd aged. I took in every curve and line in her face, the gentle sag in her cheeks, the skin on the backs of her hands that bore the faint beginnings of age spots, and my heart broke a little. Somehow my mother had changed from the always-snazzy Gus into a woman of nearly seven decades at the beginning of something that could turn out to be very scary.

My phone beeped in the kitchen where Ben had plugged it in. I laid Mama's hand back on the quilt and retrieved my phone from the desk. Sumner.

Just wanted to make sure you got home okay. Thanks for coming tonight. You are magical.

I leaned against the back of the chair and exhaled as a wave of clashing emotions coursed through my mind. The first part of the evening had been perfect—sunshine, water, Sumner, and his laughter and optimism. Then the shock of finding my driveway full of cars, Mama on the couch, Ben standing like a sentry in my kitchen.

I thought back to that moment in Twig when I considered telling Sumner about Mama and the mystery of what was happening in her mind. I hadn't wanted to make it real by speaking it out loud, but after tonight, there was no denying that something was happening. Something big and baffling and scary. Opening up to him now would make sense. After all, he'd been honest with me about his wife's death and how hard that had been on him.

But something was keeping me from going there with him—from trusting him with my full, honest self. What was it?

As I tried to think of how to respond, a second text came through. This time it was Ben.

You okay?

Just the sight of his name on the screen settled something in me. He'd taken care of everything tonight, and probably without asking a single question. A simple "thank you"—for coming to Evan's rescue, for finding Mama, for handling it all when I wasn't around to do it myself—felt empty in comparison.

From the very beginning Ben had been steadfast and unwavering in his friendship and devotion. Anytime something bad happened—if I made a bad grade, had an argument with a friend, or got in trouble for breaking curfew—he was there with the listening ear, the sympathetic words, the well-timed humor.

Maybe that was part of the reason I kept him—and his heart—at arm's length. What teenager actually valued such a strong, steady presence? I'd been waiting for a spark, for excitement, for that delicious, twitchy feeling in my stomach, all the butterfly wings flapping in tandem. As an adult, I knew those things amounted to nothing more than a flimsy wish, but as a young woman, I thought that was love. I didn't know finding a good man meant looking past the sparks and butterflies.

Ben was that good man. He'd been one then and he was still one now. Marissa was a lucky woman. I'd been lucky once too. I just didn't know it.

CHAPTER 27

*Chamomile is often thought to symbolize relaxation
and peace, but a less common meaning of this delicate
white and yellow flower is "energy in adversity."*
—LUCY LANGWORTHY, GUIDE TO FRAGRANT FLOWERS, 1945

GUS

Despite Harvis's insistence that I tell Jessie what was going on in my squirrely head, I was dead set on not telling her. At least not until I figured it out on my own. How I was going to figure it out on my own, I hadn't the foggiest, but darn it if I wasn't going to try. And darn it if Harvis didn't spill the beans to her the night I got lost.

I still wasn't sure what exactly had happened. I'd been flipping through a back issue of *Better Homes & Gardens*, looking for a specific recipe for okra succotash, when the hairs on the back of my neck stood up. At first I thought I'd heard someone at the door, but no knock came, no scuffling like someone was on the front porch. But the worried, panicked feeling didn't go away. Then it got worse, and I remembered my legs feeling antsy, like I needed to get up and move around.

Next thing I knew, Ben Bradley's hand was on my shoulder, his calm voice telling me it was time to come on home. I hadn't realized I wasn't home until that moment. Everything before and after that was a blur. I woke up the next day with an urge to make oatmeal cookies, but Jessie's and Evan's hushed voices and worried eyes told me I'd lost another part of myself. It was becoming a regular occurrence, and I wasn't ashamed to say I hated it.

Jessie had already made me an appointment with some fancy doctor, but she called and demanded they let us come in that afternoon. I tried to tell her it was unnecessary, but she waved me off. Finally she said, "Thank you," and hung up with a satisfied smile. The crease between her eyebrows deepened again the moment she turned to me. "They'll see us at ten o'clock."

"Jessie, this doctor is all the way in Mobile and it's prime shopping time. Is it really that responsible to close Twig? What if someone needs to buy something?"

"Responsible?" Her face was pink. I'd struck a nerve. "Last night Ben found you walking up the road with no shoes on, tears running down your face, unsure of how you got there or where you were going. *Weeks* ago, Harvis found you huddled on your couch thinking water was flooding your house. You know what's going on, he knows, but I know nothing." She held up a hand when I tried to speak. "I don't want to hear it, Mama. I want to hear it straight from the doctor."

The worst part was, I couldn't defend myself. She was right—I knew exactly what was happening. When my mother had died from complications from Alzheimer's and my father told me her mother, my grandmother, had died the same way, my reality settled deep in my bones: that's how I'd go too. I just assumed it would happen when I was old. Sixty-nine was not old, thank you very much. Yes, my mother and grandmother had died in their seventies, but I figured I had enough vinegar in my bones to hold it off an extra decade or two. I guess I was wrong.

The two of us arrived at the doctor's office fifteen minutes before my appointment. Evan had stayed behind to man the shop. While Jessie filled out paperwork and nervously bounced her leg up and down, I checked out the waiting room. Waiting rooms were notorious for having free stuff—or coupons for free stuff—and I didn't want to pass any of it up. Before my name was called, I managed to pocket four coupons for Bengay and a sample-size bottle of Gold Bond hand lotion.

The nurse who called us led me to an exam room and quickly took the necessary stats—height, weight, blood pressure, pulse. She held up a thermometer and I dutifully opened my mouth. She held out her hand and I held out my wrist. With two fingers on my artery, she closed her eyes and counted. Satisfied, she tapped her fingers on the iPad on her lap. "Healthy as a horse," she said. I turned to Jessie and smiled. She pretended not to see it.

We waited an interminable thirty minutes with nothing but a *Popular Mechanics* from 2015 before the doctor finally came in. Jessie greeted him warmly, but I rolled my eyes. The kid looked barely older than Evan.

"How old are you?" I asked him.

He smiled. "I'm thirty-three, Mrs. McBride. How old are you?"

I raised my eyebrows. "Did your mother not teach you any manners?"

Jessie cleared her throat. "She'll be seventy in November."

"I'm sixty-nine, thank you."

He laughed. "I like you already."

"Humph." I didn't give him the satisfaction of a smile.

After a few swipes on the iPad the nurse had left on the desk, he crossed his arms and stretched his legs out in front of him. "Let's chat, why don't we?" He then proceeded through a whole rigmarole of questions, asking me everything from what I had for dinner when I was four years old to what colors I saw when I closed my eyes to what items I'd put on a grocery list for a holiday meal.

"Why in the world do you want to know that? We're months away from the holidays."

He smiled again. He was the smilingest doctor I'd ever known. Probably due to his young age. "It's called mental cognitive status. I'm asking you questions to test yours."

"And to test it you need to know my holiday recipe list? That's personal, if you must know."

"Mother, please." Jessie only called me Mother when she was almost to her breaking point. I straightened up and ran through my ingredient list for cornbread dressing, and for good measure, my recipe for pecan spoonbread too.

He kept asking me questions. About my recent "episodes"—when I couldn't remember details, Jessie filled them in, something I both appreciated and resented. About my medications, vitamins, diet. About my use of alcohol. "None, thank you," I replied. "Although this line of questioning is making me seriously rethink that."

He chuckled and continued. Past injuries, surgeries, complications. Medical conditions of my family members, living and deceased. I shifted on the paper-covered bed. I knew that was the question that would get me into trouble.

"My grandmother had . . ." I swallowed. "Well, she had trouble in her mind."

"Oh?" His eyebrows rose a notch.

"Everyone called it Old Timer's disease. Some people said she was senile."

The doctor laced his fingers together. "Back then, not everyone knew the term Alzheimer's. And the disease is 70 percent genetic."

I fluttered my eyes closed a moment, then opened them. Jessie was staring at me hard, but I kept my focus on the doctor. "By the time my mother developed it, we knew more about it. They at least used the right term for it."

"Alzheimer's?" Jessie asked. "Mama?"

I finally looked at her. Her eyes were rimmed with tears. "Oh, baby. You had to know."

She covered her face with her hands and leaned forward.

"I wondered," she said through her hands. Then she sniffed and sat up. Her cheeks were wet and splotchy. "I knew Minnie forgot things a lot." I loved hearing her use her childhood name for my mother, who had died when Jessie was only seventeen. "I didn't know about her mom though. Your grandmother. I guess I never asked for details."

"And they weren't details I was itching to give you. Who wants to tell her daughter there's a line of Alzheimer's running straight as a ruler right through the women in her family? I wanted to protect you as long as I could."

She exhaled, blowing her bangs up off her forehead.

The doctor stood and opened the door, motioning to the nurse outside. "I'm going to have Helen take you down for a CT scan. It'll show us the structure of the brain and any shrinkage. It'll also rule out conditions that cause similar symptoms."

"What would those be?" Jessie asked. I knew what she was thinking—maybe there was something else that could be causing all this mess. Something other than the Big Thing.

"It could be any number of things. Brain tumor, aneurysm, bleeding in the brain . . ."

Jessie sat ramrod straight in her seat. I cleared my throat and tried to catch the doctor's eye.

"Given your symptoms and your family's medical history, I don't think you need to worry about those."

The nurse came in and whisked me down the hall to another room. Through a glass door stood a contraption lined with blinking lights, shiny silver, and a round contraption as big as Marilyn Rickers's Smart car.

A minute later, I was lying down on the conveyor belt with the instruction not to move a muscle. An IV in my arm shot cold liquid through my veins, and I breathed as shallow as I could while the machine clicked and spun to life. She said it would somehow take pictures of thin slices of my brain. I was just glad I couldn't feel it.

An hour later, I was in the doctor's personal office in a chair next to Jessie. All around us sat framed photos of the doctor's young and beautiful family. Blonde wife, two cherubic babies. Twins, from the looks of them. It was a wonder that this man who worked with patients with a smorgasbord of elderly brain problems went home to this family every night. Alzheimer's to baby bottles. The speed of life could still sometimes take me by surprise.

He folded his hands and gave the news I knew we'd hear. Without an MRI it was just a preliminary diagnosis, but he felt fairly confident it was Alzheimer's. Beginning stages. Impossible to estimate the progression. Could be years of casual lapses, like lately, or my brain function could deteriorate rapidly. Then he had the gall to suggest I needed supervision, as if I were a child.

"I've been on my own for quite a long time now. I think I'm just fine."

"You're not on your own. You have us." Jessie turned to the doctor. "She lives next door to me . . . well, through some trees, but still, she's the next house. She's at my house almost all day though."

"That's good. But what about nighttime? At some point, she—" I cleared my throat and he turned to me and smiled. "*You* will likely experience what we call Sundowning, or late-day confusion. Later stages of Alzheimer's cause patients to experience heightened confusion and disorientation as the sun goes down."

Jessie looked at me, likely thinking of the night before, but another shot of memory raced through me. My own mother used to pace at night. Nothing seemed able to calm her down. Not until she finally fell into a fitful sleep. Was that my future? "I can handle nighttime just fine," I said, rubbing my eyes. "That's when my shows come on."

"Mrs. McBride. This is real, I'm sorry to tell you. It's not going away. You'll need to treat it seriously."

"I'm taking it seriously, young man. I've known about this a lot longer than you have. I just don't want you to go deciding things for me. I may not have a white coat with my name in curly script on the front, but I'm well aware of how this thing works."

"Is there any medicine, or do we just . . . ?" Jessie was gripping one hand in the other, squeezing her fingers together as if they were one of those heart-shaped stress balls they gave out in the cath lab.

He sat forward in his chair, as if this was the part he enjoyed. "Unfortunately, there's no medicine to slow the progression, but there are drugs that may help lessen the symptoms. There are also clinical trials . . ."

They spent the next ten minutes discussing my medical care—drug possibilities, side effects, trials, and outcomes—as if I weren't even there. And I let them. Talking about it was exhausting.

When we finally left, the bright sunshine outside was a shock. I covered my eyes with my hand and inhaled the air that thankfully didn't smell like disinfectant and sweet air freshener. My stomach rumbled. "What do you think about Jack & Mack's on the way home? I could go for an onion burger."

Jessie shook her head and sighed. "Lord, Mama, you're acting like you just picked up a cold or a stomach bug."

"What do you want me to say?" She yanked open her car door and I did the same. "That I'm scared? That I want to scream and pound the walls with my fists? That it makes me feel weak and small and helpless?"

Jessie turned to me with wide eyes, wet around the edges. I shook my head. No, ma'am. We were not going to share a good cry right there in the parking lot. "I'm sorry to disappoint you, but I'm not saying any of that. And truthfully, I'd rather you not cry for me either. It's not like I'm dying tomorrow."

Out of the corner of my eye, I saw two nurses leave out of a side door of the office. One of them was mine. Where she'd been all business in the office—no chitchat, no extra words—now she was smiling, laughing. I crossed my arms and felt like something important had just been taken from me.

Jessie jerked the car into Drive and took us home. We were silent the entire way.

CHAPTER 28

Often used in weddings, the lily of the valley symbolizes sweetness and
purity, but it can also denote reconciliation or the return of happiness.
—DR. JULIUS GRISSOM, *THE GRISSOM GUIDE*

JESSIE

I'd always been good at holding back my tears, and that day was no different. After the appointment that morning, Mama whisked herself into the house and I barged into Twig, pushing the front door open so hard a display of painted wooden signs clattered to the floor. If I hadn't been so angry—at her, at the doctor, at everything—I would have found it funny, both of us mad as wet cats and fleeing into our separate corners to lick our fur and calm down.

Except that I didn't calm down. All day I rang up customers—thankfully no longer by hand—hauled pots and plastic crates to cars, and spread dirt and fertilizer, but my mind stayed as frantic as it had felt when I was sitting in the doctor's hard chair, my stomach twisted into a knot of nerves. Anytime I thought about the future and its unknowable years, Mama and her "It's no big deal" attitude, and the fact that I'd have to tell Evan about the diagnosis, grief banged loudly on some internal door. But I refused to open it up.

It wasn't until the last customer drove away that I cracked that door open and let the tears come. It was the sight of Mama that did it.

From the back room of Twig, as I washed my hands in the big sink, I could see her in the kitchen window of my house. She walked back and forth between the counter and the sink, likely working out her own frustrations with flour, butter, and sugar.

Then Evan walked into the kitchen. Mama rubbed her back and held a spoon out to her mouth to taste whatever concoction she'd been working on. It was a regular occurrence, nothing special about it, but in light of our new hard reality, it felt too tender for my heart to take.

I hadn't noticed anyone drive up, so when a car door slammed, I flew to the front counter where Mama kept a box of tissues stashed somewhere. I fumbled around a moment looking for something, even a napkin or spare T-shirt, to wipe my face before greeting the last-minute customer.

Before I turned around though, he spoke. "I brought you a cucumber," Ben said. "It's not much, but it's sort of a thank-you gift."

My stomach plummeted and I gave up trying to find a tissue. I used the back of my hand instead. "You don't need to do that." I didn't turn around.

"I know, but if it weren't for you, we wouldn't have cucumbers and tomatoes for our salad. And tonight we will."

I sniffed quietly, but he heard it.

"Hey, hey." He appeared at my side and turned me to face him. I knew my face was a wreck, but I couldn't do anything about it.

A car drove up outside and voices filled the air. Ben walked to the door and flipped the sign around in the window. "Sorry," he called through the window. "She's closed."

He pulled up a stool next to me and put his hand on my knee. The simple fact that he didn't ask any questions, didn't demand to know what was going on or why I was crying, made it easier for me to let go.

"I'm scared I'm going to lose my mom." I leaned toward him and sobbed, pouring all my grief onto Ben's firm shoulder. I cried until there was nothing more to pour out, until my throat felt raw and my eyes were like sandpaper. He pulled a Kleenex seemingly from thin air and handed it to me. I pressed it to my eyes, then squeezed it into a ball.

"Do you want to tell me about it?"

I did. I relayed all that had been happening with Mama over the last few months. He already knew some of it. Then I told him the doctor's diagnosis.

He didn't ask too much. Didn't try to solve anything or tell me not to worry or that everything would be fine. He just sat with me and listened, and as he did, the weight on my shoulders lifted just a little. The force of my tears had left my forehead sore and my nose stuffy, but my mind felt clear, like a mirror when you wipe away the steam after a shower.

"Do you know the first time I met your mother?"

I shook my head, surprised at his change of direction. "Probably sometime after we'd been out for a walk on the road. I don't know specifically. Do you?"

"It was just before you and I first talked—well, outside of school at least. I'd been out with the Jeep and it died on me—just like it did that day you saw me and helped. Only this day no one but your mom was around."

"And she's not one to hop in a dirty car and drop the clutch."

"Right. So I was pushing the truck past your house and she was standing by the mailbox. I waved and she . . . I don't know, I guess she smiled, but it was more like a smirk."

I laughed and wiped under my eye. "Did she say anything?"

"Oh yes. She said she'd run into my mom at the drugstore that week, and Mom told her about my new car. So I said, 'Here it is. What do you think?' Keep in mind, I was sweating buckets and my legs were covered from the knees down in red dirt."

"What'd she say?"

"She asked me if I'd ever been to Rock City."

"What?"

"Exactly. I had no idea where she was going with it, but I told her I'd gone there sometime on a field trip. She goes, 'I went there once. It's not all it's cracked up to be. Kind of disappointing, actually.' Then she turned and walked back up the driveway."

I covered my eyes with my hands and shook my head. "That sounds just like her."

Outside, clouds covered the sky, darkening what had been a blindingly sunny day. I was grateful for a little less brightness.

"I know you need to get in for dinner, but do you feel like taking a drive?" he asked. "We could just . . . get some fresh air or something."

No doubt Mama had something simmering on the stove, a peace offering after our painful morning, but I wasn't quite ready to talk.

"Sure. That sounds great."

Glory Road was quiet, as usual, as was the highway at the end of it. Highway 170 wasn't a main thoroughfare—it didn't connect Perry with any big place so there was no flood of late-day after-work traffic. Just an occasional eighteen-wheeler and a few farm trucks.

I didn't ask where we were going—I didn't care, really. He turned down a few more mostly deserted roads, then the fields behind wooden fences began to feel vaguely familiar. He slowed down next to an open gate.

"Is this . . . ?"

"I think it is," he said. "Think we'll get in trouble?"

"Probably not as big a deal for two adults to trespass than for a hundred teenagers."

He turned in and drove down the dirt path that weaved around thick trees and towering shrubs. With clouds still moving in, the shade here seemed more like deep dusk than just after seven. The path ended at the wide, grassy expanse I remembered from all those parties in high school. Back then it had been tidy, the grass mowed, the shrubs tame. Now the grass was knee high and kudzu crept up and over whole trees, threatening to swallow everything in bright-green leaves.

Ben stopped at the edge of the field, took his seat belt off, and leaned his seat back a little. I did the same, then propped my feet on the dashboard.

"Make yourself comfortable."

Ahead of us, a flock of blackbirds that had been poking around in the tall grass took off, a big black mass rising higher and higher. Just as they disappeared into the trees on the far side of the field, the sun dropped below the dark clouds. All of a sudden everything was liquid and shimmery—the tips of every blade of grass, scattered bright-yellow wildflowers, the hood of the Jeep.

I glanced at Ben just as he turned to me. The sun highlighted the angle of his cheekbone and the lighter, caramel color in his hair.

"I'm so sorry about your mom," he said.

"Thanks."

My hand rested on the seat next to me, and he reached over and covered mine with his. The warmth felt like medicine. I closed my eyes as he traced the gentle dips and rises of the back of my hand with his thumb. First my knuckles, then my fingers. Then he cupped my hand and turned it over, tracing the lines in the palm of my hand with his fingertips.

I opened my eyes. "Ben . . ."

"Hang on. Let me say something." He took a deep breath and turned his gaze back toward the empty field. "I'm about to end things with Marissa. It's time."

"What?" My heart picked up its rhythm, thumping as if I were half a mile into an evening run. His hand tightened around mine.

"Don't you . . . ? Have you thought at all . . . ?" He dragged his free hand through his hair and sat forward in his seat, then turned to

265

me. His eyes locked onto mine. "Us. You and me. Have you wondered at all if this is . . . if we've been given another chance here?"

"I . . . I don't know. You're with Marissa and I . . ."

Sumner. He was there, at the back of my mind. The image of him on the boat in the middle of the river, his face tan and smiling, his hair windblown. Holding my hand. Making me wonder if Glory Road wasn't all there was for me.

But this was Ben. Against all odds, we'd found ourselves back in the place where we first started, only this time we were adults, hardened to some extent, more fully settled as the people we were meant to be. And I still liked who he was. The same Ben with the strong shoulders and soft heart.

"You *are* with Marissa." I tried to make my voice firm, but it still wobbled. "She's Nick's mother. I can't get in the way of that. I won't."

"I've already made the decision," he said. "It's not totally because of you, although you're a big part of it. I think you've always been a part of it. A part of me. I left Atlanta so I could figure some things out. It wasn't necessarily going to be a permanent move, but now that I'm here . . . and you're here . . . I don't know. It just makes me wonder if I got in the car and landed back on Glory Road for a bigger reason than just giving Nick and me a chance to breathe for a while."

I swallowed hard.

"I don't love her. I'm not sure I could, even if I wanted to."

I tilted my head. "Why not?"

He rubbed the back of his neck, then met my gaze. "She's not you, Jess."

The sun had dropped farther into the trees, casting long, thin shadows over the edge of the field. Waning sunlight trickled into the Jeep and dust motes danced above the dash. I inhaled and leaned forward. His hand brushed my lower back, then he pulled it away.

"Do what you need to do then," I said, my voice finally firm. "When you're done, come find me."

GLORY ROAD

❧

I scrubbed my skin red that night in the bathtub, as if I could wipe away the stain of the day. Now, at the late hour, even the surprise ending only added to my exhaustion. I ran the washcloth down my chest and around the backs of my knees, and as I did, the memory of Ben's hand on my fingers, my wrist, my lower back came back to me, nudging with persistence.

I felt like I needed to catch my breath, though I hadn't been running and wasn't even breathing hard. It was like a rope was running through my fingers too fast for me to catch it. But who was pulling the rope? And why was I scared of it getting away from me?

Once the water grew cold, I sat on my bed and pulled on a pair of cotton drawstring pants and a soft T-shirt. As I brushed my hair, a knock sounded at my door, and Mama stuck her head in. "Truce?" She thrust a plate of peanut butter cookies out in front of her.

I smiled. "I guess we have to talk sometime."

She sat on the opposite side of the bed and leaned back against the pillows. She took a bite of a cookie and turned to me. "You're so full of words, they're practically pouring out of your eyeballs. Let me have it."

I sighed and leaned back next to her. "I don't want to fight about this. We have to deal with it, but it's your health, your body, your mind. We can get more details about the medicines and trials the doctor mentioned, then see what you're willing to try."

"You heard all he said about the side effects. Would you want to put yourself through the nausea, the headaches, the . . . constipation?" She spat out the word. "All that just to prolong something that's going to come anyway?"

"I don't know, Mama. I don't know what I'd do."

"Will you be mad at me if I decide not to try any of them?"

"I might. But it's your choice. And I'll get over it. I just might not get over losing you." My voice broke, and she took my hand and squeezed it.

"Yes, you will. When you have to, you will. But listen to me, Jessie." She reached over and pulled my chin so I faced her squarely. "I'm not going anywhere soon. I know what it feels like in this brain of mine, and I know I'll still be okay for a little while. When the time does come that I need some extra attention . . . well, we'll just cross that bridge when we get to it. But I will not be your responsibility."

"You'd let someone else take care of you, but you won't let me?"

"Oh, honey, it's not that I won't *let* you. It's that I don't want you to have to be the one. Don't you see? I don't want to be your burden. I want you to be free to live your life as you choose. Not to feel tied to any one place because of me."

"That's not why I'm here. I'm here because I've chosen it, not because it's a . . . a consolation prize. You know that. We both love it here. It's our home." I blew my bangs out of my eyes, frustrated that she'd insinuate that I was only here because of some sense of duty.

"And you're wrong about being a burden," I said, my gaze on the ceiling. "You'd never be a burden to me. I'm your daughter and I love you. Taking care of you would be a privilege. An honor."

"Now, don't you go making me cry."

"Have you cried about it yet? Because I've cried buckets today."

"When you get to be my age, you'll see that the years behind you stretch on for miles, and the ones ahead seem shorter every time you think about them. Something's bound to happen—not many people get the luxury of dying peacefully in their sleep. And I know where I'm going after this life, so if I get there a little quicker than I thought I would, so much the better."

I let my head fall back against the soft pillows again. "You always see things so clearly."

We both were quiet as the irony of my statement sank in. How long would she be able to think in such clear, exact ways? The tide of tears rose again, threatening to overtake me, but with her usual humor and impeccable timing, she pulled me back from the edge.

"So what's the deal with these two boys who've been hanging around you this summer? I thought you were against dating. You've sure been against any man I've tried to set you up with."

"I *am* against dating. I'm too old for that."

"And what do you call what you're doing now? Dinner with Sumner? Long drives with Ben?"

I turned to her. "How'd you—?"

"I saw you hop in his car earlier. It was like you were seventeen again, skipping off with Ben to go to the Icebox."

I shrugged. "Ben is . . . Ben's like falling into a hammock. It's soft and familiar and . . . you know it's going to hold tight underneath you." I blinked and turned to the window. Even through the glass, I could see lightning bugs winking in the dark. "Sumner's just the opposite. He has a boat in the Caribbean, he's jetting off to Scotland this week, and his house is featured in just about every magazine in the Southeast." I wiped away dampness at the corner of my eye. "He's like climbing onto a roller coaster. You strap on the seat belt, close your eyes, and take off."

"Well, there's your answer right there."

"And what's that?"

"Honey, roller coasters have never been your thing. They make you throw up."

I laughed and she joined me, squeezing her eyes closed, her face bright and lively. I laughed so hard, tears ran down my nose. At some point they may have crossed over into real tears, but sometimes grief and humor mix together so tightly it's impossible to tell them apart.

CHAPTER 29

Climbing vines can mask unsightly fences and poles, or create a lovely
vertical garden in a tight space. However, be aware that many vines
will climb absolutely anything, including gutters, roofs, and other
plants. They are always moving, always straining toward the light.
Employ appropriate pruning techniques to avoid a rampant vine.
—CHARLOTTE FAYE, MONDAY MORNING GARDEN CLUB

JESSIE

B en and I agreed to give each other time. He needed to talk to
Marissa and I needed to figure out if I really wanted to throw
myself—and my heart—into a relationship with him. Into seeing if
the regrets and yearnings that had lain dormant between us for so
long could be transformed into something real, something lasting.

With both him and Sumner out of town—Ben and Nick to
Texas to visit a client and, while they were out there, the Alamo, and
Sumner to tour St. Andrews golf course in Scotland—I had a week to
let my thoughts sift and settle. Instead of the mental chaos I expected
with everything going on in my life, my heart felt strangely peaceful.

I'd made an appointment with another doctor to discuss the
possibility of a new drug for Mama—it was only in the testing phase,
but Dr. Dudley had said it looked promising. I also secured the bells
of Ireland, anemones, and ranunculus Olivia had requested for her

bouquets, along with finalizing details of the grapevine chandelier and Harvis's arbor.

Then I took Evan shopping for a couple of new outfits for school. I'd been feeling a little out of touch with her, but to my relief, we talked and laughed our way through shopping, then lunch at Kim's Café. By the end of the week, the hard edges of my life felt softer. Deep down, I had the sense that things would be okay.

The day before Ben was due back from Texas, Evan knocked on the open door of the potting shed as I mixed a spray bottle of vinegar, Dawn soap, and a few tablespoons of salt.

"What's that for?" she asked.

"It's weed killer." I added one more dash of salt, then recapped the bottle and shook it. "The kind that doesn't leave nasty chemicals everywhere."

"If you can use that, why do you pull weeds by hand?"

I shrugged. "Sometimes I like the work. It feels good to see them disappear."

"But you could just spray and be done with it."

"Yes, you could." I smiled and handed her the bottle. "Why don't you tackle the bed under the oak out front. Just make sure you don't get it on any of the hostas. This stuff will kill anything it touches."

She held the bottle out in front of her like it was poison. "You need to send some of this stuff down to Mr. Bradley. Nick said weeds are taking over their garden."

"Really? I told him he had to stay on top of them."

"I don't think they share your love of pulling weeds by hand." She grabbed a pair of gardening gloves off the tabletop, then paused. "You know Mr. Bradley has a girlfriend, right?" It was so unexpected, I had to struggle to keep my face from giving away my shock.

"Right?" she pressed.

"I . . . Yes, I do know that."

"He doesn't love her though."

271

"What—how do you know that?"

She shrugged. "Nick told me." She turned and headed up the path that led around the front of the shop, making sure to put one foot on each mossy stone, just like she did when she was little.

I knew I should wait for Ben to come to me. After all, that's what I'd told him: *"Do what you need to do, then come find me."* But I couldn't keep myself from sending a quick text.

A little bird told me you're having a weed problem. I have a bottle of weed killer that'll take care of it.

He responded within seconds. Great. I'll come by tomorrow and pick it up. Our flight gets in at noon. Looking forward to seeing you.

❧

Saturday dawned with typical mid-August humidity and a washed-out sky. Noon came and went, and I expected to see Ben pull down the driveway any minute. I stayed busy—unloading a new shipment of annuals and helping the ladies from Perry Baptist choose flowers for a trio of baskets to take to patients at the hospital—but as the hours crept by with no sign of him, I grew impatient. I closed the shop a few minutes early, and with Mama rocking on the front porch with the new issue of *Southern Lady* and Evan finally cleaning her bedroom, I grabbed Ben's bottle of weed killer and headed to his house.

A small silver car was parked on the street in front of his house, so I parked in the driveway. Before I knocked on the door, I took a deep breath and ran my hands over the loose bun at the back of my head. As I did, the silver car snagged my attention again. Just as I noticed the Enterprise Rent-a-Car tag, the front door opened. Instead of Ben or Nick, it was a woman wearing black leggings and a gauzy sleeveless top. She was beautiful—long lashes, red lips, and wavy, strawberry-blonde hair.

"Oh, hi." She stopped short when she saw me standing on the porch. "I was just grabbing something from my car. Can I help you?"

"I—" From somewhere deep in the house, I heard Ben's voice and froze.

Her gaze traveled from my shoes to my shorts and T-shirt and stopped on the Twig logo just under my right shoulder. "Oh, you're from the garden shop." Her voice was light, with a hint of humor hidden inside. "So you're the one who got Ben on this gardening kick. Good for you. I've been telling him he needed a hobby other than just tinkering with computers." She turned and called over her shoulder. "Ben, the woman from the garden shop is here."

She turned back to me. "Thanks for helping him with his project. I was a little worried about him getting here and being bored out of his mind."

Footsteps crossed the wood floors inside, then I saw Ben's face and something inside me cracked. His eyes were wide, and his smile was tight and uncomfortable.

She reached an arm around his waist and squeezed. "I'll let you two talk shop. I'm going to see if I can convince Nick to throw me some pitches out back." She turned to me. "I used to play softball. Believe it or not, I'm still pretty good with a catcher's mitt. Oh, and I'm Marissa, by the way."

She thrust her hand out toward me. I had no choice but to take it. "Jessie." Her grip was firm and she let go quickly. Then she reached up and ran her fingers through Ben's hair and kissed his cheek. "I'll see you out back."

Ben closed his eyes.

"Nice to meet you, Jessie," Marissa called on her way through the house.

When she was gone, he moved toward me. "Jess—"

But I took a step back. "No. Don't."

"Jessie, wait. It's not . . ." He groaned. "It's not what it looks like."

273

But I was already pounding through the grass to my car. He followed close behind me. My hands trembled and I remembered the spray bottle. The stupid weed killer. I turned and thrust the bottle at him.

"Jessie. Stop."

But I couldn't. My breath was ragged and my throat was thick. I yanked open my door and climbed in. He grabbed the edge of the door before I could close it. "She just showed up. She found my flight information and was waiting at the airport when we got in."

He was still talking, explaining, but my mind went back to when I'd called him all those years ago. When I hoped he still loved me. Loved me enough to fight for me. But he didn't. Then or now.

"I can't." I stared at the steering wheel. It was easier than looking into his eyes.

I knew I was being irrational. We'd made no vows, no declarations to each other. As my eyes filled, I realized that though it—*he*—had only been a hope, a yearning, I'd wanted it more than I'd wanted anything in a long time.

I squeezed my eyes closed. "Marissa is here now. She's happy to be here with you and Nick. Go back inside and enjoy your family." Then I closed my door.

He remained there next to my car while I wiped my eyes, then backed up and drove off. He was still there when I glanced in my rearview mirror one last time.

CHAPTER 30

If you have a flower overgrowing its desired boundaries, consider containing its roots. You could try planting it in a pot or bucket under the soil, or adding a border around the plant, partially under the soil to keep the roots in check. If the plant continues to overgrow despite your attempts at control, be aware that it may just need extra legroom.
—ANNE P. SNIDER, *FINICKY FLOWERS*

EVAN

For a while now, deep down I'd felt like two different people. One Evan wanted nothing more than to wrap her arms around her life: her mom with her broken heart and her flowers and smudges of dirt on her cheeks. Her spirited grandmother with her denim jackets and fluffy meringue and strange forgetfulness. Her old house with its creaky hardwood floors, her cozy bedroom with the stacks of books and soft blankets. Life was good and familiar. Dependable in its everyday sameness.

The other Evan wanted more. She wanted to stretch and push and press. She wanted breathing room. She wanted to do things she wasn't supposed to do just to see what would happen. She wanted to test her own limits and blast everything wide open.

The real Evan saw the dangers to both those extremes. In one, I'd become my mother—maybe taking a peek at parts unknown but always returning to what I knew. In the other, I'd probably just hurt her. I knew there had to be a balance—a way to walk the line without falling into the depths on either side—but I had no idea how to find that. So I mostly did nothing. I just took life as it presented itself to me. I didn't ask too many questions, and I didn't press too hard against the walls.

Then school started.

Ruth was in several of my classes, which was fun. With my work at Twig and her family's last-minute end-of-summer vacation, I hadn't seen her much in the weeks leading up to school. On the first day we spent most of Alabama history and biology sending discreetly folded notes back and forth—I made sure to sit right in front of her— recapping the last bit of our summer.

I was shocked to find out she'd spent a lot of time with a boy named Parker during her trip to visit family in Biloxi. On torn pieces of notebook paper, Ruth told me all the important details: he lived next door to her cousin Darleen, he wanted to be a missionary in Africa just like she did, and he shared her obsession with Sherlock Holmes.

You're smitten, I wrote.

I think I'm in love, she wrote back, which almost made me burst out laughing. Sweet, obedient, devout Ruth in love with a boy she didn't know a month ago made about as much sense as ice skates in Alabama, but her next note shocked me more.

Have you heard about the party Friday? It's at some field just outside Perry. Maybe we should go.

That she'd heard about the party was one thing—not to mention the fact that I hadn't. That she wanted to go was on a whole other non-Ruth level.

And how do you propose we go about that? I reached up to scratch my head, then dropped the note on her desk. Mrs. Hughes stared at me, but I just smiled.

Gina's going, of course, she wrote back. Gina was her sister, a senior this year who, as such, had three years of professional rule bending under her belt. *You could spend the night with me and we could get a ride with her.*

I turned around in my seat. Ruth was grinning. "Seriously?" I mouthed.

"Miss Ashby. Eyes forward, please."

"Yes, ma'am."

I cornered Ruth the minute the bell rang after class. "You're serious about this?"

"Sure. Why not?"

"It's—we'd get in a lot of trouble if anyone found out."

"Then let's make sure they don't find out." She hoisted her bright-red backpack onto her shoulder.

I opened my mouth, then closed it. This new Ruth was baffling. "Okay, but . . ."

She grabbed my hand and pulled me out the door and down the hall. "It's a new year, Evan. Don't you feel it? Anything is possible."

When she said it like that, I did feel it. I did.

After that, everything fell into place. The football game that night was away, so we didn't have to worry about transportation to and from the game. I asked Mom if I could spend the night with Ruth, and of course she said yes. Ruth begged Gina to let us ride with her to the party. Gina put up a fight, but Ruth told her if she didn't take us, she'd tell their parents that Gina was going to an unchaperoned party with boys, music, and possibly alcohol. Gina had no choice but to consent to bringing her little sister and her friend along.

I ran into Nick as I left the cafeteria on Thursday. And by "ran into Nick," I mean I bumped into him so hard I dropped my lunch tray. Thankfully, the tray was empty.

He picked it up off the floor for me. "Easy," he said, handing it back. "You could kill someone with that thing." He'd been walking out with a few other guys, but when he stopped, they continued on without him. He didn't seem to mind.

"Sorry. Just didn't want to be late to biology."

"No problem. How's your first week been?"

"Not too bad. Yours?"

He shrugged. "It's fine. Different school, different kids, but somehow it's still the same."

It felt funny seeing him in a new environment. Here at school he seemed bigger. Taller, maybe. And older. All the nervousness that had leaked away over the summer came back hard.

He gestured down the hall with one hand and started walking. I walked with him, trying to think of something interesting to say.

"Are you going to the party Friday?"

He raised his eyebrows. "Thinking about it. You?"

"My friend Ruth and I are going."

"Think your mom will be okay with that?"

"Well, we, uh . . ."

"You're not going to tell her."

I bit my lip. "Wasn't planning on it."

"Better be careful there."

The bell rang, scattering everyone down the halls and through classroom doorways.

"I will. It'll be fine." I glanced behind me toward the staircase. I was late, but then again, he was too. I adjusted my backpack and tried not to look as jittery as I felt.

He gave me a half smile before heading down the hall to his class. "I'll keep an eye out for you then."

❧

I had some ideas of what the party would involve, though I didn't know exactly what to expect. Would there be any other ninth graders?

Would I be able to find Nick? Would Mom find out I wasn't just spending the night with Ruth? The unknown bothered me, but I did my best to pretend I was fine with everything. After all, this was the Evan who wanted to push and reach and live. It felt different than I thought it would—more daunting, somehow. Intimidating.

We piled into Gina's car just after dinner. She'd told her parents we were all going to a friend's house for a back-to-school movie night. A little unbelievable to me, but her parents didn't question it.

"Is that what you're wearing?" Gina asked me as she cranked the engine of her white Camry.

I'd worn a top Mom had bought me on our shopping trip. I loved it—the background was a deep emerald green and it had these little white lily pads all over it. It was also super thin and flowy, which was great since it was still roasting even with the sun down.

"What's wrong with it?" I ran my hands down the sides of my white shorts—not too short, but shorter than I was used to—and straightened the camisole I'd worn under the flowy top.

"Nothing," Ruth said, glaring at her sister. "You look great."

As soon as she'd gotten in the car, Ruth had changed from her usual knee-length skirt to a pair of denim shorts and a snug gray shirt. I was surprised to find she actually had a figure under all the modest clothes she usually wore.

She twisted around in her seat, her dark-brown hair making a wild, curly halo around her head. "It's going to be a great night."

By the time we arrived at the field, it was already full of cars. Music pumped out of speakers—a mash-up of country, rock, even some Beatles.

"I'll meet you back here at ten thirty," Gina said as we climbed out of her car. "And not a minute after. Don't think I won't leave without you." Then she was gone, leaving us with no idea what to do.

"Well, let's . . . explore, I guess," Ruth said.

We stayed to the edges of the field—the center was a massive crush of people, everyone shouting, dancing, and moving together to the music and some hidden beat of the group itself. Car after car overflowed with laughter and yells. People we didn't know smiled at us as we walked by, calling out hellos. We passed a truck with huge tires, its tailgate down to reveal a cooler with a spigot pouring out bright-pink liquid. One of the guys handing out red Solo cups stopped us. "Your hands are empty." He filled two cups and handed them to us. "Enjoy." Ruth glanced at me, then reached out and took one, so I did too.

Everything in me told me not to drink it—or at least to ask what was in it. But I shut down that rational voice and took a sip anyway. Whatever it was tasted like cough syrup and I almost spit it out, but I managed to get it down. The second sip was only slightly better.

Ruth's face was happier than I'd ever seen it. "This is amazing." She had to talk loud over the noise. "So many people! Do you think they all go to Perry?" Someone bumped into her and she held her cup away from her so it wouldn't slosh.

I was happy too, or at least I think I was. Freedom and anticipation and fear all mingled together to make a potent mix that flowed through my body and made my stomach jumpy. Something in me— probably the part that didn't want to test any limits—whispered that this wasn't the best idea, but I kept walking, kept smiling, kept sipping.

At some point I lost Ruth. She was right there beside me, then I turned to say something to her but she was gone. I thought I saw the back of her head over someone else's shoulder, but when I tried to push my way to her, she disappeared again. About that time another red Solo cup made its way into my hand. I took a sip—it was the same pink stuff, but by now it had lost most of its bitterness. It was sweet, but not too sweet, and had a pleasant tang. In fact, it was pretty much the best thing I'd ever tasted.

I kept pushing through the crowd, trying to find Ruth, but finally I gave up. Surely I'd run into her at some point. I was dancing with some guy to some song about a wagon wheel, singing loud even though I only knew a few of the words, when someone tapped me on the shoulder.

I whirled around expecting to see Ruth, but the quick movement sent my head spinning in a dozen directions. I reached out to grab the nearest solid thing, and my hand connected with a strong arm. It was Nick.

He wrapped his arm around my shoulder. "You're coming with me."

"Hey, man, she's with me." The guy grabbed my other arm, but Nick pushed him off.

"Dude! What's up with this?"

"What are you doing?" Nick asked me, ignoring the guy's frustration. He bent and spoke near my ear. "Did you know that guy?"

I shook my head but stopped when the dizziness returned. "No idea. But he was nice. I think."

"Right." He led me through the crowd, pushing away arms and shoulders as they blocked our way. I clung to his hand, then his arm. He was my knight. My prince. All the things I'd always thought were so sappy and ridiculous. He'd said he'd keep an eye out for me and he did. He found me. I was dopey with happiness.

Finally we broke out of the tight knot of people. The air was fresher on the outside, like liquid in my parched throat.

"Come on." He gently pulled me toward the entrance gate.

"Where are we going?"

"I parked near the exit. I've been to enough parties like this to know sometimes you have to make a quick getaway."

I was about to question him—get away from what?—when we arrived at his car, parked under a big tree right next to the gate. It was much quieter here. A few people sat on the hoods of cars nearby, but it was nothing like the sweaty mass in the middle of the field.

Nick reached in his open window and grabbed a water bottle. "Here." He handed me the bottle.

I uncapped it and took a sip, then shook my head. "My stomach feels kind of funny."

"A couple doses of hunch punch will do that. Let's try sitting."

We found a couple of empty chairs and sat down. My stomach settled a bit, and I straightened my legs out in front of me.

"How do you feel?"

"Great." I blinked a few times. The trees were moving a little, like I was looking at them underwater.

He laughed quietly. "Yeah, I bet."

"Did you have any of that pink stuff?"

"Nah. I take a pass on drinks that come from the back of someone's car."

"Truck. It was a big truck."

"Even better. You should probably avoid them too. You never know what could happen."

"Nothing will happen." I settled farther down into the chair and rested my head on the back. "You're here, right?"

"What if I hadn't found you? Did you even know that guy's name?"

"Of course. It was Will. Or Phillip . . ."

"Evan." His voice was urgent and I turned to him. I forced my eyes to stay open, though they were trying desperately to close. "I'm serious. You can't do this again. If you're going to come to parties like this, you have to be careful. Where's your friend, the girl you came with?"

"I . . . I don't know. She was there, then she wasn't . . ."

"You two need a better plan. You have to watch out for each other."

"What are you talking about? It's just a party. People having fun. Don't you like to have fun?" As I talked, my words seemed to slide together. I worked my lips, trying to get them to pronounce everything right, but it was useless. I reached up and felt them with my fingers. They felt normal to the touch, though I could have sworn they were three times their usual size.

"Yes, I like to have fun. And I'm sure you do too, but this isn't the right kind of fun. Not everyone's going to watch out for you like I will."

I smiled at him. "You will. You'll look out for me. You've been so . . ." I stopped. My thoughts were bouncing like Ping-Pong balls. "I like that you're here. You've made everything . . . better. Everything in my life. You're the prince." I bit down hard on my lip, embarrassed that I'd let that word slip out.

He laughed. "You have no idea what you're talking about."

"Don't laugh at me. I'm serious, I—"

He laughed again, but it was softer. "I'm sorry. I am. And I get it. You're not too bad yourself, kid."

Just then two guys called to Nick as they approached. They were laughing and jabbing each other in the shoulders like guys do. I'd never understood that. Girls never did that.

"Hey, man, what's up?" one of them said.

Nick turned to me. "Scott." He pointed to the taller of the two. "And Billy. They play baseball."

"Did you hear about Coach Terrell?" Scott asked Nick.

As they talked—something about a new job, or maybe a new dog—I let my eyes close. One spot behind my forehead had begun to ache, and as I listened to the voices and sounds around me, that ache grew to a ferocious pounding that throbbed in time with my heartbeat. I relaxed my neck muscles and tried to keep my body as still as possible. The throbbing continued though, growing worse by the second.

"What's going on with all this?" Billy or Scott asked. His voice was muffled, like my ears were stuffy. "Is she . . . ?"

She. Was that me? I probably could have figured it out if I opened my eyes, but I couldn't muster the effort it would take to pull them open.

"Shut up," Nick said.

"No, seriously," the other one said. I could tell by his voice that he was smiling. Maybe even on the verge of laughter. "What's the deal? She's your girlfriend?"

"No, she's not . . . She's fourteen. A freshman."

My stomach tightened into a ball and dropped.

"So? She's cute. Anyway, I went to prom last year with Kasey Lott. She was a freshman and it was no big deal."

Nick sighed. "She's like my little sister, man. She's a friend. That's it."

Despite my total brain-haze, his words cut through the slop and left my heart—my ridiculous crush—in clear view. So that was it. He didn't like me. Or he did, but as a sister. As a friend. Humiliation crept in, blazing on my cheeks.

I heard shuffling next to me, then Nick was pulling me to my feet. "Come on, Evan," he said quietly.

He opened the passenger door and I crawled in, then he cranked the engine and rolled the windows down. Just before we pulled out of the gate, I saw Ruth. I yelled her name out the window and she ran to me.

"Evan!" She was out of breath. "I've been looking everywhere for you. Where have you been?"

"I . . ." I turned to Nick. "I don't know."

"I'm Nick." He held up his hands as if to proclaim innocence. "I'm a friend. And I'm taking her home."

"Wait, I can't go home. I'm supposed to be staying with Ruth." Then out of nowhere, I knew I was going to be sick. I fumbled for the handle and just barely managed to push the door open before I threw up on the grass.

"Um . . ." Ruth took a few steps back. "I'm sorry, but you can't come to my house like this. My parents will kill me. Then you."

Nick put his hand on my shoulder. "You okay?"

I pressed my wrist to my mouth and nodded. I cleared my throat. "I feel better."

"Hallelujah. Let's get out of here." He grabbed a napkin out of the glove box and handed it to me. "I'll let her sleep it off, then I'll get her home."

Ruth eyed me. "Is that okay with you?"

"Yes, I'm fine. I'm so sorry, Ruth."

"Are you kidding? This was the best night ever. Except for . . ." She gestured down to the grass next to the car.

"But how did you . . . ? I mean, you drank it too."

"Only a few sips, but it was gross. I poured it out." She pushed the door closed. "I gotta go or Gina really will leave me." She turned and ran back to the other side of the field where Gina had parked. I checked the clock on the dashboard: 10:28.

I left the window down as we drove away from the field. When we got to the highway, Nick turned left.

"Wait, Ruth's house is the other way."

"You're not going to Ruth's house, remember? We've been over this."

"But if I go home . . ." I glanced down. My white shorts had a big pink stain down the front, and judging by how my hair felt when I ran my hand over it, I was sure I looked awful. Not exactly what Mom expected the next time she saw me.

"You're coming to my house." He raised his eyebrows, daring me to object. I nodded. "Good. We have the most comfortable couch you'll ever sleep on. Though I suspect you'd fall asleep pretty much anywhere."

"What about your dad?"

"I'll take care of it."

I closed my eyes again and relished the breeze on my face. My stomach was beginning to tumble again. I took a few deep breaths to settle it back down.

"How're you feeling?"

I swallowed hard. "So-so."

"Next time someone hands you a cup of mystery drink, what are you going to do?"

"Just say no?"

A half grin. "That'll work."

He turned onto Glory Road and slowed down as the car bumped gently over the dips in the red dirt.

"Why are you so nice to me? I just . . . I'm curious."

I'd been wondering it for a while, actually. I think deep down, some part of me had known all summer that he didn't really *like* me. That he was just a nice guy who liked good music and who needed someone to hang out with in a new town. Maybe I qualified because I wasn't like most of the girls in Perry and because, as he'd said, I didn't ask him too many questions. But this one was important.

He shrugged. "I don't know. I feel like I want to take care of you or something." He waited a moment before speaking again. "Sometimes I wonder what it would have been like if my dad had . . . if I had a sibling. Someone to watch out for." He glanced at me. "I guess I took it a little too far with you. I'm sorry."

"No, it's fine, it's . . . I like it. I like having you around."

He ran his hand through his hair. "Seriously though, if something happens again—not just something like this, but anything—if you need help, I'm here for you. Got it?"

I nodded, slowly this time to not upset my brain again. "Thanks."

He parked in his driveway, then cut the lights. "Now, let's get you inside. With any luck, Dad's already in bed."

We crept into the house, but as soon as I sat on the couch and pulled my sandals off, Mr. Bradley appeared from the back hallway.

"Have fun?" he asked before he saw me. "Evan. What are you doing here?" He turned to Nick in confusion.

"Please don't tell my mom," I blurted.

"She needs to stay here tonight," Nick said. "I'll run her home early in the morning, but she can't go home like this."

Mr. Bradley was watching me. "Yes, I can see that."

I crossed my legs, hoping to hide the pink stain on my shorts, then tried to smooth my hair. "She just . . . She'll be so mad at me."

"I wouldn't be so sure," Mr. Bradley said. "She won't be happy, but I don't think anger will be her first reaction."

"You're going to tell her." I massaged my forehead with my fingertips, making circles over my temples with my thumbs.

"No, I'm not. It's not my place," he continued. "But it is yours."

I groaned, let my hands drop, and leaned back against the cushion.

He sighed, then turned to Nick. "Get her a blanket and a pillow, then say good night."

"Yes, sir."

Nick did as his dad asked, then retreated to the back of the house. I lay in the dim living room and stared at the ceiling. My head still felt like it was on a merry-go-round, but if I stayed still and breathed shallow breaths, it slowed enough for me to close my eyes. I had no idea how I was going to deal with tomorrow—picking up my stuff from Ruth's, getting home without Mom figuring out what had happened, coming up with a suitable explanation for my stained clothes and tangled hair—but that was hours from now. I'd come up with something.

Then again, maybe Mr. Bradley was right. Maybe the truth was best. And here was the truth as I saw it.

1. Nick was just my friend, which sucked, but it was probably just as it should be.
2. All that pushing and stretching, all the limit testing I halfway thought I wanted? I was beginning to think it wasn't worth the trouble.
3. Still, anything was possible. Just like Ruth said.

❧

I woke up the next morning to Mr. Bradley tapping me on the shoulder. "Evan." He pulled his hand away and hitched his voice up a notch. "Evan."

I covered my exposed ear with my hand and said something that was supposed to be, "Why are you yelling?" but it came out jumbled.

"Up and at 'em," he said. "I just woke up Nick so he can get you back home. I don't want your mom to worry."

I pushed myself up into a sitting position. My eyelids felt glued together. I rubbed them hard and squinted in the morning light. Mr. Bradley's hair was rumpled on top, like he had skipped the brush when he got out of bed. "She won't worry. She thinks I'm at Ruth's."

"But she won't for long, will she?" He eyed me until I shook my head.

"Good." He stuck his hands in his front pockets and tilted his head to the side. "Everything okay with you?"

"Yeah. I'm fine. Why?"

He shrugged. "I just didn't see you as much of a party girl."

I snorted a laugh. "I'm not. Definitely not."

He pulled his lips into a thin, straight line. "Hmm."

"I know it doesn't seem that way, but I'm really not." I tugged at the edge of the blanket I'd slept under. "I did have fun though. Most of it, at least. But I think I'll stay away from the . . ." Just the thought of the pink stuff made my stomach lurch.

He smiled, then stuck his head in the hallway and called Nick's name. We both heard a loud grunt in response. He grabbed his keys off the kitchen table. "Come on. He's not getting up anytime soon. I'll drive you home." He opened up the back door. "After you."

"Did you know Nick was going to the party last night?" I asked as we neared our house.

"Of course."

"And you were okay with it?"

He pulled into the driveway and stopped. Mom was in the yard watering her plants. My head swam a little at the sight of her.

"I'm not crazy about parties in strange places. Especially places the cops used to bust when I was in high school. *Especially* not when there's alcohol around. But Nick knows the deal. I trust him as long as he doesn't give me a reason not to trust him. So far it's worked."

"That's pretty much my mom's rule too. But there's no way she would have let me go to this party."

He glanced ahead to where Mom stood still, probably wishing she'd put on some real clothes. "Try not to be too hard on her. She loves you a whole lot." He turned back to me. "I think she'd do anything to protect you, including keeping you away from a party you probably shouldn't have been at in the first place."

I opened my mouth to protest, but he continued. "Look, Nick is older than you. Three years is a big deal when you're young. When Nick was fourteen, I wouldn't have let him go either. No way."

He grabbed the door handle. "You'll have to get out one of these days. Might as well get it over with." He gave me a small smile, then opened his door.

CHAPTER 31

Water is good for your garden, but just as in life, too much of a good
thing can be a detriment. Overwatering can cause a flood and wash
away soil and necessary nutrients. Establish a regular watering pattern
and stick to it. Your plants will come to expect their daily quench,
and it just might become a life-giving routine for you as well.
—AARON IRVING, GRACE IN THE GARDEN

JESSIE

At the hottest part of the summer—usually around mid-August—I
liked to start my days with a watering hose in hand. Spending so
much time and energy on the plants at Twig sometimes caused my
own garden to suffer, but at the very least, I always made sure it had
plenty to drink. Offering sustenance to my faithful shrubs and colorful annuals left everything a little brighter and fresher.

Standing at the side of my house in my short cotton robe and
flip-flops, coffee mug in one hand, hose in the other, I found it easy
to get lost in a daze. Evan had spent the night at Ruth's, Mama hadn't
yet made the trek from her house to mine, and the road was empty of
cars. My mind was free to roam, although these days, it wasn't going
anywhere easy.

It'd been almost two weeks since I trotted to Ben's house with
my gift of weed killer. I'd willingly set aside all my misgivings, all my

hesitations, and followed what had felt like a sure thing straight to his front door, but instead, I found her.

"*She's not you, Jess,*" he'd said in his car just days before that. His words had been like a balm, like warm honey. He'd felt so solid, so real, so much of what I wanted. But seeing Marissa in his house, her arms around him, her lips near his ear—it was a stark reminder of how much love can hurt. I'd told myself years before that I wouldn't hurt again—and neither would Evan—and I needed to keep that promise.

He'd called of course—when I got home from his house, my phone was already ringing—but I didn't answer. When he sent texts, I skimmed them before turning my phone facedown. He came by the shop only once. I was busy with customers, so he'd waited on the front porch, probably thinking I'd come sit with him as soon as I was finished, but I couldn't. It was too much. Like when you opened the door to a hot oven and the heat blasted out—not burning, exactly, but letting you know a blaze was in the realm of possibility. I knew fire could remove impurities, could burn away excess and reveal the truest elements, but it could also whittle away, leaving you with nothing.

And there was Sumner too. While I was trying to shake Ben out of my heart, my memories, and my tangled emotions, Sumner was, in a way, easier. At least time with him didn't feel painful at the edges. As soon as he returned from his trip to Scotland, he'd come to my house and whisked me away to dinner. He asked me to show him the best of Perry, so I took him to Jack & Mack's, where we ordered onion burgers and root beer floats and laughed at the old black-and-white photos on the walls depicting the Perry of my childhood. Strangely enough, it wasn't that different from how it was now. Somehow time had marched on, yet stayed completely still at the same time.

I was still thinking about the old photos at Jack & Mack's when I heard the unmistakable rumble of Ben's Jeep coming up the road. I whirled around toward the path that led to my front porch, but there was no way I could get inside without him seeing me first. I stood still, hoping he'd pass by without noticing me, while at the same time suppressing an urge to do something to get his attention—wave, yell, run.

When he slowed and pulled into the driveway, I dropped the hose and turned the faucet off, using my other hand to pull my robe around me a little tighter. I took a deep breath before I turned around. That's when I noticed Evan beside him in the passenger seat. Evan, who was supposed to be at Ruth's house.

When he stopped the car, he said something to Evan and she peered at me before responding. She looked miserable, and he looked only slightly better. Finally he opened his door. I inhaled, trying to gather my strength but not feeling like I had much left. Then Evan climbed out and walked toward me.

"Hey," she said quietly.

I reached out and touched her arm. "What—?"

"I promise I'll explain later, but can I just . . . ?" She gestured to the house, then glanced back, not at me, but at Ben. He gave her a half smile. When I turned back to her, she was already climbing the porch steps and reaching for the handle of the screen door.

"What's going on? Why is she with you?"

"It's kind of a long story."

I shot him the same look I gave Evan when I knew she was keeping something from me.

"She's fine. Really. She just needs some sleep. And a lot of water. She'll tell you the rest."

I nodded and rubbed my hand over my forehead. Whatever had happened to put her in his car rather than sleeping at Ruth's, I wanted to hear it from her.

"Jessie . . ."

I hesitated a second before turning back to him, and when I did, his eyes had changed. He scuffed the toe of his shoe on the ground in front of him. "I got a note in my mailbox the other day. Someone wants to buy my parents' house."

"What?"

"Yeah. It's kind of crazy. It's this couple looking for a place to raise goats to make cheese. They said they were out driving, looking for land, and saw the old carpet and junk by the street in front of our house. Thought maybe we were getting ready to move."

"What'd you say?" My unsteady heart was pounding in my chest, my ears, my fingertips. "Did you tell them you'd just moved in?"

He stared up at the sky, then back at me. "I'm going to sell it to them. I already told my parents. Well, I asked them. They loved knowing it was someone who'd use the land well." He smiled. "The goats will probably eat my tomatoes. They were pitiful anyway. Turns out I'm not much of a gardener."

So that was it then. He'd come back, and now he was leaving again. We'd both go back to life as it should be. "But school's already started. Will Nick go back to his old school?"

He looked at me strangely. "We're not going back to Atlanta. I've actually already found a house. We'll just rent until we decide on something permanent. It's downtown, right behind the café."

"You mean here? In Perry?"

"Yes," he said slowly. "We're staying here. At least for . . . Well, I don't know how long. But we both like it here. Neither of us wants to leave. Nick will finish out the school year for sure."

"Okay." I tugged at my robe again. "What does that mean for . . . ?" Tears pushed at the back of my eyes, but the emotion behind them wasn't clear.

He rubbed his eyes. They were red and dark circles bloomed beneath them. "Marissa is gone. We ended things the night you came over. She left the next morning."

I didn't say anything.

"It was . . . simple. We just didn't make sense. We'd been trying to force this thing between us all because of Nick, but do you know what he said to me the next day when I told him we'd broken up?"

I shook my head.

A smile pricked the edges of his mouth. "He said, 'Took you long enough.'" Then his smile faded. "I know there was more than just Marissa standing between us. I know we have years of stuff to sort through. I'm not oblivious to any of that."

"I know."

He took a step closer to me. To the casual observer, it'd look like we were having a chat about the garden. Or maybe the weather. It was just as well that no one—including Ben—knew the way my heart was tumbling.

"Jess, I don't even know how we'd begin to give this—us—a real shot. Where we lay everything out in the open and say what we mean. We don't hold anything back."

I closed my eyes. When his fingers found mine and he squeezed, I squeezed back.

"What if our time has passed?" I whispered.

"What if this is the best chance we've ever had?"

I wanted to do it. I wanted to take a step toward him and close the space between us. Lean into him and erase the years.

But I pulled my hand away, though it felt like tearing away a piece of myself. I couldn't put my heart through it again. Not with Evan by my side. It was too big of a risk.

"I'm sorry." I left him there in the driveway, his arm still outstretched.

❧

For only the second or third time ever, I didn't go to work in the morning. I left the door to Twig locked with the Closed sign hanging in the window, even though it was a Saturday, usually my busiest day of the week. As the sole operator of a small business, I didn't get sick days, but I decided it was my right to take one.

Evan slept until noon, and while she dozed, I cried. I hated to do it. I felt weak, silly, like a teenager unsure of her heart or the ways of love. But I knew love. And I knew my heart. I cried for the girl I used to be, the woman I'd grown into, and the woman I'd have to be as I faced the future. This summer had emboldened me, but it had also left me feeling hollow. The ache that had been with me for years pulsed even stronger now, and I still didn't know what to do about it.

When she began to stir, I got up, splashed cold water on my face, then went to the kitchen. A moment later, I knocked softly on her door.

"Yes?"

I opened the door and held out a glass of water and a piece of toast on a plate.

Her eyes grew wide and she reached for the water. She drained the glass and set it down. Her hair needed a brush and she smelled— well, not great.

"He told you, didn't he?"

"Told me what?" I raised my eyebrows.

"Wh-what happened last night."

"No, he didn't. He left that for you. I'm getting a pretty good picture, although I would love for you to tell me I'm completely wrong."

"What do you think happened?"

I shook my head. "Nope. I'm not going to do that. You'll have to spell it out for me."

She took a deep breath and leaned back against her pillow, then told me about the party, Ruth's sister, and Nick bringing her home.

I tilted my head. "Why did Nick bring you to his house? Why didn't you just go back home with Ruth?"

She covered her face with her hands.

"Evan. Tell me."

"There was this stuff. This drink. It was pink and sweet and tasted okay. But then I threw up. Mr. Bradley let me sleep on their couch."

Her hands still covered her face. I wanted to yell at her for being thoughtless and irresponsible, but at the same time I wanted to hold her close to me, to feel her hair against my cheek and her arms around my neck. When she finally pulled her hands away, she seemed both older and younger than her fourteen years.

"Why didn't you tell me about the party? Or at least ask me about it?"

"I don't know. I knew you'd say no and I . . ." She shrugged. "I really wanted to go. Just to see what it was like."

I felt like I was stepping through land mines, treading carefully to avoid setting anything off and doing irreparable damage. "You broke my trust."

"I know. I totally blew it."

"Honey, you didn't blow it. You can't blow it with me, like it's going to be the last straw and I'm going to give up on you. That's not going to happen."

"Did you ever do anything like this? Did you ever break the rules and do something you weren't supposed to?"

I was surprised by the directness of her question, but I also recognized it for what it was—a way to link us together. To show her that she wasn't feeling anything I hadn't felt, wasn't trying anything I hadn't already tried in a hundred different ways.

I'd always wanted to be easygoing as a parent. It wasn't in retaliation of anything my parents did or didn't do—it was just that from the beginning, Evan carried herself with the air of a person much wiser than her years. So far I hadn't needed to discipline her too much, or even lay down many rules. One of Evan's gifts was an inherent intelligence and the ability to choose mostly right paths.

I realized now that my choice to let her make her own decisions— within reason—meant that I hadn't been honest about my own mistakes. And maybe the best thing a parent could do for a child was admit where she herself had gone wrong.

"Truthfully, I didn't break a whole lot of rules. Some, of course, but nothing big. But what I did was spend a whole lot of time trying to be someone I wasn't."

Evan pushed her hair back from her face and peered at me with the big blue eyes that had come straight from her father. Probably the best thing he'd ever given her. "Why'd you do that?"

I inhaled and blew the air out slowly. "I think I wanted people to like me. I wanted to be who I thought everyone wanted." I leaned toward her and whispered, "I became a cheerleader."

Evan laughed. "I know that."

"You do?"

She nodded. "Gus was cleaning out her attic one day and gave me a box of old yearbooks. Those uniforms were pretty ugly."

I feigned shock. "They were not!" She smiled. "But why'd you never tell me you saw them? You never asked me about it."

She shrugged. "I thought it was a little strange that you'd never told me you teased your hair and wore a green sequined skirt, but . . . I don't know, seeing that picture of you, it didn't really feel like you. It seemed like she was another person entirely. Not my mom."

"It's definitely not who I am now. But my attempts to fit in, to be another kind of person, didn't help me very much." My chest clenched as I thought of Ben. Those misguided attempts to be a certain kind of girl were what had kept us apart. I was sure of it.

I ran my hands over my face and tucked my hair behind my ears. "I try not to think in terms of regrets, because I really do believe everything has led us to where we are now—me and you and Mama here in this place. But I went through some hard things because of my desire to be someone else. I don't want that for you."

I took her hand in mine. Her fingernails were clipped neat and short. I brushed my fingers over her nails, remembering the tiny dots of pink polish I used to dab on them when she was a little girl. "I know you're figuring out life and who you're going to be and where you belong. Everyone has to do that at some point. You're a lot stronger than I was when I was your age. You're more sure of yourself."

Evan snorted. "I don't know about that."

I reached out and tipped her chin up with my fingers. "Yes, you are. I know you are. Deep down, you know the real Evan. Don't lose her. Other kids aren't worth it. Parties and boys and weird relationships—nothing's worth losing who you are. That little gold nugget deep in your heart. You have to treasure it. Okay?"

"Okay. Thanks."

I scooted over on the bed and lay down next to her. She curled her body toward mine and I smoothed her tangled hair back from her face. "I've been so scared of you getting older. Of you gaining your independence and not including me in your life anymore. I used to be nervous about middle school, but you sailed through that and seem to still like me."

She gave a half grin, half eye roll.

"Please keep letting me in. I'm always on your side, okay? You can tell me anything and my love for you isn't going to change. No matter what."

She nodded.

"Deal?"

"Deal."

We were both quiet a moment. The breeze from the ceiling fan rustled loose sheets of paper on her desk.

"I need a shower," she said.

"Yes, you do."

She pulled herself up off the bed and stopped at her door. "Did something happen with you and Mr. Bradley?"

"Why?" I raised my eyebrows, hoping she'd let it drop.

She shrugged. "I just haven't seen him around lately. And you seem . . ."

"I seem what?"

"I don't know. Like you're . . . not as happy as you were before school started back. Or something." She shrugged again. "And I like Mr. Bradley. He's nice."

I inhaled a shaky breath. "Don't worry about me. I'm just fine."

She reached for the door handle.

"Is there anything else you want to tell me about Nick?"

"We're just friends," she said quickly. Very quickly.

"You sure?"

"I am. And it's a good thing, I think."

"Why is that?"

She put one hand on her hip and sighed. "Boys are confusing. And kind of weird. And I just . . . I think being friends is a little less complicated."

A moment later, I heard the shower. I leaned back against her pillows again and closed my eyes. She was right, boys could be confusing. But no one said being "just friends" made it any less complicated.

CHAPTER 32

*Many plants thrive in full-sun conditions. If you have a bed with
no shade or a sunny side of the house begging for color, consider
common sun-loving flowers such as lavender, salvia, or lantana.
Less obvious choices include plumbago, perky sue, or rockrose.*
—CANDACE GOOCH, ALABAMA GARDENING FOR BEGINNERS

EVAN

I was elbow-deep in my locker Monday morning when Ruth shouted
my name over the commotion of the ninth-grade hall. The bell
was going to ring any second and I couldn't find my precal book.

"Hey!" she said, out of breath by the time she reached me. "You're
still alive!"

"Of course I am." I finally located the bright-red spine of the massive precal textbook and yanked it free from the pile of books. Two
weeks into the school year and my locker already looked like the bottom of the sale bin at the used bookstore downtown.

"Considering the last time I saw you, when you threw up on my
shoes, I have a right to be a little surprised."

"*Ruth.* Will you be quiet, please?" I glanced around to see if anyone had heard her. The last thing I wanted was to get a reputation
for . . . well, for anything. "And I didn't puke on your shoes."

"True." She shrugged. "But it was close. So did your mom find out you were at the party?"

I slammed my locker and knelt to zip my bag. "Yeah."

"Oh man. What happened? Did you get in a lot of trouble?"

I shook my head. "Not really."

Her eyes grew big. "Really? I'd probably never see sunlight again if my parents knew I'd been at that party." I fell into step next to her as we joined the crowd and made our way down the hall. "Your mom is so cool."

The truth was, I was as surprised as Ruth was. Even after our conversation in my bedroom, I still couldn't believe she hadn't grounded me. Not that she'd ever grounded me before. Then again, I'd never done anything worthy of being grounded. But if driving with Nick got me a week of cleaning, planting, hoeing, and weeding, I assumed going to a party without permission—not to mention the pink-drink incident—would definitely push my mom over the edge. But it didn't.

She did tell me I'd have to work to earn her trust back and that it would probably take a long time to do so. But more than anything, she hugged me. A lot. It was like she couldn't walk past me without touching me. If it wasn't a full hug, she was patting my arm, smoothing my hair, or kissing my forehead. Sometimes I shrugged her off—it was getting kind of embarrassing—but for the most part I was okay with it. Things had been weird this summer, and I liked that if nothing else felt the same, she did.

Ruth and I parted ways at the end of the hall—she to study hall in the library and me to studio art. I pushed open the side door next to the library and crossed the senior parking lot to the creative arts building on the other side. I'd taken art classes in middle school, but the assignments were all pretty lame. This class felt different. For one, the studio smelled good. Just like Twig had a particular scent, Ms. Landry's art studio had its own particular aroma. It could have been the paint or maybe all the papier-mâché animals she'd hung from the ceiling. I'd never thought much about art, but being in the class made me feel like I could be an artist. Even though I wasn't all that good.

"Remember, class," Ms. Landry called out. "You can't be a bad artist. You can be a lazy artist or a disinterested artist or even an angry artist, but you're not bad unless you give up on it. The art is in you. You just have to let it out."

She was going around the room passing out thick white paper and drawing pencils. Our assignment was to ask the student sitting across from us how he or she was feeling today, then draw them according to their mood. Whatever that meant. Each table had four people— two on each side—except for my table. We only had three. The space across from me was empty.

I raised my hand. "Ms. Landry?" I gestured to the empty seat. "I don't have—"

Just then the door burst open and a boy ran in. The sudden breeze from outside whisked a pile of papers from Ms. Landry's desk to the floor. "Sorry," he said when he realized the room was still and everyone was watching him. He held up a piece of paper. "I was just added to this class."

Ms. Landry clapped her hands. "Perfect." She pointed to the seat across from me. "You can be Miss Ashby's partner."

His smile dimmed a little when he saw me, but he walked toward the empty chair and slung his backpack on the floor by the desk. "Hey."

"Hey."

The rest of the class had started talking—way more than just asking each other how they were feeling. There was a certain comfort in the noise. It took away from the awkwardness of sitting across from this boy I was about to have to try to draw.

Ms. Landry stopped by our table and knelt to talk to him. I

watched as he handed her the paper, then explained how he'd requested the art class but had been placed in theater instead. He had shaggy blond hair and the longest eyelashes I'd ever seen on a boy. They were almost like a girl's or a small child's. He was thin, but his arms were tan and thick with muscle.

I glanced back up only to see he was looking right at me. So was Ms. Landry.

"Are you ready?" she asked me, her thick eyebrows arched.

"Oh, um . . . ready for what?"

She grabbed one of the pencils and held it out to me. "You have a partner now. Time to get to know each other."

She moved to the next table, leaving us with nothing but each other and the paper and pencils.

He smiled. "I'm Jack."

"Evan."

"Cool name."

"Thanks."

He pulled a sheet of paper toward him. "So, Evan. Tell me how you're feeling today." His tone was serious and he squinted, like he was a psychiatrist talking to a patient on a couch. "You can be honest. I'm here to listen."

"I—" I stopped, unsure of what to say.

Then he laughed. "I'm kidding."

I laughed too, relief flooding through me.

"This is a weird assignment." He took a deep breath. "Okay, let's do this. Seriously. How are you feeling?"

I shrugged. "Okay, I guess."

"Hmm." He kept his gaze on me as he moved his pencil across the page. "That doesn't give me much to go on."

"Sorry. I feel . . . well, I feel good."

He stopped his pencil and looked up at me.

"It's a good day." I shrugged again.

He shifted his paper and resumed sketching. It took me a moment to realize he knew what he was doing.

"Wait—you're . . . you're really good."

He didn't say anything, just kept sketching. From across the table, I saw the long lines of my hair, the angle of my cheekbone. He took longer on my eyes, taking care to fill in my pupils, then he erased a spot in each, making it look like light. In just a few minutes he was finished. He turned the page around so I could see it.

"I can't believe you just did that." It was a quick sketch, but it was me. Anyone could see it. It was . . . beautiful. "No wonder you wanted to be in this class."

He shrugged, then his cheeks flushed. "It's just—it's something I can do." He set the page on the table. "I can do two things well— wrangle horses and draw. Just don't tell my dad about the drawing."

"Why not? You're so good at it."

"Nah." He reached up to his forehead like he was grabbing the bill of a hat that wasn't there. Then he let his hand drop and fiddled with his pencil. "It's just not something he puts a lot of stock in. 'Can't make a living with a pencil.'" Jack dropped his voice low like he was imitating a man with a deep voice. "That's what he used to tell me."

"That's ridiculous. Plenty of artists make money with pencils. And paints. And . . . other things."

He slid his pencil toward me. "Your turn."

I took a deep breath. There was no way to get around the fact that I was about to completely embarrass myself with my drawing skills. Or lack of. "So how do you feel?"

"Lucky."

I laughed. "Seriously? You feel lucky?"

"Sure. I got to sit across from you. Made a new friend. Like you said, it's a good day."

I picked up the pencil and held it above my paper.

"Start with the eyes," he said. "Sometimes that helps. If you get the eyes right, the rest of it may come a little easier."

"I don't think any of it is going to come easy." I bit my bottom lip as I sketched out what I hoped was something resembling his eyes.

"You're not looking at me."

"Huh?"

"You have to know what I look like to be able to draw me."

"Right." I inhaled and focused on his eyes. They were deep blue and kind of squinty at the edges. "This is awkward." He wagged his eyebrows and I laughed.

Though it took him only minutes to complete my sketch, it took me much longer. While I drew—or tried to—he talked. About the horse farm his dad owned. About his pesky younger brothers. How he wanted to be an astronaut when he was little.

"I gave up that idea when I found out you have to be really good at math to be an astronaut. But I still love the idea of space. I have a telescope out in the top of our barn. Sometimes I'll see dozens of shooting stars in one night. Satellites moving around. It's crazy what you can see in the dark."

I hadn't realized it, but as he spoke, I'd stopped drawing. I was pulled into his voice, his stories. He talked a lot—more than most guys—but instead of being weird, it was mesmerizing. I wanted him to keep talking so I could keep listening.

"Anyway." He sat straighter in his seat. "Won't be an astronaut, probably won't do anything with art other than draw pretty girls in class. I'll most likely take over my dad's farm one day. And I'm okay with that. Although a part-time job right now would be nice. I'll be sixteen next summer and I have to pay for my own car."

"You talk a lot."

He grinned. "You're not the first person to say that."

When the bell rang, Ms. Landry held out a file folder for our drawings. "If you're not finished, you can work on them in our next class. Where you sat today will be your seats for the rest of the semester. Better get used to each other." I slid my drawing into the folder, but Jack held on to his. Outside, in the bright sunshine, he handed his to me.

"You were supposed to turn that in."

He shrugged. "I can do another one tomorrow. I want you to have that one."

"Thanks." I brushed my thumb over the edge of the drawing. It was a little strange to have a drawing of myself, but I was touched that he'd given it to me.

"What class do you have next?"

"Precal. That way." I gestured back toward the main building. "You?"

"Lunch." He turned toward the cafeteria but paused. "I saw you at the party Friday."

"What? You were there?"

He nodded. "I saw you . . . dancing." His cheeks colored again, and he shoved a hand into his pocket.

"I don't . . . I'm not . . ." I raked my fingers through my hair. "I'm not really like that. I'd never been to a party like that before. I don't dance or drink. Or anything, really. It was just a onetime thing." I didn't know why it felt so important for me to explain myself to him, but I wanted him to know the truth.

"That guy you were dancing with lives out near me. I don't know what he was doing at a high school party—he graduated last year." His eyebrows bunched together. "I don't like him at all. I was trying to push toward you to get you away from him, but then your boyfriend pulled you away." He kicked at a rock on the ground. "I was glad someone did."

I was silent a moment, digesting what he'd said. "He's not my boyfriend."

"He's not?"

I shook my head. "Just . . . just a friend."

"That's . . . Okay. I'm glad." He hitched his backpack up on his shoulder. "So, I'll see you tomorrow? You have a portrait to finish."

I laughed. "'Portrait' is taking it a little far. I'll do what I can."

He gave me a little salute and headed for the cafeteria. I took a deep breath and let it out slowly, then closed my eyes and felt the sun's rays dance on my eyelids, my cheeks, my arms. I opened them when kids began to stream past me on the sidewalk, everyone in a hurry to get to their next class. Instead of hurrying to mine, I watched Jack walk away. I felt good; he felt lucky. Not a bad way to start off the year.

CHAPTER 33

A rich and fascinating relationship exists between flowers and bees.
Bees need the blooms for sustenance, and flowers need the bees for
pollination. Consider planting bee balm, butterfly bush, black-
eyed Susans, or other bee-friendly flowers in your garden.
—LEIGH T. JACOB, *HARMONY IN THE GARDEN*

JESSIE

I was out in the orchard when Evan called to me from the back porch steps, holding some kind of slim package in her hand. Even from the far distance, I could make out the orange-and-white FedEx logo, which was strange because FedEx had already come today.

I put my hand up to my mouth and called, "Five minutes!" That's about all I had anyway before dusk swallowed the last of the day's light.

I'd been in the orchard since closing time, tending to the crab-apple trees I'd recently discovered were covered in cedar rust. Mama was convinced a poultice of coconut oil and cardamom would take care of it just as well as a fungicide, but I had my doubts. Then again, she'd been right about kitchen cures before, and I was willing to try anything. The trees were so pretty in the spring when the pink and white blossoms bloomed. Even in the winter, their bare branches were like dark, lacy fingers spread out against the pale sky.

After rubbing the last of the oil mixture onto the leaves I could reach, I took off my gloves—they smelled like Vicks VapoRub and a little like the sandy bottom of Evan's beach bag—and made my way back to the house.

Evan was at the kitchen table with notebooks and loose paper spread all over the surface, leaving her own marks on the already heavily imprinted table.

"We saved dinner for you," Mama said. "Plate's in the oven." She barely looked up from her crossword puzzle book.

"Thank you." I glanced at Evan. Raised my eyebrows. She nodded back to me and gave a quick thumbs-up. We'd developed a sort of private language of small movements and gestures over the last several weeks. It was my way of checking on Mama without her being aware of it. A silent question, an equally silent response, and we both knew whether Mama'd had another episode or if her day had been good, which these days meant uneventful.

Evan gestured to the envelope on the counter. "It must be something important. I had to sign for it and everything."

I pulled the tear tab at the top and out slid a small envelope. The paper was thick and creamy, and my name was printed on the front in elegant calligraphy. Inside was a business card bearing the name Bliss Day Spa. The words *Two o'clock Friday* were printed in gold letters.

Friday. The day before the wedding. My first reaction was hesitation. Surely I couldn't put aside my preparations—twining flowers through the grapevine chandelier, attaching the hanging jars, putting together the simple yet classy arrangements that would adorn the porch and yard of Oak House—just to be primped and pampered at a spa. That was for the bride, not the florist.

I planned to say as much to Sumner when I retreated to my bedroom to call him, leaving Mama and Evan sputtering with unanswered questions.

"I assume this is your doing?" I asked when he answered.

He cleared his throat. "I have no idea what you're talking about."

I laughed. "The spa? The appointment Friday afternoon?"

"Ah, yes. That. I took it upon myself to force a little relaxation on you. Pardon me for saying this, but you don't strike me as the kind of woman who'd book your own spa appointment. Even if you do have a wedding to attend Saturday night."

"You want me to go to the wedding? As a guest?"

"I assumed . . . Well, obviously, I *wrongly* assumed it went without saying that I wanted you to be there. So, yes, I would be honored to have you by my side for the wedding. And to treat you to the spa on Friday."

"That's very sweet of you and I'm sure it'd be . . . amazing. But I can't possibly . . . It's the day before the wedding."

"I know that, but I also know most of the work will be the day *of* the wedding, right?"

I hesitated, mentally estimating the time it would take to complete all the necessary tasks before the seven o'clock ceremony Saturday. Earlier, even, if I wanted time to get myself out of my work clothes and into something appropriate for an evening wedding.

"Come on," he said. "Olivia will be there with her bridesmaids too. She's already told me she's bringing in champagne, so I apologize for them in advance, but take it as a chance to unwind a bit. Consider it my thanks for doing all this for Olivia. And for me."

"What'd I do for you?"

He laughed, low and deep. "Well, let's see. You've made me feel young again, like a teenager who can't stop thinking about the girl he has a crush on."

"Wh-what?" He'd been so lighthearted only moments before, and the seriousness took me by surprise.

"I can't stop thinking about you." He emphasized each word. "On the days we don't talk, I spend all my time anticipating when I'll next see you or hear your voice." He paused. "You've made me realize there might still be . . . love . . . for me. I wasn't sure I'd ever feel that way again."

I opened my mouth to speak, but my brain wouldn't catch up. I had no words.

He exhaled a small breath. "I did it, didn't I? I completely scared you off."

"No, I . . ."

I couldn't help it—I thought of Ben. The juxtaposition between the two men was stark. Black on white. Where Ben was familiar, even after all these years, Sumner was intriguing and new. Ben had the benefit of history, of shared innocence, but Sumner was like a fresh, clean canvas, ready to be filled with life and adventure.

To him, I wasn't the girl who'd broken his heart, who'd married someone else. The girl who'd been broken herself. To him, I was new too.

"Jessie?"

"Okay."

"Okay—does that mean yes to the spa or coming as my date?"

"Yes. It means yes to all of it."

CHAPTER 34

When planning a garden, it's easy to become discouraged if what
you plant doesn't live up to your expectations. Maybe the soil wasn't
amended properly. Maybe the season was hotter or dryer or wetter than
usual. Maybe everything you touch seems to wilt. Remember, there's
beauty in those outcomes too. Gardening is about much more than just
growing pretty flowers. It's also about cultivating your own heart.
—SALLY JO MCINTYRE, CONTEMPLATIVE GARDENING

GUS

I woke with a start, rising from the wrought iron chair like someone had goosed me. It was late afternoon, usually the hottest part of the day, though clouds had crept in while I'd been napping.

Napping, I thought with a snort.

I was usually too busy for naps. It was just this newfangled drug the young doctor had me taking twice a day. It wasn't even FDA approved yet—just something they were trying out. Jessie seemed optimistic about it though, and why not? She wasn't the one who had to take it. I told the doctor I'd be calling him personally if all of a sudden I sprouted green hair on my chin or started quacking like a duck.

Something had woken me up, I was sure of it, but all around me was still. My backyard was almost completely shaded, hemmed in as it was by big, bushy oaks and a thick canopy of loblolly pines. Only in the back corner did the trees spread apart and leave space for the sun to push through. And that's where Tom had staked his sundial all those years ago.

It was our fifth anniversary and he made me close my eyes before guiding me through the yard to this very spot. "What do you think?" he'd asked, his voice full of pride and excitement.

I read the words etched into the plaque on the front. "It's beautiful, Tom. Thank you."

The real truth was that sundials always felt a little macabre to me—hostile even—standing there counting down the hours of a life without a care. I couldn't say that to Tom though.

There it was again—the sound I now recognized as the one that had ended my catnap.

Chug-chug-chug.

Harvis's truck clanged up my driveway. It stopped under the sweetgum tree—I could hear the balls crunching under the tires—and his door creaked open. The polite thing would have been to turn around with a smile and offer him a seat, but I didn't. An empty chair sat next to me and he'd sit in it if he wanted to.

And he did. "Beautiful day."

I glanced up at the clouds skirting past the sun. I shrugged. A funny sound came from his throat and I realized it was a laugh. I stared at him. "What is it?"

His gaze strayed to my hair, and he reached out a hand toward my right ear.

"Well, what is it, Harvis?" I wished I had a mirror to check myself in, but I tamped down the urge to give myself a quick pat down to see what was out of place. I'd never been fluttery in front of a man, and I wasn't about to start now.

"Your hair is a little . . ." He reached out again, but I swatted his hand away. When I reached up myself, I felt my hair plastered to my head, damp with perspiration from my nap. I must've had my head turned to the side, ruining all that hard work with my curlers this morning.

I tried to fluff my hair with my fingers, but it was pointless. "Looks like my hair is a lost cause. Just like my mind."

I knew what his next words would be. Something soothing, coddling, something along the lines of "Don't say such a thing. It'll all be just fine." But he surprised me.

"Good thing I don't love you for your mind."

I turned to him and cocked one eyebrow.

"I love you for those blue jeans you like to wear with the rhinestones stuck on the back."

I laughed. My heart felt like a kite spinning at the end of a string. "Oh, for Pete's sake."

He rubbed his hand over the top of his head—no cap today—then he took my hand in his, and I didn't pull away. He grew serious and looked out to the yard toward the sundial and beyond. A bumblebee buzzed next to me, pausing a moment to sniff us out, then continued on to a patch of zinnias next to the birdbath.

"The truth is," he said, "I love everything about you, Augusta McBride, and that includes your mind. If you'll have me, I'll go anywhere and do anything necessary to take care of you. To make you happy. If that's moving with you into some kind of assisted-living home—"

I sucked my breath in. A *home*? I tried to pull my hand away, but he held it tight.

"—*or* staying right here on Glory Road. Whatever you want."

I shook my head. "Is that really what you want? Because we both know how this is going to go. My mind feels okay most days, but it'll keep losing its grip until one day I won't recognize you. Or Jessie . . ." My voice broke and I put my free hand to my mouth.

"Augusta," he said gently. "Look at me."

I did.

314

"I'm not scared. It's a terrible disease and I hate it, but I'm not scared of it or you. And I'll be right by your side through the whole thing." He squeezed my hand and nodded toward the sundial. My eyes skimmed across the words for the thousandth time.

Take the gifts of this hour.

"You have a lot of gifts in your life and they're not going anywhere. And I won't either. If you'll have me."

He fell silent then, his gaze directed out to the yard. He was, I knew, giving me a moment of privacy—however long I needed—to make my decision.

But I'd already made it. "You're the gift, Harvis."

❧

That evening I found Jessie in the middle of her living room floor surrounded by boxes of mason jars and a big ball of burlap twine. I settled down on the couch across from her. "Are those for the wedding?"

She nodded and reached for another jar, wrapping twine around the middle and tying it into a bow.

"For drinks?"

"I think drinking out of mason jars would be a little too country for Olivia. No, these are for candles. I'm going to line the dock with them and set them out on the railing of the boathouse."

"That'll be beautiful. How many do you have?"

She glanced around. "About a hundred. Maybe a little more."

"Better let me help then." I reached for the scissors and began cutting lengths of twine. They slid into a pile at my feet.

"I need to talk to you, honey."

Her hands stilled. I knew the "honey" would alert her that it was serious.

"Harvis came to see me today." I took a deep breath. "Believe it or not, I think he intends to make me his wife."

"What?" Jessie's eyes were wide and she dropped the twine altogether.

"He wants to be the one to take care of me." She opened her mouth, but I continued. "Now, don't worry, I'm not going anywhere. But I've already told you I don't want to be your responsibility. At least not totally yours. You have your own life. You and Evan. Who knows what will come for the two of you in the future? And Harvis . . . Well, it turns out he's a good man. I think I've known that for a long time, but it took me a while to admit it. And he's not scared off by me losing my mind. In fact, he doesn't even love me for my mind." I laughed. "He loves me in my rhinestone blue jeans. Can you believe that? Almost seventy and making a man lose his mind over my legs in a pair of jeans. And I'm not even offended!"

Jessie laughed and brushed a tear from the corner of her eye.

"Take that, Gloria Steinem," I said.

We laughed and laughed, wiping happy and sad tears off our cheeks and chins, until it finally passed. I pressed a hand to my chest. "It feels good to open my heart up again."

"It's such a risk though. You're not scared?" I knew she was talking about all of it. Every single bit.

"I am scared." I lifted one corner of my mouth and nodded. "I admit it, I am. But if I've learned anything in my life, it's that real love is always worth the risk."

CHAPTER 35

Zinnias are traditionally a happy flower, and you can't go wrong offering a loved one a bouquet of brightly colored zinnias. In particular, the scarlet zinnia signifies constancy or steadfastness. Blue hyacinths have a similar meaning, and the two flowers together would make a striking pair.
—WARREN ELLIOTT, THE SECRET LIFE OF FLOWERS

JESSIE

After a lot of discussion, some of it heated, it was decided: Mama, Evan, Harvis, and I would make the trip to Oak House Saturday around noon in two cars so they could leave before the wedding. Harvis would put the cover on the bed of his truck and transport the grapevine chandelier and all the flowers in buckets of water. My car would carry the twine-wrapped jars and bouquets for Olivia and her bridesmaids. The three of them would help me get set up, then Harvis would drive Evan and Mama back home. Everything had to be set up by four o'clock anyway for the photographer to begin taking photos, and by that time I expected Mama to be wiped out.

She put up a stiff fight but finally gave in when I mentioned that the high Saturday afternoon was supposed to be ninety-seven degrees.

"I reckon it wouldn't do for an old lady to fall asleep in her plate of buttercream icing," she said.

I patted her hand. "No, it wouldn't do at all. By the time the thermometer hits its peak, you can be back at home with a glass of iced tea and a rerun of *The Gilmore Girls*."

"Sounds like a perfect afternoon to me. I wonder if it's too late to get Harvis hooked on Rory and Lorelai."

❧

But before I could focus too much on the day of the wedding, I had the day before the wedding, which was now my spa day. Or at least spa afternoon. I spent part of the morning helping customers choose annuals that would help get their containers through the end-of-summer heat, and the rest of my time spreading the latest batch of Patsy and Loretta's organic fertilizer in my flower beds and under the fruit trees. It was hot, smelly, dirty work, but I figured it would make me appreciate the pampering later in the day that much more.

I left the shop in the care of Evan and Mama, telling them to close up early if customers were light. I popped over before I headed out. Evan sat behind the front counter, fiddling on the laptop, and Mama was spritzing our potted lilies and gerbera daisies with soda water. She said it would make them last longer.

"What in the world are you going to do when word gets out about your little side venture of wedding flowers?" Mama asked. "As soon as photos of Miss Olivia's wedding hit magazines with your name listed as the florist, people will start calling. Mark my words. You'll need extra help around here."

"Hello?" Evan waved her hands around. "I'm right here. I can help. And check this out . . ." She turned the laptop toward me. "I've set up an Instagram account for the shop. It'll help when someone Googles your name."

"We're on Instagram?"

"Yeah, I've already posted some photos, and look—you have likes!"

She'd posted pictures of the shop itself—the overflowing window boxes and planters, the arbor covered in jasmine and wisteria, the potting shed with its blue shutters and weather-beaten cedar siding—along with photos of me wrapping twine around the mason jars and tucking peach-colored ranunculus into vases.

"Evan, these are great. Thank you for doing this."

"No problem." She turned back to the laptop, her face bright from the glow of the screen. She was focused.

"You're right. You're a big help to me. And you can do even more, if you want. As long as it doesn't take away from homework or studying. But Mama's right too. Regardless of whether we get any extra business after the wedding—and I hope we do—I need to think about hiring someone else. Just part time for now. And maybe a driver too if there are more weddings."

"I know someone who may be interested." Evan kept her eyes on the screen but ran her fingers through her hair. "He's just . . . He's someone from my art class. He said he was looking for an after-school job."

"Hmm." I watched her, trying to ascertain what this "he" meant to her, if anything. "Is he nice?"

"I think so. Yes."

"Okay. Do you want to ask him about it? Maybe he could come by one day after school and I can talk to him."

"Sure." She shrugged but couldn't hide the small smile that nudged the edges of her mouth. She tucked her blonde hair behind her ears and hopped off the stool. "I need to go take some more photos for your page."

As soon as she was gone, Mama exhaled. "Good thing you won't need to place a help-wanted ad."

"What do you mean?"

"You never know what kind of kooks answer those things. You could've brought the next Perry Strangler right here to Glory Road."

"I didn't know we've ever had a Perry Strangler."

"Well, we haven't. But you never know. At least Evan knows this boy. That tells us something about him." She was quiet a moment. "She's changed this summer. Grown up."

I took a deep breath. Any insinuation that she was growing up, growing away, made my heart hurt. But it was true, and I couldn't do anything to stop it.

❧

Bliss Day Spa was in downtown Mobile, tucked into a towering old antebellum home on Government Street. When I arrived and gave the woman at the front desk my name, she ushered me into a room at the back of the house. Sunlight flooded in from a wall of south-facing windows, and deep chairs and love seats lined the walls. Magazines and gleaming coffee table books filled baskets next to each chair.

The woman held out her hand and gestured for me to choose a seat. When I was settled, she handed me a glass of water with cucumber slices, then slipped out. I leaned my head back and silently thanked Sumner again for this long-overdue treat.

A few minutes later, the front door opened and a flurry of female voices—all talking at once—swelled in the old house.

"This must be the bridal party," the woman said, setting off a round of squeals and laughter. When they burst into the room a moment later, I stood to greet them. Olivia and I hadn't officially met each other yet, but it was obvious which one she was. She had Sumner's dark eyes and high cheekbones. She was even lovelier in person than in the photos I'd seen at Sumner's house.

"Jessie?" She raised her eyebrows when she saw me. When I nodded, she hugged me and turned to the huddle of beautiful young women behind her. "This is the woman responsible for making everything at Dad's house completely gorgeous for the wedding." She squeezed my arm. "I'm so glad you're here. And I'm sorry lunch didn't work out a few days ago."

"It's fine. You have a lot of people who want to catch up with you while you're here."

We'd made a loose plan to meet for lunch the day after she got into town, but an impromptu day trip to Orange Beach with friends nixed our plans.

"My dad can't stop talking about you. He's so excited about showing you off to all his friends tomorrow. I think he may be more excited about you than he is about me getting married!"

"Olivia." Her friend shushed her. "That's not true."

"Oh, I'm kidding, though it's true he has a thing for Jessie. But no, I know he's happy about me and Jared. My biggest worry is that he'll blubber his way down the aisle."

She laughed and we laughed along with her, but something in me felt off balance, like I'd gotten my toe hung under the edge of a carpet and tripped. *"He's so excited about showing you off to all his friends."*

A troop of women in white aprons filed into the room then and pulled up stools in front of each of us. For the next two hours, our arms, legs, and feet were covered in warm paraffin wax, oiled, massaged, and lotioned. Our nails were soaked, filed, buffed, and polished.

At some point Olivia's loudest and most outspoken and boisterous friend, Bridget, popped open the bottle of champagne and poured a flute for each of us except Olivia. For her, she poured a full glass.

"It's your wedding weekend," Bridget said with authority. "It's our job to make sure you have fun. Starting with two glasses of champagne."

While my toes soaked in a mini hot tub in front of my chair, I sipped my flute of champagne, savoring the fizzy bubbles and the sharp, crisp flavor of raspberries. Bridget circled the room refilling glasses and admiring everyone's nails. When she got to me, I shook my head and put my hand over the top of my flute. "I'm good."

She shrugged and waddled to the next girl, her pink-polished toes spread out with thick cotton pads.

Olivia downed her first glass with alarming speed, then started on her second.

"Who's driving y'all out of here?" I asked the girl next to me.

"Oh, we're Ubering. Not to worry." She tapped on her phone with still-wet nails. "The driver is picking us up at four thirty."

I tried to remember a time when I was this breezy and free. Olivia had said her bridesmaids were all roughly the same age as her. Twenty-six. When I was twenty-six, I had a one-year-old and was simultaneously trying to childproof our house and keep happy a husband who was becoming increasingly bored with me.

I inhaled and sank farther into the downy pillows at my back. Almost ten years had passed since I'd left Chris, and I was still grateful I was no longer faking my way through life.

As the girls talked about someone who was stood up and someone else's second chance, I closed my eyes. I tuned them out until the voices grew louder. I peeked an eye open.

"I mean, it's crazy, right?" Olivia's friend Madeleine asked. "To think you're picking a person—a partner—for the rest of your life. How in the world do you know?"

Despite the fact that Olivia was the one getting married—the one who'd most recently chosen her life partner—they all swiveled their heads toward me.

"Um . . ." I laughed.

"You're married, right?" Madeleine asked. "How'd you choose?"

"I think it's important to note that I *was* married." I held up my left hand and wiggled my bare ring finger. "I'm not anymore. I may not be the best person to ask about choosing husbands."

"But you must've been sure at one point, right? I mean, you

chose to marry that guy over all the others. How do you know who to pick?"

"I think . . ." I spoke slowly, trying to gather my thoughts along with the right words. "I think you marry the one who, when everything else is stripped away—money, job, arguments, disagreements—he's still the one you'd want to sit with on the porch and . . . just . . . do nothing. Or do anything." I looked down at my fingers spread out on top of the rolling cart next to me, each nail painted a smooth, glossy mother-of-pearl. Not a speck of dirt in sight. "Pick the one who matters more than all the *stuff* of life."

The room was silent and my mind tipped like a jar slowly pushed onto its side, making everything inside shift and shuffle.

Then out of the stillness came Bridget's loud voice. "Why in the world would you want to take away the stuff? That's the fun part."

Peals of laughter pierced the room. "Bridget, you're terrible!" they said, their voices once again cheerful and animated. But my mind was still on that front porch, welcoming the silence, the contentment, the exquisite pleasure of a quiet, love-filled life.

CHAPTER 36

Anytime you move a plant, you break roots, which takes away from
the plant's ability to thrive. If you decide you need to move your
plant, make sure to provide adequate moisture in the new location.
Stick to a regular watering pattern until you see new growth.
—GRACIE BROOKS, PROPER GROWING
CONDITIONS FOR GARDENING SUCCESS

JESSIE

The day of the wedding we made it to Dog River with minimal problems. The only hiccup was when a box holding the twigs and greenery tipped over after a quick stop at a red light, dumping water into the back seat of my 4Runner.

Oak House was quiet when we arrived. I knew Sumner was eating lunch with Jared and his dad while Olivia had brunch with her bridesmaids. I wondered about Olivia, celebrating her wedding without her mom there. I couldn't imagine having gotten married without Mama there to bustle around, making sure every detail was taken care of. More importantly, she'd been a touchstone, a spot of reality in a day that felt otherwise trimmed in white chiffon and wispy dreams.

We parked under the magnolia and unloaded everything. While Mama and Evan set out the glass jars along the dock—I wouldn't place the candles in them until just before the ceremony so they wouldn't melt in the heat—Harvis and I toted the chandelier down the dock to the boathouse. He'd packed every tool possible—screwdrivers, a variety of nails, hammers, wrenches, filament string, zip ties, even a huge blue plastic tarp, though I couldn't imagine what purpose he thought it might serve at a wedding.

His foresight allowed us to make quick work of hanging the wreath. A breeze lifted off the river, carrying the scent of pine and briny water. All around, birds sang and fish jumped and slapped back into the water. Aside from the blazing heat, it was a brilliant day for a wedding.

When the chandelier was in place, hung from the clear filament string with jars of tea-light candles suspended beneath, Harvis set off to find Mama. I hung the remaining greenery and blossoms along the railings and at the end of each row of chairs already set up for the ceremony. Only twenty chairs—enough for the closest family and friends. And me, though I wasn't sure I qualified as either. The other guests would be waiting in the yard to greet the happy couple for the reception.

I found Harvis, Mama, and Evan on Sumner's porch, two ceiling fans whirling on high. When I'd last seen his house, it had looked impressive, but now—cleaned, shined, and spruced for the wedding—it positively glowed.

"Mm, mm, mm." Mama shook her head and ran her hands up and down the polished arms of the antique chaise she sat on. "He has some mighty fine taste."

Harvis took off his cap and scratched his head. "Think so? Little uppity for my blood."

Mama sniffed. "Maybe. Though I could do with seeing this view every day."

He grunted. "The water's nice."

The sound of cars and then happy voices traveled to us from the driveway. I heard Olivia's bridesmaids—or more accurately, I heard Bridget—then Sumner's own laughter.

Harvis checked his watch. "Three o'clock. Just about time for our exit."

They stood and I hugged them. "Thank you for the help. I couldn't have done it without you."

"Sure you could," Mama said. "You, my dear, can do anything."

❧

With the departure of my little family—at some point this summer I'd begun to think of Harvis as family too—and the arrival of the wedding party, activity around Oak House kicked into high gear. Olivia had said she wanted things loose and natural for her wedding, and while we accomplished that with the flowers, everything else was as elegant and top-notch as anything I'd seen.

The caterers arrived with silver dome-covered trays, plates of appetizers, carving boards, crystal stemware, and boxes of French wine and champagne. The pastry chef and a small army of helpers unloaded eight layers of round cake, which they then carefully stacked on top of each other and covered with white buttercream, piped rosettes, and beading that mimicked the train on Olivia's dress.

The band—a ragtag group of guys toting speakers, a drum set, and a couple of guitars—set up under the oak tree and ran through a few short songs, then disappeared. When they returned, they wore crisp three-piece suits. The wedding planner—thankfully Olivia had hired a real one to coordinate the day—bustled around with a couple of assistants, making sure everything was in just the right spot.

With the aid of a makeup artist and a team of hairstylists, the bridal party and Olivia were getting ready in the cottage next door. While I finished the last of the arrangements and set them out in their silver pots and vases, the trio of photographers began snapping early photos, testing the light and choosing their lenses.

I finally saw Sumner at five o'clock, just as I tucked the last stem of hypericum into an arrangement for the cake table. He came up behind me and gave my shoulders a gentle squeeze. He smelled like fried seafood and a little bourbon. "Everything going okay? The flowers are beautiful."

"Thanks. I think I'm finished. There's nothing left except lighting the candles. I won't do that until just before seven." His hair was windblown and his cheeks pink. "Everything okay with you?"

"Oh yes." He glanced down at his casual clothes—khaki pants, checked button-down rolled up to his elbows, and Top-Siders. A spill of something red had left a small splotch on his shirt. I reached out and touched it.

He tried to rub it away. "I know. I have some cleaning up to do. I took Jared and his dad to the Grand Mariner for a late lunch. We ate a little bit of everything and there was a lot of cocktail sauce."

I lifted an eyebrow. "And bourbon in the afternoon?"

He laughed. "Just a little. It's not every day my daughter gets married."

I gathered my scissors and florist wire. "I know you have a house full of people. Any chance there's a shower open?"

"I'll make sure of it."

Inside was indeed full of people. The wedding party sat on chairs in the living room, many of them focused on the football game on TV. The wedding planner was working on a stain on the front of a groomsman's shirt. On my way out the front door to grab my things from the car, I passed Bridget.

"Where's Olivia?" I asked her.

"Next door, finishing up her hair. If you see her, tell her she's a wimp for giving up on her single life." The other girls laughed, and one threw a balled-up napkin at her.

I retrieved my bag and dress, then followed Sumner up the stairs. When we passed another bridesmaid coming down the stairs in a fog of hair spray mist and floral perfume, I touched her on the arm. "See if you can sneak Bridget's glass away from her. Whatever it is, replace it with Coke."

"Yes, ma'am."

When she was gone, I groaned. "'Yes, ma'am'? Do they really think I'm that old?"

Sumner smiled and led me down the upstairs hallway. "May I remind you, you called me Mr. Tate when you first met me."

I cringed. "Sorry. I was just being polite though. We'd only just met."

He shrugged and paused at a bedroom door, then gestured into the room. "This is my room. I've moved everything I need into one of the guest rooms, so this is all yours. Bathroom is right through there, and towels are on the counter."

"Your room? Are you sure? I can use the guest room. I don't mind."

"I know, but there's more room here." He reached for my hand. We both stood in the doorway, only inches separating us. Part of me wanted to take a step back to allow a little breathing room between us. "Thank you for coming today," he said. "Aside from the flowers. Thank you for coming for me."

"I'm glad I'm here. Thanks for asking me."

"It's a special day for sure. My little girl getting married. A lot of people are here to celebrate with us." He smiled. "You being here makes it even more special."

He kissed me lightly on the cheek, near the edge of my mouth, then turned back down the hall and disappeared into one of the other bedrooms.

I closed the door behind me and leaned against it, then exhaled. It was the first time I'd been upstairs in his house. Definitely the first time I'd seen his bedroom. Just like all the other spaces in his house, everything in this room was neat and polished. A long dresser was dust-free and empty of any personal belongings other than one framed photo of Olivia and a leather box holding a pair of cuff links and some spare change.

His bed was smooth, with a dark-navy duvet and crisp navy-and-white pillows—sumptuous yet still masculine. The hardwood floor gleamed in the sunlight streaming in from a window, and a sisal rug covered the floor at the end of the bed. I slid off my shoes and set my bare feet on the rug. The fibers poked and pricked the bottoms of my feet. I smoothed my hand across the duvet. My own bed, covered in a vintage chenille spread and a patchwork quilt, seemed almost childish in comparison. But, oh, it was comfortable.

I showered and dried my hair, then stepped into my dress. It was long and red—not flashy red, but more subdued, if a long red dress could be considered subdued. It had a halter top that tied behind my neck, the ties hanging down over the bare skin of my back. Delicate gold sandals and a thin gold-and-diamond bracelet of Mama's completed my ensemble.

The dress was left over from my days of galas and parties with Chris, the only dress I'd taken with me when I packed up my car and headed back to Perry. It was also the only dress in my closet even remotely appropriate for a seven o'clock wedding. It may have felt perfect for the occasion the week before when I'd tried it on, but today it felt too red, too tight. But there was nothing I could do about it now.

I brushed my hair out and fanned it over my shoulders, trying to cover as much of my exposed skin as possible, then checked the clock on the bedside table—six fifteen. With my stomach full of jumpy nerves, I opened the door and forced myself to walk, one foot in front of the other, down the stairs and out onto the back porch.

The bridal party was nowhere to be seen, likely whisked away into the cottage by the wedding planner. Guests milled around chatting and laughing on the porch and out in the yard. Someone had already lit the candles leading out to the dock, and it was a good thing, considering how many people were already there standing around with glasses in hand, apparently having started the reception early.

I scanned the crowd until I saw Sumner standing with a small group of men. His face lit up when he saw me, and some of my nervousness subsided. I inhaled and walked out into the long, lazy rays of sun. He extended his elbow and walked me down the dock toward the chairs set up in the boathouse. My work had paid off—everything was lovely. The flowers and greenery were holding up well in the heat, and small flames lit the tiny jars hanging beneath the grapevine wreath.

"I've never seen anyone so beautiful," Sumner whispered as he walked me to my seat. "Other than my daughter, of course, but I have to say that."

I smiled. "I'd be concerned if you didn't. And you don't look too shabby yourself. Seersucker suits you."

"Olivia wanted Southern, and she said seersucker was the way to go. Here." He pointed me to the row just behind the one reserved for family. "You can sit here. I'll be just in front of you. I wish you could sit with me, but my brother and Elizabeth's sisters will be up here with me."

"Of course. This is fine." Next to me were three other women dressed in various shades of white and cream. They watched us as if we were the main attraction.

"Ladies." Sumner held up a hand in greeting.

"You're looking well, Sum," the woman next to me said. "I saw your new course in Charleston last month. It's beautiful. You outdid yourself."

He grinned. "I aim to please." He turned to me and winked. "I'll find you after the ceremony."

Once he walked away, the women leaned into one another and whispered. I read through the program, trying to ignore their furtive glances that felt like daggers. I smoothed my hair over my shoulders again, feeling overexposed. And the high-heeled sandals I wore were already pinching my feet.

"Oh, fine, I'll ask her," came a whisper from the group. Then louder, "Honey, are you here with Sumner?"

"Yes, I'm his . . ." His what? We'd never talked about it. "I'm here with him."

She raised her eyebrows to the woman next to her. Then she turned back to me with a sweet smile. "And how old are you?"

One of the other women laughed while another gasped. "You can't ask that, Lily."

"Sure I can. I can ask anything I want, and she can decide what to tell me."

Three pairs of eyes settled on me, expertly arched eyebrows raised, foreheads smooth as a baby's. Before I could answer, I was saved by the first strains of Canon in D as Jared led his mother down the aisle.

"Get a look at those sequins," Lily muttered, shaking her head. "Bless her heart, she's sure not from around here."

❧

The reception was a party unlike any I had seen since my wedding to Chris. Plates of food, swishes of silk and organza, clinking wineglasses, and swells of laughter and conversation surged around Sumner's beautiful backyard like waves. Cameras flashed as Olivia and Jared cut their cake and danced to an Ed Sheeran love song.

Sumner was as in demand as Olivia was, moving confidently from group to group, holding everyone's attention, delivering laughs and handshakes. Sometimes he'd take my elbow and lead me through the crowd to another group of people he wanted to introduce me to, but other times someone would pull him away without me, and I hung back alone, which was okay with me. After a while, I camped out by the fruit and cheese table and slipped my sandals off one by one to squeeze my heels. As I reached down to rub the top of one foot, he caught my eye from across the lawn. He smiled, then winked.

Just then, an older woman paused next to me. She wore cream silk pants and a blousy sleeveless top, her neck adorned with several long necklaces. Her blonde hair was piled high on her head, showing off large diamond earrings. She followed my gaze to where Sumner was laughing with a group of men.

"So you're the one who's captured Sumner's attention." Her bracelets jangled as she reached across the table to dip a thin apple slice in the baked Brie.

"I suppose so." I'd grown tired of the quick glances and bold stares, the women talking down to me like I was a teenager out past my curfew.

"Well, best of luck to the two of you." Her smile appeared genuine enough until her gaze slid down to my dress. One eyebrow arched up, and before I knew what was happening, she reached around and pulled the back of my dress out to check the label. She clicked her tongue. "Such a cute dress." Leaving only a whisper of Chanel perfume behind, she sauntered off and grabbed the arm of a woman standing at the cake table.

The feeling started in my stomach and gradually made its way up into my chest, squeezing tight. I kept my face calm, not giving away the fact that all the air in my body had seemingly leaked out, leaving me gasping. I looked around at the sparkling evening, the lights, the beautiful dresses and people. Though I'd spent so many hours preparing for this night—the tips of my fingers were blistered from tying twine and wrapping florist wire—I had no connection to anything here. No attachment at all. I didn't fit with the place or the people, but instead of wishing I did, all I felt was a ripple of relief.

Olivia and Jared left the reception in a blaze of sparklers held by guests standing on the steps of Sumner's house and down the driveway. Sumner had tried to pull me to the end of the line next to the limo with the rest of the family members, but in the crush of people grabbing sparklers and jostling to get into position, I waved him off and found a spot by the house. My stomach was a ball of nerves, and I yearned for a moment of solitude.

Finally, after a few false starts, the photographer got into position and the new couple descended the steps. Amid the cheers and laughter and catcalls, Olivia found me and hugged me tight.

"Thank you so much for everything. It was all so beautiful." Her skin was dewy in the humid air, and her hair had sprung from its clips and fell down her shoulders in waves. As Jared continued down the tunnel of people, Olivia leaned in toward me. "You were right. What you said at the spa? Jared matters more than everything else."

Her words—my own words—were still running through my mind a few minutes later as the limo pulled away and Sumner turned back toward the house. When he saw me, his shoulders sagged and he smiled. "Hi," he said when he reached me. "I'm exhausted. Happy, but exhausted."

"I bet you are. It's hard work being the father of the bride."

"You're not kidding. My feet are killing me." He glanced at my feet. "Yours must be too."

My heels dangled from one hand, and I curled my toes in the soft moss covering the ground under the trees.

He gestured to the path that led around the side of the house. "I had them box up a couple slices of cake for me in the back. I'd consider parting with one if you're hungry."

"You know . . ." I looked over my shoulder to where my car sat under the magnolia. "I'm pretty beat. I think I'm going to head on out."

"Really?" He was disappointed, I could tell, but it was time for me to leave.

I nodded. "Thanks for—"

"Mr. Tate?" We turned to see the wedding planner hovering near the side fence. "I need you for a few moments. If you could just . . ." She pointed to the backyard.

He exhaled and turned back to me. "I'm sorry."

"Really, it's fine. Go ahead. I need to get on home anyway."

He took a step closer to me. "I can't thank you enough for being here tonight. And not just for the flowers, though they were perfect."

I reached up and touched the blush rose on his lapel. It had only just started to droop.

He took my hand and leaned down. As his lips brushed mine, the wedding planner cleared her throat. "The photographer from *Bay* magazine is here for just a few more minutes. He'd like to get a shot of you on your back porch, if that's okay."

"You'd better go."

"Good night, Jessie."

He let the planner lead him away, and I watched until they disappeared around the side of the house. Then, lifting the hem of my dress with my free hand, I carefully stepped across the brick driveway to my car. Inside, I pulled my hair up into a knot and exhaled.

I let the night air swim through my car on the way home, chipping away at the stress of the evening. Of the last few months, really. When I turned into my driveway nearly an hour later, I sat with the car off, the windows still down. It had rained at home sometime during the evening, and the scent of fresh dirt and damp grass floated through the car.

In the glow of the moon, Twig sat empty but peaceful, the old window boxes spilling over with late-summer begonias, coleus, and sweet potato vine. In my house a single light was on in the kitchen, illuminating Evan's face as she drank a glass of orange juice in front of the refrigerator.

As I peeked in on my life from the dark night outside, contentment bloomed in my chest. I had my present, which was *good*. More than I deserved. And I had my future, whatever that looked like. My life was right in front of me.

CHAPTER 37

Many say the echeveria laui is the loveliest of all the succulents, with soft, powdery blue-gray leaves and small bursts of peachy-pink blooms at the top. The most fascinating aspect of the plant is that it is very slow growing. It can take years to reach a height of only about six inches, proving the old adage that good things come to those who wait.
—WENDELL BANCROFT SR., *LATE BLOOMERS*

JESSIE

M ama, I can't make you a bouquet of just succulents. It'll look dry and . . . hot."

"Well, I'm too old and experienced for pink and frilly. You can save that for the young'uns."

I stifled a smile as she picked up her sun hat—white, not pink, and no frills to be seen—from Twig's front counter and plopped it on her head. "I know that's not your taste. Can you just let me work on it? I promise I'll make a bouquet you love that fits *you*. I need you to trust me."

She eyed me, then threw her hands up. "You're right, you're right. Flowers are your thing. You have three weeks—let's see what you can do." When I opened my mouth, she spoke over me. "And I do trust you."

"Good."

"Although I have to say, three weeks is not a long time. The last time you did flowers for a wedding, you had three months."

Mama always loved to get the last word. "Thanks for the reminder. I can handle it."

Elma Dean pulled up in front of Twig and Mama ambled to the front porch. "How you doin', Elma?"

"Do I hear you're getting married?" Elma chirped.

"I don't know what you hear, but it does seem that I am getting married." Mama did her best to hide it, but I could hear the pleasure in her voice. The pride.

"Are you going to have bridesmaids?"

"I am. My granddaughter, Evan, is going to be my bridesmaid and Jessie is going to walk me down the aisle."

"Well, that's just perfect. Birdie Davis and I have been talking. We can't use rice anymore—somehow it's bad for the birds—so what do you think about bubbles? Wouldn't that be fun?"

"What on earth are you talking about?" Mama asked.

"What we're going to throw at your wedding, of course. You do intend to invite the rest of us, don't you? Marilyn Rickers would have an absolute come-apart if you don't."

"Of course you're invited, Elma," I called out. "You're all invited."

Mama was right about Harvis intending to make her his bride. He'd approached me on a hot afternoon in late September and asked if I had any objection to them getting married.

"Harvis, I appreciate you asking me, but I hope you know you don't need my permission. You might need Mama's, but you don't need mine."

He chuckled and rubbed the whiskers on his cheek.

"I'd love to have you be a part of our family. An even bigger part." I reached out and pulled him into a hug.

"Oh, what's all this?" he asked, caught off guard. But then he patted my back. "Your mother is an exceptional woman. And I knew your daddy. He was a good man. I don't intend to try to replace him."

"I know you don't."

"All I want to do is keep Gus happy and thriving as long as I can." His eyes pooled and I squeezed his arm.

"I know you do. And you will. And she'll keep you on your toes. You know that, right?"

He laughed again and wiped at his eyes. "I do. Lord help me, I do."

❧

The ceremony was planned for 4:00 p.m. on the last Saturday in October. Mama wore a dress she'd had for years, and she loved the bouquet I made for her filled with all her favorites—dahlias, garden roses, and green-and-pink succulents. Because the wedding was so simple—in her backyard, only twenty guests, and easy lemon pound cake with whipped cream and strawberries for the "after-party," as she called it—the hours just before the wedding were calm and unhurried. She and I and Evan spent most of the day together at her house, flipping through old photos and making sure her panty hose was free of holes and her shoes were buffed to a shine.

Finally Evan headed back to our house to get ready, and Mama and I had some time alone. While she touched up her makeup, I slipped my dress on, then pulled my hair up on one side and clipped it with one of her rhinestone hairpins.

When I finished, I sat on her bed and watched her. "How do you feel?"

"My mind is clear as a bell."

"I don't mean that. I mean about the wedding. About today."

"I feel good. I'm ready."

As she leaned in close to the mirror, I thought about how strong my mother was. She'd been married once, and so happily, but it ended in such a horrible way. And here she was doing it again. She had reserves of strength and grit I couldn't imagine ever pulling from. Her own reserves seemed bottomless.

"Do you still think of Daddy sometimes?"

She turned to me and set down her mascara. "I think of him every day. Every single day."

"Really?"

"Really. Why do you ask?"

I shrugged. "I just . . . He died. You put your whole heart into your marriage with him and it ended. But you're trying it again."

She nodded. "I've had a lot of time to think about this. Your daddy had a jealous streak when it came to me—never took too kindly to any other man giving me a second glance or sounding a little too friendly toward me—but I know beyond a shadow of a doubt that he'd tell me to marry Harvis. And you know what else? I did put all I had into my marriage with him, but it turns out I still have some of myself to give away."

A tear slipped down my cheek and I touched it with my fingertip. Mama grabbed a tissue and sat on the bed next to me. "Tell me what's wrong. Is it just Daddy? Or is it something else?"

I dabbed my cheek with the tissue and sniffed. "I just don't know where you find the bravery to put your heart out there again even though . . ."

"Even though. You think I haven't thought about that? I know this could end badly. I have a disease and I don't know what my future will look like. Harvis's heart may very well break wide open. Then again I may wake up and realize I'm living with the stink of manure for the rest of my days."

I laughed into my tissue, then blew my nose.

"But you know what? The way I see it is I have to ante up again. Why put off the chance to love? Why say no to that beautiful thing when it's staring at me in the face and nothing is standing in our way?"

She reached over and tucked a strand of hair behind my ear. "You've had a hard go with love. I know that. And I want so much more for you. Not just so you can be tucked away in a marriage, but so you can know what it's like to be cherished. To experience a marriage that's whole and satisfying. I want that so badly for you."

"I'm glad you have it again with Harvis."

Her face brightened. "I can't believe my luck, to tell you the truth. A second man wants to put up with me. Who would have thought?" She picked up her mascara again and walked back to the mirror. "Correct me if I'm wrong, but I have a feeling all this talk of putting your heart out there has nothing to do with Sumner Tate."

I squeezed the tissue in my hands until it was a tight little ball. Not long after Olivia's wedding, I'd broken up with Sumner. Well, *break up* might not be the right term. That felt too young and immature for the relationship we had. Sumner was a decent man with a good heart. His just wasn't a life I saw for myself or Evan. And I wasn't willing to rework our life to make it fit with his. He was gracious, of course, and kind, and he didn't make me feel bad for making the decision I needed to make for my family. I knew he wouldn't.

"Are you thinking of someone else?" Mama asked.

I looked over at her.

Just then the back door opened and Evan called through the house, "Mom? Gus? It's time."

❧

Evan, dressed in a white linen sundress and sandals, walked down the back steps and toward the rows of chairs set up under the shade trees to the side of Mama's backyard. We couldn't see the guests from where we waited on her back porch, but Elma Dean stood at the

340

bottom of the steps and served as a guide to tell us when to begin our walk. After a moment, she pointed to us and gave a signal best suited for an air-traffic controller.

"Are you ready?" I whispered to Mama.

"I'm ready if you are."

We began our slow way down the steps and toward the gathering of friends in the yard. As we rounded the corner, Mama's hand on my elbow tightened. Harvis stood at the end of the aisle with a wide smile, tears streaming down his weathered cheeks. And there, on the back row, sat Ben.

CHAPTER 38

During times of dormancy, the ground appears quiet and empty,
as if it were doing nothing but waiting for spring. However, this
couldn't be further from the truth. The dormant earth does wait, but
silent, invisible work is taking place. Microorganisms are working,
breeding, and eating. They, along with sun and rain, make the
earth richer, ready for a new season of planting and growth.
—VIRGINIA PEARCE, *THE WATCHFUL GARDENER*

JESSIE

I was running hard, my legs pumping, the cold air filling my lungs and making them burn. When I got to the end of the road, I stopped for a moment to slow my breathing, then turned around and ran back toward my house. I'd woken that morning with the urge to move, so instead of waiting until evening to run, I started early, with only one steaming cup of coffee in my belly.

I blinked my eyes in the chill. Wetness pricked the corners and stuck to my lashes. It was only seven thirty, a Saturday, and cold air funneled down Glory Road in the morning sunshine. An early season cold front had pushed through overnight and blanketed everything in a thin layer of frost that made every surface sparkle. The sun was intense though, and it wouldn't be long before the frost melted away and the temperatures crept up.

I breathed in deep, soaking in the stark and rugged beauty. Deep down, I think I always knew I'd stick around this place. This red dirt. These tall pines. All of it welcoming me each day in whispers and soft breezes. Glory Road was where I belonged. I'd stuck my stake in the ground like a country-crossing pioneer. This was my piece of earth and nothing would pull me away.

❧

A couple of hours later, I'd showered and dressed and sat on the porch with a bag of pecans next to me on the top step. The faint aroma of wood smoke tinged the air and two bowls sat at my feet—one with cracked shells, the other with plump pecan halves. I had a metal nut-cracker, but I also liked to do it the old-fashioned way. My dad had been the one to show me how to squeeze two nuts together until they cracked, revealing the meat inside. My fingernails were stubby and dirty from peeling the shells off, but I was pleased at my progress.

Harvis had requested pecan pie for our Christmas feast in a few weeks, and Mama said she'd make it for him as long as someone else shelled the pecans. "That kind of manual labor doesn't mix well with my manicure," she'd said, snappy as ever. I told her I'd shell them for her if she promised to show me how to make the pie. If I was lucky, I'd even get her to write down the recipe for me.

Behind me, the screen door opened and Evan appeared. She stuck a section of newspaper in front of me, too close for me to read it. I dropped the shells in the bowl and leaned back to see the page clearer. It was the front of the About Town section, and Sumner's chiseled face smiled up from a full-page spread. The headline above the picture read, "Sumner Tate, President of Tate & Lane Golf Course Design, hosts party for the recently completed Riverside Golf Community."

"He could have at least asked you to do the flowers for his party."

She snatched a handful of shelled pecans before I could swat her hand away.

I folded the paper and handed it back to her. "I think I've done enough flowers for him for a while."

"Think you'll ever see him again?"

I inhaled the cool air and reached for another pair of pecans. "I don't know. Probably not."

"And you're not sad about it?" She picked up a couple of cracked shells that had fallen on the porch and dropped them in the bowl.

I shook my head. "No. I'm not sad."

"Hmm."

I glanced at her. "Yes? Any more questions?"

"Nope." She grabbed one more pecan from the bowl and turned back to the door. "It's way too cold to be out here," she said, but then she stopped just before she went inside. "Oh, is it okay if I go to the Icebox in a little while?"

"I thought you just said it's too cold."

"I won't be in my pajamas when I go."

"Sure. Are you meeting Ruth there?"

"No, Jack. We're collecting rocks for this project in our art class. I need your rubber boots too, if that's okay. We're going to wade out into the water to get the shiny ones at the bottom."

Too cold to sit with Mom, but not too cold to keep her from stepping into freezing cold water with a nice boy. "It's fine with me."

The screen door slammed behind her and the porch was quiet again. Mama and Harvis were up the road at her house—at *their* house—cleaning out the fireplace so Harvis could start an all-day, slow-burning fire. My daddy used to love keeping a fire like that in the fireplace. He'd start one anytime the temperatures dipped below sixty degrees.

I smiled. Daddy would probably be grateful for Harvis taking care of Mama in her sunset years.

Harvis had been the one to suggest moving into her house instead of uprooting her to his house. "It may make things easier later," he'd said to me. "No sense in adding to her confusion by putting her in a house she doesn't know."

Mama was so lucky to have him. We were lucky to have him.

I froze when I heard a familiar rumble coming up the road. At the sight of the man behind the wheel, my heart pounded in my chest so loudly I could hear it in my ears. I brushed the pecan shells from my hands and stood, watching him roll to a stop under the trees.

The last time I'd seen Ben was the day of Mama and Harvis's wedding. We didn't say much more than hello that day—he'd been in the middle of packing up his parents' house and said he couldn't stay long.

It was an excuse—yes, he was selling his parents' house to the farming couple, but he probably would have stayed longer if things hadn't been so muddled between us. He hugged Mama though and shook Harvis's hand. As I watched him walk away, Harvis came up behind me.

"He's a good boy, that one."

Ben called me the night before he moved. I wanted to answer, but the old fear was still there—the fear that kept me from reaching out and grabbing the sure thing in front of me. The fear that I'd break again. In the end I waited too long and the call went to voice mail. I listened to it the second the message showed up on the screen.

"We're heading out tomorrow," he'd said, his voice quiet. "I just wanted to let you know in case you see my car passing by a lot. We're not using movers, so it'll take several trips." He paused, then exhaled. "I'm sorry I didn't stay longer at the wedding. And I'm sorry I messed everything up. Maybe I . . . I don't know. I really thought this time would be it for us. I wish . . ." He broke off again. "Don't get too excited though. I'm sticking around for a while. I think Perry has sunk its teeth into me again, for better or worse."

Evan continued to see Nick at school, of course, and she'd given me updates about their new house in downtown Perry. Nick had invited her over to see it a couple weeks ago. That night she'd told me how Ben had tried to set up another vegetable garden in the backyard.

"It's so pathetic, Mom. He really needs help."

Now Ben opened his car door and walked toward me. He paused several feet away from the bottom of the steps as if gauging my reaction to him. He wore blue jeans and a plaid flannel shirt with the sleeves rolled up and a fleece vest over it. His dark wavy hair, his beard, his eyes were all the same. He was so . . . himself. So enduring.

He shoved his hands into his pockets. All my nerve endings stood at attention. Ready. Eager. But I waited.

He opened his mouth to speak, but then he hesitated. He hung his head for a moment, then raised it, his gaze settling on my face. "I used to know everything about you. What made you laugh, what made you upset. The way you bounced on your toes when you were excited about something." He smiled. "I knew the real you. Underneath everything you layered on yourself, I knew who you were inside."

He reached out a hand, then let it drop to his side. "It's been twenty years, Jessie. I want to know you again. I want . . . *you*. So much it hurts. That has never changed. Not since the very first day."

I closed my eyes and exhaled. They were just words, but they settled down deep inside me, in that place that had felt empty for all these years. He'd been the missing piece. The whole time. And here he was, standing in front of me, slipping into place.

"I know you said you couldn't do this, but . . ." He shrugged. "I can't do it without you. I don't want to. And if you tell me to leave, I will. I promise you won't hear from me again, but I just—"

I shook my head and he stopped. "I don't want to do it without you either."

His shoulders dropped, a weight of almost visible tension slipping from them. A longing inside me ached so forcefully, it made me want to cry. I wanted to pull him to me and keep him close.

"May I?" He gestured to the steps.

I nodded.

We both sat on the top step, the bag of pecans between us. He reached in and grabbed two, then leaned forward and rested his elbows on his knees, turning the pecans over in his fingers. "I was so scared you . . ." He shook his head like he didn't want to say the words.

I reached over and took his hand. It was warm and dry in mine. "Twenty years."

He nodded. "I know it's a long time."

"But not too long."

He turned and studied me, his gaze traveling across my face like cool air. When I kissed him he made a small noise of surprise, then returned the kiss. It was warm, tentative, curious, as if we were two people finding each other for the very first time. And in a way, we were.

He pressed his forehead to mine and held both my hands in his. His eyes were bright. I bit my lip and smiled, and the smile he returned lit up his face.

I'd always thought I wanted to be carried away by love. But my eyes saw differently now. I needed firm ground beneath my feet. A foundation tested and solid. Rooted. And that's what I had. Roots. I had them with Mama and Evan, and we were growing more. This man sitting next to me, joining me, filling me up, was proof of that.

A crisp breeze stirred the air, rustling the leaves on the ground and lifting my hair until it tickled my cheeks. In front of us red dust settled back onto the road, obscuring Ben's tire tracks, leaving the ground fresh and untouched. Ready for whatever came next.

ACKNOWLEDGMENTS

To the team at Thomas Nelson—Amanda Bostic, Allison Carter, Kim Carlton, Becky Monds, Jodi Hughes, Paul Fisher, Matt Bray, Jocelyn Bailey, and Laura Wheeler—thank you for your support, guidance, and kindness to me over the past several years. Publishing with you has been such a sweet experience. Thank you to the sales team for working so hard to get my books into the hands of readers everywhere. Thank you to Julee Schwarzburg for your eagle eye and for keeping my characters from all that smiling and nodding! To sweet Kim, thank you for your unflagging support of *Glory Road* and for helping me make the story as rich as it could be. Working with you has been so much fun. Thank you to my agent Karen Solem, whose calm and unruffled attitude is a good balance to my flustered tendencies! Thank you for your wise guidance through this third novel. I'm thankful you're on my side.

Thank you to Leslie West and everyone at the Homewood Public Library for your support of my books, for asking me to come to your book clubs, and for the large tables and quiet space to work. Thank you to Alabama Writers Connect, as always. Thank you to Anna Gresham for being my friend in both writing and life. Thank you to Tricia Cordell for information about growing veggies, to Keith and Micki Peevy for answering questions about Dog River, and to Jon Culver at Sweet Peas Garden Shop in Homewood, Alabama, for letting me pepper you with questions about operating a small plant nursery. Thank you to Patti Henry for continued support and friendship (and great conversation on an impromptu six-hour car ride).

To book clubbers everywhere who have invited me into your homes and libraries in person or through the magic of technology: my love for you knows no bounds! Truly, it's such an honor to be asked to join in the fun for an evening to chat, eat, drink, and laugh. Thank you for reading my books and for extending the invitations.

To the community of book bloggers and reviewers who love books with such fierce passion, thank you for all your love and support and for inspiring me to keep writing so you all can keep reading!

Thank you to librarians who do so much to foster the love of reading, especially the librarians who love my children (and, by extension, me): Mrs. Woodruff, Mrs. Morgan, Ms. Laura, Ms. Mary, Miss Cristina, Miss Molly, Ms. Alicia, Ms. Laurie, and Ms. Meg.

To my sweet family, especially all the Kofflers and Dentons, thank you for being so excited for me as I continue to wander down this road of writing books. It's so much fun to do life with you. A special thanks to my father-in-law, Joe Denton, for all the bags of "Papa peas," the shelling of which gave me the jumping-off point for this story. (Not to mention my purple fingers.) And to my little clan—Matt, Kate, and Sela—thank you for loving me and putting up with me. I love you dearly. Thank you especially to Matt for being my voice of reason and calm patience when I tend to jump and startle and generally lose my cool.

Thank *you*, dear readers who hold this book (or device) in your hands and read the words I work so hard to put together. If not for you, these stories and characters would not be out in the world, so thank you for reading and for passing my books along to friends, sisters, daughters, mothers, and even a few husbands and fathers.

Heavenly Father, this adventure has been one blessing and surprise after another. Thank you for using my stories to shine light into dark places and for allowing people to connect through the world of books and reading.

DISCUSSION QUESTIONS

1. The setting of this book is a red dirt road in a small town. It's quiet, most of the neighbors have known each other for decades, and not much changes. Even as time charges forward, there are still towns like this all over the South— and across the country. Does the setting in *Glory Road* remind you of any place from your own life?

2. When the book opens, Jessie is only mildly aware of her mother Gus's memory lapses. As time goes on, Gus's difficulties become more apparent and concerning. Do you have any experience with walking through a similar situation with a family member? Did you walk that road alone or were there others around with whom you could share your fears and questions?

3. Jessie's daughter, Evan, is a young teenager experiencing new sensitivities and emotions as she's figuring out the world and her place in it. Jessie's plan for tackling these teen years is to talk less and listen more. If you've been through teenagerhood with a child, did you find yourself trying to come up with new strategies to connect with your teenager? What worked and what didn't?

4. What did you think about Jessie's relationships with Ben and Sumner? Did you see similarities between Sumner and her ex-husband Chris? Did you understand her pull toward both men? Were you rooting for one over the other?

5. Jessie has a deep-seated fear of letting herself love again.
   How do her ex-husband Chris, her younger years with Ben,
   and even her father's death play a part in her fear of getting
   close to someone else? In the end, what was it that allowed
   her to move beyond the fear and let her heart love again?
6. When Evan is out running with Jessie, she thinks about how
   she can sometimes see what her mom must have looked like
   as a child. She says, "If you can still look like your little girl
   self when you're grown, do you still feel little? Like you're
   playing pretend and you really don't feel like the adult
   everyone thinks you are?" Can you identify with Evan's
   thoughts and questions? Have you ever, even for a moment,
   felt like you're still your younger self trapped in an adult body
   with adult responsibilities and expectations?
7. Let's talk about Harvis and Gus. How are their personalities
   different, and why do you think they meshed well despite
   their differences?
8. Despite being fiery and independent, Gus ends up letting
   Harvis in and leaning on him for strength. Given her
   declining health and unpredictable future, why do you think
   she did that? What gave her the courage or strength to admit
   she wanted the companionship and needed the help?
9. Do you understand Gus's desire to keep Jessie from feeling
   the burden of having to take care of her own mother? Do
   you understand Jessie's insistence that it wouldn't be a
   burden, but a privilege? Many people are familiar with
   the responsibilities of being a caretaker of an older family
   member. If you feel comfortable, share an experience
   you've had that's similar to or different from Jessie and Gus's
   situation.
10. When Jessie was younger, she thought love was "sparks and
    butterflies." By the end of the story, she's realized her need

for firm ground and a solid, tested foundation. Can you think of a time in your life when, like Jessie, you thought love was about that initial spark and the fluttery feelings? How did your view change? Or is it somehow a combination of the two?

11. The quote at the beginning of chapter 38 talks about times of dormancy in the garden, and how while the earth is waiting, "silent, invisible work is taking place." How does this relate to Jessie's life? Do you have any experience with quiet times that prepared you for something bigger?

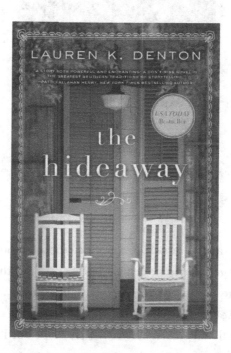

From the author of the *USA TODAY* bestseller *The Hideaway* comes a new story about families and mending the past.

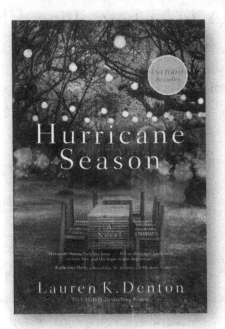

"A poignant and heartfelt tale of sisterhood, motherhood, and marriage, *Hurricane Season* deftly examines the role that coming to terms with the past plays in creating a hopeful future. Readers will devour this story of the hurricanes—both literal and figurative—that shape our lives."

—KRISTY WOODSON HARVEY, NATIONAL BESTSELLING AUTHOR OF *SLIGHTLY SOUTH OF SIMPLE*

AVAILABLE IN PRINT, E-BOOK, AND AUDIO!

THOMAS NELSON
Since 1798

ABOUT THE AUTHOR

Photo by Angie Davis

L auren K. Denton is the author of the *USA TODAY* bestselling novels *The Hideaway* and *Hurricane Season*. She was born and raised in Mobile, Alabama, and now lives with her husband and two daughters in Homewood, just outside Birmingham. Though her husband tries valiantly to turn her into a mountain girl, she'd still rather be at the beach.

❧

LaurenKDenton.com
Instagram: LaurenKDentonBooks
Facebook: LaurenKDentonAuthor
Twitter: @LaurenKDenton
Pinterest: LKDentonBooks